MARTINA DEVLIN

THREE WISE MEN

HarperCollins*Publishers*

This novel is entirely a work of fiction. The names, characters and incidents portrayed in it are the work of the author's imagination. Any resemblance to actual persons, living or dead, events or localities is entirely coincidental.

HarperCollins*Publishers*
77-85 Fulham Palace Road,
Hammersmith, London W6 8JB

www.**fire**and**water**.com

Published by HarperCollins*Publishers* 2000

Copyright © Martina Devlin 2000

Martina Devlin asserts the moral right to
be identified as the author of this work

ISBN: 978-0-00-651458-9

For my parents,
Frank and Bridie Devlin,
who always make me feel the centre of their universe

PART ONE

CHAPTER 1

Kate props an elbow on the ledge above the hand-basin and concentrates on drawing a steady line around her mouth with her new rust-coloured lip pencil. She's slapping on the face she chooses to wear, as opposed to the one dumped on her by the arbitrariness of genes, for a rendezvous with Jack. And lip-liner is integral to the operation. She snapped up three pencils when she spotted them in Clery's – plums are in vogue and you can't find autumn shades to save your life. Not that lip-liner is technically a life-saver, but it comes a close second. It's certainly giving her mouth the kiss of life.

Kate is preparing for her farewell to Jack's arms, as well as the rest of him, and she can't apply herself to the task until she applies her make-up. A woman has to look her best to do her worst to a man; imagine if he went home relieved. Like a lemming that couldn't find a cliff.

Her lips are within half an inch of perfection when the phone rings, causing a painted-on wobble instead of a pout. She contemplates ignoring the source of the interruption, reconsiders when it strikes her the caller might be Jack changing the time they're to meet, and bolts from the bathroom before the answering machine gobbles any message.

The caller is Mick, her friend Gloria's husband, and he's virtually incoherent. Kate has to make him repeat his story twice before she establishes that Gloria's been rushed to hospital with a ruptured ectopic pregnancy. Whatever that is.

It must have required the full ER team from Mick's garble. Thirty-six hours without sleep are taking their toll on him. Kate, only barely assimilating the news, realises she's still clutching her new lip-liner and grinding the pencil tip against the body of the phone. Bronze Babe is smeared between redial button and microphone. She and Gloria have been intimates for a million years, since they were cast as two of the three wise men in the Primary Two nativity play; another friend, Eimear, was the third.

'Which hospital is Gloria in? I'll go straight in to see her,' she offers.

Mick advises against it, to Kate's relief when she remembers her only way of contacting Jack to cancel is by catching him in the office – a call to his home is never an option. Not unless she's intent on setting out the welcome mat for trouble.

'Leave it for now, she's still not able to have visitors: the tears start tripping her as soon as she lays eyes on me,' says Mick. 'They operated on her in the middle of the night and it's been a massive shock. We didn't even realise she was pregnant. I was too shaken to let you know sooner but Gloria's just asked me to give you and Eimear a ring – I've already told her family. Eimear's my last call, then I suppose I'll head off and find something to eat. I haven't much of an appetite, to be honest. You've no idea what a jolt this has been; it's the first time I've had to phone an ambulance.'

Guilt pricks at Kate. She ought to volunteer to meet Mick for a drink, she's known him even longer than Gloria and he sounds in a state, but she's psyched up for her parting is such sweet sorrow number with Jack. And even if she doesn't pull it off tonight she can plant the seeds . . . drop hints about how the end of the line is only a few stops away. In the meantime she can't bring herself to renounce the euphoria of an evening spent in her lover's company. Mick must have other friends who can keep an eye on him.

'I'll drop in to see Gloria before work tomorrow,' she promises; and conscience salved after a few consolatory truisms, returns to her dating ritual preparations. Game on.

Kate knows she should feel restrained by Gloria's hospitalisation but decency is purged by jubilation at the prospect of Jack's undivided attention. Her reflection smiles giddily at her as a wave of exultation bubbles up from her diaphragm and catches in her throat. He drenches her with gladness, simply the thought of him makes her laugh aloud. It's enough to be able to look at Jack, she wouldn't object if there was never any touching. Actually, that's a fib; she adores the stroking, but it's not the alpha and the omega.

'Listen to me with my Latin tags. I should forget about being a lawyer and think about being a friend,' she reminds herself.

Kate's aware – and only hazily concerned by the realisation – that she's dwelling on the anticipatory pleasure of being with Jack without sparing a thought for Gloria, comatose and attached to a drip. She'll make it up to her tomorrow; she'll transform Gloria's room into a bower. Meanwhile she should be plotting the direction her tryst with Jack will take.

She's decided to end their affair, although not because it's turned stale – a flashback of Jack's lean brown fingers cupping her cheek swims before her eyes and she tingles with anticipation, losing her train of thought. 'Concentrate,' she wills herself, a woman needs to be rehearsed before an encounter with Jack. He has a propensity for bringing the curtain down on the rational processes. Jack O'Brien tends to make you feel more and think less.

That's why she's wearing her dating underwear. Kate has no intention of ending up in bed with him but to be on the safe side she slipped on a particularly sheer matching set after showering. Jack always notices and comments as he eases them off, it's worth occasionally imagining you've stumbled into playing the leading lady in a porn movie for the pleasure he takes in it.

On Jackless days she slings on whatever comes to hand – even her boyfriend Pearse's boxer shorts when she's cold – but if Jack's in the vicinity Kate prefers the comfort of the uncomfortable. Style over substance is the coda, which is just as well because there's virtually no substance to what she's wearing.

But back to the task ahead. She daubs at the shaky patch on the lip-line front and contemplates options in the staple declarations department. There's that threadbare standby, 'Let's agree to say goodbye now before anyone gets hurt,' closely followed by, 'We owe it to our partners to call it a day.' She has a sneaking fondness for 'We both knew this liaison had built-in obsolescence' but is wary of fielding it in case Jack accuses her of pomposity.

Kate giggles. 'The sure-fire way to scare a man off is to tell him you're ready to have his baby.'

But carrying his child – or anyone else's – is unimaginable. Besides, she doesn't want to put the wind up Jack so thoroughly that he's caught in a typhoon; what's required here is a regretful parting of the ways potholed with might-have-beens.

Even as she rehearses, Kate instinctively recognises her chances of pulling off a dignified exit-stage-left are on a par with the likelihood of nomination for a Nobel Prize. Jack only permits disengagement when he's ready; anyone else's requirements do not compute. He confessed once that he ended or engineered the conclusion of every single relationship he embarked on. Apart from his marriage, which still purports to be watertight in Jack's version of his first-class cruise through life.

This time she's going to take the initiative, vows Kate, scrutinising her face and deciding it will pass muster. God, but it's time-consuming, this business of packaging yourself for an affair. The rules preclude turning up in mangy jeans and a windcheater, it has to be glamour every time. As sound a reason for bailing out as any dilatory – but better late than never – notions about loyalty or morality. She could have waded through Bertrand Russell's *History of Western Philosophy* with all the hours lavished on blending, shading and defining a face that would never, not ever, earn a second glance when Jack's wife was in the vicinity.

She'll call a halt tonight for sure. Fortified with this sense of clambering a few rungs up the moral ladder, Kate activates the burglar alarm and closes the front door behind her. Then she has to de-activate it to retrieve a coat – in her exhilaration at knowing she'll be within Jack's ambit in ten minutes, less if she trots, she forgets that she needs another layer. He might proclaim himself enthralled by her skinny freckled arms but he won't be quite so smitten by goosebumps lurching upon them.

That's a characteristic of Jack, she thinks as she hurtles down the stairs. He fosters oblivion. Which just about sums up her attitude to Pearse. She has a disgraceful capacity for amnesia where he's concerned. Make that mental obliteration.

Her boyfriend – although Kate doubts Pearse was ever a boy because he was born middle-aged – is currently visiting his mother in Roscommon. This has allowed her the luxury of an hour in the bathroom reinventing her appearance for Jack's delectation, allied to the elimination of any obligation to construct a plausible excuse for heading out dressed like a slut on a week night. Thank heavens for Pearse's mother's unsteady turn the other day propelling him westwards.

Jack isn't in The Odeon when Kate arrives; she's disappointed, searching the bar decorated with a nod in the direction of a thirties theme. Then again, Jack is never there first. She always forgives him because she doesn't want to sound girlie about having reservations at hovering in a pub on her own. The Odeon is more central than the places they usually meet but Jack calculated it was safe because it attracts a young clientele, plus the lighting is so subdued you need a torch to find the marbled bar. And there's a sea of bodies bobbing around Kate so unless Moses shows up to part them, the chances of someone recognising her are remote to zero.

Kate is swirling the dregs of her red wine with burgeoning discontentment when Jack strolls in.

'You look gorgeous.' He unleashes his most intimate smile. Her resentment evaporates.

'Let me order you a refill,' he adds, stroking her back lightly with circular movements. 'Is that a new lipstick? Have I told you yet how sensational you look? How come you look extra fabulous tonight?'

'I had an early night last night,' laughs Kate, warmed by his main-beam attention. 'It's down to sleep, the ultimate beauty aid. No, come to think of it that's plastic surgery. But sleep must run the scalpel a close second.'

Jack looks faintly bemused as he leans an elbow on the bar and asks for two glasses of red wine. They arrive in miniature bottles and he carries them to a pair of curving cream leather armchairs which miraculously disgorge their occupants just as he searches for a place to sit. Life operates that way for Jack, reflects Kate, as he touches his glass to hers.

'Here's to wine and women, we'll pass on the song,' he says.

'To wine and men,' she responds. 'Although a man is only a man but a good glass of wine is a drink.'

'You purloined that from somewhere,' he accuses her lightly.

'Cannibalised it,' she shrugs. 'That's as acceptable as invention.'

Time to play the goodbye girl, she reminds herself minutes later as he crowds her, leaning across the table and gazing at her lips so intently she starts to wonder if she has a red wine rim around them. Covertly she rubs between nose and upper lip while pretending to adjust her ankle boot, then prepares to extract one of her guillotine lines from the ready-prepared store. But Jack distracts her by lifting her hand and running his thumb against her inner wrist.

'Feck it,' she decides, 'I'll tell him we're finished after we have sex. No point in ruining the evening.'

It seems churlish to raise the subject in the languorous afterglow of their lovemaking, especially when they have unfettered access to her apartment with Pearse's absence. Instead of biting the bullet Kate swallows it, along with her good intentions, and snuggles up to Jack who's radiator warm.

She's slumbering contentedly when he leaps up, dislodging her head from its perch on his shoulder and complaining she should have kept an eye on the time.

'Eimear will go ballistic if I wake her arriving home at 2 a.m.,' Jack whines, looking considerably less alluring with a crossly furrowed forehead and one foot in his underpants than he did a few hours earlier.

Kate regards him with a distinctly unenamoured expression as he cannonballs around her bedroom scooping up articles of clothing. She thought men were supposed to fall asleep after climaxing, not trash your room. Right, this is it, he's brought it on himself – she's ready for endgame. But Jack isn't.

'Listen, we have to talk,' she begins.

'Not now, baby girl; order me a cab, would you. And, um, you couldn't lend me a couple of notes to pay for it – I forgot to hit the hole-in-the-wall machine today.'

Automatically she dials up one of the local firms and hands him the price of his fare. By which stage Jack is dressed, prepared for flight and has regained his grip on the sixth-sense charm he operates.

He bends over the bed, cooing: 'What did you want to talk about, Katie-Kate?' and covers her face with feathered kisses which completely divert her from following her own advice delivered in front of the bathroom mirror. Oscar Wilde had the right idea about good advice: Pass it on. As precipitately as possible.

'Share the joke, baby girl,' murmurs Jack, by now licking her inner ear.

But before she responds the front-door buzzer sounds the taxi's arrival and he bounds away like a greyhound out of the trap.

Kate scowls, punching the pillows, and contemplates having that chat with Jack over the telephone. He can't trickle exactly the optimum quantity of saliva into her ear over the phone. Honeyed words are as much as he can manage there. She'll call him tomorrow.

The last conscious thought to strike Kate, as she nods off, renders that phone call unlikely.

'I don't honestly want to end this affair with Jack, that's why I'm having such trouble doing it. Just because Jack belongs to Eimear doesn't mean I can't share him – if we're discreet.'

CHAPTER 2

'I'm having an affair.'

The words dangle in the air, flaunting as temptingly as a Christmas bauble. Gloria's instinct is to take them down and examine them, just as she always longs to handle glittery tree decorations – touch them to check if they're real. She's lying in a hospital bed, a captive audience. If in doubt say nothing: that's her mother's advice. Gloria ignores it.

'Who with?' she asks Kate.

'With Jack,' responds Kate, feigning interest in the wilting floral arrangement on Gloria's locker.

The news is so startling it almost – almost – distracts Gloria from her own problems. Now she does take her mother's recommendation to heart, although only because she's too dumbstruck to speak. Kate glances at her covertly as she strips expiring foliage from the vase of moon daisies and seizes the silence as an invitation to elaborate.

'We're in love, Gloria. Neither of us planned it but it happened and now' – she blushes – 'we find we can't live without one another.'

'And love invents its own laws?' Gloria's tone is caustic; she's regained her power of speech and a sense of outrage along with it.

The stain on Kate's cheeks deepens, clashing spectacularly with her red hair. 'We know we're doing wrong,' she admits. 'This is such agony, ecstasy too, but agony. I can't erase Eimear from my mind.'

'You managed very nicely when you leapt into bed with her husband.'

'Oh, Glo, don't be angry with me, I know I'm a wicked temptress who deserves to be ducked in the village pond.'

Kate beats her chest in such mock-pious atonement that Gloria can't help but smile. Just for a nano-second; this is no laughing matter. She hurriedly resumes her stern expression.

'What were you thinking of, Kate McGlade, taking up with your best friend's husband and you with a man of your own at home?'

Kate bows her head in comic humility, hoping for an encore of the smile, but Gloria is relentless now, appalled at the impact her deviancy will wreak on their triumvirate.

'This is serious, Kate; this is beyond serious, you have to stop seeing him immediately.'

'I can't,' she wails, rumpling her hair until it's standing in peaks. 'It's the real thing, he's my Coca Cola lover.'

'Well then,' forecasts Gloria, 'prepare for Armageddon. And you'll probably have your cornflake-box crown confiscated.'

They each wore one, sprayed gold and decorated with fruit gums, twenty-six years ago as the Three Wise Men. Trouble is, they grew up to be Three Unwise Women.

But Gloria's losing sight of her own troubles with Kate and she's not ready to shed that comforting blanket of misery just yet – especially not to tackle a situation as explosive as this. A dear little nun who calls for an uninvited visit is just about to remind her of them. The sister totters into the room, sees another figure by the bedside and starts backing out, but Kate (natural born coward that she is, thinks Gloria) insists she has errands to run and she'll call by later.

'There's no need,' Gloria tells her.

'Holles Street Hospital is only around the corner from me, it's no bother, Glo. I'll bring you some flowers – these ones need urgent medical attention,' Kate bribes her.

'Make it freesias,' she barters. 'And don't think I've finished with you yet, you've a shopping trolley full of explaining to do.'

Kate settles the nun in a chair by Gloria's bedside and scuttles off, pulling faces at her behind the tiny sister's back. Gloria shakes her head: The woman's beyond redemption – one minute she's chanting *mea culpas*, the next she's behaving like a skit of a schoolgirl.

However she has a guest to take her mind off Kate's bombshell, one who looks like she's been paying hospital visits since the days of dancing at the crossroads. Not that nuns went in for much of that, unless of course they were late vocations. Gloria studies her covertly as she speaks: integrity and sincerity shine from the nun's eyes; she's in her mid-seventies, no veil, neatly cropped hair, silver band on her wedding ring finger, mysterious stain on the front of her black dress. Gin or vodka?

As she listens she stems a rising impulse to slap her visitor – a sting to shock her into silence. Gloria looks at her clasped hands on the bedspread and concentrates on controlling them. The nun is talking about God's will and how he moves in mysterious ways; Gloria nods whenever she looks directly at her and wraps fingers around fingers, pressing until white blotches spread across the surface of the skin.

'There's a reason for everything, even if we can't yet see it,' explains the visitor in tones Gloria hopes to be conclusive.

'Indeed there is, sister,' she agrees dully.

Fourteen years of convent education are no preparation for forcibly ejecting elderly nuns from your hospital room. Besides she's leaving now – no, it's a false alarm. The nun lifts her bag from the floor but instead of standing up she's rooting around for something.

Amazing, notes Gloria. You can spend a lifetime in a convent, devoting yourself to God and good works, but there are certain female traits that can never be sublimated and the instinct to cram handbags to the hilt is one of them.

The nun tracks down what she's searching for and produces it with a magician's flourish: a holy picture showing the Madonna and Child. Gloria holds it limply. Our Lady is wearing her usual impractical blue nightdress – who decided the poor woman always has to be kitted out in bedclothes anyway? The small blond toddler in Mary's arms looks like a right handful, no chance of persuading him to eat his greens if he doesn't feel like it.

Mother and tearaway have their hands joined in prayer peaks and at the bottom of the card is an invocation, 'Holy Mary, Mother of God, pray for us sinners.'

Even the Virgin Mary has a baby, Gloria thinks sourly. The nun settles herself back in the chair and she stares at her mouth as it opens and closes, opens and closes.

Can the nun direct her to where the Holy Spirit will impregnate her? Otherwise she may as well leave. It doesn't even have to be a child of God, an ordinary one will do.

A nurse's head appears around the door. It's Imelda, Gloria's favourite one. She and her boyfriend are saving up to emigrate to Australia but they keep having to postpone the departure date because of sessions. Either it's a session for a brother's birthday or a session for a friend's wedding (that can run into week-long celebrations) or a session for their engagement. Sessions are what make life worth living for Imelda but they don't help her and Gerry the Guard save for their Outback odyssey.

'Doctor Hughes is about to make his rounds,' she announces, a prim figure in her nurse's white. You'd never think this was the girl who bartered a pint of Guinness and her uniform badge for the male stripper's lurex thong at a hen party last week, claiming she wanted Gerry the Guard to try it for size. Gloria looks hopefully at her but is unable to signal the necessary distress flare.

Fortunately Imelda's talents don't begin and end with partying like there's no Gomorrah. A glance at the patient's face shows an unnatural brightness in the eyes. Instead of bustling off, Imelda comes into the room and helps the nun to her feet:

'I think it's time we gave you a drop of tea, sister, we'll have you worn out with all the visits you're paying.'

No wonder they call nurses angels, thinks Gloria. If Imelda weren't engaged she'd marry the girl herself. Of course she's married already, and the wrong sex to pledge herself to someone called Imelda – at least here in Ireland. Still, she feels a rush of love for the nurse in that instant.

'Here we go, sister.' Imelda beams down into the older woman's face as she lifts her bag and attaches it to the bent arm.

'Well, maybe a cup of something would be pleasant,' concedes the nun, allowing herself to be led.

She hobbles to a halt as she passes Gloria's bedside and pats a hand, not noticing the bone poking through the knuckles.

'I hope I've helped you, dear. It's good of you to let me talk to you. You'd be surprised how many people don't want to be bothered these days. They tell me they've lost their faith, as though they could misplace it like a spool of thread.'

'Thank you for your trouble, sister,' whispers Gloria as she potters off.

'I'm the world's biggest hypocrite,' Gloria wails to the empty room.

She buries her face in the pillow, not knowing if she hates this inoffensive nun or herself more. The misery wells up and splashes down her cheeks. It's not fair, she sobs against the starch. The worst sort of pillow talk. But even weeping requires energy that she can't muster – the tears peter out and she's left with a thumping headache.

Imelda lands back with the doctor, who glances at her blotchy face and decides to jolly her along. Gloria imagines him dressed like Ronald McDonald handing out balloons.

'Now, now, we can't have this moping, there'll be plenty more babies,' he booms.

Imelda sits beside Gloria and holds her fingers in her capable, calloused nurse's hand – Gloria is amazed at how needily she clings to it.

'This is only a temporary setback, you'll be pregnant again in no time,' insists Dr Hughes.

Feck off, you quack, she says, but only inside her head. She feels better and a twitch that could pass for a half-hearted smile chases across her face. The doctor is delighted with himself.

'Sensible girl,' he nods, flicking through her notes.

He's headmasterly, jowly and heavy-handed with the after-shave. A few checks and he's on his way.

'I'll be seeing you in the maternity ward one of these days,' he calls from the door.

Not if I see you first, you scut, she says, but naturally it's only inside her head again.

Kate and Eimear arrive simultaneously: Kate is weighed down with bribes – a stack of magazines in her arms as well as flowers – while Eimear proffers a box of chocolates so large she should have applied for planning permission.

'God love you, Gloria, you've been through the wars. How many pints of blood did they pump you full of? I wonder whose blood it was? I hadn't a notion ectopic pregnancies were so serious – that you can actually die from them. You're not going to die on us now, are you, break up the trio?'

Kate rattles through this without so much as drawing breath, she always did take life at the gallop. Eimear is quieter, she perches on the edge of the bed and looks steadily at her friend's wan face.

Gloria sees Kate's game, she's trying to pretend she didn't visit her earlier. While Eimear struggles to open the window – it's painted shut – Kate gives Gloria a cautionary look, taps her finger against her lips and says loudly, 'Mulligan here and I bumped into each other by the front desk.'

As she gushes on about what a fright they've had, Eimear leans across, whispers, 'Poor you,' and touches the invalid's hair. It's exactly what she needs. The stroking soothes her, she has a little wallow, then, when Eimear murmurs, 'Such bad luck,' she's ready to be brave.

'Good luck, bad luck, who knows?' Gloria gives an elaborate shrug.

They stare at her a moment before laughing aloud – nervous peals, admittedly, but better than none at all.

'Good luck, bad luck, who knows?' they repeat, mimicking the shrug.

It's their mantra, the three have parroted it for years when one of them has a setback. Unbelievably it does cheer them up.

Gloria is almost enjoying their visit. Perhaps that's an overstatement, since she'll never rejoice in anything again, but they do distract her from her misery – and from Kate's atomic conversational gambit of a few hours earlier.

'How'd you end up with a private room?' asks Kate, as she rips the cover off Eimear's chocolates. 'You could fly from Dublin to Florida and back for the price of a couple of nights.'

'Mick's job at the bank gives us free health cover.'

Gloria is vague, she's scrutinising the contents with the due gravity such an outsized package of cocoa solids deserves. Chinese farmers could probably grow enough rice to feed a family of eight on a patch of land the size of this box. The chocolates are called Inspirational Irish Women and they make their selection from such luminaries of Hibernian womanhood as Lady Gregory and Countess Markievicz. Kate chooses Maud Gonne so she can tell her Belfast hospital story again.

'Remember the summer you worked as a domestic in the

17

Royal?' Gloria prompts her and she's in like Flynn with the rest of the story.

'One of the regular domestics was called Maud and if anyone asked for her when her shift was finished, I used to tell them, "Maud's gone," and then double over,' she recalls. 'None of them ever seemed to get the joke, they just thought it was a mistake to take on light-headed students.'

'Which it was,' interjects Eimear.

'Which it was,' agrees Kate. 'The amount of pinching that went on was serious. I still have a conscience about the breast pump I stuffed into my holdall – I didn't even know anyone who was breastfeeding. I ended up dumping it in the Lagan one night.'

'You were young and stupid,' consoles Eimear. 'Weren't we all.'

'What's my excuse now,' Kate responds.

It jolts Gloria back into a recollection of her friend's transgression. How can she giggle with Eimear about student high-jinks when she's behaving like a low life with her husband? This needs sorting – only not just yet. She aches too much to concentrate on anything but her own hurt.

She watches her friends as they chatter, flicking through magazines and reading her get-well cards. Kate's guessing who they're from by the pictures on the front. She lifts one that reads 'To My Darling Wife' in gold lettering and says: 'Next-door neighbour? The boss? No, it has to be from the cat.'

'You fool,' Eimear slaps her playfully.

If only she knew, frowns Gloria, there'd be nothing light-hearted about that blow. But she can't be the one to tell her. Can she? She sucks on a ragged fingernail and tunes out of their conversation, content simply to have them there in the room with her. Her two best friends. They interpreted it as a sign when they were chosen for the nativity play: they'd been singled out to become a troika.

Ostensibly the roles went to the girls because they were the tallest in the class and the likeliest males, providing curls and dimples could be overlooked. But they knew better – it was meant to be. When three girls have been through the Loreto Convent school play together, wearing scratchy cotton-wool beards, it forms a bond. How they swanned about in their cornflake-box crowns.

Gloria is six again and decked out in her mother's ruby quilted dressing gown, trailing sleeves and trailing hem. Eimear was the black wise man and wore not just a crown but a turban too. Of course you're only meant to have one or the other but when Eimear saw her friends' gilded concoctions she threw a tantrum until the nuns gave in to her. And that took some scene because nuns aren't ones for giving in: it sets a damaging precedent.

Eimear carried the gold, Kate the frankincense and she had the mirror. That's what they called it, initially by mistake and then as their first private joke. Gloria still has a photo of the three of them, looking bashfully exotic in their cobbled together finery, with Sister Thaddeus – the play's director, casting manager and costumier – exposing an excessive quantity of gum alongside. She came from Dublin, the finest city in the world she claimed, and none of them could contradict her. At six you don't tend to be well-travelled.

'How far is Dublin from Omagh?' they asked.

'A hundred and twelve miles,' she said – an immeasurable distance.

After the nativity play they became a trinity. Three was their lucky number: there were three of them, that's one trio; they were the three wise men, that's another; each of them was six, that's two threes; and they were all born in September, the ninth month, three threes.

As teenagers they fantasised about forming one of those all-girl singing trios and taking on the pop world: Eimear as their lead singer, the blonde one that everyone could fancy,

Kate and Gloria mopping up the stragglers – Kate with her copper hair and Gloria with her nearly black. Something for everyone in the audience. It never went beyond a few rehearsals of 'Leader of the Pack', with the girls cooing about meeting a biker in the candy store in dire American accents. Everyone sings in brutal American accents in Irish country towns, it's the rule. They had their name picked out before the first rehearsal: The Unholy Trinity.

They were inseparable all through school, then diverged to colleges in Belfast, Dublin and London – but it was only a trial separation because they all ended up together in Dublin. That was down to Eimear's machinations because she kept sending the others ads for jobs cut out of the Dublin papers.

'We might as well have conceded defeat the first time she mentioned us moving to Dublin because Eimear always gets what she wants, she's one of life's winners,' reflects Gloria. 'I'm one of life's runners-up and Kate doesn't even bother going under starter's orders because she's not in the same race.'

Being stuck in hospital is an example of how she always falls at some hurdle or other. She wants a baby and becomes pregnant – so far so good. But it's not a viable pregnancy, to use that delightful medical term fielded by Dr Hughes, so instead of a baby she ends up with an ambulance ride at 3 a.m., an operation and a chunk out of a fallopian tube. She thinks she'll have a slash of a scar too, from the peek she took when Imelda was changing her dressing, although she doesn't like looking at it. The place where they cut her baby out.

Mick was throwing up while they operated on her. Hospitals have that effect on him.

Mick's her husband of eight years, the man she's loved since a teenager. Wouldn't you think they could take Dr Hughes' advice, crassly expressed though it is, and push on with rupturing her other fallopian tube or planting a baby in the right spot? Not if her Michael has anything to do with it. He's saying they have to take a break from babymaking, a proper break, until she mends – and Gloria has the distinct impression he means from sex as well as procreation. Not that she necessarily wants him to climb on her here and now in the hospital bed but she'd like to think there'd be some cavorting this side of the menopause.

'The trouble is,' she broods, 'I'm dealing with a man who looks relieved at the idea he's under doctor's orders to tuck his wife into the far end of the bed and drop a chaste kiss on her forehead.'

To add insult to injury she has a nun who tells her what's happened is God's will, a doctor who predicts she'll go on to produce a brood of seven and, the final ignominy, a bedpan below her backside. Which she's actually grateful for. But at least the nurses are human and there's always Kate and Eimear to bring her chocolates and set her laughing. Although it hurts her right side when she does, the missing-tube side where her baby clung fleetingly to life.

CHAPTER 3

Kate visits Gloria, whispering that she's ducked out of work for the afternoon. An undertone implies a sense of guilt but it's obviously not an emotion she's familiar with.

Look at her, she can hardly wait to talk about The Revelation – Gloria's already labelling it with capitals because it's so sensational. She's seething with Kate, partly because she senses a furtive glee, even as Kate claims to feel like Judas.

Kate can't stop mentioning Jack's name, she breathes the word lingeringly, describing the affair in bodice ripper-speak – her heart skips a beat when she sees him and her legs buckle beneath his kisses. Gloria thinks she might at least make an effort to avoid clichés if she's determined to force her to sit through this. As far as she knows, Kate's never read a Thrills and Swoon in her life but you'd swear she was reared on them from her engorged prose. Anyway, between the irregular heartbeats and unreliable legs, the crux of the matter is that Kate's conscience is interfering with her big clinch close-ups.

'I don't want to hurt Eimear,' Kate sighs.

'Should've thought about that before you played Open Sesame with her husband,' Gloria remarks.

Kate turns a reproachful gaze on her. 'I didn't come here for a lecture, Gloria.'

'I hope you didn't come for absolution either.'

She's becoming increasingly incensed by Kate – she's risking the triumvirate, measuring a fling with Jack above more than twenty-five years of friendship. And in a dark recess, a part of her consciousness she can scarcely bring herself to acknowledge, Gloria is jealous. Jack's so glamorous: a lecturer at Trinity College, a published poet, a regular on chat shows, and to cap it all he looks like Aidan Quinn. The first time she saw him her pulse kept time with the *Riverdance* score but she'd never dream of casting a glad eye in his direction, not only because he belongs to her friend but because he's too dazzling to be interested in her.

Yet here he is having it away with Kate who's no better looking than herself. Of course Kate has the red hair, some men are pushovers for that, usually dodgy ones, Kate claims. Gloria supposes it has to be the intellectual appeal, she's a lawyer and witty in a flippant way, with brains to burn. Mind you, Kate's obviously set fire to more brain cells than she can spare if this stupid adventure is anything to judge by. But since when did intelligence stop people making complete eejits of themselves.

'They don't have kids, it's not as if I'd be breaking up a family home,' Kate justifies herself.

'So you're thinking of galloping off into the wide blue yonder with him.'

Kate drops her eyes before Gloria's challenge and a pause drags into a silence.

'Not really,' she sighs finally. 'I know it has to end but I feel as if I've wandered into a room with no doors marked exit. I'm fond of Pearse, it's just that Jack is so irresistible.'

'Pearse. I wondered how long it would take before we got around to Pearse,' Gloria yells.

He's the man Kate lives with, an old dear who's knocking on a bit, but she knew that when she moved in with him. Or rather, invited him to move in with her. He lived some miles outside the city in Skerries, a seaside spot favoured by families but not much use to party animals, according to Kate.

23

Gloria feels her friend is getting a bit long in the tooth for this goodtime girl malarkey but Kate turns huffy if she intimates as much.

'The night is young and so am I,' Kate insists after an evening out, when the others are desperate for their beds. She makes them feel like social outcasts if they attempt to slope off home at midnight.

'Don't worry, pumpkins are in this season,' is her rallying cry as she tries to reconvene the team at some drinking den where staff reverse the Wedding Feast of Cana miracle with the wine served.

But back to Pearse.

'I'd prefer to leave Pearse out of this,' says Kate.

'I'm sure you would but he's part of your life,' Gloria snaps.

'My insignificant other.' Kate pulls a face.

'Behave yourself, Kate, you're living with him, he deserves better.'

'I know, he deserves a wonderful woman who'll make him delirious with joy for a lifetime and I can't do that. Even without Jack in the frame I couldn't do it. But with Jack . . .'

Gloria meditates. There's nothing romantic about Kate and Jack betraying Eimear because they've fallen in lust and confused it with love. However she raises the white flag.

'Look Kate, I haven't the energy for this, I haven't the strength for my own problems let alone yours. Since you're determined to confess, why don't you get your completely insincere act of contrition off your chest as quickly as possible and give me some peace. How did you and Jack discover it was your life's mission to have two hearts beating as one?'

'Initially I was flattered by his interest – I'd never have imagined I could be Jack O'Brien's type. I decided he was having a rush of blood to the head and it would simmer down but it's been three months now and we're still crazy about each other. Let's face it, he could have anyone he likes,' Kate concludes in that pathetic, tremulous voice Gloria finds so out-of-character – and so infuriating, 'and he chose me.'

'Come on, Kate, you can do better than that,' she admonishes.

Kate expels air noisily. 'I suppose Jack winkled his way into my affections at a vulnerable time. Pearse was hammering away about how we ought to get married, since we've been living together for four years and how he'd like to have a few kids. I said where's your hurry, sure men can have prostate operations and hip replacements and still produce babies. But Pearse said fathering them was all very well but being able to bend over and pick them up was another matter entirely.

'Jaysus, Glo, it was babies, babies and more babies with the man, he was obsessed. He couldn't understand why my biological clock wasn't ticking, like most women's over thirty, and I said if I heard it ticking wasn't I bloody well able to tell it to shut up. I . . . oh God, I'm so sorry, Gloria, I was forgetting about you – talk about insensitive.'

Gloria shrugs. 'People can't tiptoe around me forever,' she manages, although a few more days of fancy footwork would be welcome.

Kate continues: 'I was feeling harassed and then I bumped into Jack one day in Grafton Street and before I knew it we were in the Shelbourne with Irish coffees, gossiping and laughing about nothing in particular – and then all of a sudden he leaned over and pushed my hair out of my eyes and we both knew.'

'Knew that you were about to cheat and lie and abandon a friend?' demands Gloria. 'You're mad, you're dealing with a man who thinks trust is only a word that applies to his pension plan, and you're no better yourself, Kate McGlade.'

Gloria can't mask her rage. How dare anyone else be happy when life has kicked her in the stomach and then aimed its Doc Marten at the side of her head for good measure.

Kate shrugs. 'Since when did you turn judge and jury,

Gloria? You must remember what it's like to be in love. How the more you feel the world is against you, the more you cling to one another. Yes, I feel guilty, but I also feel I'm bursting with life.'

'It's a wonder you've never been caught out – people know each other's business here, this is a city the size of a village,' says Gloria.

'We're very careful,' replies Kate, but Gloria arches a dubious eyebrow.

'You'll be walking up the street hand in hand one day when you're supposed to be at a conference in Edinburgh and you'll bump into Eimear or Pearse or both,' she predicts.

Another silence falls between them, not the comfortable quietness among friends but a brooding stillness. Gloria ruptures it at last.

'Why are you telling me all this, Kate? Eimear's my friend as much as you are. Do you expect me to keep a secret like this from her?'

Kate twists her mouth – it could be a smile, it could be a grimace.

'That's your business, Glo. I confided in you but if you choose to go to her . . .' her voice tails off.

Gloria is amazed. A thought is materialising in her dazed brain and she can't quite acknowledge it: it's as if Kate wants her to tell Eimear, then the decision will be out of her hands.

There's a rattle at the door and the afternoon cup of tea and two dull-dull-dull digestives arrive (have they never heard of Mikado biscuits?) delivered by Mary, one of the domestics. Gloria has yet to catch her without a smile as wide as the street, despite the fact she has breast cancer – everyone has their story to tell and there are no secrets in a hospital. She winks and leaves a second cup for Kate, although she's not supposed to supply visitors.

'What should I do?' asks Kate, as soon as they're alone.

26

'Break it off and keep your mouth shut, there's no point in salving your conscience at the expense of Eimear's peace of mind,' Gloria orders. 'Nor Pearse's,' is an afterthought.

'You're right.' Kate nods, adding sugar to her tea, although she hasn't taken it since she gave it up for Lent sixteen years ago. They all abandoned sugar at the same time to subjugate fleshly desires (Sister Xavier's idea) and leave them as thin as rakes for Easter (Eimear's contribution).

They chat desultorily for ten minutes more, then Kate lifts her coat. Impulsively Gloria delays her.

'Tell me, Kate, is it worth it?'

Her face is radiant. 'God, yes. I'm miserable and torn and full of self-loathing but I also feel extravagant, exhilarated, energised.'

'Sounds as though you're high on Es,' Gloria puns – but Kate doesn't notice.

'I feel as though anything and everything's possible. A kiss from Jack is a hundred times more exciting than full-blown rumpy bumpy with Pearse, though he's the most loyal man a woman could ask for. He could find me spread-eagled in bed with Jack sweating on top and still he'd try to believe the best. Like Jack drugged me or he'd walked through the wrong front door and mistaken me for Eimear. I despise myself. But not enough to want to stop.'

'You are going to stop, though, aren't you?' Gloria insists, more stridently than she intends, but here's her own world knocked to kingdom come and Kate's having sex with some-one she shouldn't be and relishing every humpingly fantastic minute of it.

'I must stop, I know that,' Kate agrees and, blowing a kiss, she's gone.

Shortly after 5 p.m., Mick turns up. She contemplates telling him about Jack and Kate but dismisses it on the grounds that he might blurt something out or even turn whistle-blower deliberately. Men don't feel the same way about keeping secrets as women do.

Instead she talks about the mastectomy faced by Mary, the cheerful trolley lady, and once he's worked out which one she is he's suitably interested. It's astonishing how much you can know about a person you don't know.

She watches him defy the shape of his mouth to decimate one of the digestives she saved for him in a single bite and wonders how she'd feel if he were having an affair.

Provided it wasn't Kate or Eimear she could handle it. Of course, she acknowledges, she's probably being complacent because she can't actually picture it happening. She may fancy Mick (or at least she must have once), but she can't imagine many other women panting to grapple with him.

He has a faintly seedy air, not the academic dishevelment of Jack, the 'I'm so engrossed in intellectual matters I can't remember to push a comb through my hair' approach; Mick's is the 'What's a comb anyway?' outlook. And he's put weight on – there's a perfectly formed pot belly wobbling over his trouserband – with more to come, she suspects.

'Would you listen to me, and I'm supposed to be his nearest and dearest,' she scolds herself.

There's another reason why she doesn't tell Mick about Kate: he grew up next door to her, he'd never want to believe ill of Kate, he thinks she's the bee's knees.

'I must stop using Mick's expressions.' Gloria is alarmed at the thought of becoming a Tweedledee/Tweedledum version of her husband. The entire Tyrone Gaelic football team (their home squad) are also the bee's knees, except when he loses money on them; Gloria hasn't felt she's the bee's knees in Mick's eyes for the longest time.

They met through Kate, who revealed the impossibly exciting news that he fancied her long before he had the nerve to say so himself. They had their first kiss when she was sixteen and sex on his twenty-first birthday. That was a mistake, he was too fluthered to know his lad from his big toe but she felt she owed it to him. Her gift-wrapped body to unpeel. Except he treated it the way most people behave with wrapping paper. Nevertheless they became engaged a couple of years later and Gloria was the first of the trio to wed, at twenty-four.

That's a slice of the reason why she's jealous of Kate, she's put it about and Gloria hasn't used it half enough. She wishes she'd tripped the light fantastic with a few more partners when she had the chance, but Mick was always there in the background and before she knew it she was parading down the aisle in white. Not exactly a virgin but not what you'd call experienced either.

Mick wants kids too. He and Gloria delayed it because of careers and buying houses but when she turned thirty they decided the time had come.

'The time has come, the walrus said, to talk of many things,' whispers Gloria.

She and Mick don't talk of many things any more, especially not of cabbages and kings. Still they're unanimous it's time now. Except, instead of pregnancy, they had a puzzled year of trying and failing, of buying ovulation kits, of tracking her cycle like it held the answer to the Third Secret of Fatima. Which, as everyone now knew, was an overrated secret anyway.

Gloria frowns. You spend your twenties frantically trying to avoid pregnancy and your thirties even more frenziedly trying to engineer it. Somebody up there's having a belly laugh at the lot of them. Who'd have guessed the only sure-fire way to get pregnant was by being a teenager in the back of a borrowed car.

Mick and she thought they'd cracked it last month when no period came for almost two weeks after it was due – but then she had a bleed, ten days of feeling sorry for herself, followed by an emergency admission to hospital a few days ago with her ectopic pregnancy. The surgeon explained about ectopic pregnancies to Gloria, the one who removed a vital section of her right fallopian tube and a minuscule foetus with it. The surgeon held up his baby fingernail to show her its size.

Even after his explanation Gloria felt she needed clarification. Mick brought in a dictionary so they could look up what had happened to them.

It said, 'Ectopia: condition in which the foetus is outside the womb.'

Gloria reflects on this bald definition, pondering its accuracy and inaccuracy. It doesn't say anything about bleeding internally as you lie beside your husband, thinking your neck and shoulder aches are caused by the awkward position you've adopted all day in bed to accommodate stomach cramps – pains caused by the blood saturating your insides and being forced up your body.

It doesn't say anything about trying to wake your husband, who sleeps like the dead, about not being able to move until finally by some atavistic spark for survival you crawl to the edge of the bed, topple out and your husband starts up and calls an ambulance.

It doesn't say anything about the visitors who blithely assume you can press ahead and have another baby when you're feeling better, because you still have one fallopian tube, or about the nurses who hug you and show they understand your world has juddered to a standstill, even as they charge about running a hectic ward.

Definitions lull you into a false sense that things are explicable. But maybe the older nurse who suggested she plant something to remember her baby by was right. A holly bush to rhyme with Molly – that's the name she'd have chosen for a girl. She senses she was a girl, her fingernail-sized nearly life.

CHAPTER 4

Eimear is slumped at the bottom of Gloria's hospital bed and it doesn't take a Sam Spade to detect she's been crying. On anyone else it would look blotchy and unappealing, on Eimear it's tragic and captivating.

'I know you have your own troubles, Glo,' her voice is brittle, 'but I have to turn to someone and telling you is like keeping it in the family. Jack is seeing someone else.'

Gloria is alarmed. 'Eimear, I find that hard to believe, isn't the man besotted with you.'

'Jack's the kind of man who can love you to bits but still shag other women.'

'And have you any idea who she might be?' Gloria enquires cautiously.

'Probably one of his students or maybe a colleague, I don't care a great deal who she is to tell you the truth. It's not the woman but the deed that bothers me.'

'Have you tackled him about it?'

'No, I'm planning to do it tonight.' Eimear's expression is sullen. 'I've had my suspicions for a while but no proof. Then this morning I opened his credit-card statement and found he'd spent the night in a Dublin hotel when he told me he was in Cork at a poetry festival.'

Eimear slings her bag on the floor with the degree of venom usually reserved for skirts with broken zips and continues: 'I rang the hotel and they confirmed it was a double room.

Clumsy of him, wasn't it? I thought adulterers were supposed to cover their tracks by using cash. Maybe he wants me to find out, save him the nuisance of confessing.'

She mopes while Gloria tries to think of something positive. Before she can dish up the platitude of the day, Eimear adds: 'I know he's been with a woman for some time – there's a smell about him that's different and he's paying me more attention than he's ever bothered to before, showing me his poems and asking what I think of them. Of course I always say they're magnificent, isn't that what he wants to hear, where's the point in suggesting he lob in a rhyme once in a while. It only gets him all het up and exasperated.'

Eimear has never been a fan of Jack O'Brien's work. His brooding looks, yes, his earning power, yes, his television appearances, yes, his ability to make every woman feel she's the most fascinating creature he's met, yes – his poetry, ho hum.

'So you're definitely going to thrash it out with him tonight,' asks Gloria.

'Don't you think I should?'

'Not necessarily. What if it's a fling that's been flung? What if he was just getting something out of his system, or it was a one-off aberration, or a drunken mistake he's trying to put behind him?'

'You mean let sleeping dogs lie?'

'Exactly!'

'Or lying dogs sleep easy,' mutters Eimear, but the venom has ebbed from her voice.

She doesn't want a scene, she prefers everything serene and ordered. The three of them do, they're Librans after all.

'I brought you the *Irish Times*.' Eimear ransacks her bag, just like the nun. The paper is located under a can of hair mousse and she reaches it over, then heads immediately for the sink in the corner of the room to scrub her hands.

'Newsprint everywhere,' complains Eimear.

After she leaves Gloria checks the date on the front of the paper: excellent, it's a Saturday (you lose track of days in a hospital) so there'll be birth announcements. She turns to them at once.

Two Clares, an Aoife and twins Gemma and Joseph. Hmm. Aoife has potential. There's also a brace of Seans, a Patrick and a Sarah. Patrick's lovely but he'd end up a Paddy. She scans the list of parents' names and is relieved to find she doesn't know any of them.

Another set of twins, Richard and Alison, catches her eye.

'Good God above,' she rants, 'it's bad enough other women having babies without managing two at once; no wonder there aren't enough to go around for the rest of us.'

She's still wading through birth weights and welcomes from brothers and sisters when Mick walks in.

'Eimear phoned last night and said she'd be in this morning,' he tells her.

'Been and gone,' replies Gloria as he leans over to kiss her. On the forehead again. Does the man think she's had her lips amputated?

Gloria surreptitiously turns the page so he can't see Birth Announcements but Mick isn't fooled.

'I don't believe it, you're not at that again, Gloria, you'll do your head in.'

She toys with the idea of tears but hasn't the heart for them.

'I was only taking a quick look at some names.' She smiles brightly. 'What do you think of Aoife?'

'I think you should have your head examined putting us both through this. What are you doing, picking out names for babies after what's happened to the two of us.'

His tone is so vexed she feels aggrieved.

'You're not the one who needed a massive blood transfusion, you're just the one who snored like a pig until I was knocking on death's door.'

He throws her a reproachful glance. 'It's mentally unbalanced, reading up on baby names at a time like this. You'll push yourself over the edge and I'll be left to gather up the pieces.'

She realises it's madness but she can't help herself, it's like picking a scab – she knows it won't help the healing process but there it is on her knee insisting on being fiddled with.

Perhaps if she could say this to Mick it would help but she doesn't, she rolls over and faces the door, her back towards him. Lunch arrives and she leaves the tray untouched.

'You must eat,' he insists, 'you'll never get well otherwise.'

'I'm not hungry,' she pouts.

'Force yourself.'

'No.'

'It's criminal to waste food like that.'

'You eat it if you're so concerned.'.

'I didn't come to hospital to eat your lunch,' he objects.

'Well what did you come for? It certainly wasn't to cheer me up or distract me with news or keep me company – from what I can see you came to lecture me and order me about.'

Mick lifts his coat. 'I'll call back later when you're feeling calmer; this is a difficult time for me too you know.'

He compresses his lips into a paving crack and stalks off.

Gloria removes the cover from the lunch plate – vegetable curry. Trifle to follow. She leaves the curry, eats half the trifle – 'A drop of sherry would work wonders for you,' she addresses the bowl – and switches on the television. Imelda calls by with some medication and mentions that she'll be discharged on Monday. She also reveals that the Australia fund is seriously depleted as a result of last night's session.

'Another hen party?' asks Gloria.

'No, leaving do for one of Gerry the Guard's schoolfriends New York-bound to make his fortune.'

'So you gave it some welly.'

'I gave it some shoe – I lost one, don't ask me how, and Gerry the Guard had to piggyback me up the garden path but he slipped on ice and we ended up skittering about all over the place – he got me there in the end though it was more of a slither than a manly stride. They don't have that snake on the Garda Siochana crest for nothing.'

Imelda bounces away, fresh-faced, but reappears within seconds. 'Call for you, Gloria, I think it's your mother. I'll wheel the phone in.'

Gloria's spirits lift at the prospect of a maternal chat but it turns out to be her mother-in-law, the real Mrs McDermott. She's not the worst in the world but Gloria isn't in the humour for her.

'Lovie, I know exactly how you must be feeling,' bawls the voice on the end of the line. 'I lost two babies myself before Mick came along, bless him. You never forget a miscarriage, no matter how many babies you have afterwards.'

'That's a comfort,' Gloria thinks bitterly, holding the phone a few inches from her ear.

'Oh, it was hard in my day, sure enough,' she bellows, 'you had to get on with it if you lost a baby.'

Her mother-in-law continues in this vein for five minutes, while Gloria fantasises about hanging up and claiming they were disconnected.

'Still, I have my boys and I wouldn't trade them for the world. You should always remember this about babies, lovie, if they don't make you laugh they'll never make you cry.'

'Margaret,' Gloria interrupts, desperation lending her fluency. 'You've no idea how much I appreciate your call, it's helped so much. But there's only the one phone on this corridor and I can't monopolise it. I'm going home soon, I'll ring you then.'

'Are you indeed? I'll pop down and visit you, so. I have the free travel since I turned sixty last year.'

Somebody up there has really got it in for her. Gloria sends the telephone trolley clattering against the wall and prepares to treat herself to another wallow, she's earned it. So they're turning her out on Monday: out to the tender mercies of a mother-in-law determined to be supportive if she loses her voice in the process, and of a husband who can't bear to touch her. Gloria's grown curiously attached to this sloppily painted orange hospital room although she's shed tears in it, raged at Mick in it, leaked more tears in it and railed against life in it.

She contemplates her departure. Time to count her blessings instead of sheep, that's what Bing Crosby recommends and he wouldn't give you a wrong steer. On the plus side: she'll have her own things about her, and didn't Maureen O'Hara stress the importance of that on behalf of women everywhere in *The Quiet Man*. On the minus side: no nurses, fewer visitors and she'll have to make her own tea. She confides in the bedside locker: 'Maybe I'll send Mick out to Arnott's for a Teasmaid, it can be my coming-home present from him.'

Except he doesn't want her home, he prefers her safely out of the way in hospital.

CHAPTER 5

Eimear always expected to be implacable if she discovered Jack straying. No wavering, no listening to excuses, no nonsense. Funny how wrong you can be. She still can't bear to listen to his explanations, she finds it offensive enough that it happened without hearing the gory details to salve his confessional binge. Describing the affair makes the woman flesh and blood, she prefers her shadowy. Anyway, Eimear couldn't care less about her rival.

'Stop, she's not a rival, this isn't a competition for Jack O'Brien's affections,' she shrieks, equanimity in splinters.

Now what brought that on, she frets into a soothing Baileys with ice, leftover Christmas supplies. She's rationalised this, it's his infidelity that bothers her; the other woman hasn't cheated and lied, Jack has. The other woman hasn't ignored any pledges, Jack has. Eimear has no quarrel with her. She empties the dregs of the bottle into her glass, can't be bothered adding more ice, and wishes Jack O'Brien's other woman disease-ridden and bankrupt. Is that too extreme? She contemplates moving on to the remnants of the Tia Maria and decides it's not extreme enough. How about disease-ridden, bankrupt and bald.

Perhaps she should make some coffee and pour the Tia Maria into it. To heck with coffee, it dilutes the alcohol. Jack's other woman, the one with hair falling out in clumps if hexes work, is no sister of hers whatever the sisterhood claim. Eimear trails the liqueur over her tongue and glances at the clock: drinking at 11 a.m., see what Jack O'Brien has driven her to. Aided, abetted and bloody-well-chauffeured by a woman.

She vacillates between a rational need to understand and an irrational urge to bludgeon someone, preferably her husband but the other woman will do very nicely too. If women are all meant to be sisters, why do some of them allow themselves to become susceptible to married men? Sibling rivalry obviously, female emancipation means empowerment, so that when you envy another's toys you snatch them off her. No room for maidenly modesty here. Eimear contemplates her unknown challenger: it would make her smash and grab easier if she dumped Jack and she doesn't propose to do anything so convenient for her machinations.

But she does intend making him suffer for a while. Her strategy is that tried and tested formula, the silent treatment, coupled with separate meals and even more separate beds.

He's lucky they're still sleeping under the same roof.

A memory intrudes on Eimear's punishment scheme, lurching into her thought processes and tickling a reluctant laugh; Kate always called Tia Marias 'Tina Maries' because she overheard two old dears order that once. The giggle turns into a snuffle and then a sob.

Eimear drags herself back from the brink and stands up, sending her chair clattering. She recaps the bottle so forcefully she loses a fingernail; it's drinking in the morning that's making her feel weepy, not this wobble in her relationship with Jack.

But she's going to chart it back on course now and that means showing him the error of his ways. He relishes his home comforts, let's see how he likes it when they're unavailable to him.

'This is a war of attrition,' Eimear advises the Baileys

bottle in the instant before catapulting it into the kitchen bin. 'Whoops, forgot to recycle. Ah, so what, the world has stopped turning – doesn't matter if the environment is banjaxed.'

She slumps back at the kitchen table, cradling her cheek with the heel of her hand. It's peculiar, she reflects, how few men have any stomach for the kind of skirmishing that women excel at. Recriminations he can handle, tears he can handle, but silence and sulking and ignoring him? He's actually accused her of mental cruelty.

Their conversation went like this:

Jack: 'What sort of a day did you have?'

Eimear: Silence.

Jack: 'I said what sort of a day did you have, Eimear?'

Eimear: Silence.

Jack: 'Is it a crime to make conversation now?'

Eimear: Silence.

Jack: 'Answer me, is it a fecking crime to make conversation now?'

Eimear: 'Do you have to repeat everything twice but with expletives for good measure?'

Jack: 'At least you're talking to me.'

Eimear: Silence.

Jack: 'Come on, Eimear, do you want blood? A pound of flesh? I've said I'm sorry, I've tried to make it up to you, you can't bear a grudge forever. Tell me you forgive me and I'll never look at another woman again, so help me God. I'll give my lectures in blinkers, I'll cross the street if I see a skirt approaching, I'll stop kissing my mother if that's what it takes.'

Eimear: Silence.

Jack: 'You're a cold piece and no mistake. This is cruelty, deliberate and premeditated. At least what I did was in the heat of the moment. You're a hard-hearted witch and you're savouring every minute of this. I bet you're delighted you caught me out, it reinforces that innate sense of superiority you have.'

(She leaves the room.)

He's right, Eimear admits now, curled foetus-like on the bed. She is gratified at having Jack in the wrong in a ditch and herself sitting pretty on the moral high ground. Except she loves this man, desperately, although he's cheated on her and will again given half a chance.

'He doesn't even need half a chance, quarter would do him,' she snivels. 'He's one of those libidinous men for whom one woman is never enough, there's another conquest around the corner and she's always more exciting than whoever's waiting at home.'

Eimear prepares to abandon herself to the luxury of tears, but realises within seconds that her turquoise silk tunic is in danger of being dripped on and sniffs to a halt. Instead she decides to go and talk to Gloria, she's always to be relied on for tea and sympathy.

She throws on a coat, lifts her favourite umbrella, painted with cats and dogs plummeting from the sky, and is soon striding along Herbert Park towards Ranelagh. Eimear realises she should have phoned first but she can't bear the idea of the bell pealing out, unanswered, in Gloria's redbrick terrace – at least walking there is using up some of the nervous energy agitating within her.

'Of course I knew he was a flirt when I married him, it's something he can't help,' she tells Gloria while they're waiting for the kettle to boil.

Eimear intended to restrain herself until they were sitting down with a teapot in front of them but she can't hold her tongue.

'Put him in a room with a waxwork of a woman and he'll still try to chat her up. Mostly he isn't even conscious of it. I never found it threatening in the early days – I used to treat it as a lark, you marry a character and how can you complain when he behaves like one, but I don't feel so tolerant any more.'

'Maybe you've been too patient,' suggests Gloria guardedly, elbows on the kitchen worktop, green eyes clouded with concern as she watches her friend.

'Exactly!' Eimear sounds over-excited. 'It's time to make a stand, lay down some ground rules I should have made sure he was clear on from the start. I'm facing facts now. I listed them at the back of that *Medieval Women at Work* diary you bought me for Christmas, Glo. Shall I run through my checklist?'

'You brought it with you?'

'No, I know it off by heart.' Eimear paces as she reels it off:

'Fact one: There's no woman Jack wouldn't shag, apart from you and Kate. He'd never have the nerve to approach you two because you'd give him his marching orders and fill me in on his manoeuvres. Dear God, why am I thinking in military metaphors? Maybe I'm watching too much *M*A*S*H*, you see what marital discord visits upon a woman.'

'Eimear, come and sit down, the kitchen isn't big enough for prowling. I'll wet the tea and then we can discuss it calmly. Would you like some camomile? It's calming.'

Eimear ignores her, up and down the galley kitchen she parades, wheeling sharply left by the broom cupboard and back to the marble wall-clock above the door.

'So you and Kate are out of the loop – a twenty-six-year friendship matters to women, thank heavens for some constants. But every woman apart from you is a potential threat. Fact two: Jack loses interest in an easy victory – it's the thrill of the chase as far as the bedroom door that he enjoys, what happens on the mattress is neither here nor there to him. So whoever he's seeing shouldn't feel too confident: the relationship has a built-in self-destruct factor. As soon as she said yes to him he was hunting for the parachute string. Fact three: Jack has to be punished for humiliating me. I'm doing that now by treating him like a flatmate who's reneged on his share of the rent money one month too many. By being civilised but remote – actually withdrawal of affection isn't very civilised but it's only temporary. And it achieves results.'

Gloria touches her elbow and guides her unobtrusively to the breakfast bar, pushing her gently on to a stool. Eimear doesn't pause as she counts off her list on the fingers of one hand, an over-wound clockwork toy.

'Fact four: I can't keep up this war of attrition forever because it's damaging the marriage. Not as much as he harmed it with his runaway willy but enough to dent the bodywork. And it's misery to keep it going, he hates it but I detest it too – you automatically open your mouth to say, "You'll never guess what happened to me today –" and it's an effort to clamp it shut again. Fact five: I have to make him think he's won me over against my better judgement, that I've caved in to his blandishments. Jack believes in the myth of his charm, he probably can't understand how I've held out so long against him.'

Her fingers curl automatically around the china sunflower mug Gloria slides into her hand, she swallows a sip of tea and the camomile seems to halt her manic inventory, even before it hits her bloodstream. Gloria heaves a sigh of relief but it's premature.

'Fact six: A baby would be useful at this point both to shore up the marriage and confirm my status – he can cavort with as many floozies in as many jacuzzis as he likes but the mother of his children is a woman apart. That will always be my ace of hearts.'

Gloria's own heart shrivels at the mention of babies, her loss palpates within her, but Eimear doesn't notice – her eyes are fixed sightlessly on the pottery fish mobile dangling from the shelf stacked with cookery books.

Eimear's mouth curls with distaste. 'My Clinique total skincare package can only keep me competitive for so long against the under-graduates. I know I have looks but other women have them too – girls ten years younger than me now but who'll one day be twenty and thirty years younger. Fresher and softer and easier on the eye, breathless when he notices them and grateful when he beds them. Bastard.'

She hunches over her tea while Gloria silently curses Kate and wonders what to say that won't provoke Eimear into another frenzied bout of itemising. She may find it therapeutic but it's not doing much for Gloria's emotional state. What Eimear needs is reassurance, with her cover-girl looks she's probably never been upstaged by another woman before. So tentatively she tells Eimear that Jack has probably learned his lesson and advises her to forgive and forget.

'Whoever he was seeing is probably ancient history now,' says Gloria.

(I'll make sure she is.)

Eimear listens, sipping her tea. Gloria's such an innocent, she thinks, she believes in happy-ever-afters. She can't accept that men and women shaft each other, especially men, who apply the shafting literally.

Already she's feeling guilty at having steamed over to Ranelagh to confide in Gloria. Especially when she belatedly recalls something Kate mentioned on the phone the other night: there's a chance Gloria's completely infertile.

'Apparently her other fallopian tube is kinked and those winsome little sperm can't paddle their way around tricky bends,' Kate told her.

Eimear wishes she'd gone to St Stephen's Green to confide in Kate instead of blurting all this out to Gloria; but even in her distraught state she instinctively realised she stood a better chance of catching up with Gloria than Kate. Kate's been avoiding Eimear lately, the phone call featuring Gloria's faulty fallopians (shame you can't return them to the manufacturer) turned out to be five minutes snatched between meetings instead of the meandering dialogue Eimear was anticipating.

'She lives for work that one, I don't know how Pearse puts up with it,' Eimear frowns.

Yet he worships Kate, he'd pluck the moon out of the sky if she asked for it. Still, even for a workaholic she's been hard to pin down. Which is why Gloria has to bear the brunt.

'Glo, I shouldn't have come over here to whine at you, it's your bad luck I'm not the bottled-up bottle blonde I usually pride myself on being.' Eimear is apologetic.

'Good luck, bad luck, who knows?' responds Gloria, more from a sense of duty than fun. 'Anyway, you're not really a bottle blonde: you were fair as a child.'

'I'm behaving like an egotistical child talking about me, me, me when you've more than enough to contend with yourself right now – Kate told me . . . I'm so sorry, I know how much you wanted a baby. How's Mick taking it?'

Gloria shrugs. 'Other people's difficulties are great for distracting you from your own.'

Eimear's embarrassed she was tasteless enough to reveal her master plan to make Jack a father – time enough for revelations when she has a stomach that wobbles like Mick's.

'It's just I've no one else to turn to, that's why you're taking the brunt of this, Glo. I've tried talking to Kate but she seems alarmed when I raise the subject,' sighs Eimear.

'Does she indeed,' responds Gloria.

'Funnily enough I first mentioned it on the same night you were rushed to hospital with your ectopic pregnancy. No, not funnily enough, there's nothing amusing about almost losing one of your oldest friends.'

Eimear leans across the breakfast counter and rests her forehead against Gloria's for a few seconds. Gloria feels so many conflicting emotions that she's grateful for the momentary respite of that caress: self-pity at her own plight, sympathy for Eimear's, fury at Kate.

Both are lost in thought. Gloria surrenders herself to self-commiseration; she's convinced it's better than occupational therapy in limited doses. Eimear drifts back in time to the trendy wine bar with Kate where they shredded reputations along with beer mats over luke-warm Chardonnay. They were waiting for Gloria but on the night her ectopic pregnancy screamed for attention, she wasn't able to make it out of bed, never mind to Dame Street.

'Can you believe the name of this place? The Put A Cork In It,' asked Kate. 'Why do wine bars always have ridiculous punning names – is it written into their leases?'

Eimear shrugged. 'You're the legal expert. Hair salons are just as guilty if you're thinking of reporting anyone to the taste police. Any sign of Glo? It's not like her to be late.'

'She could be caught in a logjam if she's coming by bus; at this stage of the evening the lanes are no use and it's access-all-areas for traffic,' said Kate. 'How many bottles of wine do you reckon it will take tonight before our tights spontaneously self-ladder?'

Eimear laughed and suggested they order another in the interests of scientific experiment. However she hadn't eaten properly all day and the wine shot straight to her tongue. The words hurtled out of her before she realised she was about to utter them.

'Noticed anything unusual about Jack lately, Kate?'

Kate was laughing so hard at the dismal efforts of a couple of suits at the next table to attract their attention that it took a few seconds for the question to register. Immediately it did, she placed her glass carefully on the table and gave Eimear one of her headgirl looks. Despite her freewheeling single-mingle reputation, Kate's conservative streak meant she occasionally played shocked when Eimear and Gloria least expected it.

45

'Unusual as in . . . ?' she asked.

'Shifty, shady, up to no good. Developing a touch of the Mike Baldwins.'

Kate picked up her glass, brought it to her mouth and set it down untasted. Eimear sensed panic. Maybe Kate had her suspicions about Jack and never mentioned them on the shoot-the-messenger principle; perhaps she had even seen him with someone else. Possibilities whirled in Eimear's mind – there had to be a reason for the persistent claim that the wife was usually the last to know.

Eimear tugged so hard at a strand of blonde hair that Kate expected to see a clump detach itself from her scalp. 'Kate, I must know. Have you seen him with anyone?'

Kate had never heard this pleading note in Eimear's voice before. Guilt overwhelmed her and she exploded. Tearing strips from the wine bottle label, she hissed: 'Isn't it time you took a reality check, Eimear? You've the perfect marriage, remember, no one can touch you.'

Eimear was dumbfounded but the rage evaporated as quickly as it materialised and Kate continued, more moderately: 'Don't start imagining problems, Mulligan; your life is the stuff of colour supplements.'

Turning playful, she topped up Eimear's glass and said, 'Let's see, you've vacant possession of a husband so handsome he should be slapped with a government health warning: Admiring Jack O'Brien For Too Long Can Seriously Damage Your Opinion Of Other Men. You own a des res in leafy Donnybrook . . .'

'Leaky Donnybrook – all those trees plus the Irish climate add up to drips every time you walk down the street.'

'There's your fulfilling job tending to books at Rathmines library' – Eimear hazarded an unconvincing gargoyle impression – 'a mother-in-law safely relocated to Youghal and beyond casual visits, no children to leave chocolate fingerprints on your off-white matching sofas –'

'Vanilla matching sofas,' Eimear interrupted.

'If your interior designer says so. Any more blessings? There's the hair, of course; as nearly natural as anyone born outside of Scandinavia can expect, the toe-curling tribute from hubby on his last book of poetry, dedicated to "My inspiration, my life, my wife" and, um, I'm running out of ideas. Mulligan, you've been short-changed.'

'I surrender,' giggled Eimear, misgivings about Jack allayed. 'I admit it, I'm a woman beloved of the fates, no one could ask for more than I have.'

'I'd like that in writing.' Kate signalled for more wine before the bottle was halfway drained.

'Reinforcements,' said Eimear.

'Send reinforcements, we're going to advance,' responded Kate.

'Send three and fourpence, we're going to a dance,' Eimear finished the joke for her.

'That's the trouble with knowing people for twenty-something years: there's no secrets left, even your quips are shared. But it's comforting too.'

'Anyway,' said Kate, 'moonlight and roses have to turn into overcast skies and decaying flowers sometimes. If only to relieve the monotony.'

'I suppose,' admitted Eimear, although mentally chafing against it.

'And isn't Jack up against a deadline on his new collection? Doesn't he develop a furtive streak, sloping around at all hours of the day and night when he's hunting his muse?'

Eimear reflected. It was true; only a few days earlier Jack had sharpened half a dozen pencils and retired to the study with the determined air of a man about to grab creativity by the throat and shake a sonnet or two out of it. But a jarring thought intruded. Jack never talked about work in progress, so how did Kate know . . .

'Kate, how on earth are you aware that Jack only has a

few weeks left before he must hand in his manuscript to the publishers? I wouldn't have mentioned that to you; he has it drilled into me never, not ever, to discuss unfinished work.'

Kate radiated ridicule. 'So Jack's made you take a vow of silence, signed you up for a contemplative order? Or has he had your lips stapled together? Something must've slipped out, you know the loosening effect the demon drink has on an old alcofrolic like you. Anyway, men are off the agenda, this is supposed to be a testosterone-free zone. You know, Gloria is more than just unfashionably late. I'm going outside to ring her on my mobile and demand an explanation for her no-show.'

Kate rummaged in her bag for a fluorescent yellow phone – bought, she claimed, because it made her imagine she was sitting under a coconut tree drinking daiquiris – and slipped off her stool.

'Don't empty the bottle while I'm gone, you lush. And don't accept any drinks from strange men unless they're buying champagne.'

Eimear hauls her mind back to Gloria's kitchen. 'It makes me shiver remembering it, Glo. There we were, joking about conning drinks out of flash guys who leave their credit cards behind the bar, while you were lying in a pool of blood not able to reach the phone.'

'The bleeding was internal, Eimear. And at that stage I wasn't in a life-threatening condition – serious to critical, possibly.'

Eimear cringes at the caustic undertone.

She returns home from Gloria's in a happier frame of mind, persuaded that she's overreacting to Jack's trademark flakiness. It's a little more pronounced than usual but not excessively so, surely. But the next day he mentions that he needs to call by college for an hour or two although it's a Sunday, and her misgivings are back, multiplied like weeds during an absence. She pulls out the incriminating credit-card statement and stares at it. The transaction listed beneath his hotel room rental catches her eye. Drat, she was hoping the Fiorucci T-shirt mightn't appear until next month – Jack would explode when he saw the price.

'You paid HOW much for a T-shirt? I don't care if there are cherubs on the front, there'd need to be the complete heavenly choir of angels for that price.'

Wait a minute, Eimear checks herself, she doesn't need to take abuse about overspending from a man tasteless enough to use their credit card to fund his slap and tickle. This bill's as damning an indictment of her husband as finding a used condom under the bed. Now why did she have to think of bed, it's a tiny step to the mental picture of Jack in bed with another woman. The permutations whirl around in her brain.

'So much for "with my body I thee worship"!' She crumples the statement and flings it on the floor. 'He's on his knees to more than me, that's for sure.'

Eimear half-heartedly peels potatoes for Sunday dinner. She wishes she were more like Kate, who insists she'll live and die a spinster of this parish; Eimear used to think spinsterhood was a shameful fate, something that stamped you with a big red reject sign. Now she can see there's a lot to be said for the single life. At least if she were unmarried, Eimear wouldn't lie in the bath torturing herself with images of her husband splashing in the suds with someone else or sharing her toothbrush or shaving so he doesn't rasp her when they kiss. Or brushing her hair, his seduction speciality.

It's not the sex she minds it's the intimacy. That's a lie, she objects to the sex too. When the pictures of him with this faceless woman – she's always featureless, but with long, sit-upon hair as blue-black as the feathers on a crow – become too detailed she slides under the bath water and hums until the rush of blood to the head blocks everything out.

The potatoes are boiling in a saucepan, waiting to be mashed within an inch of their lives, and Eimear is still brooding on Jack's affair. Now she's wondering where he goes to shag them – hotel rooms, maybe? No, that would show up on his credit card and there's been just the one hotel so far. Obviously he only chats up women with their own flat. She imagines the conversation:

'Excuse me, you tantalising creature, do you live at home, share with friends or are you self-sufficient? Because there's something about an independent woman I find irresistible . . .'

The potatoes are boiling over; she doesn't notice as the water sizzles around the electric ring and the saucepan lid rattles a tetchy tune. Maybe she's partly to blame for the way Jack is, perhaps there's something missing in her that he has to search for elsewhere. Some womanly component that the great geneticist in the sky left out:

'Let's see, Eimear Mulligan, she's getting the face, the size 10 body and the lifelong friends. That doesn't leave room for much else – fair's fair, it'll have to do her.'

Eimear realises she's being inconsistent, in one breath wishing she'd never married anyone, let alone Jack, and in another hating every woman he's ever spared a glance for, from under those heavy black brows of his.

'He plucks grey hairs out of them, that's how conceited he is.' She drags a hand through her neck-length bob. 'I do it for him, that's how feeble I am.'

But she doesn't want to be consistent, she wants to feel secure again.

She even tried going to church last Sunday, something she hasn't bothered with regularly since she was a teenager. She sat there for almost an hour and let the words wash over her without listening to their meaning, but there was a comforting sense of familiarity. Eimear thought about Mass again this morning but decided against it – she'd feel hypocritical. She burns to punish Jack, not hear a Christian message: forgive

us our trespasses as we forgive those who trespass against us.
Screw that. She wants him to suffer. To fall down and break
his crown and then she'll be the one to bathe it with vinegar
and brown paper. She'll be the one he needs.

CHAPTER 6

Eimear studies herself in the mirror and acknowledges her face is different, it's definitely changed. It looks like a pregnant face to her. She knows that's technically impossible, since his sperm won't have collided with her egg yet, but she and Jack made love last night without using protection and she instinctively feels there'll be a baby. It's just waiting to be conceived. Everything was perfect: she was mid-cycle, she lay quietly for twenty minutes afterwards – Jack thought she'd nodded off – and she willed her body to be fertile. She's still concentrating on it, thinking fecund thoughts.

She intended sulking for longer with Jack but she read her *EveryWoman* to bring herself up-to-date on babymaking techniques, she knows there's more to it than some soggy collision between the sheets once you're past thirty – Gloria's experiences have taught her that. The section on contraception reminded her how to count up her ovulation cycle and it emerged last night was peak practice time so Jack was off the hook. Saturday night fervour was required.

Eimear allowed him to believe he was being masterful when he swept her off to bed and demonstrated how apologetic he was. He wanted to show her a second time but she was concerned he'd jiggle the sperm already despatched and send them off-course so she persuaded him to save his ardour for this morning. Which he did. Now she's securely aware of a back-up convoy of sperm trekking after the advance guard.

'Hope they've a decent sense of direction.' She smiles secretively.

Babies remind her of Gloria. Not only are her fallopians officially kaput, there's a chance Mick has a low sperm count. The great geneticist in the sky is trying to tell them something, thinks Eimear, then immediately feels churlish. She'll call by to Gloria's tomorrow, cheer her up. Kate seems too busy to do it, she's behaving oddly, even by her own erratic standards. She's obviously having problems with Pearse, it must be the age gap rearing its head: Pearse is a good fifteen years older than Kate – his exact age is shrouded in mystery, Gloria and Eimear routinely quip they'll have to read his date of birth off his gravestone.

Eimear's noticed that Kate has taken to referring to Pearse as 'the oul' fellow', as if he were her father or some ancient neighbour. A few years ago she was singing the praises of the more mature man, now you'd swear he was too decrepit to put one foot in front of the other. Let alone manage a bit of the other.

Eimear rings Gloria with her latest theory, which emerged fully formed ten minutes earlier. Gloria is attempting to mark some exam papers and isn't in the humour for speculation but Eimear cajoles her into listening.

'Really, Glo, it makes perfect sense when you think about it. Kate's manoeuvring Pearse into a marriage proposal.'

'Kate doesn't believe in marriage,' Gloria objects.

'Flamboyant militant talk, all very well in your twenties but you march to a different tune in your thirties. We both know she presents herself as this free spirit who's escaped matrimonial shackles – we're the stereotypes who sold out for a day in a princess frock – but I suspect she's ready to settle down now. She's just not sure how to admit she wants to belong to an institution she's spent the past decade deriding as outmoded and degrading.'

'It's a theory,' agrees Gloria. 'An unconvincing one but a theory nevertheless.'

'How can you write it off?'

'Look, Eimear, remember how she wouldn't even stand bridesmaid for either of us? That's how anti-marriage she's always been. She said it gave the best man the notion he had a right to snog you and the father of the groom would lose his head completely and try to feel you up.'

Eimear shudders, recalling several slow dances in a dress-to-suppress with Mick McDermott's appalling brother Johnno. All in the name of friendship. Kate, meanwhile, was free to swan about in an elegant two-piece with a hat and crocodile heels instead of specially dyed pumps. 'Then when it was my turn three years ago, and you were my maid of honour –'

'Oh yes, the bold Kate, allegedly so insulted at the idea of an off-the-shoulder bridesmaid's flounce or two, jam-tarted up in a black-and-white dress that was completely strapless. Talk about double standards – hers are positively double-jointed.'

'That's why it will be quite a laugh when Kate caves in and has a wedding day of her own with Pearse in tow,' insists Eimear.

'You're mental, I'm going back to my exam papers.'

Kate's a puzzle with her bouts of secretiveness and her offhand moods, thinks Eimear, as she drags out the vacuum cleaner to give her stair carpet the once-over. She's never been as reliable as Gloria, as keen to maintain the threesome. Sometimes she seems to buck against their friendship.

Jack arrives home early as she's replacing the machine in the cupboard and sets about persuading Eimear to take a shower with him.

Jack, in a bog accent: 'Ah go on, go on, go on.'

Eimear: 'I haven't loaded the dishwasher yet.'

Jack: 'I haven't loaded you yet, for that matter, not since this morning.'

Eimear: 'Jack! You never used to be so crude.'

Jack: 'You know you like it.'

Eimear: 'Well maybe I'll step in and scrub your back when I'm finished in the kitchen.'

Jack: 'Make sure you do or I'll be down to find you, dripping water all over the hall carpet and exposing my virile body to the neighbours opposite.'

Eimear visits Gloria, convinced there can be no doubt she and Jack have made a child because she's six days late and her period is never overdue. But her inner complacency – she attributes it to the premature onset of maternal serenity – is pockmarked by Mick and Gloria snapping at each other about trivia. It's embarrassing being in the same room as them.

Mick has a habit of displaying a foot of lower calf when he sits down, his trousers ride up abnormally high. Today it seems to infuriate Gloria disproportionately, she's forever telling him to pull them down.

'Eimear doesn't want to look at your hairy legs,' she complains, and he hitches them down but up they creep again. After two or three times Gloria loses it.

'Mick, would you ever put your legs away,' she all but screams and he yells at her to have a bit of manners and then she really screeches, saying he's not the man to teach her because he wouldn't know manners if they stepped up and bid him good day. Back and forth they go, totally oblivious to Eimear.

They really are on the skids, thinks Eimear, they can't even be bothered to hide their fights. Mick and Gloria are niggled by everything the other does. He pretends not to hear her and makes her repeat every request twice, while the box of Maltesers Eimear brings as a gift is material for a jibe from Gloria about his weight.

'We'll have to ration you to just a few of those, Michael,

the bathroom scales can't take much more abuse. You'll be had up for cruelty to household appliances.'

Marriage can have a bizarre effect on love, shudders Eimear. Still, she's not looking for romance, Jack's sperm are enough and they've done their job. Thank heavens for athletic sperm and priapic husbands. Now what are the chances of her being able to slip out quietly and leave Mick and Gloria slinging insults like rocks?

Eimear's period arrives on day eight. She's awakened by the sensation of blood trickling down her leg and knows even before she's conscious there's a reason she should stay cocooned in sleep – her brain is telling her to enjoy her pregnancy a few minutes longer. Except it isn't a pregnancy, it's simply wistful thinking. She held off the bleeding for a week, that's how determined she was, but she couldn't postpone it forever. The period can't be thwarted when there's no baby to dam the flow and the blood comes slithering and blobbing. It repulses her, some of it smears on her hands and leaves a stale smell as though it were penned up too long in her body. She rummages for tampons but discovers her supplies have run out.

When her stomach cramps ease she phones in a sick call to Mrs Hardiman, the head librarian. It's a mental health day, not one for lying in bed, so she catches a bus into town (when one finally arrives – Dublin Bus doesn't believe in pampering its passengers with a regular service) and heads straight for the shopping mecca of Grafton Street and Brown Thomas.

Its basement houses her favourite lingerie department. She fondles the teddies and baby dolls – such innocuous names for such seriously wicked underwear – and holds them along her body to judge their impact. She's determined to choose the wispiest silks and silkiest wisps she can lay her hands on, even some provocative cutaway pieces she'd normally dismiss as too high on the slagheap index to consider. She wants to be ready for Jack when her period's over. Stripped for action. Eimear's mouth twists as she reflects on Jack's predilections. Nothing too tasteful, he's indifferent to her café-au-lait camisoles. He prefers them red and lacy or black and sheer.

Brevity is the soul of underwear, he continually tells her; it's not his rule of thumb in life, however, because his poetry rambles on interminably. Still, at least she knows how to press his buttons.

'I'd almost despise you for being predictable if it weren't so useful, Jack O'Brien,' she remarks.

A middle-aged woman a few feet away starts putting considerably more distance between them. Steady, thinks Eimear, she's speaking out loud again – it can only be a matter of time before the men in white coats arrive.

When she's upset she comforts herself by shopping. Admittedly that's her response to boredom or depression too. The best therapy is retail, she's fond of saying – a new pair of shoes are cheaper than a visit to the shrink and you have something to show for your money to boot.

'Can I help you, madam?'

An assistant with purple lips and matching nails interrupts Eimear's meditation, she rouses herself and finds she's wringing a push-up bra between her hands. No wonder the girl intervened, there's a madwoman damaging the stock.

'Yes, do you have this in any other colours?' She makes an effort to seem normal.

'No, only black. It comes with a choice of French knickers or a thong to match.' She gestures to the alternatives.

Eimear looks at them. Very Jack. 'I'll take both.'

In for a penny, in for a pound.

Eimear catches sight of the swimwear as she pays at the till. A wave of nostalgia engulfs her for the cheap holiday packages to Corfu and Menorca she took with Gloria and Kate, before she and Jack discovered Tuscany and the South of France.

The three girls used to scorch themselves on the beach by day and sizzle at waiters as they drank themselves senseless by night. Sublime holidays.

She's suffused by a longing so acute, it's akin to grief, for the days when boyfriends were temporary arrangements, babies were something they popped pills to avoid and all they wanted out of life was a doss of a job that paid megabucks. And maybe a ride from Aidan Quinn – all of them worshipped him.

'He's the only male the three of us fancied simultaneously,' murmurs Eimear. 'None of us has the same taste in fellows, it's probably what's kept us friends for so long.'

That's one certainty: Gloria, Kate and herself will never fall out over a man.

CHAPTER 7

'Have you heard about hyacinth bulbs in olive oil – they're supposed to be the ultimate aphrodisiac.' Gloria is poking at her fettuccine.

'Can't say I have,' replies Eimear. 'But surely the best place for hyacinths is the flower-bed. What are you supposed to do, eat them? Rub them over your body? Over your lover's?'

'The article didn't specify,' admits Gloria. 'Perhaps you chop them up and sneak them into his salad.'

'Another wizard wheeze bites the dust. Jack never touches salad, he calls it rabbit food.'

Besides, thinks a gratified Eimear, he's ardent enough as it is, she doesn't need love potions to lure her man to bed. 'I can't see Mick smacking his lips over hyacinth bulbs,' she adds. 'He seems more your meat-and-two-veg character.'

'He won't slip on the nosebag unless there's spuds on the table,' confirms Gloria. 'And nobody can cook them like the real Mrs McDermott. Mick and she belong to a mutual admiration society. He even notices when she has a different coloured rinse in her hair – I could get a skinhead crop and it wouldn't register, but she slams in some lowlights and it's: "Mammy, all the fellows at the bank will be asking for an introduction to my good-looking sister."'

She stabs at the pasta.

'They say a man who's kind to his mother will be kind to his wife.' Eimear essays diplomacy.

'Who's "they"?' demands Gloria. 'They've obviously never been married.'

The pair are having lunch in an Italian restaurant opposite the library where Eimear works, to cheer Gloria up – Mick's mother's been staying for the weekend and she needs to let off steam. It's not that she dislikes her mother-in-law but she resents the way Mick behaves around her. Every visit is marked by an incident; this time it centred around a takeaway fish supper Gloria fed her the first night she arrived.

'I was only back teaching a week and I could just about manage that, I wasn't able to face the supermarket as well so there was no food in the house to cook,' wails Gloria. 'The real Mrs McDermott didn't mind, she said it made a change from proper food. But Mick claimed it was an insult to his mother to serve a carry-out and he sulked at me all weekend.'

Pig, thinks Eimear.

'He only wants the best for his mother,' says Eimear.

'If that wasn't bad enough, the real Mrs McDermott insisted on going out into the front garden every time she wanted a cigarette. I kept telling her I didn't mind if she smoked in the house but she said my lovely home would reek for days afterwards. She stood on the doorstep in full view of the neighbours puffing away. It made me look like a house-proud harridan.'

'You used to like her.'

'I used to like Mick,' responds Gloria.

'She's gone now.'

'Mick isn't.' Gloria beheads a mushroom.

Eimear pushes away her spaghetti carbonara and lights up a cigarette.

'You could try lingerie,' she suggests. 'Hyacinth bulbs in olive oil sound like a long shot but satin works every time for me.'

She pictures, with satisfaction, the keyhole-cut number she has lined up for active service that night.

'Sounds like you and Jack are enjoying a second honeymoon.' Gloria looks wistfully across the table, her pallor pronounced against the dark shoulder-length hair.

'He's being very . . . attentive.' Eimear tries not to smile like a cat at the cream.

Gloria wants to say something but has trouble finding the words, all she manages is a lame, 'Just don't take him for granted, Eimear.'

Eimear is flippant, remembering their passion last night – and the night before that.

'He's putty in my hands, Glo. You want to get yourself up to Brown Thomas, they've slinky numbers there that Saint Patrick himself couldn't resist. He'd be inviting back all the snakes to Ireland as the lesser of two evils.'

'Can't be bothered. I couldn't care less if Mick never laid a finger on me again. I used to be mad for it but now I'd rather take *Hello!* magazine to bed – who needs jiggery pokery with all those celebrity home interiors to drool over.'

'We must mention it to their marketing people,' suggests Eimear. 'They can emblazon "Better Than Sex" across the cover, it should double their sales. And on that high note I must clock back in at the salt mines. Michelle can't go off on her lunch break until I'm back from mine.'

'Is that the Michelle who always has a copy of *Wuthering Heights* in her bag?'

'The same. She says Emily Brontë's characters are so wretched they cheer her up – her own life seems blessed by comparison. Any time she feels depressed she takes out the novel and dips into Heathcliffe and Cathy's gaping voids instead.'

As they leave the restaurant, Eimear sees a bus that passes by Trinity College. Impulsively she decides to skip work for the afternoon – she'll ring in with an imaginary migraine – and boards the bus, deciding to surprise Jack. She's spurred by the thought of Heathcliff and Cathy; there's no need for her and

Jack to behave like star-crossed lovers over one lapse.

Dodging the traffic, she crosses College Green and heads in through the front arch, past the inevitable knots of students and tourists congregated there. By the porter's office she almost collides with Kate.

'Eimear, what are you doing here?'

'Snap.'

Kate shuffles her feet shiftily and Eimear notices she's perched on high heels – self-conscious about her height, she usually wears loafers.

'I wanted to buy some *Book of Kells* postcards in the shop – I thought I'd frame them and hang them in the hallway of the flat,' says Kate finally.

'In your monument to minimalism?'

Well might she look evasive.

'Give us a look at them,' prods Eimear.

'Wait till they're framed, you'll see the full effect then,' promises Kate. 'You should stop by the shop and have a look at their *Book of Kells* computer mouse-pads – talk about the ninth century colliding with the twenty-first. I nearly bought one just for the heck of it. But then I thought better not – it'll only encourage their suppliers. Next they'll be flogging us video games with Vikings attacking monasteries and the scribes scrambling to find hidey-holes for their manuscripts.'

Eimear purses her lips. 'Works for me. Do you fancy grabbing a coffee and we can plan the game out and try to patent the rights?'

'No time, Mulligan, I'm late for a meeting.' And Kate blows a kiss and bolts.

Eimear clatters across the cobblestones, towards the campanile under which Jack proposed to her one star-strewn night after a ball at the college. He looked like a matinee idol in his dinner suit and she hired a silver dress with a fishtail train that tripped her up when they danced. Jack told her she shimmered like a nereid in the moonlight and produced from his pocket a diamond solitaire that fitted her ring finger to perfection.

She's suffused by a rush of joy as she passes their bell-tower and veers right towards the English department.

On the ramp outside the door, where the students throng for cigarettes between lectures, she spies Jack's distinctive tall frame. He doesn't see her – he's short-sighted but too vain to wear glasses. Eimear is about to call his name when she notices he's deep in conversation with a petite dark girl of maybe twenty with a nose stud. She's wearing an ankle-length Indian dress and the mirrors sewn into the lavender cloth sparkle in the sunshine. Books are clutched against her chest and she's so dainty she has to bend her head back at an awkward angle to gaze into his face.

Eimear watches them. She could simply be one of his students and yet there's an intimacy in their stance, as bodies surge around them, that disquietens her. Jack lifts one of her arms away from the books, pushes up the loose sleeve and checks her watch. Eimear's stomach somersaults: it's a meaningless gesture and yet eloquent. He holds on to the wrist, stroking it gently, smiling down at the chest-high dark head.

Eimear wheels around and tramps away, past the campanile, past the porter's office, past the bus stop. Walking, walking, walking.

CHAPTER 8

Jack's lying so still, Kate panics and lowers her cheek to his mouth for reassurance. False alarm: his breath rustles against her skin. He's sprawled diagonally across the bed, one arm outstretched, hair plastered into tufts, enveloped in the sleep of the unjust. He always naps in the aftermath of their lovemaking; sometimes his eyelids droop with indecent haste immediately after he's quivered, gasped and rolled over on to his side, sweat-coated body slithering from her grasp. Kate doesn't object to his withdrawal, although she misses the reassurance of contact, because it offers a chance to study him.

She never tires of admiring her lover, although he doesn't look his best unconscious. His face needs its eyes open, brown eyes gleaming roguishly or swimming with invitation or pleading like a small boy's. As if aware of her scrutiny, he turns his face towards the pillows and burrows in.

She transfers her gaze to the bedroom of her flat, blinds drawn against the afternoon sun, a trail of jackets, shirts and socks leading from door to bed. Pearse is in Limerick on business today and won't be back until the last train – she must clear up their lovemaking debris before then. Kate's attention is caught by Jack's striped boxer shorts dangling from the lower bedpost; she fantasises about washing them and storing them in a drawer with her own underwear but regretfully abandons the idea. She can't send him home knickerless to Eimear.

'Baby girl.'

One brown eye is glinting. Jack's awake. He shields the other eye against a dust mote-peppered ray of sunshine that's sneaked through the curtains, the gesture lending him a raffish air. She ruffles his hair, quoting: 'One-eyed Jack the pirate chief/was a terrible fearsome ocean thief/he wore a hook and a dirty look . . .'

Jack interrupts before she can finish the verse, learned for the town *feis* at eight and all but forgotten until now.

'Hey, I'm the poet around here, remember.'

He wags his finger, then pulls her close for a kiss. He's less than keen on ditties – poetry should be treated reverently, not dashed off in a fit of merriment.

'Got to run, baby girl.'

Jack is already hunting for his boxers, while Kate is still in post-kissing swoon.

When he first called her baby girl, she cringed – wouldn't you think a poet could come up with something more original. Dean Swift invented a new name, Vanessa, for his lady-love. But baby girl's grown on her now.

Jack is talking as he steps into his trousers.

'Have to shoot back to Trinity for a meeting and I promised Eimear I'd be home early, she needs a hand with something or other.'

'A dinner party?'

'That's it, a dinner party. Did she mention it to you?'

'She invited me – Pearse too, obviously – but I declined.'

'Why don't you come, baby girl?' Jack breaks off from buttoning his shirt. His voice dips huskily: 'We could play footsie under the table, I could give you a quick grope on the pretext of leaning over to refill your glass, we could volunteer for washing-up duty and go a-courting in the kitchen.'

'No Jack, it's bad enough we're doing this to Eimear

in hotels, borrowed apartments and offices the length and breadth of Ireland without taking it right into her home,' protests Kate.

'You've developed a conscience all of a sudden.' He tucks his shirt into his trousers with impatient movements.

'Not all of a sudden. I've always had a conscience about what we're doing. You help me ignore it most of the time.'

'Come here and let me help you forget again,' he coaxes, arms wide open, and before she know it she's flat on her back with Jack on top and Eimear shoved to the dimmest recess of her mind.

Eimear. Kate considers her friend as she stares at the ravages that lovemaking has wreaked on her face. Obviously there's the glow in her eyes that magazines always talk about when they write those 'Sex – The Fun Alternative to Exercise' articles but her skin is raw from Jack's lunchtime stubble and a spot is threatening to erupt on her nose.

'Of course, Eimear never gets pimples, her face is a no-go area,' she mutters, debating whether to squeeze or simply use concealer on the intruder.

Her mind drifts back to the Eimear she first met. Some little girls are rosebuds, impossibly gorgeous from the tip of their long curling lashes to the top of their perfect patent pumps, forever looking like they've just been primped by the Mammy for a photograph. Eimear belonged to that variety.

Kate's mother would tell her, 'Beautiful children don't end up beautiful adults.'

Mothers don't have a clue, she couldn't have been more wrong in Eimear's case; she became more alluring, not less, the older they all grew.

Kate squeezes toothpaste on a brush and bares her gums for inspection. She and Gloria are attractive on a good day – that's a word they have to describe girls with teeth that are white but crooked or hair that's a pretty colour although it just hangs there. She slaps some concealer on her nose – this is ridiculous, she's still getting freckles and spots at thirty-two.

Kate bangs the bathroom door after her; wouldn't you think it could be one or the other at the very least. She thought she was finished with both by the time all three of them exited their teens on a flourish, vowing never to drink Snakebites again. At least not on the nights they'd be going on for a curry.

But you don't become more grown-up in your twenties, all that happens is you're better at masking the pimples. And in your thirties, well, then it's major repair time – more than spots require masking; the lines and furrows are only the tip of the iceberg, you've secrets to hide as well. Kate takes the stairs down from her flat three at a time, in too much of a rush to wait for the lift to the ground floor.

She cuts through St Stephen's Green, an oasis in the heart of the city centre, hands tunnelling into her pockets as she lectures herself.

'I'm saying "you" but I mean me – you see how adept I've become at fooling myself. Me, I, *is mise, moi, mio*. I'm the one with secrets to hide. I have the trappings of adulthood: a partner-slash-lover, a mortgage, car loan, espresso machine, interest-free credit repayments on a dishwasher, wine in the rack that I leave there untasted for oh, weeks at a time. I'm kidding plenty of people with this mature adult pose but I'm not taken in myself.'

Inside, she's sixteen again, gangly, spotty and ignored by boys, the one member of their troika with no dates and no prospect of any. Glo had her Mick and Eimear had anyone she liked but all Kate had was the two of them and they edged her out as soon as Mr Maybe came pounding up the path.

Kate dodges the tourists thronged around buskers on Grafton Street and quickens her pace towards her Dame Street office – her secretary Bridie will be nursing her fury at Kate for vanishing on a two-and-a-half-hour lunch-break. But Eimear continues to preoccupy her. Eimear was always special, a Charlie's Angel. They were all three of them lanky for their age but tall on her was willowy, she was a gazelle.

'My love is like a gazelle, see how he comes . . .' Kate quotes.

Gloria chose that as a reading at her wedding and Kate and Eimear were doubled over trying to bank down the guffaws. Glo never was one for catching on to double entendres. That's what you get for taking your inspiration from the Old Testament with all its begetting, they did nothing but rut. Mick may be a dear but he's no gazelle.

Kate never understood why Eimear didn't become a model instead of a librarian. Tall on her is frail; tall on Kate is a heifer. Kate's father says she has solid child-bearing hips – to his generation that's a compliment but she'd swap them gladly for a share in Eimear's Waterford glass fragility.

Kate climbs the stairs to the reception at Reynolds, MacMahon and Reynolds, irritation welling up alongside a mental vision of Eimear's swanlike appearance – even her neck is long and curved. Not that Eimear sets any store by it; she seems indifferent to her looks, she was always unimpressed by people who gushed about them Maybe the reason they've been friends for so long is because they never flattered Eimear. Kate and Gloria simply acknowledged at the start that Eimear was sensational and then forgot about it, just as they recognised Kate would never pass O-level art and Gloria would never step out with anyone except Mick.

'The Toners have been on the phone again about their house sale, Kate. That makes the third time today.'

Bridie regards her boss reproachfully over her half-moon spectacles. She's extremely capable, has been with Reynolds, MacMahon and Reynolds for thirty years, and Kate worships her. But right now she's making her feel like an errant schoolgirl.

'I'll get straight back to them,' she promises, 'would you

dig out their file for me? And maybe, if it's not too much trouble, a mug of coffee?'

Bridie tosses her head and grunts something Kate hopes to be an affirmative.

Bridie's tetchy, as well she might be. She has to keep covering up for Kate when she slopes off to meet Jack, lying not just to the clients but to her partners as well. The conveyancing has gone to the dogs since she and Jack discovered horizontal lunches.

'She can lump it,' mutters Kate, closing the office door and dragging her mind from Jack to the Toners. Are they the Rathfarnham couple who're selling up and moving to Greystones or the Glasnevin pair who're cashing in on the Dublin property boom and moving back to the North?

Their file lands with a thump on the desk, followed by a mug of coffee – the one with a cracked handle. Bridie probably chose it deliberately in the hope she'd scald herself.

She opens the file industriously while her disapproving factotum adjusts the blinds but as soon as she retreats Kate's mind drifts back to Jack, replaying their lunchtime encounter. She fills her senses with her lover, luxuriating in him.

A sliver of Kate that hasn't yet strayed into the force field of Jack's magnetism feels reservations about his casual infidelity: 'If he can do it to Eimear he could do it to you,' reasons an annoying voice she can't still. But the inconvenient intrusion of common sense is ignored and the turmoil overlooked because her senses are intoxicated, she's lolling in a languorous haze and she can't think clearly beyond the next caress. She willingly subordinates herself to his hands, his lips, his weight – and for a woman raised on the premise of female independence, this abdication of responsibility is addictive.

Pearse materialises in her mind's eye, souring Kate's daydream. Not in a guilty way, she simply feels exasperated. She was the first to kiss him, for heaven's sake. If they'd hung around waiting for him to take the initiative they'd still be at the hand-holding stage. They were seeing each other for a couple of weeks when she decided it was time he claimed her as his own. Fat chance. They saw a film (Pearse leaped like a cat when she brushed his thigh with her hand in the dark), then they had a few jars and went back to her place to drink the wine he bought over the counter at the pub.

They ended up on the sofa necking enthusiastically; still, when Kate stood up, adjusted her top and said it was time for bed he put his coat on and showed every sign of taking this as a dismissal. The sap. She had to throw modesty to the winds and say, 'Hold your horses, big fellow, there's room for two in there,' before the penny dropped. Kate supposes she must have found it endearing once.

Now she's bored with that diffidence – she'd like Pearse to be more assertive. But he wouldn't know how to be masterful if his life – or his relationship – depended on it. She's the one who always has to complain in restaurants if the food is cold, that's the role she's drifted into with him. It would be nice to be babied like Eimear for a change but that'll never happen for her.

She's not one of those women that men feel the need to pamper. One boyfriend told her he believed she'd be offended if he helped her into her coat, as though it implied she were incapable of looking after herself. He didn't last long. Kate's never been mollycoddled – that's what comes of being a woman with hands and shoulders as wide as a man's. She has neat little feet though, size four, which is tiny for her height (5 feet 10 inches), Pearse says it's a wonder she doesn't topple over because they're hardly big enough to balance her. Eimear has size seven feet, hah!

Even Jack, who fetches and carries for Eimear as though she'd shatter like an eggshell if she so much as lifted a shopping bag, cheerfully tells Kate she's a fine strapping armful of a lass.

70

'Would you feck off, I'm only two inches taller than Eimear,' she complains, but he treats it as a joke.

'There's a lot more of you to love,' he laughs, grabbing her waist and massaging the excess flesh with a leer. Men think they're flattering a woman when they're sending her screaming for the nearest set of bathroom scales.

She's never seen Eimear weigh herself, she wouldn't give a second thought to the calorie-counting misery that consumes most women. Eimear has no appetite: the cigarettes help, but she's never seen her study a cream bun with naked longing or work her way through a slab of chocolate as though rationing is about to be declared. Eimear is languid about food – she'll take a biscuit if it's offered but forget to finish it. Obviously Eimear's the one with the food phobia, not Glo and herself, for all their stuffing and starving. But it takes more than a feeling of self-righteousness to squeeze a woman into a size 10.

'No wonder Jack is straying,' says Kate. (Oops. Is the intercom switched on or off?)

She can't imagine Eimear wolfing into croissants dolloped with apricot jam in bed with Jack and deliberately dribbling some on to him so she has to lick it off. Not that Kate's found an opportunity to do that with Jack yet but she has nothing against it in principle.

'Admittedly I have no principles where Jack is concerned.' She spins around in her adjustable chair for the pleasure of feeling light-headed. With Pearse she'd probably complain that they'd never wash the stains out of the sheets.

'Shall I try to reach the Toners for you now, Kate?' Bridie's voice crackles over the intercom. (Rats, it was on.)

'Not just yet thanks, Bridie; there are a few details in the deeds I have to sort out first.'

Kate is pseudo-businesslike. She shuffles the pages, determined to make the Toners and their seaside cottage her priority, but within moments she's sunk in her reverie again.

Although they're a trio, she and Gloria have always been

closer. There's an imbalance in friendships where one of the members is drop-dead gorgeous and the others are drop-dead ordinary. They didn't feel jealous of the chosen one but they were aware she was different. Different as in better, different as in luckier: she had an edge. Eimear was allowed to get away with murder all her life and simply accepted it as her due.

She and Gloria rolled their eyes as Eimear sailed through a potential crisis, blithely unaware of the possibilities for disaster, while they doggy-paddled in her wake. Sometimes benefiting, it has to be conceded, from knowing this exquisite creature. Fellows would talk to them in the hopes of an introduction, they were guaranteed a certain level of popularity on her account.

That's why the trio never extended to a foursome or beyond – Gloria and Kate were always suspicious that people wanted to be their friends as an entrée to Eimear and Eimear herself was serenely indifferent. She has the two of them, that's friendship sorted.

Her attitude to Jack is the same: she married him, what more could he ask for? 'She's never spontaneously affectionate,' he complains. 'If you suggest a cuddle she weighs up the consequences of whether or not it will crush her blouse.'

Kate savours it when he's mean about Eimear, his complaints help justify her disloyalty.

She flicks her intercom switch to 'off' and pretends to speak to her secretary.

'Could you make a note of this please, Bridie. Eimear brings out the best in people but she doesn't have that effect on me. I'm adept at dissembling but I hate her – I've loathed her for years.'

CHAPTER 9

'Gloria on line one for you, will you take the call?'

Bridie's voice buzzes in and frog-marches her back to reality.

'Glo, how's life?'

'Same as ever.' Her voice sounds quavery, like someone who's been crying.

'Mick all right?'

'Same as ever.'

Kate's suspicions are confirmed, there is a wobble, tears have recently been shed.

'That bad?' she jokes, but Gloria doesn't manage even a pretend giggle.

'Eimear tells me she invited you and Pearse to dinner tonight but you won't come.'

There's accusation now, as well as a tremor.

'This is supposed to be a democracy, it's not mandatory to accept dinner invitations. Anyway it's not a case of won't, it's can't. Pearse has a work party on and I promised I'd turn up and lend him some immoral support.'

'Oh.' Gloria sounds mollified. 'Why didn't you tell Eimear that, she says you just snapped a refusal and claimed you were dashing out and couldn't talk.'

'What's so terrible about that? I was in a rush. Eimear's being awkward, you know how she likes everything her own way. She probably decided on this dinner weeks ago but never bothered checking with either of us because she assumed we'd drop everything for her.'

'I have no everything to drop, I'm only too pleased to escape the house,' responds Gloria. 'Are you sure there's no way you can avoid this work do? I promised Eimear I'd try and persuade you to change your mind.'

'I've been neglecting Pearse lately, I want to try and make it up to him,' Kate lies slickly. At least the first half is true. She lowers her voice conspiratorially. 'You know what I mean, I can't go into details over the phone.'

'Right, of course, I'm glad to hear you and Pearse are getting along better. Why don't you come over tomorrow afternoon, Mick's at a match and we'll have the house to ourselves.'

'Why not,' agrees Kate. 'You can tell me why you've been crying while you're at it.'

'Just the usual baby blues.'

Kate hesitates, it's difficult to know how to comfort her. She tries flippancy.

'Time to switch to baby pinks, those blues are too depressing.'

Gloria rewards her feeble attempt at humour with a chuckle. Then she adds: 'You'll never guess who my mother was talking to in the supermarket the other day – Miss McGinn.'

'Amo-Amas-Amat McGinn?'

'The same. She was asking after Eimear,' says Gloria.

'Naturally, she was her pet. I was the one who ponged out her class.'

Kate has three older sisters and became selective about perfumes from an early age, there were always crates of the stuff lying around. She'd wear nothing but Channel 5, as they called it, at a time when most girls her age were still squirting on the Parma Violet scents. It didn't render her any more seductive, but it gave her a certain cachet in school.

'Remember how she'd say, "Would the child who smells

like a city tart's boudoir kindly go to the lavatory and scrub herself down,"' recalls Gloria.

'Is she still seeing Ronan Donnelly the estate agent?' Kate quizzes Gloria.

'So my mother says, and still no sign of a ring. That makes it a thirty-five-year courtship, give or take a year.'

He was a source of fascinated speculation, this man licensed to snog their Latin teacher. He'd take her to the pictures on Friday nights; her hair always had that just-shampooed sheen on Fridays. They used to imagine their encounters. Eimear was best at imitating them.

'I love you, Maura,' she'd proclaim ardently in her Mr Donnelly voice and then she'd hold up a warning hand in Miss McGinn guise, as he reached to embrace her.

'First you must decline love,' she'd command, putting him through his amo-amas-amats. His reward would be a juicy smooch. They all made kissy-kissy noises at Eimear before collapsing in fits of giggles.

'Of course with the benefit of experience we know now that a permanent courtship doesn't make Miss McGinn odd in the least, it leaves her one of the sanest women in Ireland,' says Kate. 'It gives her all the advantages of a man in her life without any of the disadvantages. The only mystery is why more women don't do a Miss McGinn.'

Gloria is unconvinced. 'If life was so wonderful, how come she was always in a grump?'

'Speaking of wonderful lives, I have to get back to my enthralling job. See you tomorrow, Glo.'

As she replaces the receiver, Kate spies an *Evening Herald* folded on a corner of her desk. She flicks straight to the star signs and reads Libra. There's some space-filling drivel about Saturn in ascendant then it cuts to the chase:

'A day to tread warily because nasty surprises are possible,' she reads aloud.

She doesn't like the sound of that, but before gloom settles she spots the date on the paper – it's yesterday's. Good, she's off the hook for today. Now she really must get on with the Toner conveyancing.

Chance would be a fine thing. Kate's concentration lasts all of sixty seconds before paralysis of the little grey cells sets in. The Toners may be champing at the bit to move but they won't be any nearer completion today. Kate resigns herself to the inevitable, picks up a pencil and starts doodling.

Eimear Mulligan, she's writing – not Eimear O'Brien, her friend's married name. Her insides are churning as she thinks of Eimear, she may hate her but she loves her too.

She loves her when they're together but hates her when she's with Jack, maybe that's partly guilt, her mother says you always detest the person you've wronged.

'Between my mother and Gloria, I'm knee-deep in this bloody homespun wisdom,' she chafes.

When she was six there was none of this equivocation: she'd have given Eimear her cornflake-box crown if she asked for it. Kate draws spiky crowns across her doodle pad, then tears the page up.

She took Jack from her friend because she could. Jack the blue-eyed boy, Jack the white-headed man, Jack the ace, Eimear's Jack.

It was meant to be a fling, she was never supposed to find out. Of course Eimear still doesn't know – but the game has changed and the rules along with it. She believed she could hug to herself the secret glee of Jack's defection. Kate and Pearse would be invited to Donnybrook as usual, she'd see Jack pouring drinks, complimenting his wife on a delicious meal, resting his arm lightly around her shoulders as they described holidays and discussed kitchen extensions. They'd look the perfect couple and Kate would know, and exult in her knowledge, that Eimear's life had the potential to be as miserable as anyone else's for all her Barbie charm.

Her watertight scheme sprang a leak when she and Jack

fell in love. Kate found it just about believable that Eimear's Jack would fancy her, men were always calling her sexy, but beyond comprehension that he'd insist he wanted her for longer than a night or two. That he'd insist he needed her from here to eternity.

'Eimear's everything I'm not,' she protested one night as they lay in a tangle of sheets and limbs.

'Exactly,' he agreed, nuzzling her instep. Her instep! Pearse probably wouldn't know how to find it let alone kiss it.

'But she's exquisite and talented and as flawless as . . .' Kate gabbled.

'As flawless as a marble statue and twice as cold,' Jack finished her sentence. 'She goes to bed with me as a favour, not because she can't help herself. I want a woman who's real, who has scars' – he traced a thin line along her chin, the legacy of riding a bicycle without brakes – 'who has a stomach and lips and breasts' – he licked each part of her anatomy as he itemised it – 'a woman who's not afraid to eat and drink and enjoy life.'

Kate hugs the intoxicating memory to herself. But another call comes in and Bridie doesn't even go through the motions of asking her if she's free to take it, she slams it through.

'Isabel Eccles on line two,' she snaps.

When Kate lifts the receiver she hears a burst of Waterloo – she's been put on hold.

'Abba as elevator muzak – whatever happened to "Green-sleeves"?' Kate wonders aloud.

Abba reminds her of being a teenager with the three of them locked in Eimear's bedroom, experimenting with glitter eyeshadow and ransacking the wardrobe. It was there they had their first puffs on a cigarette, menthol, because Eimear reasoned the minty taste wouldn't leave them with bad breath. Eimear acquired the knack of smoking without turning the butt soggy almost immediately but Kate and Gloria were slower on the uptake. Eimear told them they shouldn't get hooked because women who smoke have wrinklier skin. .

'She's a twenty-a-day girl herself while Glo and I never did acquire the habit,' says Kate, severing the connection while Abba's vocal cords are still in full throttle. 'And naturally, her complexion is still as clear as a morning in May.'

Kate taps on the intercom, intent on currying favour.

'Why don't you head for the hills now, Bridie, you've put in some late nights recently.'

Bridie doesn't need telling twice, the extra half-hour will give her a head start on the other working mothers in the supermarket queue.

'I do have to nip into Dunnes for tonight's dinner,' she admits, although her enthusiasm is deliberately muted so that Kate needn't imagine she's won over. Kate's been slacking for the past few months and Bridie is exasperated at covering up for her.

Jack's face swims into Kate's mind again; until he came along she was feeling disillusioned by her countrymen's amorous technique.

'Mind you,' she acknowledges, 'they can talk any girl into a bedroom, I'll grant our lads that, they have the gab. But then they want to race through all the heave-ho part as though their time is precious and it's being frittered away. You might squeeze a little post-coital sweet talk out of them if they imagine they're in love but, smitten or not, before long they're thirsting for a pint of draught. Preferably in male-only company.'

Jack's Irish but she excludes him from the herd. He's not so much attached to the sod as to behaving like a sod, even Kate recognises that – still, it makes him all the more seductive when he sets out to seduce. He's an incomparable lover, he has the soul of a poet. Of course it's for his body she goes to bed with him, she giggles.

But Eimear's jingle-jangling inside their triangle and Kate

knows she can't keep out of her way forever, just like she can't keep her secret indefinitely. She's longing for it to be out in the open. And dreading it.

CHAPTER 10

Kate has never seen Gloria so angry, not even in hospital when she confided about her Jack-attack. Kate knows why she's doing it, Gloria's focusing on her misdeeds as a distraction from her troubles with Mick, but Gloria wallops into her so viciously that she goes on the defensive. So much for the girlie afternoon she thought was lined up: gallons of tea, a slice or two of Gloria's speciality ginger cake, perhaps some mind-numbing drivel about babies and a few snide remarks about Mick but nothing Kate couldn't handle.

'Fine, Gloria, have it your way, I'm the wicked witch from the west. Just because I fell in love.'

Gloria is savaging her about pretending she was trying to smooth everything over with Pearse yesterday. Serves her right for confessing that she's going to ask him to move out, acknowledges Kate – whoever said confession is good for the soul was on the wrong track. It's bad for the eardrums; Gloria's complaints are giving her a headache. But she can't carry on juggling Pearse and Jack any longer, the affair has taken such a grip she can't conceive of it as an adjunct to her life any longer. Jack has become her centre of gravity.

Gloria's unimpressed. But who's Miss Moral Majority to criticise her when she's leading Mick McDermott a dog's life? And he was her friend before he was Gloria's poodle, she needn't think Kate's automatically going to take her side.

'You promised me you'd call a halt, Kate, you agreed you were being stupid.'

'I don't want to call a halt, it's gone too far for us to casually break it off.'

'You don't think you're being selfish, rating your own happiness above Eimear's?'

'She'll find someone else, with her face she'll be fighting them off. But I only have one chance at a Jack, don't you see that, Glo? We're in love.'

Kate's begging her to understand but she turns her face away.

'Love,' Gloria spits the word out. 'It makes me sick. People say they're in love as though that excuses everything. "I'm about to wreck your marriage but don't blame me, it's love." "I'm about to set your life on its heels but don't blame me, it's love." Love doesn't give you the right to turn your back on your friends or to please yourself at somebody else's expense. Remember Celia Johnson and Trevor Howard in *Brief Encounter*? They didn't run away to start a new life together, they looked each other fair and square in the eye, remembered their obligations and said their farewells. They didn't even have a ride.'

'More fool them,' Kate fights back. 'Happiness has to be seized and clung on to for dear life and defended against all comers. You don't feel cosily self-righteous for doing the proper thing, you feel abandoned and depressed and an idealistic fool. Anyway, what's brought on this sudden flurry of interest in my affairs, or more specifically my affair? You haven't wanted to hear a word about it since I talked to you at the hospital.'

'It's Eimear,' sighs Gloria. 'I'm concerned about her.'

Kate is unrepentant. 'She's a big girl, she can fend for herself. All her life people have been doing her worrying for her, they can't resist that translucent appeal she exudes.'

'You never used to be so unyielding,' snaps Gloria. 'If this is love it doesn't suit you. Eimear's our friend and she needs us. She was there for you when you were desperately hunting for your first tenancy, holding your hand when you were knee-deep in rejection letters and convinced no one would give you a chance. And she's been there for me through this fertility misery, although I know she's at her wits' end with anxiety about Jack's womanising.'

'What womanising? There's only me,' Kate objects but Gloria pulls a face and she falls silent. Gloria takes up the cudgels again.

'I don't see how you can live with yourself knowing you're the reason for that strained look on her face. She's up to forty cigarettes a day now and I doubt she's eaten a meal in a month, I haven't seen her with anything more substantial than a sandwich. You've put me in an impossible position, telling me about you and Jack, I'm Eimear's friend as much as yours.'

Kate sighs heavily: 'Look, can we drop this, it's been a long week and I'm tired. Why don't you dig us out a Hollywood musical for the video – something with Fred Astaire or Gene Kelly in it.'

Her olive branch is rejected. Gloria looks earnestly at her troublesome friend, misery spilling from her eyes. Kate has always envied her those eyes – they're colleen-in-a-film-script green, not the muddy hazel that passes for it with some people. Kate wishes for the zillionth time that she wasn't stuck with blue ones. Eimear's are blue too but they're dazzle-you-at-ten-paces azure, hers are standard issue, no embellishments.

'Kate, even if you and Jack do gallop off into the sunset together, do you honestly think he'll be any more faithful to you?'

Kate laughs. 'Well of course he will, you sap. For starters we have a great sex life and Eimear's the original cold fish, you should hear . . .'

'Spare me the details, at least extend that much loyalty to Eimear.'

'Look, Glo, I don't know where you stumbled across this superior attitude. I don't accept I'm ruining Eimear's life, her marriage is in the Rocky Mountains anyway – I'm simply the catalyst.'

'Delusional as well,' mutters Gloria but Kate ignores her.

'Don't you think your time would be better spent trying to paper over some of the cracks in your own marriage instead of interfering in Eimear's? Mick's a grand lad, as happy-go-lucky as they come, but you've reduced him to a study in melancholy. His family are worried about him, or so his mother told mine during a lull in one of their over-the-fence offensives on Mrs Regan's good name. The McDermotts are convinced he's caught some disease because he's lost so much weight and . . .'

'He has a pot belly,' yells Gloria.

'. . . he's become withdrawn and incommunicative which isn't the Mick McDermott we all know and love.'

'Speak for yourself,' she responds.

'That much is obvious,' says Kate. 'Clearly there's no love lost between the two of you, so how you can even contemplate going for test-tube babies is beyond me.'

'Why do you insist on calling them test-tube babies, like something from the seventies? It's IVF treatment, in vitro fertilisation, assisted reproduction, a little medical intervention; nothing sinister, nothing miraculous, just modern medicine doing its job.' Gloria's face colours like a strawberry cone with outrage.

'Still,' Kate points out, 'a couple who can't sit in the same room together for more than five minutes without bickering aren't the most obvious candidates for babies. It strikes me that you're focusing on me because you can't bear to look at your own problems, which are, I don't mind telling you, my sweet, pretty bloody serious.'

Gloria reaches Kate her coat and walks pointedly to the front door. Kate longs to apologise abjectly, the best way to say sorry in her experience, and remind Gloria they always swore they'd never fall out over a man. But she walks past her without a word.

Jack's worth it, he has to be worth it.

'Anyway, Mick won't let us have the treatment,' Gloria whispers as Kate steps on to the path. 'There'll be no test-tube babies for me.'

Kate hesitates, turns back, but Gloria closes the door.

She sits in her car without turning the key in the ignition. She was never in love before Jack. The nineteen fellows, men, call them what you like, she slept with before him don't count. She may have told one or two she loved them, she may possibly have meant it at the time, but it wasn't love, nor a close second. Sometimes it wasn't even lust, more a case of Kate exercising her right to have sex whether she wanted to or not.

It caught her by surprise, this falling in love with him. She didn't realise she had, until Jack said it first. When he told her, it felt as though a thumping hangover had been wiped out, his words were a double dose of paracetamol. As for Pearse, well, she does have a conscience about him but he's better off without her. He was her hedge against loneliness; he knew that because she was always honest with him, but it doesn't reflect well on either of them. She glimpses Gloria's strained face at the window as she drives off.

It's a week later. Jack and Kate meet in a pub in Upper Leeson Street and he says two words even more overwhelming than the 'I love you' words she still finds incredible to believe.

'Eimear knows.'

Kate is simultaneously delirious and devastated. She wants Eimear to know, it's a relief she does, but now she'll think ill of her and that takes some living with. Not impossible, but it's tough. Formidable for Jack too, he looks like such a bewildered boy that Kate wants to hug him and reassure him. The pub's more full than they expected so she's only able to hold his hand discreetly under the table. No point in half of Dublin knowing along with Eimear.

At least she doesn't have to try and comfort him over the phone. It's their life-line, their love-line, the phone. The mobile phone anyway, they never dare rely on land lines – too easy to check calls. The thought of last number redial propels Kate's heart halfway up her throat.

But Jack's admission isn't as damning as she fears – or as heavenly as she hopes – Jack's a drama queen at times. Eimear doesn't know the identity of the other woman, just that there is someone else. He claims he wanted to acknowledge Kate, fling her in Eimear's face to wipe the self-righteous smirk off it, but he didn't feel he had the right to name names without consulting her first.

Kate's puzzled. 'But she knew you were seeing someone before, when she made you eat dinner on your own and deliberately ironed the front creases out of all your trousers. You know, around the time when Gloria was in hospital.'

'True, but she thought that was just a fling with a student and we could put it behind us – she lavished attention on me for a while, as though she'd been consulting one of those "How to Tease, Squeeze and Above All Please Your Husband" manuals. Now she's convinced I'm having a proper affair' – Doesn't he mean 'improper'? thinks Kate – 'and she's turning malicious on me.'

His brown eyes glint appealingly and Kate murmurs the sympathetic words he expects. She ignores a twinge – Jack is her reward for these tortures of betrayal that prick her when she remembers how ill-served Eimear is.

Kate knows she sounds like a lovesick teen when she talks about him but she can't help it, that's exactly what she is: lovesick. She has an ache inside her when she's not with him. It's a sharper pain than the one she feels when she thinks of Eimear.

'Same again?'

A suddenly cheerful Jack goes to the bar for another round of drinks, all he wanted was a little sympathy but Kate can't brighten up so quickly. She sees Eimear in the bottom of her glass, she's looking reproachfully at her. Kate shifts the slice of lemon so it's covering her face. She'll lose Eimear when she goes off with Jack, she's resigned to that. It's not easy to turn your back on a lifetime's friendship but anyone would if they could exchange it for a lifetime's love. Wouldn't they?

At least she'll still have Gloria. Sort of. Not that she's too enamoured of Kate but she's still talking to her, which counts for a lot at the moment. Pearse is gone, he packed up all his possessions into two or three boxes and left her his pasta maker. She'll never use it but where's the point in flinging kindness back into his face. Gloria claims he overlooked it instinctively – she believes if you leave something after you, then you'll always return to that place. In which case Kate is due back in half the airports and train stations she ever passed through, but there's no quibbling with Gloria when she spouts her folklore. For a townie she's remarkably rural.

She wishes Eimear knew about her and Jack, the same way you long for a visit to the accountant to be finished with. You recognise you'll feel better after you've sorted out your taxes but there's still the receipts and invoices to wade through and your teeth grind at the prospect.

She half-thought Gloria might have told Eimear all those months ago in hospital but she never said a word. Maybe she respected it as a confidence but Kate wouldn't have minded if she squealed.

The worst part of this affair – even the word makes her feel soiled – has been the furtive sneaking around. Some people find that exciting; she's well informed on the subject because she buys every magazine which promises to lift the

86

lid on affairs: 'Tears Before Bedtime – And Afterwards Too' or 'Top Ten Have-It-Away Hideaways' or 'Other Women: A Breed Apart'. Or the scariest one of all: 'We Cheated On His Wife, Now He's Cheating On Me'.

Kate feels sinful in a way she thought she'd put behind her; sin's a state of mind, or more specifically a state of not minding, she reasons. But she feels like a Magdalene when she remembers Eimear. Except she manages not to think of her too much. If she strays into Kate's consciousness she pours a glass of wine or switches on a television soap. Nothing like TV Land doom and gloom for distracting you from real life.

'Love makes you selfish, Gloria's right about that,' whispers Kate. 'Someone always gets hurt and it's not going to be me.'

PART TWO

CHAPTER 11

'House sharing at thirty-odd is no joke. Here I am in my thirty-third year and I can't even call the roof over my head my own. It's unnatural. By this age you've developed your little oddities, hence the name. You're not thirty-even, as in living on an even keel, you're thirty-odd as in just plain set in your ways and getting more solidified by the week.'

Gloria pauses to draw breath and Kate hastily rearranges her face into a sympathetic expression.

'I have a theory about thirty-odd,' continues Gloria, with the determination of someone who's saved up a week's worth of resentments and is determined to off-load them. 'By this stage you've taken out a mortgage on a house or flat you can't abide any more, bought matching pottery jars marked tea, coffee and sugar, as though you're so mentally deficient you can't remember which container is used for what, had passionate debates about colour schemes in some desolate warehouse of a DIY centre . . . turned into somebody you were mocking only a few years earlier. And what's worse, you like it. You parade your eccentricities with pride, talk about them in the third person, lend them genetic credibility by tracing them back to grandparents.'

Gloria adopts a Tipperary accent, for no other reason than it's the only rural one she can manage: '"I'm a divil in the morning, you can't hold a conversation with me till I'm on my second cup of coffee – my mother was the same." "The house can go to rack and ruin just so long as I'm able to keep the garden looking tidy – my grandfather spent every spare second outdoors himself."

'Now here I am, suddenly required to house-share. Pitched back into buying small loaves of bread because a large one goes stale before you can finish it. Back in the dark days of noticing and objecting (but detesting myself for it) when your friend drinks all the milk and never replaces it. Complaining, too, but feeling like a wrinkly, at her habit of playing the radio at full blast as she showers in the morning.'

Kate decides it's time to intervene. 'Call this a wild guess but are you finding life as Eimear's lodger the teensiest bit stressful?'

Gloria nods and bites savagely into the cheese-on-toast lunch Kate has rustled up for both of them – it's her stock in trade, her cooking doesn't run to anything else apart from scrambled eggs. Solidified to concrete consistency in the microwave.

'Mind you,' Gloria carries on more moderately, 'I can't seem to please Eimear either. I daren't set anything down, it's "Don't leave your mug on the cream carpet – if it spills I'll never erase the stains." So I tell her, fairly mildly considering the decibel level I've been subjected to, that if there was any space at all on the table I'd use it.

'She chooses to interpret this as criticism of her plants – and while it's true, as you know, Kate, she has foliage clambering over every available surface, spilling from ceramic strawberry pots and terracotta troughs, on their own they wouldn't be so bad. The melee is compounded by the bowls of potpourri, the vases of flowers, both dried and fresh, the candlesticks with candles she never lights because wax is so messy and the coffee-table books she never opens in case she creases the pages. But try telling Eimear this, she's in full flow about the therapeutic value of greenery.'

Gloria subsides, Kate heaves a sigh of relief, but then Gloria recollects another grievance.

'And don't get me started on Eimear's feng shui fixation: she shrieks if you leave the bathroom door open – apparently it means your money will trickle away. Or does that happen when you forget to close the loo seat? – I end up so confused.'

'I wish I had a spare room to offer you, Glo,' says Kate, wishing nothing of the kind because she doesn't want her friend's disapproving features on hand when Jack's in the vicinity.

'Wearing ear plugs to block out the noise as you and your fancy man cavort about the flat? Do me a favour, Kate. Just because I'm keeping your grimy secret doesn't mean I approve of you two. Although I'm starting to see that Jack may have some justification in kicking up his heels, life with Eimear is so regimented.

'I can't even talk to her about it. The trouble is, it's her house and that gives her the upper hand. Unspoken, but hanging in the air, every time you handle a plate cavalierly or leave footprints on the kitchen floor, is the reproach that it's her china you're risking and her floor you're muddying. I can't leave a scum ring on the side of the bath overnight any more, even when fully intending to clean it in the morning. I'll find her on her knees with the Jif in her hand and a martyred look on her face. I can't dump a few dishes in the sink or a pile of ironing in the utility room, everything has to be done at once. It's her religion. Tomorrow is never another day.'

Kate is delighted to hear Gloria wade into Eimear, it makes her feel even more justified in pursuing this relationship with Jack. But Gloria's resentment is already ebbing.

'Then again, Eimear gave me a home when Mick and I decided we needed time out. Actually it was me who decided it, Mick was opposed to the idea – he said couples who separate never solve their differences. They just find they can live without each other. I suppose he's right: even if you return to the marital home there's a sense in which something has been smashed.

'You've acknowledged the reality that the marriage might not be permanent, that maybe you won't live happily ever after, and the genie is out of the bottle. Marriage starts on the basis of two people saying they want to be together always, right? Now one or both of them are prevaricating: "Wait a minute, I need to think about this again."'

Gloria's head sinks on to her hand. What a shambles their lives are reduced to; she suspects Eimear's glad of the company, despite chafing at her untidiness. Eimear's been rattling around in her show-house since she and Jack had the mother, father and second-cousin-once-removed of all bust-ups when she discovered a packet of condoms in his wallet. He moved into rooms at Trinity College; he wanted to rush straight over to Kate's but for once the woman showed a smidgen of sense and suggested they let the dust settle first.

Gloria looks Kate in the face. 'Eimear misses Jack, you know.'

Kate immediately turns defensive. 'I didn't ask him to move out – we're not even living together. His decision to leave Eimear had nothing to do with me.'

Gloria sighs. It's a pickle fit to make your heart break – if it wasn't already cracked between the jigs and the reels. She half-smiles, that's a saying of her father's.

'Would you give my head peace, it's turned with the lot of you between the jigs and the reels. I'm off to Mulholland's for a bit of peace and quiet,' he'd complain.

Their mother rounded on the children when that happened.

'You see what you've driven your poor father to? Sending him out on a night like this to a public house, when he has a decent fireside of his own to sit at.'

They never dared point out it was her nagging he was running from, not their cowboy and indian shoot-outs.

It was her father who insisted she should be called Gloria. That's a Protestant name in her part of the country – it doesn't take a fidget out of them in Dublin where nobody worries if you're from one side or the other unless it's northside/southside of the city. The only sides now are financial . . . *tiocfaidh ar* bank balance. But names are logos in Tyrone, markers of identity; of division too. Eimear and Kate – safe choices, no problem working them out, but Gloria's a puzzle. Mallon says something and Gloria contradicts it. It's not clearcut, people feel uneasy.

Gloria's father named her after Gloria Swanson and her sister Marlene was named for Marlene Dietrich – he loved those old Hollywood black and whites. There's also a brother called Rudolph and it has nothing to do with being born at Christmas.

'You may not grow up glamorous, girls, but at least your namesakes had it oozing from their fingertips,' their father would tell Gloria and Marlene.

Not much of a vote of confidence from the man supposed to be your biggest admirer but he meant well.

Where's the allure in names like Bernadette or Teresa or those other beacons of purity they were supposed to be modelling themselves on, Gloria wonders. Agnes was another name the nuns approved of – apparently Saint Agnes was stripped naked by her pagan jailers but God sent angels from heaven with a piece of cloth to preserve her modesty.

Agnes Kearney, who sat in front of Gloria, would cringe every time that story was mentioned. She counts back: there were two Teresas and three Bernadettes in her class, including Bernadette Lynn, who did everything humanly possible to prove she had no aspirations towards canonisation – to the delight of half the fellows in the youth club.

Gloria inspects Kate with heightened interest across the

toasted cheese crumbs. There must be something magnetic about Jack to send Kate off her head like that. There has to be an overwhelming reason why she couldn't retain herself, like her innate sensuality responding to his incessant demands and leaving her in a haze of intoxicated befuddlement.

'Stop it, stop it, stop it,' Gloria shrieks mentally, sidling off to use Kate's bathroom. 'I'm getting myself all worked up speculating about a friend's love life, it's indecent.'

Anyway, it's all conjecture because she's never encouraged Kate to discuss her sheetside shenanigans – but everyone who knows her agrees she's a goer. 'A ride and a half,' as Mick puts it. Although how he'd know is beyond her.

Mick was only insistent about sex before they married. There was a noticeable sliding off after their grand day out and her ectopic pregnancy was the straw that broke the camel's hard-on. Left it limp, anyway; it may not be permanently inactivated but she's not the girl to fix it.

'Woman,' she corrects herself, leaning on the hand basin. 'I must stop referring to myself as a girl, if only on the grounds of accuracy.'

They've made love four times since her ectopic; that's four times in five-and a-bit months. A rate of not even once a month. According to Gloria's February issue of *Image* magazine, couples who've been together for a few years settle down to an average of twice a week. So someone, somewhere, is getting all her turns. She was never that bothered about jiggery pokery until she realised she wasn't going to have it unless there were twenty-eight days in the month. 'Enjoy this, my pet, it'll have to keep you going for the rest of the year.' The less she's allowed her conjugal rights the more she feels entitled to them.

She's not even sure you can count all four sessions since he lost his erection halfway through the last effort. Effort was the operative word, his heart clearly wasn't in it and neither, as it transpired, was his lad. She broods. It's not a pleasant experience to find your husband has lost his erection halfway through work in progress. There you are, legs akimbo, having quite a nice time really, when you suddenly get that shrinking feeling followed by the sinking one. He pumps on for a while, as though neither of you have noticed anything unusual, but eventually he concedes defeat.

Then of course he's desperately upset, manhood compromised, so you end up cuddling him and saying it doesn't matter when it does. Especially as he doesn't offer to distract you. Especially as you're not convinced he'll be ready to play house with you in the foreseeable future. Not on his track record.

After that, Mick seemed to operate a sexual shutdown. Gloria considers. It's entirely possible he takes himself in hand after she's fallen asleep but she's discovered no evidence of it.

'Let's see a counsellor,' she suggested.

He slammed the door on his way out.

'Mick, we need expert help,' she insisted.

He slammed the door on his way out.

'I'm at my wits' end,' she pleaded.

He slammed the door on his way out.

'I'm leaving you,' she threatened.

He slammed the door on his way out.

So here she is in Donnybrook with Eimear, sleeping in her spare room on cream linen sheets and eating her meals off primrose pottery. Gloria misses her own embroidered duvet covers and her own willow-pattern plates. She ran away with nothing more than her make-up purse, some clothes and her pillow. She can't sleep on any other pillow, this goes everywhere with her.

Gloria wanders back along the hall to Kate, stacking dishes in the kitchen sink.

'Any word from Mick?' Kate calls over her shoulder.

'Not a dicky bird.'

She's been staying with Eimear for a fortnight and Mick has only contacted her once. That was the night after she moved out, when he rang up and ordered her to get a grip, she was mentally unbalanced and she should come straight home and stop dragging friends into their problems. Now who could resist an invitation like that.

Kate turns around, drying her hands on a teacloth. 'Maybe he feels contact should come from you, Glo – after all you're the one who jumped ship.'

Gloria focuses on the jet earrings set dancing by the way Kate's holding her head. She's watching Gloria with an expression of affectionate concern but Gloria doesn't notice as she ruminates on Kate's suggestion. It's forcing her to consider her motivation more narrowly than she's allowed herself.

Does she genuinely want to save her marriage or is Eimear and Jack's split the equivalent of the butterfly's fluttering wings in Ballaghadreen that spark an earthquake in Bombay? Not to mention a marital severance in Ranelagh.

CHAPTER 12

'I've thought it over, Mick, and it's the only way I'll come back to you,' Gloria says levelly, bracing herself for a row. She's not disappointed.

His face turns magenta as he yells: 'It's insulting, it's degrading, it's bestial, it's treating me like a sperm bank.'

'I don't see that, it's not as if I want to get pregnant by any piece of testosterone on legs, it's not as if I'm walking down the street pointing to the first man I meet and saying, "You'll do nicely, big boy." It's not as if I'm selecting a suitable sperm donor based on his IQ. I want your baby, Michael Patrick McDermott's, my husband's, the man I've loved since I was sixteen. I want us to be a family.'

'But you're telling me that the only way you'll come home to me is if we shell out for fertility treatment,' he protests.

'So it's the money that's bothering you.'

'No, it's not the money, Gloria, it's the way you're going about this I don't like. You're doing it entirely back to front. Any sensible person would sort out their marriage before they'd ever contemplate something as drastic as intravenous fertilisation.'

'You see, you know so little about it you can't even be bothered to get the name right,' she snorts. 'What do you think I am, a druggie hooked on babies?'

So much for her mental promise not to lose her temper and descend to trading insults.

'Don't be so superior, Gloria, you knew what I meant. You've latched on to this treatment as though it's the miracle cure but what happens if it doesn't work, have you thought about that? Just because you empty your bank balance into the hands of some specialist doesn't mean you'll walk away with a baby.'

Gloria pauses before responding, determined to haul the conversation back on to an even keel. 'Of course I know there's only a one in four chance but why shouldn't we take it, why shouldn't we be among the lucky 25 per cent?'

Then irritation takes over: 'You're always so negative, Mick McDermott, you need to take a risk. We have no chance of a baby at the minute, at least this gives us something to hope for. Live dangerously for once, why don't you. I'd have thought it would've suited you down to the ground, you don't even have to kiss me this way, you get to be a father without any of the bother. And we all know what an effort it is for you.'

He leaps up, face contorted with rage. 'I wondered how long it would take before you harped on about that. You've blown it out of proportion, just because I couldn't perform to suit you that once when I was tired.'

'Whatever. Now how about leaving your legendary caution to one side and taking a chance on medical science?'

Mick is still furious. 'I don't mind taking chances, it's typical of you to paint me as some kind of tippy-toed big girl.'

'The prudent virgin,' Gloria muses. Mischievously of course.

There's murder in his glance but he steadies himself visibly. 'I'm not overly cautious, I just like to be aware of all the possibilities first. And you can wipe that supercilious smirk off your face, Gloria. What gives you the right to call me negative when you're the one laying down all these conditions for continuing with our marriage?'

'Sit down, Mick. It's not conditions, just one.'

'And a hefty condition it is. You're blackmailing me into

100

something I'm not sure I want to do,' he hops from one foot to the next.

'Well, let me know when you are sure, you know where I'll be.'

'Burying a knife between my shoulder blades with your friends from the sisterhood on hand to mark the spot.'

He flings himself into the sofa opposite rather than joining Gloria on the one she's occupying in Eimear's sitting room. Her friend has gone to an art exhibition to afford them a chance to ransack their relationship for a solution. Gloria refused Mick's suggestion they meet in their own house – there's no way she's setting foot over that threshold until he agrees to try for a baby and she doesn't mean by scrutinising thermometers and calendar dates. They're way past that stage.

Gloria tries to reassure him but takes the wrong tack: 'Why would the three of us waste our time gossiping about you? You're developing a paranoia complex.'

'No wonder, when I hear Eimear Mulligan or O'Brien or whatever she calls herself has been going around telling people I have a low sperm count,' he splutters.

'Of course she hasn't, I don't know where you get these notions from,' she protests.

Mick pantomimes disbelief.

'A neighbour commiserated with my mother about it, as it happens. The poor woman was mortified, being approached by a venomous old biddy agog to discuss the contents of her son's testicles. So if it travelled all the way back up to Omagh then you can be sure tongues have been wagging freely in Dublin. And you're the only one who knew about the sperm test so it's a dead cert it went from you to Eimear and then she broadcast it on the RTE news bulletin.'

'Mick,' says Gloria as patiently as she can manage, 'you know very well your sperm count was checked and found to be normal.'

The outrage level continues to soar.

101

'I know that and you know that but someone's got hold of the wrong end of the stick and my reputation is being smeared to hell and back and Eimear's the odds-on favourite. Now that her marriage is over she's trying to put the evil eye on yours.'

Gloria inhales deeply. 'Mick, you're being unjust – and what's more you're straying completely off the point. Now can you turn your attention to deciding if our marriage is worth enough to you – if I'm worth enough to you – to have a baby. That is,' she corrects herself, 'to allow medical science to help us have the baby I thought we both wanted.'

'And if there's no baby there's no marriage, right?' He folds his arms.

'If you must put it that way.'

As he rocks back and forth on his sofa, Gloria is distracted by the sight of his stomach, still a pudding-sized hillock above his trouserband but no longer the mountain range it once was. Come to think of it, there are no fleshy gaps between his shirt buttons. Good God, has he lost weight? And how could he manage that when she's certain he's been living on takeaways since she left him? She realises she's just accused him of changing the subject but she can't help herself.

'Mick, are you on a diet?' she demands.

He looks smug. 'No, the weight's been peeling off me since you stormed off into the night. Granted, I don't have as much of an appetite as I used to, I have a lot on my mind.' He looks sanctimonious. 'I may need to buy some new trousers soon.' Sanctimony turns to triumph. 'A size down,' he adds, in case she hasn't grasped the significance.

'I'm delighted for you, you look grand on it,' she tells him, ignoring the spasm of fury that all her efforts to persuade him to go to a gym or eat the odd salad failed but as soon as she's not around to cajole there's a visible difference.

'Thanks,' he says. 'I wish I could say the same for you but you look pale and tired.'

'I'm not sleeping so well,' she admits.

'Eimear wouldn't be the easiest flatmate either, she's too particular. Take a look at this place' – his eyes wander critically around the pastel living room – 'it's like a showpiece. There's no unbuttoning your waistband and getting comfortable in a house like this. It's a wonder she didn't tell you to keep me in the kitchen.'

'Mick,' she says, 'I really think we should leave Eimear and her house rules out of this. The bottom line is I want a baby, I need one, and IVF is our only chance. I'm ready to go for it, are you willing?'

Infuriatingly, Mick avoids a straight answer. 'What about adoption? That's an option we haven't discussed.'

She screeches: 'We're not talking about adoption here, we're talking about fertility treatment.'

'Maybe we should be talking about adoption, it sounds a lot more straightforward than messing with your hormones.'

Through gritted teeth she enunciates: 'Mick, I have nothing against adoption, certainly it's something we should investigate, but right now we're discussing fertility treatment and that's a mammoth issue on its own without tacking adoption on to the end of it. I'm not ruling out adoption, but I also want to try for a baby of my own, and I need your co-operation for that.'

Gloria slumps back, exhausted.

Mick demands: 'What if you have the treatment and there's still no baby. Does that mean you'll head off again, that you'll decide the marriage is over a second time? What guarantees do I have?'

She's smouldering. 'There you go with your speciality, being negative, you're so cautious I want to shake you. There are no guarantees, just hopes. Have you never heard of nothing ventured nothing gained? This is ridiculous, we can't even talk about a baby without being at each other's throats. It's definitely all over as we are now, but there's a chance we can work our differences out with a baby.'

'So you're prepared to use a child as a pawn? That's despicable.'

'I didn't mean it that way.'

Gloria inhales and exhales slowly, willing herself to calm down.

She continues: 'Look, we've known each other more than half our lives, we believe we can be happy together – we were once.'

Mick pounces. 'Exactly, so let's work at being happy again and leave this baby business alone until we're sure of the basics.'

'Sweet Lord but you could teach Hamlet a trick or two about procrastination. I don't have time to leave it alone, I'm thirty-three this year. Your chances of this treatment working are better the younger you are. I'm old already, my womb and ovaries are ageing every day. My mother had me when she was twenty-five, my granny had her when she was twenty-two. Even if I get pregnant first time I'll be in my thirty-fourth year before I have a baby, I'll be ancient among all the other mothers in the labour ward.'

Mick puts his arms on her shoulders and gently shakes her. 'Get a grip, Glo, women have babies into their forties these days. You're young still, another six months or even a year won't make much difference.'

She pushes him away. 'It might, I can't take that chance. I need to feel I'm doing everything I can right now.' Her voice rises, she's becoming hysterical. 'Why are you against me, why do I feel I'm the only one in this relationship who wants a baby?' Tears prickle against her eyelids and she turns her head so Mick won't see them and accuse her of being unstable or over-emotional or any of the other techniques he uses to end discussions he's uncomfortable with. She jabs a finger into the hollow at each side of the upper bridge of her nose, a trick to thwart the tear ducts.

Mick's voice sounds calm now that she's the one getting upset. 'Stop being so confrontational, Gloria, you know I'd like to be a father too. But launching head-first into IVF treatment in these circumstances is not just wrong, it's dangerous. You're not thinking clearly, you're overwrought. Come home, let's glue our lives back together and then we'll see where we are.'

Her voice trembles despite her best efforts. 'I've told you my condition for returning home, I'm not changing my mind. Either we go together to this open meeting for infertile couples at the hospital next week or I'll post my wedding ring through the letterbox.'

'That sounds suspiciously like an ultimatum, Gloria.'

'That's because it is an ultimatum, Mick.'

His face leaving the room is streaked with sorrow.

As the door closes, Gloria loses the slim control she has over her emotions and liquid spills down her cheeks in hot, damp trails, dangling along the chin line before plopping on to her shirt.

When Eimear returns, her face is blotchy but she's cried out – curled up on the sofa and staring vacantly at the door handle.

'Is it safe to come in?' Eimear calls from the hall. 'Are hostilities in progress or has a peace deal been hammered out?'

Her light-hearted tone turns to surprise. 'You're sitting in the dark, Glo,' she exclaims, 'the curtains aren't even drawn.'

Eimear switches on a lamp and Gloria shrinks from the beam.

'Gloria, what's happened to you? I knew I shouldn't have gone out, I should've waited upstairs in case you needed me.'

'I'm grand, Eimear, I probably look worse than I am. I've

just been moping, I meant to wash my face before you landed home but I didn't manage it.'

Eimear looks at her steadily, then gives her a hug, murmuring, 'Poor little Gloria'; Gloria leans against her inhaling Oscar de la Renta. They rest quietly, arms wrapped around each other, then Eimear disengages, pats her shoulder and says, 'I'll put the kettle on.'

Gloria feels a pathetic urge to pad after her, not to let her out of her sight, but she remains on the sofa listening to the kitchen sounds.

Eimear emerges from the back of the house with a pot of tea and a plate of Jaffa Cakes. She feels her spirits rise – there are few crises which cannot be addressed with Jaffa Cakes, they took the three of them through wobbly exam results, wobbly bank balances, wobbly love lives. Gloria decimates two in rapid succession before she's able for conversation.

'Big crowd at the gallery?' she asks casually.

Eimear looks mildly surprised at this conversational gambit, she's expecting the dirt to be dished on Mick but Gloria's not ready for that.

'So-so. Actually, I only stayed a few minutes, then I sloped off to see an Al Pacino film at The Screen. Knocking on a bit but he's still undeniably gorgeous in a short sort of a way, he rolled his eyes a lot and chased taller women.'

'He wouldn't have to chase me too hard,' Gloria manages half-heartedly.

'Me neither. I'd develop a sprain.'

Eimear watches Gloria out of the corner of her eye.

'Mick called around,' Gloria says finally.

'I gathered as much.'

'We had our usual shouting match. Your neighbours must be cursing us.'

'They've had it too quiet since Jack moved out; they probably miss the pair of us barging at each other.' She shrugs.

106

'Isn't it better than *Fair City* and they don't have to put up with advert breaks.'

Eimear passes the biscuits and asks: 'Did you raise the fertility treatment with Mick?'

'I did.'

'And he wasn't enamoured of the idea?'

'That's putting it mildly. I'm a blackmailer, I'm neurotic, I'm using him as a sperm bank, I'm a silly moo who should come straight home and put all this nonsense behind me. I'm everything except the truth, which is a woman who desperately wants a baby with her husband.'

'So he said no?' Eimear lays a sympathetic hand on her arm.

'To tell you the truth I'm not sure what his answer is. He argued the bit with me and he flounced out but he didn't say no exactly. I'm sure I would have remembered an uncompromising no. All that stays with me is the hatred and the accusations. Maybe he wants to think it over, he has until next week. I suppose I'll just have to sit it out and wait to hear from him – or not.'

'There's hope then,' presses Eimear.

'I suppose,' Gloria concedes.

'He'll calm down and see sense, you can be certain he will. Sure hasn't he been devoted to you for centuries, he'll not give you up without a fight.'

'It's the fighting that wrecks me,' she tells Eimear. 'Every last inch of me is exhausted, I want peace and quiet for a change. Life doesn't have to be full-scale war, other people seem able to settle their differences amicably – maybe there's something in the chemistry between Mick and me that makes us essentially incompatible. We're fine as long as everything runs smoothly but toss a problem or two underfoot and we start floundering.'

'Gloria, you're exaggerating,' says Eimear. 'You're feeling depressed and everything appears bleak. You and Mick have been disgustingly blissful for years and years, the rest of us have been consumed with envy at the pair of you, and believe me you will know joy again. It's only natural that a couple who've had their hopes of parenthood thwarted should come a little unstitched at the seams but you'll work it out for the best, honestly.'

'Do you really think so?' she asks doubtfully.

'I don't think, I know,' insists Eimear. 'I have this theory that everyone has a certain amount of bad luck to wade through in life; some people seem to encounter it in one fell swoop and other people have it spaced out. Maybe you're in the swoop category, this could be all your bad luck lumped together and you'll have no more to worry about.'

It's an explanation that appeals to Gloria. A reluctant smile flashes across her face, followed by the irresistible impulse to say her party piece: 'Good luck, bad luck, who knows?'

Eimear grabs her with a laugh, almost sending a teacup clattering – which would have upset her far more than Gloria – and as she straightens the clock chimes 1 a.m.

Eimear yawns. 'Time for bed, said Zebedee. You have the bathroom first, Gloria. I'll carry this tray through to the kitchen.'

Gloria is on the top stair when the phone rings. She peers over the banister as Eimear answers it – a call so late can only mean trouble.

'It's for you.' Eimear sounds scared. 'It's Mick.'

CHAPTER 13

Mick's been drinking and his words are slurred. Gloria's instinct is to tell him to ring again at a more civilised time and replace the receiver forcefully (Eimear doesn't like it slammed). But before she severs the connection, Mick's disjointed string of words rearrange themselves into a cohesive sentence.

'Gloria, it's your father. He died half an hour ago. Your brother's just phoned here looking for you. He was in a call box and didn't have much change so I said I'd get you to ring him.'

'Stop your nonsense, how can Daddy be dead, he isn't even sick. Away to your bed and sleep it off.'

'Gloria, I know I've been drinking but I'm not drunk and I'm not hallucinating. I have a phone number for you, it's the hospital pay phone. Rudy's there now waiting to hear from you. Your father collapsed on his way to bed, your mother called an ambulance but he was dead on arrival. They believe it may have been a heart attack.'

As Gloria dials and waits for the phone to peal out in a corridor of Omagh's hospital, she's still expecting her brother to answer and say: 'He's fine, he took a bit of a dizzy turn and they're keeping him in for tests.'

Eimear hovers anxiously but Gloria doesn't speak to her, she's too preoccupied with the drumming in her chest and eardrums.

The receiver is lifted on the sixth ring.

'Is that you, Glo? I was outside having a fag.'

'Never mind the fags, Rudy, what's happened to Daddy?'

'Did Mick not tell you – he's dead, Gloria.'

His voice sounds reedy, the Tyrone accent heightened by emotion. Dead becomes two syllables, each as ugly as the other. Rudolph chatters on.

'There were only the two of them in the house. He was watching some sports highlights on television, then he and Mammy said the Rosary, she asked him if he wanted tea and he said no, he didn't want to be getting up for the bathroom in the night. He stopped the cuckoo clock so it wouldn't disturb him and headed for bed – Mammy told him she'd sit up and finish her library book, she only had a chapter left.'

He pauses for breath, shallow gulps; Gloria waits with preternatural calm while he continues: 'Mammy hadn't read more than a few lines when she heard a crash, she sprang into the hall and saw Daddy had fallen, he was holding on to the banister, slumped three stairs from the top of the landing. She ran up to him, he seemed to be having difficulty breathing and she panicked when she saw his face: it was like parchment.

'She phoned an ambulance and rushed back to his side. Then she held his hand and talked to him, about the weather, about the Maeve Binchy novel she was reading, about the bulbs she had ready for planting in the garden. She thought she ought to whisper an act of contrition in his ear on his behalf and just as she finished she heard the ambulance siren. She had the front door open before they were parked and while they were taking him out she rang me to meet her at the hospital. By the time I arrived it was all over.'

'Where's Mammy now?' asks Gloria.

'She won't leave him, she's sitting by his bedside, she never takes her eyes off his face.'

'She isn't on her own, is she?'

'No, Noreen's with her,' Rudy reassures her. 'I'm still trying

to track down Marlene in London, I've rung everyone I can
think of and I've left a message on her answerphone. I had
trouble enough catching up with you.'

Noreen is Rudy's wife, she and her mother-in-law are great
friends and Gloria's fond of her. Still, it's galling to think she's
comforting her mother when Gloria's 112 miles away.

'I'll be straight up, I'll pack a bag,' she promises rashly,
forgetting that she left Mick with the car as well as the house
and all its contents when she walked out.

'Gloria, it's a three and a half hour drive, you'd be better
off with a good night's sleep. Come up in the morning.'

'What sleep are any of us likely to get this night? I'll see
you in a few hours – I'll make straight for the hospital.'

'We may have taken Mammy home to bed by then.'

'If you're not there I'll know where to find you but I want
to see Daddy first.'

'Whatever you think best – and, Glo, drive carefully.'

'I'll run you up,' offers Eimear, as she turns away from the
phone. 'It won't be the most comfortable journey in my old ·
Beetle but at least we'll get you there.'

Gloria is too grateful to demur; the alternative is to swing
by Ranelagh and liberate Mick's car.

'I'll throw a few changes of clothes in a bag,' she tells
Eimear, already halfway up the stairs.

The phone rings again and Eimear answers it. Gloria hears
her speaking and the tinkle of the disconnection as she roots
for anti-perspirant in the bathroom.

'That was Mick, he offered to drive you up tomorrow.'
Eimear materialises at the door. 'He's over the limit or he'd
do it tonight.'

Over the limit's an understatement, Gloria thinks, but she's
too distracted to do other than shake her head and say, 'I'd
prefer to go tonight.'

She can find nothing – where's her sponge bag? Never
mind, she shoves everything into a plastic carrier. A bottle

of mouthwash clatters into the bath as she ransacks the shelves.

Eimear hovers hesitantly in the corner of her field of vision.

'Gloria, do you think we should say a prayer?'

She looks at her blankly.

'For the repose of your father's soul,' adds Eimear.

Gloria is reminded of the formula: 'Eternal rest grant to the souls of Brian and Mary Gormley and Patrick and Clodagh Mallon, oh Lord, let perpetual light shine upon them, may they rest in peace, amen.'

But that's the prayer they say for her dead grandparents, it has nothing to do with her father.

She resumes packing. Eimear backs off when she sees her face, mumbling something about hunting out her weekend bag.

Father O'Kane is talking about the man lying in a toast-coloured box to the side of the altar – Gloria assumes it must contain her father since they chose it for him. Chose is an exaggeration. Donal Downey the undertaker – also landlord of Mulholland's pub – said, 'This model is our most popular one,' and Rudolph and she nodded. She can't connect the person the priest is talking about with her father. It's the same cleric who performed her marriage ceremony, Father O'Kane; she remembers him joking to Mick that if he smelled so much as a hint of alcohol from his breath he'd abort the wedding service. Except he wasn't joking.

Her father liked Father O'Kane, he said the quickest Mass of any priest in the parish: twenty-one minutes on weekdays; forty-four minutes on Sundays when his hands were tied by the choir. Gloria's father approved of speedy priests, he groaned when they had a young one assigned to the parish because he'd be full of sincerity and determined to extract every ounce of meaning from the service.

Mick is sitting beside Gloria, he's been shadowing her

since the removal of the remains – that's how they refer to her father now, as remains – to the church yesterday. She doesn't want Mick throwing his arm around her and answering questions on her behalf, it seems hypocritical in view of their separation. But Mick argues it wouldn't be fair on the family to give them something else to worry about. Eimear and Kate are in the pew behind her. Kate hasn't stopped crying since Mass started, Gloria can hear her sniffling and the rustle as Eimear passes her tissues.

'May the divine assistance always remain with us . . .'

Father O'Kane's voice cuts through her musings but only for a moment.

Already she's distracted, off at another tangent. Gloria remembers a fellow from her final year in Queens called Hugh Devine who used to claim it was his family's intercession being importuned during the Mass.

She glances past Mick to her mother, a dry-eyed stranger in her new black hat, and thinks of the surprised-looking young woman in a knee-length white dress and veil, holding a prayer book, in the wedding photograph at the top of the stairs. Gloria's mother seemed younger than twenty-three, like a teenager dressing up as a bride for a fancy-dress competition. Her father was twenty-seven, ill-at-ease in his navy suit – the photo is black and white but he never bought anything except navy suits all his life – and his normally wavy hair was slicked back and compressed to his head, only a wayward curl above the right eyebrow escaping.

And then, virtually obscured by a pillar beyond her mother, she spies Jack. He's kneeling near the side entrance to the church, face in his hands, but there's no mistaking his solid frame and the set of his head. Initially taken aback, Gloria reassesses her response and is immeasurably touched; she tries to remember if he ever met her father but can't. Belatedly she thinks of Eimear – and Kate. Then shrugs mentally. Jack's made the effort out of respect for her bereavement, irrespective of how his gesture (never mind his presence) might impact on the women in his life, and she won't slight him for it.

He approaches her as she leaves the church and wordlessly envelops her in a bear hug. An enthusiastic social kisser, she can never recall Jack embracing her in this way. Gloria inhales tweed and aftershave, something else too, something indefinable. Pheromones, perhaps, although surely not at her father's funeral . . . As they disengage she catches Eimear and Kate watching them. Jack sees them too and seems determined to avoid both.

'You must come back to the house for something to eat later,' she tells him, automatic words she'll use to dozens of well-wishers within the half-hour.

His hands linger on her shoulder for a moment. 'Gloria, I can't, I have to be back in Dublin by later afternoon. But thank you for the invitation.'

'Thank you for coming,' she responds, social niceties carrying her through a cloak of bleakness as the coffin shouldered by six men passes her. Her eyes stray past Jack to the honey-brown box saturated in wreaths. There's a touch on her elbow, it's Mick, and when she looks back Jack has melted away.

'Wasn't that Eimear's Jack?' he asks. 'Decent of him to come the length.'

Eimear's Jack. That's debatable, thinks Gloria. Equally debatable if he's Kate's. Then she loses interest in everything but the necessity to pick her steps with care as Mick guides her to the funeral car, before stepping up to join Rudy and her uncles at the coffin. Women don't tend to walk behind coffins in these parts, they say it's not fitting, although the Walsh sisters did after their mother died. But then, there weren't many men in that family. Mick approaches her again at the graveyard. Kate and Eimear have their arms around Gloria but they move aside.

'I've decided I'll come to that hospital meeting with you on Thursday, Gloria,' he whispers.

'Right, see you there,' she answers distantly.

She's just thrown a rose on top of the disappearing box her father is lying in – the man who told her the story of the Children of Lir every bedtime and promised her a swan for her eighteenth birthday, but in the meantime bought her a white felt duck (he couldn't find a swan) to cuddle to sleep with.

'Couldn't I collect you and take you there?' Mick asks.

'Whatever you like,' she agrees, watching the gravediggers watching the family. They can't begin their work till the mourners leave.

'So I'll see you on Thursday evening at Eimear's.'

'Fine,' she nods, impatient for him to move away. He lingers but she's saved by her Auntie Kathleen who descends, bosoms a-quiver, demanding that Gloria recount every last detail of 'poor Jamesie's final moments'. As if she didn't know it all already better than anyone.

'He never lived to collect his pension,' sighs Auntie Kathleen. 'How's your poor mother taking it?'

'The lack of a pension or the lack of a husband?' asks Gloria, rather meanly, but Auntie Kathleen affects not to hear.

Eimear and Kate are shoulder to shoulder for the first time in Gloria doesn't know how many months. It strikes her with the force of a blow that this is the first time she's seen them together since her ectopic. The trio have sloped away to Mulholland's for a quiet drink, without neighbours and schoolfriends approaching for the 'I'm sorry for your loss'/'I know you are' ritual.

Mulholland's was her father's home from home, although he wasn't a heavy drinker – he used to have the odd bottle of Guinness here to lubricate his card-playing. Gloria is drinking one now to toast his memory, although it's a vile concoction. She envies her companions their white wines, if she can just sink a few more inches of this she'll be on the pig's back. Her mind coils backwards to childhood as she sips.

Gloria (aged eight): 'Where are we now, Daddy?'

Daddy: 'We're on the pig's back.'

Gloria (a minute later): 'Are we on his shoulders yet, Daddy?'

Mammy: 'Don't go climbing on the back of your father's seat, Gloria, you'll spoil his concentration and have us all killed.'

Gloria: 'Where are we now, Daddy?'

Daddy: 'We're on his shoulders, honeybunch.'

Gloria: 'And you'll let us know when we're on his forehead and sliding down his nose, won't you, Daddy, won't you?'

Mammy: 'How many times do I have to tell you about climbing on your father's seat, Gloria. Rudy, take your finger out of your nose. Marlene, if you think you're going to be sick roll the window down.'

Daddy: 'I will of course, Gloria, you'll be the first to know. But we've a few more miles to go yet before we're on his neck, never mind sliding down his nose.'

They decamped to a caravan in Mullaghmore for the first fortnight in July every year – that way they'd avoid the marching season – and she doubts if a single journey to the Sligo seaside went by without the distance being measured on the pig.

'If I can see the bottom of this glass of Guinness I'll be on the pig's back,' Gloria promises herself. 'Hold your nose and think of Ireland, woman.'

Eimear speaks as Gloria's swigging determinedly. 'I saw Jack talking to you outside the church.'

Gloria nods.

'Did he have much to say for himself?'

Gloria shrugs.

'I didn't notice him back at the house,' continues Eimear.

'He wasn't there,' says Gloria.

Now Kate takes up where Eimear leaves off, neither of them able to let it rest.

'Did you know Jack was coming, Glo?'

Gloria shakes her head.

'You must have been surprised to see him.'

She shrugs again.

'Did he have to get back to the city in a hurry?'

'Said he needed to be somewhere by late afternoon,' volunteers Gloria. 'I appreciated his coming, it was a kindness I didn't expect.'

Kate and Eimear nod in unison, each delighted by this spark of human decency from a man they both love although aware he doesn't just have feet of clay – it's shins, knees and thighs too. Gloria senses their chagrin that he spoke to neither of them; would they ever get some perspective into their lives and stop obsessing about bloody Jack O'Brien, she thinks, swirling around the creamy liquid in the bulbous glass with its distinctive harp stamp.

She has a brief respite, then Kate picks up the threads of their earlier conversation. The one unshadowed by Jack – but tinted by darker nuances.

'It's a terrible idea, Glo.'

'Beyond terrible,' agrees Eimear. 'The timing's banjaxed. Give it another couple of months and see how you both feel – you're bound to be emotionally confused.'

'Exactly,' nods Kate. 'You and Mick should have a break, go lie in the sun and drink daiquiris until you feel stronger. A funeral takes it out of you, you think you're coping and then wallop, it hits you like a lorryload of cement.'

'You're on automatic pilot now,' interjects Eimear. 'It will be weeks before reality bites. Just head off the two of you, put some space between yourselves and all this.'

'Quality time,' says Gloria.

'Just so,' they exclaim in unison, delighted she's seeing sense.

'Fuck quality time.' Gloria empties the glass in one final draught. 'Here's to you, Daddy. Another round, Patsy,' she signals the barman. 'But make it three white wines this time.'

He brings the drinks over. 'I'm sorry for your loss.'

'I know you are.'

At least he doesn't try and shake her hand. Gloria sips the sauvignon, which trails sourly along her tongue after the Guinness, and gathers up the threads of the conversation again.

'All we're doing is going to an open meeting for couples interested in assisted reproduction, I won't be bringing a specimen bottle with me and tricking Mick into discharging his manhood into it,' she tells them. 'We need information. If we don't get it at Thursday's meeting we'll have to wait months for the next one. Then months before they can start us off on the treatment. I don't have an infinite number of months, I want to get this show on the road. *Sláinte*.'

She knocks back her wine and looks challengingly at her friends.

Kate stands and walks away. At the bar she reaches over a note and returns with three slim glasses. Patsy arrives a moment after, uncorks a bottle of sparkling wine and pours each of them a foaming beaker. Kate lifts one.

'Here's to Nasty Spumanti,' she toasts. 'And may the next time we drink this be at your baby's christening.'

The three clink glasses.

'To babies,' agrees Eimear. 'May you have the fattest ones in Dublin and may they all grow up to be brain surgeons and film stars.'

CHAPTER 14

Eimear phones Kate to complain.

'Gloria meant what she said after her father's funeral, she's really going home to Mick purely and simply to have a baby with him – not that there's anything pure or simple about it. She's just told me she's moving back to Ranelagh tomorrow.'

'So the IVF open meeting went well,' says Kate.

'Must have, it's all systems go on the babymaking front. Incidentally, she insists we're to refer to it as assisted reproduction. Such a daft name, it makes you think of couples having marital relations in little rooms with someone in a white coat hammering on the door, calling, "Need a hand in there?"'

'Eimear,' Kate protests, 'she's married to Mick, it makes sense for them to sort out their differences and they'll never do that while Gloria's in your spare room. More to the point, they'll never have a baby that way either which seems to be their priority.'

'It's Gloria's anyway.'

Eimear knows she's being selfish but she prefers the status quo. When Gloria mentioned fertility treatment at her father's funeral Eimear didn't take her seriously. Bereavements can have a destabilising effect, some people are carried away with an urge to replace the lost life with a new one. Others just want to do anything to take their minds off their grief. One of her fellow librarians told Eimear he couldn't wait to get home from his mother's freshly filled-in grave so he could drag his wife off to bed. By the scruff of the neck if necessary. Either a panic attack or some kind of life affirmation, she assumed.

'I was convinced Gloria would think better of it as soon as she was safely back in the real world with me in Dublin,' Eimear explains to Kate. 'Besides, fertility treatment is the sort of undertaking that requires two volunteers, not one able seaman and another who's been pressganged.'

'But we both toasted her in Mulholland's, we clinked glasses and wished her triplets,' Kate points out. 'I thought you were all in favour of it.'

Kate's usual extravagant gesture over cheap bubbly.

'I played along, I didn't want to come across like Cassandra, but this will all end in tears,' predicts Eimear. 'Come over and help me talk some sense into her.'

'I'll come over but I can't promise anything. It's not up to us to interfere. What are you afraid of, Eimear? She can't live with you forever, even if she never goes back to Mick. Besides, you drive each other demented.'

'What's Gloria been telling you?'

'Nothing, but it's obvious the two of you weren't cut out to share a window box let alone a house.'

Gloria can't wait for Eimear to plunge the coffee before she fizzes over with plans.

'Kate, have you heard I'm moving home tomorrow?' says Gloria. 'Mick and I are determined to make it work this time. Besides, we need to be interviewed by a doctor and a counsellor from the unit before they'll accept us on the programme and we're not going to present a convincing case if we don't even share the same address.'

'Why are you going back to him? I thought we were agreed we didn't need men.' Eimear looks sulky as she doles out the coffee.

120

'Except as occasional playthings,' interjects Kate.

'We need men for babies,' replies Gloria. She reaches for the milk jug and adds: 'Even an IVF baby.'

'I always was hazy on letters,' admits Kate. 'That stands for infertile, involuntary . . .'

'In vitro fertilisation,' says Gloria.

'Is that the same as test-tube babies?' asks Kate.

'That's right, they're the only sort I can have.'

She brightens visibly as she turns technical. 'Mick's sperm rendezvous with my eggs in a dish in a laboratory, hopefully producing embryos, which get zapped up my insides and then I cross my fingers that they'll convert into babies.'

'Romantic, isn't it.' Kate pulls a face.

'I've had it with romance,' storms Gloria. 'I don't care how antiseptic it is, I don't care how many doctors and nurses prod me around, I don't care if Mick feels like a walking sperm bank, I don't care if we never have sex let alone a candlelit dinner again, if this is what it takes to have a baby then I'll do it.'

She's breathless by now and radiating defiance.

Eimear is ashamed of her ungracious reaction to Gloria's news – it's a selfish combination of 'If I can't have babies then no one else should be allowed to' and annoyance that other couples can work out their differences but not Jack and herself.

Kate is straight down to practicalities. 'I hear it's expensive. Is there a long waiting list? And will they do it for you in Ireland or do you have to slope off to England, the same as if you're having an abortion?'

Gloria has the answers at her fingertips. 'Yes, it's pricey but so's a cruise or a kitchen extension and nobody blinks an eye if people have those. We're advised to budget for three attempts; I'm cashing in an old endowment policy and that ought to cover it. I shouldn't have to wait more than a few months and yes, they will do it in Dublin – we approve of making babies here, after all. We'll never keep our laurel wreath as the European city with the youngest population if we don't replenish stocks.'

'So the money's coming from you – that could cause problems later,' notes Kate. 'Wouldn't it be better if Mick contributed? It might make him feel more a part of it.'

'Listen, he can contribute all he likes,' says Gloria, 'I don't care who pays for the treatment, it's not some power trip with me. What's important is that the money's there and I don't have to wait while we apply for a bank loan or sit on some health board waiting list until my hair turns grey.'

'Mine's grey already,' says Eimear, in a clumsy effort to drag the conversation away from babies – they make her think of Jack.

'Body hair as well?' enquires Kate.

'Do you mind!' Eimear rolls her eyes in pretend-disgust. 'I just have a few grey hairs under my fringe, nothing my hairdresser can't handle.'

'Ah, the tumultuous-tressed Terry from Curl Up and Dye,' breathes Kate. 'Tell me, Mulligan, does Terry ever go to the salon in civvies or is it always the full drag-queen spangles and fishnets?'

'I think I saw him once in jeans,' she ponders, 'but they had puce satin kick-pleats. And he was also wearing a gold sequinned belt and matching stilettos. Does that count as dressing down?'

'I work with someone who remembers him at college when he was Terry Terrible, lead singer in a punk-meets-Goth-meets-missed the boat band,' volunteers Gloria. 'She said he was gorgeous.'

'He's still gorgeous,' Eimear promises.

There's a lull, then Kate wonders aloud what happened to change Mick's mind about IVF.

'He wants me back so we're able to negotiate. I've told him

it's the IVF and me, either he takes both or none of us,' says Gloria.

'Hey, you've learned how to play hardball,' enthuses Kate.

'It's no game,' Gloria is heated. 'I want a baby. It's not like wanting a new coat or a new house, it's a real need and pain like no other – it's a bereavement, a cavern, a stomach-churning ache. People seem to assume this is about some selfish urge to replicate yourself but it's not. I'd adopt a baby tomorrow if I could, except no one wants to give them up for adoption any more. What am I supposed to do? Buy a foreign baby on the black market? This is something I can do right now. This is something I AM doing right now.'

'Way to go, Glo!' Kate pretends to wave a football scarf between outstretched arms. 'I've never seen you so assertive, this biological clock of yours is obviously having a positive effect on you.'

'So, Gloria and Mick and baby make three,' says Eimear, 'another of those lucky trios.'

Gloria nods. 'I always did like odd numbers.'

'So he's definitely agreed to go through with it?'

'Why wouldn't he?' Gloria's adrenaline is pumping. 'He's not the one who'll be shot full of hormones so her ovaries go into overdrive, he's not the one who'll have daily injections up the backside and surgical instruments shoved up the fanny, he's not the one who'll have to walk around with two or three embryos inside, willing them to cling on – all of them or one of them or any combination you like – pleading and bargaining with God that they'll survive. Please, God, let them take root and I'll never ask you for so much as a lost set of keys again. All Mick has to do is jerk off.'

Eimear and Kate are torn between admiration and horror. Kate recovers first.

'Gloria, your language has taken a turn for the worse

since you started reading up on this IVF business,' she says, sham-severely.

'It has, hasn't it,' replies Gloria, decidedly pleased with herself. 'But look, I'm the one who has to go through it, not him.'

'He'll have to go through it with you,' Kate points out.

'A bit of hand-holding,' she shrugs. 'It's hardly in the same category.'

'I think you're being a little hard on him,' Kate disagrees. Gloria tosses her head.

'How do you know so much about IVF?' Eimear asks. 'You can't have gleaned all that exquisite detail about injections in the rump from a brochure.'

'I've visited someone who's been through it three times – a neighbour put me in touch with her.'

'Great. Don't her babies make you miserable though – broody?'

Gloria regards Eimear bleakly. 'She doesn't have any babies. She had three tries and three failures.'

'Poor woman,' murmurs Eimear; dimly she hears something similar from Kate. 'And . . .' she hesitates, on uncertain ground now, 'are you still going ahead with it, even knowing . . .'

'What choice do I have?' Gloria sounds jaded. 'It's maybe no babies one way and definitely no babies the other.'

For a while, they simply sit there. Then Kate stands up and switches on the radio, as John Travolta and Olivia Newton-John insist, 'You're the one that I want.' The three of them adored *Grease*, they went to see the film four times until pocket money supplies dried up. That was back in the summer of '78 – they even took to wearing ankle socks but they didn't catch on in Omagh. Too draughty.

'My granny used to say St Anthony was the man to get things done so long as you paid for his favours,' says Kate.

'I don't need to pay for sperm, Mick will give me his free,' replies Gloria.

'Most men would, they're remarkably spendthrift with their favours,' adds Eimear, thinking of Jack. Far from charitably.

'If you pray to St Anthony and promise him you'll slip the parish priest a hefty wedge, you're guaranteed to be stepping out in stretch-waist trousers in no time,' says Kate.

'Stretch-waist trousers, life couldn't be so cruel,' shudders Gloria.

'You'll wear them and be glad of them,' predicts Kate. 'I've been through pregnancy twice with my sisters, remember.'

'How much do you think I should promise St Anthony, Kate?' she asks.

'How much is your treatment? Offer him a percentage of that, ten per cent or something.'

'It's two grand plus the cost of the drugs but you can claim that back from the health board,' replies Gloria.

'Ten per cent is two hundred pounds,' works out Eimear. 'St Anthony's rates sound high.'

'My granny never discussed his charges but I doubt if she ever offered him more than a half-crown,' says Kate.

'That's twelve and a half pence, and there are no half-pennies any more,' Eimear interprets again. 'Which will buy a third of a pint of milk or a couple of those winegums you love, Glo. Anyone know how much a pint of milk was when we were seven so we can convert the money?'

'Don't be a sap,' they chorus. 'Seven-year-olds don't go round buying pints of milk with their pocket money.'

'Maybe there's a halfway point between half a crown and two hundred pounds,' suggests Gloria.

'Mind you,' interjects Kate, 'my granny probably never asked Anto for anything more than a missing ring. It's hardly in the same league as providing a baby.'

'How about thirty pounds, would that do the trick?' Gloria anxiously scans their faces.

'That sounds about right,' Eimear tells her, although she hasn't a clue.

'Look at it this way,' says Kate, 'you're spending several thousand pounds, the odd thirty here or there won't make much odds.'

'That sounds like you're telling me I should give him more,' replies Gloria. 'Do you think thirty pounds is too stingy?'

'No, thirty's a good round number. Although so's fifty,' says Kate.

'Fine, I'll promise him fifty. You'd make a great fund-raiser, McGlade, the church doesn't know what it's lost in you.'

After they've waved Kate off Eimear admits: 'I may have to consider the St Anthony option myself if I'm ever to persuade Jack to come home. Don't know what I was thinking of kicking him out, it's a damn sight easier to smash something than to patch it up.' She sighs and massages the back of her neck. 'Oh, Glo, I'm going to miss having you around to untidy the place once Mick whisks you off home to your Ranelagh hatchery.'

Gloria takes over the massage operation, the gentle movement of her fingers belying the brusqueness of her tone. 'Get up the yard, Eimear, I drive you to distraction.'

'You keep me company.'

'I can still do that, I'll be around every night giving you progress checks, you'll be sick of the sight of me.'

Eimear turns and takes Gloria's hands in hers.

'Tell me truly, Glo, does Mick honestly think IVF's a good idea or is he going with the flow?'

Gloria's mouth purses over her teeth. 'You know how men are. He's not enamoured of the notion but as soon as there's a baby to show for it he'll think it was his call all along.'

'And if he doesn't?'

'Then I'll be a single mother. But at least I'll be a mother.'

CHAPTER 15

'Make a wish,' orders Gloria.

'I don't know what to wish for,' protests Eimear.

'Don't tell me you have everything you want in the world, Mulligan,' Kate raises an eyebrow.

'Far from it, I can't boil it down to just one.'

'But you're only allowed one wish,' Gloria reminds her.

'That's why I want to get the wording right, maybe edge in two wishes for the price of one.'

'I've already made my wish,' says Kate.

'Are you certain-sure you're allowed to wish here, Gloria?' checks Eimear.

'Where else would you wish but on an angel?' asks Gloria, reasonably enough.

Which is why the friends are standing at the foot of Killiney Hill, on the outskirts of Dublin, stroking one of the wings on the giant angel, and a fine fellow he is. If ever an angel could make your wishes come true it's the Killiney statue – he's a bronze, athletic specimen with a bare chest. Not one of your wimpy asexual marble models in a nightie.

Eimear reads the lettering on the base of the statue. 'Bad news, girls, he's not an angel at all he's Daedalus. We'll all spiral into freefall if we expect him to make our wishes come true.'

'Good news, bad news, who knows,' responds Kate. 'It's true he fell – but he also flew. I'd as soon take my chances on Daedalus as Raphael.'

127

Gloria glances back at the road. 'Bono lives around here somewhere, I bet the angel helped out with a few of his wishes.'

Kate is scornful. 'You don't honestly think he came up to the statue and said, "How about a number one hit, big fella? There'll be something extra on the collection plate for yourself."'

Gloria adopts a hurt expression. She always was one skin thinner than the others but Eimear's noticed that she seems to have shed another since her father's death, you can't tease her about anything. Kate wanders off to tug at some bushes while they make their wishes.

'All done?' she calls back. 'We'd better start climbing if we want to see the view before it mists over.'

They trail after her, Gloria carrying the rug, Eimear with the nibbles and Kate setting a cracking pace with the wine in her backpack.

'What did you wish for?' Gloria asks.

'You know I can't tell you, it won't come true if I do,' Eimear points out.

Gloria looks crushed.

'Let's try guessing what Kate wished for,' she suggests to distract her. 'I bet she wants Pearse back, that's why she's in such a foul mood. She's sorry she let him slip through her fingers.'

Gloria gives Eimear a sidelong look. 'I doubt that she does want Pearse back, I think it's a dodo between them.'

'What makes you so sure?'

She hesitates, then laughs and fakes a croaky voice. 'I'm the old crone of the woods, I know all, I see all.'

'But do you tell all?' jokes Eimear.

Gloria returns to her normal voice. 'My lips are sealed. What did you wish for? I hope you remembered my mother's advice: "Be careful what you wish for, it might come true."'

Kate overhears and stumbles, unnerved.

128

Eimear doesn't notice, she's concentrating on her wish: a jumble of winning Jack back and pretending the split never happened and promising not to pay attention to his roving eye if he returns and willing him to lose his flirtatious ways – but then he wouldn't be Jack, would he, and heavens above, if the angel can make sense of that morass then he must be a supernatural being.

As for Gloria . . . you don't need to be a genius to work out what a person is hankering after when they embark on fertility treatment. They're wishing on the magical doctors, on the enchanted medicine, on the spin of the dice – it's all down to luck.

At the summit, hearts pumping after the climb, the girls shade their eyes and gaze out at Howth, Ireland's continental drift, deceptively close across a narrow stretch of water. It's a Viking name and doesn't it just sound like one.

'It's Viking for port,' says Eimear.

'What is?' asks Kate.

'Howth.'

Kate giggles. 'You can just imagine the longships rowing into the headland and all these strapping lads in horned helmets leaping out with their long blond plaits flying. "You have rape, Olaf, I'm on pillage patrol and Erik's taking care of plunder." And Olaf going, "Oh no, not rape again, I'm barely recovered from the last session. Can't I do plunder for a change?"'

Eimear joins in the fun. 'All the villagers start fleeing and the maidens are saying to each other, "The bad news is, the Vikings are coming." "What's the good news?" "The Vikings are coming."'

'Good news, bad news, who knows?' calls Gloria, semi-prone on the ground, where she's arranging the rug. 'Chuck us the corkscrew, Kate.'

Wine on a sunny day is a truth drug, Eimear reflects. You start off thinking, 'I must go easy here,' but after the first glass you couldn't care less. Besides, they're supposed to be bonding, the three wise men as a threesome having fun for a change. Like before.

'Should you be drinking in your condition?' asks Kate, refilling Gloria's glass.

'What condition would that be: hopeful? Self-deluded? Drugged up to the eyeballs? Anyway I'm having half-half –' she waves the Ballygowan bottle – 'so I'm only going to end up half as tipsy as you two.'

'But you're twice as susceptible to the demon drink,' Kate points out, 'so that makes us even-stevens. And you don't know what effect your sniffer plus booze might have on your system.'

'Give her a break, Kate,' intervenes Eimear. 'None of us are driving, we're getting the Dart back into town, and I don't see what harm a couple of glasses can do the girl. She's only just started her sniffer, it's hardly had time to work its way into the pores yet. Here, Glo, dote, have something to soak up the drink.'

'Gobbles!' Gloria shrieks, with more enthusiasm than a few olives deserve, commandeering the plastic pot and rolling over with her face towards the sun. If she had a tail it would be wagging.

'You do have your sniffer with you, don't you, Glo?' adds Eimear and Gloria nods sleepily.

She has to carry the sniffer about with her, it's to be taken every six hours day and night to suppress her hormones. Then they can inject her with a new set of hormones conducive to kicking her ovaries into overdrive. That way she'll produce ten eggs in the month instead of just one and there'll be ten chances of an egg being fertilised instead of a solitary one.

'I'm becoming quite an expert on this IVF lark,' remarks Eimear.

'There don't seem to be many larks about it,' responds Kate.

They lean back against a rock, eyes closed. After a while, Eimear opens hers, sips and casts a speculative glance at her companion.

'So, Kate, how's life treating you?'

'Can't complain.'

'You know how to take it on the chin. Lost your devoted acolyte, Pearse, and you never once whine – it's simply business as usual.'

'Pearse and I were a temporary arrangement.'

'If four years is your idea of a temporary arrangement you have extraordinarily high expectations for permanence.' Eimear splutters into her wine as a laugh catches in the hollow of her throat.

Kate joins in and a companionable glow spreads between them. Gloria has nodded off – they're not surprised, she sets her alarm clock for 4 a.m. every night to spray hormone suppressants up her nostrils.

'After a relationship turns sour, there's such an overwhelming sense of relief when you're finally free that it carries you through the times you might be feeling regretful or lonely,' volunteers Kate.

'That's only if you want the relationship to be over, Kate. If someone else makes a unilateral decision and ends it for you then you're not exactly bathed in blessed relief.'

'Sorry, Mulligan, that was self-obsessed of me,' she whispers. 'How are you holding up? I know I haven't exactly been a tower of strength for you to lean on but that doesn't mean I haven't been thinking of you. And Gloria keeps me posted on your state of, um . . . on your state.'

'You were going to say state of mind, weren't you,' Eimear tells her. 'My state of mind's in a state of chassis. But it's nothing a good wallop of alcohol can't straighten out.' She leans across and opens another bottle.

'Alcohol never solved anything,' says Kate and Eimear looks up in surprise, it's not like her to moralise. 'But it

131

makes you forget what it was you wanted solving in the first place.' Kate holds out her own glass with a wry smile.

'I think we've lost Gloria.' Kate nods across at their dozing friend balancing the olives on her stomach.

'It's the dawn chorus alarm calls, she finds it tough getting back to sleep.'

'I know, I hope it's worth it.'

'She and Mick think so, I don't know who else can judge,' says Eimear.

'I'm not sure Mick does but that's between the two of them, we can only wish them well,' says Kate.

'Aren't you turning mellow in your old age.'

'It's the wine, it takes the whine out of life,' she puns, and they hold their hands across the top of their glasses to contain the plonk while they giggle.

'Kate.'

'Mmmm.'

'I have a theory about you.'

'Jaysus, a teory, dat's dangerous territory,' she says in her desperate version of a Dublin accent. 'All right, Mulligan, hit me with it.'

Only Kate calls her Mulligan, it strips years off her when she hears the name, it reminds her of her old life. She doesn't even think of herself as Eimear Mulligan any more, she sloughed it off so easily to become Eimear O'Brien, married to Jack O'Brien, the catch of their generation who slipped through her fingers.

'You've a new man,' Eimear tells Kate.

Kate spills her drink down her linen tunic.

'Or you fancy someone and you're hoping he'll step forward as a replacement for Pearse,' Eimear amplifies her hypothesis. 'That's why you aren't bothered at being borderline thirty-three and single. It's easy to be manful about being manless when there's a dreamboat hoving into view on the horizon.'

132

Eimear empties her glass triumphantly and retrieves the olives from Gloria's front.

'Fancy an oliver?' she proffers the container but Kate doesn't notice, she's frowning with concentration.

She jolts forward, directs a brilliant smile at Eimear and says, 'I could never fancy an oliver, I'd keep remembering Saint Oliver Plunkett and his shrunken head in Drogheda. He'd be moving in for the clinch and I'd be thinking about doll-sized desiccated heads and blessed martyrs and' – she spits the name out – 'Oliver Cromwell, which naturally would make me remember warts and decapitations. None of which,' she rounds off, 'are conducive to snogging.'

Their snorts wake Gloria, who drowsily asks whose character they've just lambasted, and then anxiously wonders if she's been snoring.

'Like a trooper,' Kate tells her.

'No, you swear like a trooper,' objects Eimear.

'Feck off, I don't,' she says, and they dissolve again.

It's only as they're packing up to leave – there's no more woeful sight than empty wine bottles – that Eimear remembers Kate side-stepped her theorising about a new man.

'So do you have your eye on someone?' she asks as they take a last look at Howth with its des res dots strung along the coastline. No Viking marauders, thinks Eimear, but what can you expect, sunshine *and* a floor show?

'What makes you imagine that?' responds Kate, bending to tie her laces.

'Why do Irish people always answer a question with another question?' tuts Eimear.

'You mean like you've just done,' says Gloria, coming up behind them.

'It's a fair cop,' shrugs Eimear. 'It makes sense to assume you've another man in mind – if not in body, Kate. You look exactly the same post-Pearse as you did during-Pearse and women between men always use it as an opportunity to cut their hair or dye it or buy a trendy new wardrobe.'

'Excellent work, Holmes.' Kate breaks into applause. 'But how do you account for Gloria's identical appearance despite her hiatus from Mick?'

'That's because it was only a blip, she never made the break and never had any intention of doing so,' replies Eimear.

'Feel free to talk about me as if I'm not here,' offers Gloria.

'Whereas your split from Pearse, my dear Kate, appears to be final and irrevocable,' continues Eimear.

'So I'm supposed to race out for a blonde rinse to support your theory?' challenges Kate, draping her arm across Gloria's shoulders.

'No, I can't imagine you as anything other than a redhead.' Eimear steps back and studies her friends, posed against the clifftop like a postcard from the edge.

'I think Kate would suit a fringe,' Gloria speculates. 'I read an interview with Jilly Cooper in which she said fringes were great yokes for covering up wrinkly foreheads and distracting attention from crow's feet around the eyes.'

'Thanks for the vote of confidence, pal.' Kate pushes her playfully.

'You look grand as you are,' Eimear tells her, for there is a radiance about her – maybe it's the halo of sun bouncing off her hair.

Kate's flustered, she never could take compliments. 'You said that as though you meant it, Mulligan,' she responds.

'It's my new ploy, post-cynical cynicism. I make outrageous statements in a sincere voice and nobody knows when I'm taking the Michael. Clever or what?'

'Fiendish,' Kate congratulates her. 'Last one down the hill's a sissy.'

'We're girls, we're allowed to be sissies,' protests Gloria bringing up the rear.

'Sister Xavier didn't lavish all that attention on us to turn out a race of sissies,' Kate calls over her shoulder. 'How's my London derriere holding up, Eimear, would it still inspire songs?'

She's inordinately proud of her bottom, she had a little op when she lived in England to tighten the cheeks and needs constant reassurance that it was money well spent.

'Loo-kin' good, Billy Ray,' says Eimear in her hillbilly voice, reaching out to pat her neat rear. 'I sho' do gotta get mahself one of those new-fangled jobs sho' nuff.'

'Ah, leave it out, weren't you born with a London derriere,' she responds. 'You didn't have to trek over the water for one.'

The laughter is punctured by a roar from Gloria. 'Oh no, nobody reminded me to take my sniffer and I'm half an hour late. Oh God oh God oh God, I have to get to the bottom of the hill before I can inhale. Let me past you, Eimear.'

'Calm down, Gloria, five more minutes won't make any difference,' says Kate but Gloria continues to panic.

'I'm going to buy another alarm clock and carry it with me, it's the only way,' she moans.

'Gloria, I'm sure the sniffer times are only guidelines, I can't see how a little local variation will banjax your treatment,' says Eimear, catching up with her.

'I know, I know,' she keens, 'but what if it does matter? What if I'm risking the whole process by my carelessness? I have to do everything I can, just as the doctors and nurses have to do everything they can, that way we minimise the chances of anything going wrong – don't you understand?'

'I do, dote, I do,' Eimear tries to reassure her as the angel comes into view. 'Now, Gloria, sit down by your metal man there and catch your breath, you won't inhale properly if you're panting.'

She throws herself on to the ground and Eimear holds her hand while Kate crouches alongside her.

'In out, in out, in out, gently now,' advises Kate. 'No, not yet, put the inhaler down, you're still gasping. In out, in out, in out. Good woman, now the other nostril. Don't stand up yet, give it a minute to sink it. Are you allowed another wish on Daedalus on the way down, Eimear?'

'Doubt it, that sounds greedy,' Eimear demurs. 'Isn't greed one of the seven deadly sins?'

'That's Catholicism,' Kate objects. 'What has wishing on big bronze angels at the bottom of Killiney Hill to do with Catholicism? It's pagan and that shower knew all about excess – sure they invented it.'

'When you put it like that . . .' shrugs Eimear. 'Still, I'll give it a miss. Ready for the off now, Glo?'

They help her struggle to her feet.

'Home again, home again, jiggidy jog,' Gloria murmurs.

'Nursery rhymes. Is this second childhood regression already?' Kate speculates, as they set off along the road to the station.

'Maybe. Sure, isn't adulthood overrated?' says Gloria, walking only slightly unsteadily.

They adopt positions either side of her just in case.

'Ah, come on now, no maudlin sentimentality,' objects Kate. 'We couldn't wait to be grown up and leave home. We couldn't wait to bang the school gate. We couldn't wait to shake the dust of Omagh off our feet.'

'Omagh means virgin plain,' observes Eimear.

'Mick says that's because it was full of plain virgins,' from Gloria.

'Right, and they were all in his class at the Christian Brothers school,' agrees Kate.

They're still giggling as the Dart station comes into view.

CHAPTER 16

'I wonder why we bother with men at all. They have blue cheese breath and emery board skin,' Eimear starts the ball rolling.

'They roll their socks up inside their underpants and never throw away T-shirts,' suggests Gloria.

'They leave mouldy sandwich crusts under the bed,' Eimear puts in.

'They fill the kitchen bin with takeaway curry containers and draw the curtains on sunny Saturdays so they can watch sports on television,' comes from Gloria.

'They pinch your nail scissors to tame the jungle spouting from their noses,' Kate shares in the fun.

'They sit on the lavatory for hours reading newspapers when you need the sink to wash off your face mask,' says Eimear.

They wait for Kate to lob in another contribution but the nail scissors complaint seems to have exhausted her stock of grievances.

'The trouble with men is . . . they're not women,' concludes Eimear, waving her ice-cream spoon authoritatively. She's trying to eat more and smoke less, starting with ice-cream as an essential food source.

So far the experiment has been successful. Ice-cream plus airing grudges seem as Utopian a way of spending an evening as any invented. No woman in her right mind could fail to count herself lucky for breaking free of one of those oafs, they agree – or at least Gloria and Eimear are in accord, Kate seems unconvinced.

'Men and women were never intended to cohabit; to spend time together occasionally, fine, to chain themselves to each other for a lifetime, not so fine,' Eimear announces over the dripping tubs.

They're revolting and being revolting, eating straight from containers. Gloria nods, although Eimear can't think why since she's gone back to Mick – maybe she's being supportive. Or perhaps living with Mick again has shuffled her deck of cards into something approaching reality. Then again, she could simply be engrossed in her pecan fudge flavour.

A wave of misery sweeps over Eimear, one which even brown bread ice-cream (tastier than it sounds) can't avert. If life without Jack is such bliss, how come she feels as if she's doing penance? Don't tell her this is one of those sins of omission the nuns used to warn them about.

'Jack's found someone else,' wails Eimear. 'He told me so on the phone when I offered to have him back. Can you believe it, I rang my fornicating husband volunteering to forgive him, convinced he'd have had enough of the single life by now, and he tells me it's only a matter of time before he moves in with his new girlfriend.'

Kate drops her coconut ice-cream and Gloria throws her a reproachful glance.

'You're well rid of him, Eimear,' says Gloria. 'Remember what a nuisance men are – monopolising the TV remote control and breathing curry fumes all over you, we've just been discussing how much better life is without them.'

'No, I need a man,' groans Eimear. 'The bed's too big, the living room's too tidy, the bathroom's too clean, the house's too quiet.'

'You don't need to take Jack back for company, advertise for a flatmate,' suggests Gloria, who drove her to distraction, at ramming speed, when they shared. She's irritating Eimear now with her girl guide suggestions.

Day after day she had Gloria with her, 'I wonder if Mick remembered to pick up his dry-cleaning – he needn't expect me to remind him,' and Gloria with her, 'There's meat in our freezer needs using up but no way will Mick cook a meal for himself, not while there's a chipper at the bottom of our street.' Eimear was starting to wonder why she left the man at all. She longed to tell her to cut along home to him, she might as well do it sooner as later, but Gloria would have taken it the wrong way – probably because there wasn't a right way to take it.

'God, I'm such a bitch,' she cries aloud, and the others exchange puzzled glances.

Eimear hates herself for her mental diatribe against sweet little Glo, who listens for hours on end when she feels ready to implode with rage and jealousy. Who else can she talk to, Kate's never around and there are some things a girl can't tell her mother. Eimear attempts to visualise the scene at home as she pours her heart out about Jack's double whammy, the affair and the split.

'You remember that fellow who was waiting at the top of the aisle when I swanned up in a gown that cost nearly a month's salary? Well, I know he seemed keen on me at the time but it turns out he prefers someone else and he's been giving her one – or 101 – behind my back for months.'

Oh yes, her mother could cope with that. Not. At least Gloria isn't shocked when she talks about how much she misses Jack and how she'd like to punch him and stroke him and punish him and kiss him. Have him back again.

'So what about a flatmate, would that help?' repeats Gloria.

'I've an empty bed, an empty fridge, an empty freezer now that we've liberated the ice-cream, an empty bank account and an empty life. How's a flatmate going to improve my pathetic lot?' Eimear bawls in a frenzy of self-pity.

Gloria and Kate make soothing noises.

'Knowing Jack, he can't believe his luck at finding himself single,' Eimear fumes. 'Oh, his new squeeze may think it's true love, that once-in-a-lifetime lightning bolt from Mount Olympus, but I wouldn't get too comfortable with the poetic professor if I were her. He's keen on falling in love but he isn't strong on staying power, especially if it means he might have to resist temptation. He's all for listening to his heart – except his heart speaks with forked tongue.'

Yet still Eimear wants him to come home. Every so often she's walloped by a wave of nostalgia for the first year of their marriage when they'd spend all Sunday in bed, with one of them making forays to the kitchen for emergency rations. They weren't just making love, although there was no end of that – they were cuddling and dozing and listening to the radio and reading newspapers and talking, talking, talking.

Eimear finds herself remembering their lovemaking in elaborate detail, the slithering mass of limbs and lips without beginning and end. She dwells on it constantly. She fantasises about waking up in bed one night to find him touching her.

Jack be nimble, Jack be quick, Jack jump over my candle-wick bedspread.

'Why won't he give us another chance, we used to be so perfect,' she complains.

'I have to be leaving,' says Kate.

'Don't go, you two are meant to be cheering me up,' protests Eimear.

'Maybe it'd be better if she left,' says an unusually tight-lipped Gloria.

'What are you dashing off for – what can be more important than comforting a friend who's set her heart on wallowing?' sniffs Eimear.

'I have some business to finish, I'll catch up with you again,' Kate is evasive.

'Don't go,' pleads Eimear. 'We can have hot chocolate with melted marshmallows next.'

'Not the hot chocolate with melted marshmallows bait,' groans Kate. 'It's a ploy to make me fat and spotty, admit it, Mulligan. That way I'll never dare show my face outside the door and you'll have as much company as you want.'

'Precisely,' agrees Eimear. 'Now sit down while I check the fridge for double cream.'

Kate pulls her coat on regardless and heads for the door. Her mobile phone shrills in the hall and as she answers it she looks straight at Eimear and blushes. That's one of the problems of red hair, she's always complaining to Gloria and Eimear, you never cure yourself of this tendency to colour up.

'It's her new man,' Eimear whispers to Gloria. 'Kate always reddens where fellows are concerned.'

'Has she admitted to a new boyfriend?' asks Gloria.

'No, but she hasn't denied it either which is proof enough.'

'I'm on my way,' mutters Kate and unlatches the front door with a cheery, 'Be seeing you, lads.'

'Not so fast, you brazen hussy,' remonstrates Eimear. 'You're like the favourite on the home straight at Leopardstown. Who was your mystery caller and where are you meeting him? Spare us no details, as your oldest friends we're entitled to know everything.'

'There's nothing to know, it's just someone from work I'm liaising with on a special report for the partners. We have to run through some statistics.'

Eimear is relentless. 'Kate, if you're intent on lying, have the decency to make it convincing. It's 8 p.m. on a Saturday night, there is no one in Ireland, no one on the face of the earth, no one in this solar system, checking statistics with a colleague from work right now. So who is he?'

'It's approaching deadline, we have to hand the report in by the middle of next week,' mumbles Kate. 'Besides, what makes you think it's a "he" I'm meeting? As a matter of fact, it's a woman solicitor, Isabel Eccles. She has an office on the floor above me. You've often heard me talk about her, we meet for coffee sometimes.'

'Why won't you tell us about this new man,' persists Eimear. 'You needn't feel embarrassed that we'll think it's too soon after Pearse or that I'll be upset because of Jack. I'm glad for you, we both are – aren't we, Glo.'

Gloria is silent, Kate shuffles awkwardly.

'I think it's magnificent that one of us is out there dazzling the male population and making some man beg for his date on a Saturday night,' Eimear presses on. 'Gloria and I aren't exactly stalwarts of the sisterhood at the moment, with me on my knees to Jack to come home and Gloria trailing off without a word of complaint for check-ups on her own because Mick doesn't like hospitals.'

'Mick's not the worst,' Gloria defends him.

Kate drops her bag with a resigned air and reclaims her former seat.

'You win, Mulligan, I am seeing someone else,' she agrees, lifting her ice-cream spoon.

'Aha! I thought as much. Shoot, I'm all ears.'

'This I have to hear,' mutters Gloria.

'It's a problematic situation,' explains Kate. 'I'm wild about him and he's wild about me but he's married to someone else.'

'And she doesn't know?' prompts Eimear.

'That's right, she imagines the marriage is simply going through one of those ups and downs that married people say is normal. The rough with the smooth, the good with the bad, drivel like that. She has no idea about me.'

'Some women are dense,' breathes Eimear. 'If it were me I'd know. Even if there was no evidence, I'd know.'

'So you can see why there's not much point in unveiling Mr Right, producing him like a white rabbit from a magician's hat, when it might all go pear-shaped at any moment.'

'I thought you said you're wild about him and he's wild about you,' objects Eimear.

'An untamed pair and no mistake,' hisses Gloria. Kate ignores her.

'It's . . . complicated,' she says. 'I don't know what's going to happen with us, so it's better to stay low key until I see where we stand.'

'Shouldn't that be lie?' asks Gloria.

Eimear looks at her in astonishment, she's never seen Gloria snipe like this.

'I'm not lying,' insists Kate.

'But you do a lot of lying around with your man, what's his name, don't you? What did you say his name was?' Gloria's face is the picture of innocence.

'I didn't,' answers Kate evenly. 'Least said, soonest mended.'

'Broken hearts aren't so easily mended, neither are broken faith or broken trust.' Gloria is like a demon, her hormones must be playing her up, thinks Eimear. 'I'm sorry for his wife; what about you, Eimear?'

Eimear feels she has to take Kate's part, Gloria is giving her such a rough ride.

'Maybe she deserves everything she gets. Is she a battle-axe, Kate, does your man slink about in mortal terror of her?'

Kate looks edgy as she responds: 'She's beautiful but she's a handful. I think they've simply come to the end of their road. Some roads take fifty years to travel and some only last three or four years. Theirs is finished.'

Gloria snorts. 'Sounds to me like yours is an unapproved road.'

Her outburst hangs in the air unanswered. Eimear glances from one friend to the other, surprised by Gloria's antagonism and by Kate's acceptance of it. Normally she gives as good as she gets but she seems willing to allow Gloria unlimited leeway tonight, she must realise the hormone treatment is having a poisonous effect on her.

'What about the wife?' continues Gloria. 'Is she aware that they've come to the end of their road or is she still wearing hiking boots and striding uphill in the hopes he'll catch her at the next bend?'

'What is it with you two and your laboured analogies,' Eimear tuts. 'This conversation is taking an extremely peculiar turn. Enough already. Kate, head off and enjoy your date – you can tell us all about him when you're ready but I'm sure he's wonderful. And you, young lady,' she turns to Gloria, 'are in dire need of hot chocolate with melted marshmallows on top.'

'Have you and Kate had a tiff?' Eimear asks later, over steaming mugs.

'No, she just jars my nerves sometimes, she's so selfish,' shrugs Gloria.

'Which is more than can be said for you, dote,' Eimear squeezes her shoulder. 'You're loyal to a fault.'

She realises Gloria's anti-Kate bluster has been directed at shielding her from the harsh reality of other people having happy relationships.

'Let's crack open some more marshmallows and I'll tell you again how my life's ruined,' jokes Eimear, as they slurp. 'I'll have to ask Kate for some pointers on getting over one man and getting under another.'

CHAPTER 17

Eimear stands at the front door and looks at Kate as though seeing her for the first time. A sixth sense tells Kate this is no social call and she braces herself. She watches her friend warily, noting the uncombed hair and the rumpled shirt – a sure sign of distress, Eimear even presses her tea towels. Eimear hovers, fingering her car keys like worry beads, then she speaks.

'Is it true?'

The words are monotone. Kate doesn't need to ask what she's talking about; her stomach embarks on a rollercoaster ride around her body and various possibilities flit through her mind. She contemplates lying, trying to explain, closing the door without answering and hiding behind the sofa.

But she abandons each alternative. Instead she looks directly into Eimear's achingly bright blue eyes, the colour of someone swimming in chlorinated water, and nods because she can't trust her voice to work.

Kate waits for Eimear's reaction. Pallid to begin with, Eimear blanches visibly at this affirmation. She's longing for a denial, even one so risible that only a fool could believe it, but Kate is facing her and brazenly admitting to an affair with her husband. She isn't so much as blushing. Kate's the reason Jack doesn't love her any more and the knowledge is beyond endurance.

Emotion so compelling surges through Eimear that she

totters; she gropes with her hand towards the door post to balance herself. Instinctively Kate reaches out a steadying hand and Eimear recoils. Eimear realises that she can't manage this scene after all – she thought she could confront her Judas friend but she can't even bear to breathe the same air as her.

Wordlessly she flees to the lift, determined not to break down in front of Kate, who's had everything else but she won't take her pride. Eimear jabs at the buttons, pressing all of them, suffused with fury at the mechanical object that's supposed to carry her away from this humiliation.

Kate dithers over whether or not to chase after her – to offer some kind of excuse. But she recognises that her need to justify herself is illogical; Eimear's entitled to feel resentment. She's loath to fuel Eimear's sense of grievance with a public spectacle. Perhaps silence for now might be the best option.

Common sense always operates better in theory, however, and Kate is immeasurably moved by the incomprehension on Eimear's face. Perhaps if she could make her understand . . . She steps hesitantly towards the quivering woman stabbing at lift buttons.

'Eimear,' Kate begins, as it arrives, 'come inside the flat and talk with me, don't leave like this. We've been friends too long to throw it away, let's try and salvage something. I love you, Mulligan.'

Eimear looks back at Kate, reproach welling from her eyes. She's touched by the nickname, by the affectionate tone, she glances towards the apartment's open door and is drawn to it – perhaps Kate has an explanation after all. One she can bring herself to believe.

'Jack and I,' begins Kate and the words sting Eimear. It should be Jack and HER, not Jack and Kate. The lift mechanism whirrs as the door closes and Eimear springs through the narrowing gap.

'Hijacker!' She spews the jibe at Kate.

As though, thinks Kate later, she'd boarded Jack illegally and taken over the controls, reprogrammed him to fornicate with her and lie to his wife.

The lift door slides across Eimear's face, still resolutely tearless. 'At least I didn't cry in front of Kate,' she tells herself as she weeps with all-consuming self-pity on a bench in St Stephen's Green, just out of sight of Kate's living-room window.

Back in her apartment, Kate is shaking. She pours herself a tot of neat vodka and gulps it down, then sinks on to the floor, curling in a foetal position alongside the coffee table. Kate can't believe she and Eimear have finally come face to face over Jack. That it's over and Eimear's gone. Out of her life after twenty-six years.

She rings Jack at college but he's in a lecture, she leaves a message saying he's needed at home urgently but it's hours before he arrives back. Aeons alone in which Kate drinks more Finlandia and rewinds the terse encounter with Eimear.

She thinks about calling Gloria but decides that would be selfish – Eimear is probably pouring out her heart to Gloria, she can wait for Jack. Where is he anyway, why hasn't he responded to her SOS?

'Jack will make it better,' she promises herself, rocking backwards and forwards against the marble-topped coffee table.

Jack is less reassuring than she expects, however. He pounds through the door, frantic to know the nature of the emergency, and is dismissive when Kate tells him.

'I thought something like this might happen,' he admits. 'It had to come sooner or later – at least it's behind you now.'

'How did she find out?' asks Kate.

It's only been nine days since he moved in with her – what was it about threes in this friendship. Ex-friendship. She was hoping for a longer period of grace – or should that be disgrace?

Jack looks shifty. He turns away and starts fussing with his briefcase, then he glances cautiously at Kate and admits: 'I told her.'

Kate is speechless. She reaches for the vodka bottle and finds it empty – such a time to run out. By dint of Herculean effort, she speaks slowly and calmly.

'Jack, I've just had a searing visit from Eimear, it was an encounter you could have prepared me for but didn't. I think I deserve a reason. What in the name of God made you tell her and why didn't you discuss it with me first?'

Jack shrugs. 'She took a Stanley knife to my Patrick Kavanagh first edition.'

'So you decided to land me in it?'

'It wasn't so much a decision as a knee-jerk reaction. I called around to the Donnybrook house to collect some belongings to keep here – I want to feel your flat is my home – and I discovered the book in shreds. I told her then, I didn't think of the consequences.'

He exudes penitence and Kate lays his head on her lap, stroking the thick black hair. She's the one in need of comfort but she struggles against this reaction and concentrates on Jack, soothing away his feelings of guilt. Willing herself to love him enough not to mind about Eimear.

Jack bends her neck towards him so he can reach her lips and she's compliant, waiting for the amnesia of passion to exert its blinkered hold on her. They move to the bedroom but their coupling is perfunctory; the adrenaline fails to function as an opiate this time. He sleeps in her arms and Kate lies awake with a cramp in the elbow cradling his head. Be careful what you wish for . . .

CHAPTER 18

She's young, not much more than a child. Flushed from drinking champagne – probably her first taste of it – and euphoric in the spotlight of his undiluted attention. Lissom body, from the glimpse Kate catches, there's no substitute for youth.

'Oh my God, it's your wife!' gasps the infant lover.

Kate feels as outraged as a wife. Why should they have the monopoly on betrayal?

'Of course it's not, silly – put your clothes on,' replies the chivalrous Jack.

He follows Kate out to the living room, zipping up his flies.

'Couldn't you at least have taken her to a hotel?' she asks. Deceptively mildly, judging from his reply.

'Baby girl, it wasn't premeditated, it just happened. It has nothing to do with what's between you and me,' he protests, attempting to wrap his arms round her.

Kate backs off, for his touch smarts as much as his casual dismissal of philandering.

'If it wasn't premeditated, how come you brought her to my flat?' she challenges him. 'Don't tell me she just wandered in off the street, started peeling off her clothes and you thought, "Mustn't look a gift mare in the mouth."'

'Bitter words from such a sweet mouth,' coos Jack, advancing, arms extended like the Christ statue in Rio de Janeiro.

'I deserve them but' – and here comes the part Kate finds truly unforgivable – 'I can explain everything, it's not what it seems.'

'I knew I shouldn't have agreed to you moving in with me,' she spits, fending him off. 'I turned into Eimear for you when that happened, didn't I? As soon as your clothes were in the wardrobe and the laundry basket and on the ironing pile you reverted to type.'

Bitterness threatens to engulf her. 'More fool me, I should have realised the leopard never changes his spots, he simply changes his prey.'

Jack adopts the little-boy-lost expression she's always found irresistible and says with his sweetest smile, 'You're the only one that matters, baby girl.'

'So this isn't the first time, is it?' She wills him to deny it.

He shrugs, palms outward, a repentant smile contorting his features into something quintessentially repugnant.

'You've only been living here with me a few months. Wasn't I enough for you? Am I too old, too tired, too boring?' she's pleading with him now as her voice sinks lower than her plummeting heart.

'It's nothing, you're taking this out of proportion,' he insists, still managing to look bewildered. 'She dropped by for some advice on an essay and we were a little carried away, it must've been the champagne.'

'Why did you need pink champagne to read an essay in the first place, Jack O'Brien? I've heard of rose-coloured spectacles but this is ridiculous.'

He rubs his chin and changes tack. 'This would never have happened if you took a leave of absence like we discussed.' His voice has a petulant note. 'You know I need attention when I'm writing.'

'Also when you're reading, eating, walking, driving, watching television, taking a bath and whistling down the wind,' Kate shrieks, her voice hoarse – she thinks it's an overwhelming anger but it might be something else. Hurt cloaked in fury, say, or grief masquerading as outrage. Time enough to lick her wounds, for now she has to dance to the cliché tune.

'How could you do this to me?'

Jack's boyish mask slips. 'Get off your high horse, Kate – you did it to Eimear.'

Appalled, she stares at the semi-clad stranger propped nonchalantly against her bookcase.

'We never romped in her home – in her bed,' she objects.

'Oh, so there are shades of right and wrong, are there?' he says pleasantly. 'You cheated on your friend but you stuck to certain rules invented by yourself and that made it all right.'

'It was love with us, not sex.' Kate shakes her head in disbelief.

'Love,' he elongates the word, perverting it. 'Lurve.' Again he protracts it. 'Love washes everything white, it's our emotional Persil. We can behave any way we like so long as it's in the name of love. Love conquers all – right, baby girl?'

'Don't you dare call me that,' she shouts, incensed beyond measure at his inappropriate use of their special term of endearment.

Jack laughs and her rage ferments; a blonde head appears around the bedroom door.

'I'll be off now, thanks for everything,' mumbles the girl, edging towards the hall.

'It was his pleasure,' Kate says nastily – a cheap shot, but what the heck.

'I'll see you at tutorial, baby girl,' smiles Jack, with a sideways glance at Kate as he murmurs the last two words.

Kate is icily calm now despite the physical pain palpating within her. People talk about hearts breaking but what actually happens is they explode and the splinters jab at you lacerating kidneys, spleen, stomach lining. She's just another of his baby girls and she has a foreign object inside her chest which is swelling and rupturing and is about to rip through the skin. The scene from *Alien* in which a monster bursts out of John Hurt's belly pops into her mind and she can't help herself, she laughs aloud.

Jack is relieved and joins in.

'Good girl, I knew you'd see sense. We're great together, don't let this misunderstanding spoil what we have.' He moves towards her again, smelling of semen and another woman's perfume.

Kate lifts her coat and bag. 'I'm off to see a film. I want every trace of you removed by the time I get back.'

Still he looms in front of her, teeth glinting, convinced his overwhelming charm can hypnotise any woman.

'If you touch me I'll hit you,' she warns.

He reaches for her anyway.

'I mean it, Jack.'

He tries to kiss her.

She slaps him across the face; almost immediately a crimson mark flares on his cheekbone and she gazes at it, aghast. So intent on staring is she that she doesn't see what's coming. Like for like.

Jack cuffs Kate back, part of the blow catching her on the ear and leaving a ringing noise. She stumbles, more from shock than the force of his slap.

Somehow she makes it to the front door, down the stairs and on to the street. By her Spitfire car, her legs buckle and she leans against it. A spasm grips her and she vomits over the windscreen. Dully she watches the baby food puree of semi-digested Spanish omelette and chips oozing across a windscreen wiper.

It started with a kiss and ended with a slap.

'I deserve that blow,' she whispers. 'It's my punishment for duplicity with Eimear, for abandoning Pearse, for falling for a con man like Jack. The only lessons you remember in life are the harsh ones.'

She welcomes that slap. Gingerly, Kate touches her face. It's burning but it doesn't hurt.

She crouches down and examines her face in a wing mirror. By the orange glow of the street light, she detects a fiery weal which seems to cover her entire cheek. She's puzzled by its size, where did such an enormous blemish spring from?

Kate opens the door of her much-loved green car, dubbed the Hurtle Turtle within hours of purchase, climbs in and lies awkwardly across both seats, twisted around the gear-stick. She lets her hair float on to the injured cheek, enjoying the silky sensation of the strands.

'Thank you, Jack, you've made it simple for me – now there'll be no regrets,' she whispers. It's severance made easy.

The chill awakens Kate. She tries to sit up but is too stiff to move. As she lies, disorientated, she hears birdsong and then the distant roar of traffic. It's brighter than she's accustomed to – did she forget to draw the curtains? Was it one of those deliciously self-indulgent nights when she collapsed into bed without removing her make-up and the top layer of clothes? Slowly the truth percolates through her sluggish haze – she fell asleep in the car. Her watch indicates 5.10 a.m. Kate hobbles out and drags herself up the stairs to her flat. At the front door she hesitates – he might still be there. All she wants is a shower and clean clothes, she can't handle a scene.

The flat is mercifully empty so she retreats to the bathroom and turns on the shower.

The water stings as she lifts her face to the jet, Kate cries out and jerks backwards. Rubbing at the steamed-up bathroom mirror with a towel, she sees a scaled down map of France welling below one eye, purple and green and blue. Inside the ear there's caked-in blood. This will need medical attention. Good, her pain will help atone for Eimear's.

In the bedroom she mechanically peels the sheet from the bed and lifts the champagne bottle. It's empty – Jack must have had a glass or two while he packed. She wonders which is the girl's glass, there are no lipstick stains on either. Kissed off before they reached the fizz, she thinks tartly. Or so young she doesn't need make-up. Even more tartly.

Kate sinks on the bed, clutching the bottle. Imagine falling in love with a man so tacky that he'd steal your champagne to seduce another woman and not even chain the door to prevent you walking in from work early and catching them. It's a farce. All she needs now is for the butler to appear, minus his trousers, and intone, 'His lordship's compliments, ma'am, cocktails will be served on the terrace at seven.'

Then she spots the pants half-hidden down the side of the mattress. She lifts them gingerly by the label, reluctant to make contact with cloth: they're a pair a child might wear, white with a pattern of tiny pink flowers. No wonder the girl spent so long in the bedroom dressing, she was probably on her hands and knees searching for these.

She considers posting them to the literary editor of a national newspaper with a note: 'The latest poetic offering from the prolific Jack O'Brien' or framing them and sending them to his office with a caption reading: 'Another trophy bagged by Black Jack.'

The reverie entertains Kate as she walks to the kitchen bin and drop the pants into it. She turns away, wheels back and peers into the bin. Still there. She lifts the teapot, always to be depended on for a few mouldering teabags and stewed tea, and empties the remains over the pants. Now they're not so white, now they're not so juvenile-looking. She spies a wheaten loaf sticking out of the bread-bin, crumbles a few slices on top of the gunge and steps back to admire her handiwork.

Consoled, Kate finds she has an appetite for coffee. She plugs in the kettle and makes a mug of instant, drinking it through one side of her mouth – even then it smarts – while she phones the doctor for an appointment. It's still so early that she's clicked on to the answerphone; she decides to turn up at the surgery and wait.

Next she rings Gloria, just awake and bleary, suggesting they meet for lunch. Gloria vacillates, grumpy from the early call and her disapproval of Kate's affair.

'I've some news to share, news about Jack and me,' Kate entices her.

Curiosity overcomes Gloria's instinct towards censure.

Now Kate digs out a pair of sunglasses – isn't that what battered women are supposed to wear, to hide the evidence, to protect the man. The cheek throbs where the frame rests on it.

'You're handling this very well,' Kate encourages her semi-disguised reflection in the hall mirror. She has to keep busy so she doesn't think about Jack. But he trickles into her mind as she flicks a comb through her sleek copper hair, still damp from the shower.

'I had the wrong kind of Jack-attack,' she tells her reflection.

The doctor, a woman who's treated her for five years, takes in the bruise and Kate's brittle demeanour.

'What happened?' she asks.

'Lovers' tiff,' shrugs Kate.

'Do you want to talk about it?'

'Not much.'

'It doesn't have to be with me, I could refer you to someone,' she suggests.

'Maybe.'

'In the meantime I'll make a medical report on this. You'll need it if you want to press charges.'

Kate is taken aback. Press charges. Speak to the guards. Complain about her treatment. She deserves this blow, she's owed much worse than the back of a man's hand across her face for the way she behaved towards Eimear.

'I haven't thought that far ahead, I just need to get through today,' Kate tells the doctor.

The older woman adjusts her glasses and looks at her carefully.

'It's your decision. But remember, a man who'll hit once will hit again. Other women could be hurt too.'

Kate nods and accepts her prescription for painkillers ('Don't mix them with alcohol'). She's not like those women you read about who stay with men after they repeatedly rough them up, didn't she give Jack his marching orders as soon as she saw him in his true colours, the monochrome of a cad? Didn't she land one on him before he retaliated?

Gloria isn't convinced. Over lunch, she lectures her friend.

'You can't have this on your conscience, you must get the law on him. What if he hits his next girlfriend and she ends up in hospital? It would be partly your fault for staying silent now – this isn't about revenge, it's about justice.'

'Gloria, I don't have much of a case, I hit him first,' protests Kate.

'A tap on the cheek, he hardly felt it. He's not the one walking around in dark glasses, he's not the one who went to the doctor's. Let's see, Jack's four inches taller than you and three or four stone heavier, that's hardly a fair fight, now, is it?'

'Did Eimear ever mention him hitting her?' asks Kate, sipping her gin and lime through a straw.

Gloria shakes her head. 'Never. But they say women are so mortified that they hide it even from their best friends.'

'Ashamed to be beaten?'

'Yes, and ashamed they'd stay with a man who could raise a hand to them. He has them in his power twice over. That's what it's about, mastery and submission, threat and silence.'

156

'What about you and Mick?' asks Kate.

'Mick? You must be joking, he's a pussycat. He'd cross the road at the first sign of trouble. There's times I want to shake him until he rattles to generate a response but he's never touched me, he hasn't a violent bone in his body.'

'So you think Jack may have hit Eimear but she feels obliged to cover up,' persists Kate.

'Look, Kate, I couldn't say one way or the other. That's something you'll have to ask her yourself.'

'That should be straightforward enough, considering she hangs up if I ring, slams the door in my face if I call, uses my letters as firelighters for all the response I get from them and is generally treating me like a pariah.'

'Which you deserve,' points out Gloria.

'Which I deserve,' concedes Kate.

She looks pleadingly at Gloria.

'Couldn't you speak to her for me, tell her Jack and I have disintegrated, lay it on thick about how truly, madly, deeply sorry I am and maybe you could just drop in the episode about him punching me one when I interrupted his fun and games with his latest playmate.'

'You're shameless, Kate,' Gloria reprimands her.

'Granted, but it might help her to know I got what was coming to me.'

'I can't believe you mean that. No woman deserves to be walloped by a man, not for any reason on earth, understood?'

Gloria's voice is rising with anger and the other diners are watching them covertly. The waiter undulates over to their table. Under normal circumstances the pair of them would be giving him the eye, he's easy enough on it, but they're too distracted to bother.

'Everything all right, leedies?' he asks in his sexy French accent. You can bet he's from Drumcondra.

'Tray bong,' responds Kate, 'especially if you lob another

couple of gins in our direction when you get half a chance, cherry.'

He withdraws with a grimace that could pass for a smile on a stormy night. Surely it's not her French accent that pains him; Kate's gratified at the possibility as she sips noisily through the straw.

'I said, do you understand?' repeats Gloria.

'Certainly I do, there is no justification for a man to raise his hand to a woman but I'm eternally grateful to Jack for doing it to me.'

'Because?' prompts Gloria. 'And this had better be good.'

'It's left me feeling I might be able to look Eimear in the eye again,' she explains. 'It can only be the one eye because my other's closed over.'

'Are you incapable of ever being serious? Do you have to turn everything into a joke?'

'Incapable.' Kate considers the word. 'Not capable, unable, incompetent. Yes, I think I am incompetent, an incompetent in the business of life. As for joking, well, it strikes me that life is no laughing matter, which is why there's an imperative on all of us to chortle at it as often and as loudly as possible. And that, my friend, is the gospel according to Kate McGlade. Make of it what you will.'

'You're hopeless. I'll speak to Eimear for you; God knows if she'll listen but I'll give it a lash,' she sighs. 'I trust you've learned your lesson now – men may come and men may go but friends go on forever. Unless you cheat on them.'

Kate composes her face into a mask of decorum.

'Don't turn all sugar and spice with me,' Gloria warns.

'Ah, Glo, it's not as if I've made it my life's mission to slither around stealing husbands,' protests Kate. 'This was an aberration, a never to be repeated error of titanic proportions. Now throw me a life jacket, for the love of God.'

'For the love of Eimear,' she corrects Kate. 'It's doing her no good at all, this moping around wishing she had Jack back.

Maybe now she'll see him for the slug he is – if you ask me, you've both had a lucky escape. I thought bounders like that went out with plus-fours and monocles.'

Kate empties her glass with a rattle of ice cubes. 'You, Gloria, are a star. I may not be good for much, but I'm superb at picking friends.'

CHAPTER 19

Kate's indulging in an unpleasant bout of self-analysis. It's obscene, here she is in a fertility clinic giving the glad eye to a prospective father, a few weeks after the love of her life cheats on her. Outrageous behaviour, nearly as bad as sharking down a labour ward. There he is, doing the caring husband bit, holding his wife's hand and bending his face towards hers as they sit in the waiting room until it's time for her embryo transfer.

Kate is watching them because he seems so concerned and she seems so dependent on his solicitude. Her name is called, they both stand up but the nurse tells him only his wife is needed yet – she'll collect him later.

'Send positive vibrations,' urges the wife as she's led away.

'Vibes already on their way, my pulse,' he promises.

Kate is eavesdropping, as everyone does from boredom in these places, when he looks her straight in the face. And instead of turning away, he carries on staring. She glances away, then back again – and he's still watching her. Poor woman, Kate feels sorry for her, behind that wall with a surgical instrument holding her insides open, and her husband busy channelling his vibrations towards the wrong womb.

Still, there's something dashed attractive about him, as they say in old-fashioned novels. He has a young face with prematurely grey hair and judging by the long legs stretched in front of him he must be six feet and a couple of spare inches. The clincher for Kate is his flying jacket: call her predictable, but she's always had a passion for pilot types. So instead of doing the decent thing and walking away for some water from the cooler, she stares straight back at him. No flirty lash lowering and raising, just a level gaze.

He smiles and a dimple appears in his left cheek. Smiles are next to impossible not to respond to, it's instinctive to grin back. Which she does. He stands up, he's on the point of walking across to her, when the nurse reappears.

'Liam, you can go in to your wife now.'

And that ravishing arc of teeth is unleashed on the nurse. He follows her without a backward glance. She watches as Mr Come-Fly-With-Me blows out of her life – not that he really entered it but he was a man with potential. Potential to throw her overboard, it's true, but they could make a few glorious waves together en route to the shipwreck.

'Control yourself, McGlade,' mutters Kate.

She's sitting in the fertility clinic with the sole purpose of being a rock of support for Gloria – not to eye up the clients. She realises she's probably Gloria's third choice steadier, since neither Mick nor Eimear, doyenne of the hand holders, could make it. She may even be fourth or fifth on the list, best not to enquire too closely. Best simply to ooze steady-eddie reliability and behave impeccably.

Naturally Gloria isn't in the waiting room while the oral propositioning scenario is unscrolling. Life could be worse, thinks Kate, she could be married to a desperado like that Liam fellow instead of only catching his eye. He's the sort of man who's a prime case for castration never mind reproduction – people with genes like his should be banned from replicating them. Her own aren't much better.

'Do people have many more appointments after the embryo transfer?' Kate asks when Gloria returns to the waiting room from her blood-letting.

'You're ahead of yourself, I have to finish producing eggs,

have them extracted and then fertilised before ever we get to the embryo transfer,' she responds.

'Right, of course. And then what happens after the transfer? I suppose you're back in here every day being monitored.'

'You're taking an uncommon interest in this.' Gloria eyes Kate suspiciously. 'No, after the embryo transfer they don't want to see you again until you're pregnant – or have reason to believe you might be. But all that's weeks away yet for me.'

Kate sighs as she considers Gloria and Mick's relationship. They can scarcely bear to look at each other, she can't imagine how they think they're going to rear a child. Still, Kate rationalises, she's hardly in a position to cast aspersions. Ah feck it, why not cast a few aspersions. Gloria and Eimear are making a right mess of their lives. Not that she can claim to be the expert but at least she knows she makes a pig's ear of it, regularly, and always admits it. The way they've always carried on you'd swear sweet fulfilment glowed from every corner of their relationships.

She knew there had to be some brimstone mixed among the treacle, nobody could be constantly ecstatic all the time. In Eimear's case she had proof positive via her husband's pillow talk and as for Gloria – well, she's known Mick longer than Glo and Kate can see the man is miserable. Men aren't as adept as women at showing a brave face to the world.

Probably they're the better for it, she's not sure how it benefits you to conceal unhappiness instead of addressing it or even giving in and having a moan to a friend.

'You know something, Gloria,' says Kate, 'men don't know the meaning of monogamy. It's too cruel a rule, they whine. They think variety is the spice of life. Even if they're married to a Miss World or a supermodel they'll still give the au pair a quickie if it's on offer. I don't even think they see one-offs like that as infidelity, it's just a little lapse. A day off for good behaviour.'

'Jack's dolly dalliance still rankling?' asks Gloria, not particularly sympathetically.

Kate wrinkles her nose. 'Jack's no worse than the rest of the mob, he just has more access to girls. He probably didn't even see that afternoon in the right bed with the wrong woman as infidelity, certainly not to me let alone Eimear. He'd never have dreamt of confessing it. Scratch the surface – no, scratch his face while you're at it – and the chances are you'll find a Jack in nine out of ten men.

'Confessions are for major affairs as far as men are concerned and even then they'll only admit to them because (a) they want to leave their wives and are tendering the affair as the reason or (b) they've been rumbled and imagine a *mea culpa* will generate automatic forgiveness. "I've done my part by confessing, now you do yours with the absolution. Bless me mother for I have sinned."'

'You sound like a woman who doesn't like men very much,' Gloria observes, watching out for the nurse who'll call her back in for her scan.

'Oh, I do,' Kate contradicts her. 'But liking them doesn't mean you're blind to their faults. Liking them doesn't mean you treat them like women – you can't, you need to regard them as a totally separate species who operate by different rules. You see, women think men are breaking the rules when they have affairs but they're not necessarily. A man might not believe he's doing anything wrong – and most don't till they're discovered – and even then he's sorry for his blacklisted status and the recriminations rather than for the adultery.'

'Maybe we want too much,' offers Gloria, remembering how Mick pleaded pressure of work yet again as he declined to accompany her to the fertility clinic. He gets the jitters if he as much as steps through its door. She knows he wants a baby but he seems reluctant to acknowledge the unorthodox way they're going about it, even to himself.

'You mean we want a saint *and* a scholar but we're only

allowed either or,' says Kate, thinking of Jack. 'We'd all be a lot more content if men and women simply accepted we viewed everything differently – and I do mean everything, from loo seats being left up to whether or not monogamy's an optional extra.'

Kate shivers as she glances around the clinic, this place gives her the creeps. All these people desperate for a junior version of themselves – or worse, their partner. Imagine being 100 per cent responsible for another human being for eighteen years or so, you're a hostage to fortune. There's days she doesn't even like being responsible for herself let alone someone else.

She eyes Gloria with curiosity as her friend extracts a *Hello!* magazine from the jumble on a nearby table. Parenthood is the ultimate life-insurance and that's what Glo is investing in. You have a child so you won't be lonely in your old age, so someone will visit you in your sheltered accommodation or give you a granny flat in their house. Maybe it's Gloria's way of dealing with a fear of nothingness: even if there's no after-life and no reincarnation some part of her will carry on.

Kate shrugs. People say it's selfish not to have children, as though you're committing a social solecism by swanning around spending all your money on yourself when you should be buying nappies. What's wrong with spending money on yourself? Don't you earn it yourself? Whatever happened to free choice?

She makes a mental note to stop off at Urbana and buy herself something frivolous as soon as Gloria is scanned and despatched.

'The trouble with instant gratification,' she addresses her companion, 'is that it doesn't happen quick enough for me.'

'Hedonist,' replies Gloria.

'Each to their own. Some people might say you're a maso-chist for putting yourself through this. Not' – she adds hastily as Gloria's face crumples – 'that I'm one of them.'

(Something frivolous AND decadent, Kate promises herself.)

This shoulder to lean on business is making her feel like she's propping up the heavens. But she owes Gloria, so move over Atlas.

CHAPTER 20

'I think the flowery drawers you dumped in the kitchen bin swung it for Eimear,' reveals Gloria.

'Really? Why's that?' Kate is delighted but puzzled.

'I can't go into it here, people are listening,' hisses Gloria.

'These women are having all manner of distasteful procedures done to them, it's our duty to distract them,' she shoots back, but Gloria flaps crossly at her and she's forced to wait.

It's four months later and they're at the fertility clinic again for Gloria's second try – the first was a strike but Kate's forbidden from mentioning it on the grounds it might be bad luck.

'And no feeble jokes about "good luck, bad luck, who knows?"' Gloria instructs her. 'I had enough of putting a brave face on it during that week Mick and I spent in New Orleans after the first failed IVF. All that Mardi Gras merry-making only depressed me.'

Mick's conjugal hand-holding, marginal in their debut innings, has trailed off noticeably so Kate is back in the tastefully decorated waiting room, sitting alongside tastefully dressed couples. Maybe Mick's opting out so his hopes don't ride too high, Kate thinks.

'Come along, let's pour some sugary tea down you,' she bosses Gloria as she returns from her scan moaning about how much blood she's had syringed out of her tired veins.

'I don't take sugar,' she complains.

'Come on, let's get some chocolate biscuits down you,' Kate alternates, heading for the canteen with Gloria's handbag bouncing alongside hers at the hip. She's noticed women always follow their handbags and sure enough, Gloria trots after obediently.

'You said the flowery drawers swung it for me,' Kate reminds her, giving her the grace of a sip or two of tea first.

'It's true,' swallows Gloria. 'She couldn't care less when I told her about Jack belting you and about how your face was a rainbow for weeks on end and how you had to have stitches to a cut below the eye –'

'I don't remember any stitches.'

'I had to invent something, the woman was like an iceberg. I was laying it on with a trowel,' protests Gloria.

'Fair enough. Except it made no difference, did it?'

'None,' agrees Gloria. 'You've been whore non grata for months, which wasn't exactly easy for me with everything I've had on my plate, though you've never heard me complain.'

'You're a living legend, I salute you, oh exalted one, now despatch me from my misery.'

'So I've had months of warring best friends, when what I need most in my life is serenity,' continues Gloria, 'then all of a sudden last night she mentioned your name. Yours, She Who Must Be Obliterated.'

'What did she want to know?' interrogates Kate, twirling a loose button on her reefer jacket.

'Just how you were and if you were seeing someone and whether Jack had ever been back in touch with you – gossipy stuff.'

'And what did you tell her?'

'You know all the answers already, Kate. Oh, all right, to please you. I said you were in mourning for a lost friendship, a relationship you always valued but had stupidly jeopardised in a moment of madness, that you were devastated when Jack told you it was only sex between the two of you and that despite everything he preferred Eimear's body to yours.'

'Was I comatose when he imparted this gem to me?' Kate is so indignant she rips the button off her jacket.

'Artistic licence. Anyway she seemed to mellow and started reminiscing about the triumphant days of the triumvirate and finally she asked me for her favourite story again.'

'Not her favourite story,' groans Kate.

'Oh yes,' Gloria's eyes sparkle. 'The bedtime tale in which Kate turns her key in the lock to find Jack naked on HER sheets with a voluptuous teenager, drinking HER champagne and with two used condoms from HER bedside table on the floor beside them.'

'Thanks for reminding me about the condoms, I'd forgotten that succulent morsel.' Kate's expression is as sour as her voice.

Gloria smiles beatifically. 'It's been a softening up process on Eimear, trust me.'

'You're not a doctor,' Kate finishes the sentence for her.

'Anyway,' Gloria continues, reviving with each sip of sweet tea, 'I suddenly remembered that detail about the young one's flowery whatsits down your mattress. I hadn't told Eimear about them before and she was riveted. I had to mime how you picked them up by the label and carried them to the kitchen bin at arm's length, fantasising about how you could use them to embarrass Jack. She was in kinks. Then I had to pretend to throw in teabags and wheaten bread and tomato ketchup –'.

'There was no ketchup,' objects Kate.

'No but there should've been. And there I am opening and closing the kitchen bin in Eimear's house and she looks happy for the first time in months.'

'Glad to have been of assistance,' snarls Kate.

'You owe her,' retorts Gloria. 'But the best part is, she decided that anyone who finds her rival's smalls down her mattress, and not even vampish ones at that, is more to be pitied than scorned. Added to your discovery of him marking a student's essay in your bed, it won her over.'

'Actually he'd just finished his scoring, they were refreshing themselves with my champagne – which he never replaced,' Kate points out.

'So the good news is, Eimear's ready to let you have your cornflake-box crown back,' concludes Gloria.

'I'm a wise man again?'

'Probably. You may have to eat some humble pie first, Kate, you did something virtually unforgivable and I'm amazed Eimear's magnanimous enough to see you again.'

'Have you arranged a meeting?' she asks.

'Indeed I have,' responds Gloria. 'Mick's off to the Mammy's this weekend. He claims it's to give my topsy-turvy hormones breathing space but I know right well he wants to be near at · hand for his friend Marty Colton's stag party. You remember Marty, don't you? In fact, didn't you have a ring-a-ding with him once?'

'That was Eimear,' Kate lies without a twinge of conscience.

'Anyway, the end result is I have the house to myself and I'm organising a chick fest. Be there or beware. Absentees have their reputations savaged.'

'I don't have a reputation to lose.' Kate pulls a face. 'By chick fest, do you mean loads of us?'

'Relax, I'm exaggerating,' Gloria is reassuring. 'It's just the terrible threesome. I thought I should be there to referee any disputes.'

'Glo, I could kiss you, in fact I will.' Kate grabs her and makes loud mwah-mwah noises, to the unconcealed interest of the entire canteen.

'Just a minute,' she breaks off, 'do you feel well enough

for cooking? You said the treatment's leaving you like a limp rag this time around.'

'True,' nods Gloria. 'But since when did chick fests involve serious slaving in the kitchen? I'll order in pizzas and glare balefully at you two as you knock back the wine.'

'Not long to go now, pet,' Kate pats her hand. 'In three or four weeks you'll either be wellying into it yourself or you won't want to because even the smell of booze will have you sticking your head down the toilet.'

'I want you clear on one point,' announces Eimear, immediately Kate walks into Gloria's house. 'I don't believe that Jack hit you and you have to stop telling people he did.'

'I can show you the doctor's report if you like,' offers Kate, slumping on to the sofa. Jaysus, she thinks, here two seconds and already she's under attack.

Gloria shoves a glass of wine into Kate's hand and pulls a face at her; she assumes the eye-rolling and mouth-stretching are meant to be interpreted as 'Put up with this, it'll be over soon.'

'I've no doubt you can,' agrees Eimear. 'But a report will only indicate that you had a nasty blow to the face, not who struck it and under what circumstances. For all we know, you could've walked into a door deliberately to whip up support.'

'I was a sight for weeks on end, am I madwoman enough to voluntarily lacerate myself?'

'I'm not sure what you're capable of any more. I want your word that you won't ever mention this story about Jack attacking you again. You could do his career irreparable harm.'

'Just because I don't talk about it doesn't mean it didn't happen. And aren't you the supportive wife, I'm impressed by your loyalty to him.'

'Ex-wife-to-be,' Eimear corrects Kate. 'My solicitor, a piranha of a man especially chosen for his overbite, will argue for a share of his royalties from the books he published while we were an item. The figure he has in mind is a most promising one. So, you hurt Jack, you hurt me. Where it really hurts, if you catch my drift.'

Kate is dazzled. 'Mulligan, you're as tough as old boots, I'm lost in admiration.'

Gloria, meanwhile, is looking fondly from one face to the other, as though delighted by two pupils who've learned their lessons well.

'Will I dial up a pizza now or will we watch a bit of the video first?' she asks. 'I've rented *Jerry Maguire.*'

'But you know none of us like Tom Cruise,' exclaims Eimear. 'I thought you were going for the new Woody Allen.'

'True,' agrees Gloria. 'But I had a dream about Tom Cruise two nights ago and I need another look at him to see if we've seriously underestimated him all these years.'

'An erotic dream?' enquires Kate, setting down her (empty) wine glass in the hope the movement will draw Gloria's attention to it. It doesn't – when she's not drinking, she's convinced everyone else glugs too quickly.

'As a matter of fact it was,' blushes Gloria, chewing an end of her dark hair. 'Even during the dream I remember thinking, "I'm not supposed to fancy Tom Cruise." So I'm at this party and for some reason I'm the centre of attention, then Tom Cruise comes in and he looks lonely. I feel sorry for him and stroll up for a chat and we just click. He asks if I'd like to go on somewhere because he isn't in the mood for a crowd.'

This dream needs lubrication, decides Kate. She wanders across to the table and takes possession of the wine bottle, pausing to top up Eimear's glass en route. The bottle is not leaving her side until it's sacrificed every last drop of its contents.

Gloria is still burbling about her Cruise missile. 'So he makes me a cup of coffee and –'

'Wait, I missed something crucial,' interrupts Kate. 'Did you go home with him?'

'Too right, he has a chauffeur-driven car with a mini-bar waiting outside for him and we're swept away to this mansion with TCs entwined on the security gates and I say, "TC for Tom Cruise?" and he explains they're TGs for *Top Gun* which underwrote the house.'

Even Eimear is looking fidgety at this point. Kate catches her eye and indicates the bottle, Eimear slips across to join her on the sofa.

Gloria is impervious. 'I'm thinking it's strange he has Bewley's instant coffee in his kitchen cupboard but I don't mention it in case he claims to have Irish roots and I have to listen to hours of his family history. So we sit at the breakfast bar and he tells me the reason he's unhappy is because he and Nicole Kidman have split up.'

Eimear fills their glasses, leaning back against the sofa to whisper, 'The child's mad, we must be kind to her.'

Gloria is gazing raptly at Tom Cruise's face on the video cover. 'I say I haven't heard they're separated and he tells me it's still a secret, she's on location in Mexico filming a remake of *Fun in Acapulco* with Brian Kennedy in the Elvis role –'

'You have very explicit dreams,' butts in Eimear.

'– and when she comes back they'll make a statement. Meanwhile Tom Cruise is lonely and he feels strangely drawn to me. "You have kind eyes," he tells me.'

'Works every time,' interjects Kate. 'The "you have kind eyes" line – it's never known to fail. Napoleon used it on Josephine, Michael Collins used it on Kitty Kiernan, President Kennedy used it on Marilyn Monroe, my next-door neighbour Eoin uses it on all his pick-ups . . .'

'What a pair of cynics you are,' complains Gloria. 'Anyway, I'm thinking it's probably a mistake going to bed with him because I'll be nothing more than a one-night stand but I

172

decide what the hell, I can deal with feeling like a groupie tomorrow. Tonight I'm sleeping with Tom Cruise.'

She stops, just as it's getting interesting. Eimear nudges Kate.

'And did you?' she prompts.

'Oh yes.'

Silence.

'And do you remember the details?' wonders Eimear.

'Oh yes.'

Silence.

'So how was it, Glo?' Kate bursts out.

'He was a sex god,' she says complacently. 'I never knew rapture like it, I was tingling when I woke up.'

'Where was Mick, could you not ask him to do something about the tingling?'

'He sleeps in the spare room these days, my 4 a.m. alarm calls annoy him,' Gloria replies matter-of-factly. 'Anyway, shall we watch *Jerry Maguire?*'

'Wait,' protests Eimear. 'When did you have this dream? Two nights ago, right? Did you have it again last night?'

'Afraid not.' Gloria is regretful. 'I went to bed early thinking, "Ready when you are, Tom," but there was no sign of him. I'm hoping' – she looks at the others archly – 'the video might propel him back into my subconscious.'

'Tom Cruise is Cancer,' says Kate. 'Cancer men are sensitive lovers. They're completely devoted in their relationships and sentimentality was invented by them.'

'You carry the most amazing pile of trivia around in your brain,' says Gloria. 'Well, Tom time, I'll just slip the video into the machine.'

'Hold your horses, woman, pull up a Ballygowan and let the dream doctors analyse your nocturnal fantasies,' insists Eimear.

'I don't need them analysed, I'm frustrated and hallucinating about a film star,' Gloria is dismissive. 'I bet I'm not the only woman in this street, never mind this town, at the same malarkey.'

'No, that's the obvious interpretation.' Eimear shakes her head. 'Maybe you've superimposed Tom Cruise on to Mick and you're secretly hoping to reclaim the ardour you once tasted with him.'

Kate looks dubious here, while Gloria is positively sneering.

'I've a better idea,' says Kate. 'Tom Cruise isn't your type and you're not a one-night-stand sort of gal, yet you toddled off home with him because he looked sad. You're projecting your own misery on to someone else and hoping they'll be sympathetic towards you. That "you have kind eyes" line is the giveaway.'

Now it's Gloria's turn to look dubious while Eimear sneers.

'I know, I know,' says Gloria. 'Inside my staid exterior there's a passionate woman bursting to emerge. I'm the centre of attention at this party, I evacuate with a film star, we have fantastic jiggery pokery and I don't care if he dumps me afterwards. I'm doing a *carpe diem*.'

Both Eimear and Kate look dubious at this stage.

'Slam in the sacrificial lamb,' Eimear instructs Gloria. 'We'll give Tom Cruise one last chance to prove he's attractive in *Jerry Maguire*.'

'Pizza first,' Kate puts in. 'I vote we have one with everything on it, in honour of Glo's bout with a sex god. It's the nearest I expect to come to rapture this side of the menopause.'

'Missing your blissful sessions with Jack, are you?' enquires Eimear, as Gloria hunts out the pizza-delivery number.

Oh-oh, thinks Kate, I'm not out of the woods yet.

'No, I'm glad that's all over, I hated myself for betraying you.' Kate looks levelly at Eimear, blue eyes regarding blue.

'I forgive you,' Eimear tells her and Kate heaves a premature sigh of relief.

'But don't ever think I'll forget.'

CHAPTER 21

'So what do you think of them, Gloria?'

Gloria hesitates. 'I'm no great judge of poetry, Eimear. Have you shown them to Kate yet?'

'No, yours are the first eyes to rest upon my artfully artless musings.'

Gloria spreads out the pages in front of her, sheet after sheet covered in Eimear's slanted pen-and-ink script, and angles for time.

'I never knew you were interested in poetry, when did you decide you had a collection inside you?'

Eimear treats her to a radiant smile. 'It came to me one night, in a flash of inspiration, when I couldn't sleep. I hopped out of bed for a pen and paper and then snuggled back down under the duvet with my Fungus the Bogeyman hot-water bottle and started scribbling. The words flowed as if someone else was dictating them, I hardly had to search for a rhyme. I just seemed to know instinctively that daily retching would go with oh-so-fetching' – she points to a poem entitled 'Bulimia For Beginners' – 'and that raspberry ripple would be perfection with one erect nipple in "The Naked Ice-Cream Seller".'

She's animated as she studies her work, vanilla bob pushed impatiently behind her ears. Gloria hardly knows how to explain the poems are mad, bad and dangerous to show to anyone but lifelong friends. Even then it's risky, they're certainly making her re-evaluate what she knows about Eimear.

Luckily Gloria doesn't have to deliver an opinion as Eimear snatches back the folio and combs through, searching.

'Here,' she produces 'Loving You is Murder' and starts reciting:

'You killed our love, so I'll kill you
You savaged it, like I'll savage you
You spat on me as I stretched prone
Now prepare to feel saw on bone
There will be pain, it will hurt me too
There will be blood, I'll bleed too
You'll writhe and beg in your death throes
As I hack at fingers and sever toes
And lover, that final spasm
Will be our farewell orgasm'

It's creepy. Gloria listens with mounting horror, and as Eimear finishes on an elated flourish, sapphire eyes alight and satin cheeks a-glow (all that verse has her thinking like a Hallmark greeting card), she's trying to work out how to reach the door without passing directly by Eimear.

The poet is expectant.

'It's . . .' Gloria trails off, destitute of inspiration.

'Yes?'

'Unusual.'

Will that do? It seems it will.

'Precisely,' agrees Eimear. 'And the circumstances in which I wrote it were unusual too.'

Her voice lowers. 'Gloria, I dreamed that poem. I fell asleep after writing in bed one night and dreamed I was reading a collection of poetry with my name on the cover. I turned to page three and this was on it. I woke up and remembered it exactly, I jotted it down immediately and here it is, the work of my subconscious.'

Eimear, you have a warped subconscious, says Gloria, if

this is how it operates I'd pension it off. But the words are only inside her head.

Aloud, she enquires: 'So you think you might try to get these published?'

Eimear chuckles. 'Of course I will, you sap. I didn't chew my nails ragged for an audience of one. I'm going to ring Jack's publisher.'

Good God, she's lost the plot completely.

'Would he want to publish two O'Brien poets?' Gloria quibbles. 'And even if he did, imagine meeting Jack in the reception at Abbot Press – might that not be awkward?'

'We're civilised people,' says the woman who's set a lover's dismemberment to rhyme. 'He is still my husband you know, it takes the best part of five years to get a divorce in this thrustingly modern country of ours. If I can't say a calm "good day" to my own husband once in a while, it's a poor lookout.'

'That sounds fair enough,' agrees Gloria. 'But Jack's publisher might not be the ideal one for you all the same – your work probably has more, er, feminist appeal, it's not exactly mainstream like Jack's.'

She frowns at the word feminist.

'I don't mean that pejoratively, Eimear,' hastens Gloria. 'But you know, all of these poems do seem to be anti-men.'

'Where are they anti-men? I love men,' she objects.

'Well, here where you compare the ice-cream seller to a perverted Pied Piper of Hamelin, luring little girls on the basis of a ninety-nine for some sixty-nine. And here, where your bulimic woman thinks if she's thin enough men will find her desirable, so she starves herself skeletal and lies on her deathbed asking for a mirror.'

Eimear frowns, considering the evidence. 'So I might stand a better chance of having these published if I approached Bitchin' Babes or All Girls Together or some of those slipstream houses?'

'I'm no expert,' shrugs Gloria. 'But they might be worth a call. Of course you'd probably have to change your name back to Mulligan if you're making a pitch as a radical right-on poetess.'

'Poet,' she interjects. 'Poetess is derogatory.'

'Right, poet. The poet Eimear Mulligan.'

'Oh no,' she shudders, 'I never liked Mulligan.'

'Or you could decide to write it off altogether,' suggests Gloria. 'Regard this poetry exercise as healthy therapy for an unhealthy phase and move on with the rest of your life.'

'Absolutely not.' Eimear's outraged. 'I've lived with a poet long enough to know there's nothing to it except lashings of self-belief and a thesaurus at your elbow. If a messer like Jack can be a poet then so can I.'

'But why would you want to do exactly the same as him?' Gloria is bewildered. 'Go off and be a painter or a sculptor or a mountaineer if you want to show him, but you're taking him on in his own backyard, people are bound to make comparisons and you'll always come second.'

'You're so wrong.' She's impatient, the words spilling out. 'Jack will be fuming when he realises I can write poetry too. He detests competition, he's convinced he's the greatest living poet in Ireland and history will set him alongside Yeats in the lyrical firmament, while the rest of the pack are rhymesters who hit it lucky once in a while. He's always reading extracts from Heaney or Kennelly and dripping so much scorn on the pages it's a wonder they don't disintegrate from unadulterated acid. If there's one thing that puts the fear of God in Jack, it's the emergence of a new poet. He's petrified some hotshot is going to come along and prise his laurel wreath off him.'

'And that's what you're hoping to do?'

'Of course not, Glo, I just want to put the wind up him. Obviously as the erstwhile wife of an established poet I'm guaranteed a certain amount of attention. Critics will mention the book, if only to maul it, and every review will describe me

178

as the estranged wife of the poet Jack O'Brien – they may even call me the wronged wife or the deserted wife.'

Her eyes sparkle as she admits: 'I win both ways. Either the critics loathe the poems and Jack is tainted by association, or they go into raptures about them and he sits chewing his fingernails in his Trinity eyrie while I'm lionised as the poet in the family.'

'My, my, Eimear O'Brien, aren't you the girl.'

She inclines her head slightly, accepting the homage. Gloria isn't clear that it is tribute exactly, she's uncertain how to feel about this vengeful valkyrie. She's not someone she'd like to end up on the wrong side of, that's for sure.

'I thought you were almost over Jack, you hardly mention him these days.'

'Revenge is a dish best eaten cold, I'm sure Don Corleone said that in one of the *Godfather* films,' Eimear murmurs.

'Revenge is so unladylike.'

Eimear erupts into raucous laughter, answer enough, but she expands her response anyway.

'Being ladylike, my sweet Gloria, is highly overrated. Besides, who defines ladylike? Once it was ladylike to pluck your hairline for a high forehead, once it was ladylike to slap white paste on your face and have the skin eaten away with lead poisoning, once it was ladylike to squeeze your body into a corset that starved you of oxygen and had you fainting at every turn around.'

'That was centuries ago,' Gloria demurs.

'It's not so many years since it was ladylike to wear white gloves in public, to wear mantillas to Mass, to stay at home and raise your children, to conquer your fleshly desires since men couldn't be relied on to control theirs,' Eimear continues. 'Ladies didn't go into pubs or smoke in public or cause a scene. But I'm going to create a huge scene – not a brawling match. Don't worry, Glo, I won't march up to the lecture theatre and heckle Jack in front of those students he loves so much he has

179

to shag them. All of them. My scene will be confined to the written page. And I might even make a few quid out of it, buy a frock or two to flounce around literary soirees in.'

Gloria hugs her. 'Eimear, do you know what you are?' she tells her.

'What?'

'You're a survivor.'

'That vote of confidence deserves a cup of tea.'

They're drinking it when an alarm goes off. Eimear leaps like a frightened rabbit; so much for female empowerment, smiles Gloria.

'It's only my clock,' she calms the twitchy poet. 'I carry it about in my bag now, in case I forget to sniff.'

She produces the banana-yellow box, resets it for six hours' time and squirts hormone suppressants up each nostril. Her head throbs, she has a permanent migraine on this treatment.

While she rests, waiting for the pain to subside, the doorbell rings.

'It's one buzzer after another here,' complains Eimear, padding out to the hall. A male voice rumbles, then Pearse appears in the doorway.

Gloria leaps up and goes to kiss him, vacillates, then offers a cheek anyway. His lips barely graze it.

'Pearse, how lovely to see you, don't you look well,' she gushes in her uncertainty. 'You've obviously been sunning yourself somewhere exotic, you don't get a tan like that in Bray.'

'Only Cuba,' he radiates false modesty.

Only Cuba, you may as well say only Timbuktu. Gloria and Eimear pantomime going 'ooh-er' at one another behind his back.

'Business or pleasure?' Gloria enquires.

Pearse works for a travel company and is often sent abroad, although William Hurt's *Accidental Tourist* isn't a patch on him. He abhors being away from home.

'I had some business on the island and then I stayed on for a few days,' explains Pearse. 'I wasn't expecting to find you here, Gloria, but I'm delighted – it's two for the price of one.'

Eimear is far from enchanted at his clumsy analogy but decides to play hostess.

'We're just having a pot of tea, will you join us?' she invites and disappears into the kitchen without waiting for his answer.

Pearse balances on the edge of a chair and folds one leg over the other, displaying pastel socks that match his pale blue linen suit – a colour obviously chosen to highlight his tan. When he and Kate were together, he never wore anything unless it was grey or brown and Gloria doubts if he had so much as a linen handkerchief to his name.

'So how have you been keeping, Gloria? You're looking well.' His habitually apologetic voice punctures the silence.

Looking well? That's a big fat lie, she knows she looks dire but anyone would on IVF treatment. Still, one untruth deserves another.

'Oh, I'm the best,' she fibs back.

Eimear returns with a cup and saucer – visitors are never given mugs in her house – and a plate of Mikado biscuits.

'I didn't know you had spring-sprongs,' Gloria is aggrieved.

'Emergency rations,' explains Eimear.

'Am I an emergency then?' asks Pearse, looking gratified at the possibility.

'I didn't mean it like that,' Eimear frowns. 'It's just handy to have something put by for visitors.'

'What she means,' Gloria interprets, 'is that she doesn't like to give me Mikados too often because of my idiosyncratic manner of eating them.'

'You mean you nibble off all the marshmallow and save the jam until last,' says Pearse.

She nods.

'That's what everyone does,' he shrugs, 'there's nothing eccentric about that. I munch through them like that myself, although not in public.'

'You see,' Gloria rounds accusingly on Eimear. 'For years you've been telling me there's something atavistic about it, now I discover I'm perfectly normal and you're the oddity.'

Eimear ignores her. 'Milk and sugar, Pearse? Just milk. This is a welcome surprise, it's been an age since we saw you.'

'Best part of a year,' agrees Pearse pleasantly. 'Since Kate ditched me for your husband.'

Eimear is still holding the teapot, a honey-coloured teddy-bear. The teddy has to be temporarily decapitated to fill the pot, which always strikes Gloria as an unsatisfactory arrangement. Eimear pauses in the process of refilling Gloria's mug, silence stretches between them. He drinks his tea placidly. Gloria can stand the tension no longer.

'That was hardly Eimear's fault,' she protests.

'But I hear the three of you are still friends,' he remarks. 'A cosy little set-up.'

This is so unlike Pearse, he's never aggressive; Gloria and Eimear exchange disturbed looks.

'Why did you come here, Pearse?' enquires Gloria.

'I could say I was just passing and thought I'd drop in,' he answers. 'But that wouldn't be true. Or I could say I had some books belonging to Kate that I wanted you to return for me, but that wouldn't be true either. I'm here because I want you to pass on a message.'

'Couldn't you have left it on her answerphone or scribbled her a line?'

He bites into a Mikado, chews and delays his reply. While his jaws move, Gloria scrutinises the Cuban tan – on reflection it doesn't suit him, his skin's too leathery and the wrinkles have become more pronounced.

'I could have done,' he admits. 'But I thought Eimear might enjoy telling her, I thought she was entitled to it. Kate did, after all, treat both of us quite nastily. You may have turned the other cheek, Eimear, but you must still bear a tinge of animosity towards her. No? Not the tiniest flicker?'

'Give us your message and we'll make sure Kate is aware of it,' Gloria orders but he doesn't seem to hear, he's watching Eimear closely.

'Eimear, tell Kate she did me a favour,' he intones, like someone's who's memorised a lesson. 'Tell her I can never thank her enough for lying and cheating and opening my eyes to her true character. Tell her I've met someone else now, a caring woman who loves me for the man I am, not the man she'd like me to be, and that I'm consumed with bliss.'

He smiles mirthlessly. 'We're getting married in a couple of months. Obviously Kate will understand that I can't invite her. Tell her I hope she finds true happiness herself one day, as I have.'

Eimear stretches out her long legs and stands up. 'You have to get over her, Pearse.' She shakes her head. 'I've put Jack behind me, you need to do the same with Kate.'

He rises too.

'But I have put her behind me; I've just told you, I'm getting married.'

'What you said and what you meant are worlds apart,' she disagrees. 'Go home to this woman who loves you and try to deserve her love. Don't gamble it by chasing over here to let Kate know she's lost her chance with you. The fact you're so avid for her to hear you're marrying someone else speaks volumes.'

'You're wrong, you couldn't be more wrong,' glowers Pearse. 'You seem to be implying that I'm still in love with Kate when I'm not.'

'Pearse,' snaps Eimear, 'lie to anybody you like but don't lie to yourself. Now go away, marry, invent a new life for yourself. Be happy. Naff off out of it like a good lad.'

He does as she suggests, leaving a trail of coconut crumbs in his wake.

'You said "naff",' Gloria challenges her, after they've watched from the window, giddy as schoolgirls, while Pearse stomps off. 'Princess Anne says that.'

'She said it once to some photographers, we don't know it's a daily utterance.'

'You were magnificent,' adds Gloria.

'I know. Kate doesn't deserve a friend like me.'

'Will we ring her up and tell her?'

'What a sensational friend I am?'

'No, about Our Man in Havana coming around to reveal his nuptial intentions.' Gloria gloats as she imagines Kate's reaction. 'Won't she relish this: "Tell her I hope she finds true happiness one day, as I have."'

'Poor woman.'

'Kate?'

'No, the bride-to-be,' says Eimear.

'It might work out, you never know. She must have some power over him, Kate could never have persuaded Pearse into a baby blue linen suit,' Gloria points out.

'Kate would never have tried.'

'It looked well on him with his fair hair and the tan, Eimear, apart from the suit being on the crumpled side.'

'You mean he was on the crumpled side. Kate's well rid of him, he's too wrinkly for her.'

'Let's ring her now,' urges Gloria, 'it'll be such a hoot.'

Eimear dials but after two shrills, Kate's answerphone crackles on.

'She always makes it sound as though she's off at a rave when she's not at home, how do you inject such a suggestion of high living into a recorded message?' grumbles Eimear.

'Practice,' Gloria tells her. 'Do you mind if I ring home? I want to remind Mick to take the casserole out of the freezer,

184

he'll be so engrossed in the match he'll have forgotten and it will be midnight before we have any dinner.'

Eimear reaches her the receiver and flops on to the sofa, TV guide in hand. When Mick answers the phone, Gloria can tell immediately he's been drinking heavily. Her heart sinks: it's only midday. This means trouble.

CHAPTER 22

Gloria drives home as quickly as she can through the heaving Saturday lunchtime traffic, stomach in knots, ready for the row any fool could detect in Mick's voice. A bottle of Power's is sitting on the coffee table in the living room; the cloying scent of whiskey fills the air – Gloria has always deplored Mick's habit of leaving his bottles uncorked as though he won't need the cap again. Once a bottle's opened it's meant to be finished, that's his outlook.

The toilet flushes and she hears his footsteps treading heavily overhead. His frame fills the doorway, eyes blinking indignantly. He's still dressed in the *Father Ted* T-shirt he wore to bed last night.

'What have you to say for yourself?' he challenges Gloria.

'It's early in the day for whiskey.'

'The day is long and so's the bottle.' He pushes past and slops a few inches into his glass.

'I'll make us some coffee,' she suggests.

'There's no "us" about it.' He eyes her in a confrontational way.

She retreats. 'Then I'll make myself some coffee.'

'There's still no "us", though, is there?'

Gloria can see a vein throbbing on his right temple, the one that always erupts when he's hitting the bottle.

'There's only you and what you want, that's all that matters, isn't it, Gloria?'

186

'Mick,' she steels herself to speak mildly, 'I'm going to make us both a coffee and I'll rustle up a sandwich for you since you probably haven't eaten since breakfast, then I'll come back and we'll talk through whatever's troubling you.'

Gloria wants to bolt for the kitchen but manages to lift one leg and then the other at a normal pace. She holds the kettle under the tap: Oh God oh God oh God, not again.

They have a deal: hostilities suspended for three IVF attempts, animosities pushed to one side while the common goal is pursued. Except it's not a common goal, it seems to be only her chasing it, and this is too hard to manage on her own. It needs two people working at it: one to undergo the treatment and the other to hold your hand and promise you a happy ever after. It doesn't have to be true, just say the words and ease you past the next injection, the next scan.

Mick feels excluded: her body, her treatment, her fixation. 'You're doing this for you,' he accused her last week.

'I'm doing it for us,' she pleaded.

'You're impossible to live with,' he accused.

'My hormones are being tinkered with, be patient with me,' she pleaded.

'You don't even want me to come to the hospital with you,' he accused.

'Of course I do, but I know it isn't easy for you to manage time off work and I don't mind going on my own,' she pleaded.

'You only came back to me for a baby,' he accused.

She fell silent.

In a few days' time they'll be ready for a second egg extraction. Already Gloria can feel her ovaries swell, her stomach is slightly distended and she's uncomfortable in trousers. She tries to blot out the first failure, the crushing disappointment when she bled the night before she was due for a pregnancy test.

'Focus, focus, focus,' she chants, leaning against the worktop.

The kettle has long since boiled but she makes no move to spoon granules into the waiting mugs. She can't let herself think about the first failure when she's in the middle of a second attempt. But Gloria is unable to suppress the memory, it floods back.

The anaesthetist has crinkly eyes, they smile at me above his green mask as he slaps my hand repeatedly, searching for a vein. It seems odd to feel a wave of affection for a man who's walloping the back of your hand. He's the only one in the operating theatre I don't know. The doctor and nurse at the bottom of the table are both familiar from my regular checks in the past month. I'm flat on my back, knees apart, but they chat as though we're all lining up in a supermarket queue.

'Mick's outside waiting for you,' says the nurse. 'He seems worried about his parking meter but I told him we wouldn't be long.'

It's Jackie, my favourite, she has a tortoiseshell kitten called China Blue and we talk about cats whenever I come for scanning and to give blood.

'Give' is a misnomer – they prise it from my reluctant veins. The blood-letting is the part I hate most, they syringe it out of me at every appointment. I know they need it to store my eggs in, I don't begrudge it for the babies, but I still cringe as it's taken.

'I'm such a coward,' I winced apologetically once as a nurse approached with a needle.

'Cowards don't have IVF treatment,' she replied.

'They do, they just whinge about it more.'

She laughed and plunged the needle in, while I closed my eyes and concentrated on not pulling away.

The crinkly-eyed anaesthetist has found his vein and now he's stroking my arm . . . the comfort of strangers. Did he see my bottom in this unbelievably silly open-backed hospital gown as I climbed on to the trolley, I wonder, as I float

188

off. It's only an Omagh derriere, not a surgically enhanced London one.

It feels like seconds later when I'm back with Mick, a cup of sugary tea in my hand.

'I like this, put more sugar in it,' I instruct him muzzily.

He's excited. 'They extracted thirteen eggs, Gloria, that's three more than average. The medics seem very pleased with you. You should've seen where I had to masturbate while they were working on you – it's just a little room with no facilities. They offered me a magazine for "stimulation", but I said no, it didn't seem right. It was bleak in there I can tell you.'

What were you expecting – dancing girls?

My brain asks the question but my tongue can't help out with the verbalising.

In the next cubicle I hear a woman being dressed by a man. Rustle, rustle, murmur, murmur. The man ends each sentence with 'darling'. She was the first one into the operating theatre, there are four of us up for extraction today. It's like being at an upside-down dentist's.

Jackie's head materialises through the curtains.

'Knock knock,' she says.

'Who's there?' I answer.

'Only me.'

'Call that a punchline?' I complain.

'How's this for a punchline: Gloria, you can go home as soon as you've finished your tea. Take it easy for the next two days and we'll see you back on Wednesday for the egg replacement, provided everything goes according to plan. Ring up tomorrow to check that fertilisation has taken place.'

'You mean it mightn't?' I'm alarmed.

'It probably will,' she soothes. 'Mick provided his sample while you were in the operating theatre, I'm sure everything will be hunky dory.'

The head disappears.

'David Bowie had an album called that,' I tell Mick.

189

He looks at me anxiously.

'Hunky Dory.'

'You're rambling, Glo, it's the anaesthetic. Finish your tea and we'll get you home to bed.'

'A hunk a hunk a burning love,' I sing in a squeaky voice.

Mick removes the teacup from my hand and pulls a shirt over my head.

'Did you say you were making a sandwich?' Mick's voice, calling from the living room, jolts Gloria from past to present.

'Coming right up,' she shouts back and opens the fridge door in search of ham, the only sandwich filling Mick tolerates. The eggs catch her eye and she's back with the thirteen specks of eggs marked McDermott in a laboratory of the Rotunda hospital. That was four months ago. Seven of them fertilised but they only needed three, that's as many as the experts return to the womb.

It's a different doctor replacing the eggs, only now they're forty-eight hours old and embryos; no anaesthetist is needed this time.

'They're good quality embryos,' says Jackie, making conversation.

I'm relieved, although until this second I had no idea that embryos were graded like fruit and vegetables.

The fertilising doctor doesn't speak much, she's concentrating on my vagina. Mick is waiting outside with his newspaper.

'There,' says the doctor. 'Lie quietly for twenty minutes and then you can go home.'

'Is that it?' I'm astonished.

'It only takes a few minutes,' smiles the doctor, unpeeling her rubber gloves.

'We'll send Mick in to you,' Jackie tells me. 'Three good-quality embryos,' she beams at him.

He throws her a look of incomprehension, as though she's just announced: 'The mother ship is waiting, we must leave your planet now, earthling.'

'Tell me when twenty minutes is up,' I order, to give him something to do. He enjoys chores like that, he checks his watch and nods.

'So you're pregnant now,' he says when we're alone.

'Pregnant? Not quite, I just have three embryos inside me. We won't know if I'm pregnant for a couple of weeks.'

He virtually carries me to the car, clips me into the seat-belt and drives along in third gear to the fury of every car behind us.

'Dublin drivers – cowboys the lot of them,' he frowns, but as he speaks he hits a pothole and my head bounces off the car roof.

'Jesus, Mary and Joseph, I've miscarried,' I bellow.

Mick pulls over in front of a set of traffic lights – cue more honking from behind. 'Have you? Are you bleeding? What's happening?'

'I don't know, but it's no thanks to you if I have lost them,' I shriek. 'Just watch where you're going and get me home in one piece.'

'The important thing is to stay calm,' he says, as he pulls out in front of a bus which has to do an emergency stop. 'I've moved the television set up to the bedroom so you'll be snug as a bug for the next few days.'

Mick stands at the kitchen door, outrage emanating from every inch of his not inconsiderable bulk. 'My stomach thinks my throat's been slit.'

Gloria starts and shuts the fridge door, there's a pool of water at her feet where something leaked from it. 'We've no ham, would you take a cheese sandwich?'

'I suppose I'll have to, but only if you toast it. Give us that coffee to be getting on with.'

191

As she spoons granules into a mug, her mind flits back to that week, an endless seven days of waiting and hoping and believing.

The days pass with daytime soaps and crossword puzzles (the simplex version, I can't manage those cryptic beasts), visits from Kate and Eimear, but separate ones because we're still at loggerheads, which suits me fine because it doubles my company, and phone calls between Omagh and Dublin. Even my feckless sister Marlene rings from London, ostensibly to enquire after my health but in reality to foist offensive baby names on me. Like Imogen.

By day six I'm starting to feel cautiously optimistic, by day nine I'm working out the baby's star sign, by day fourteen I'm wondering whether to use caterers or go to a restaurant for the christening party, by day fifteen I truly feel like a mother-to-be – I go for my pregnancy test on day sixteen. Mick is caught up in my excitement, part of it all now at last.

'Can you feel anything?' He stares at my uncovered stomach.

'No, it's like a late period except that you definitely know you're growing a baby.'

He grins. 'We're growing a baby.'

I grin back.

'Would you like a neck massage, Glo? I saw you rubbing at it earlier as though you'd twisted it.'

'That would be lovely, Mick, I'll just use the bathroom first.'

I sit on the toilet seat for decades. Traces of pink are mixed with my urine, the early-warning signal of a period. It's a mistake, I'll look again and it will be clear-coloured. I gaze into the bowl and see pink splashes. I touch myself and my fingers are stained.

Pink makes the boys wink. My father used to say that whenever I wore a pink top, then he'd wink with exaggerated slowness and I'd wink back.

I drag myself to my feet and walk towards the bedroom, where Mick is waiting for me.

'I was nearly coming to look for you, you were ages,' he says. 'Ready for that neck rub?'

'I'm bleeding,' I say.

His stare is bewildered.

'There's no baby, I'm bleeding,' I repeat.

Tears well exquisitely slowly from Mick's eyes and trail down his face, snot bubbles from each nostril. I watch him dispassionately for a moment, then I pull him towards me and he weeps on to my chest. They're sobs now, noisy, gulping, snorting howls of anguish.

'We gave it our best shot, at least we tried,' I stroke his hair. 'The odds are against you, we knew that when we started.'

'I really thought it had worked,' he gasps as he cries. 'You were so confident, you had me believing it as well.'

'You need to be confident to go through something like IVF. You may realise there's only a 25 or 30 per cent chance of success when you start but you push that knowledge aside once you're in the middle of it – you tell yourself all this pain is front-loaded experience, it will be worth it when you hold a baby in your arms. It's called self-preservation. A willing suspension of disbelief.'

Mick's tears seem to be easing, he lies still against me, a crushing weight but I carry it.

'We'll do this again as soon as they let us and it'll work next time,' I promise him.

'Do you really believe that?'

'I have to believe it, Mick. If I don't, who will?'

'I'm not sure I'm able to go through it a second time,' Mick whimpers against me.

'Of course you can,' I say dully. 'If I can do it so can you.'

I don't cry for two weeks, but when the tears come they trip me. I weep for every toe I stubbed, for every test I failed, for every dress I spoiled, for every snub I suffered, for every cross word flung at me. I mourn the father I lost, the husband I'm losing, the three embryos that can't or won't lodge in my womb.

I cry in bed every night so long and so pitifully that finally Mick loses patience. He tries to comfort me and can't: I don't want his arms around me, I want my own around a baby.

Gloria is weeping again now, into the coffee mug on the kitchen worktop, she's clutching the speckled pottery, cradling its warmth.

'You're in a bad way,' says Mick.

'I know,' she agrees. 'It's those hormones again.'

'You're not well enough for this treatment, we should have waited longer between attempts.'

'We had the holiday in New Orleans, that was a break for us before trying again,' Gloria reminds him.

'Some people leave it a year before their second go, to recover their strength and their marriage. A couple of months isn't long enough, Glo.'

'It's all a lottery anyway,' she shrugs. 'We might as well press on. I couldn't put it out of my mind for a year, every month I'd be thinking, "Another wasted month."'

Mick sighs like one gazing into the abyss. 'This is kill or cure. You'll either have a baby or wreck our marriage.'

It's a fair trade, she says, but only inside her head.

'You should've listened to me, Glo, when I said let's take a break from this fertility business but you just pushed ahead and made the appointment to start all over again. I'm not married to a woman, I'm married to an IVF handbook. This is not what I want.'

'Mick, please, I have eggs growing inside me, they think I'll be ready for extraction in a few days. Now's not the time to question whether we should be doing it – we ARE doing it, take a reality check, I need your support right now.'

'But if it doesn't work this time we take a real break,' he insists.

Gloria is suffused with rage.

'What do you mean "if it doesn't work"? You're the most negative person in the stratosphere. Everyone else has husbands holding their hands each step of the way, I have one who doesn't even think the treatment will be successful – and then hasn't the decency to keep his doubts to himself. Have you any idea how completely, utterly and desolately alone I feel? How desperate, how isolated, how loveless?'

'You have your friends, you're always off whispering secrets to them and excluding me from your circle,' he yells back.

'Yes, I have my friends, praise be to God I have my friends because I have no one else to rely on, I don't have a husband, that much is clear.'

'You mean you don't want a husband.' His face is close to hers and contorted with hate. 'Well, you carry on, you have your precious eggs extracted, but don't come looking for sperm from me. The bank is closed.'

He doesn't mean that, Gloria thinks, as she slides on to the floor, too rattled to stay on her feet any longer. Mick has slammed out of the house without a jacket, and she can see rain drizzling through the kitchen window.

'I hope he catches pneumonia and dies,' she mutters. 'I hope he's in one room of the hospital gasping his last as I'm in another giving birth to twins.'

The notion is so ridiculous, she laughs humourlessly. He'd be nine months dying from pneumonia for starters.

Fury courses through her, energising, healthy ire.

'He can keep his sperm,' she fumes. 'I'll use donor sperm, I'll ask another man to oblige.'

She casts around for a suitable candidate.

'Pearse is too spooky, Marlene's boyfriend's in London,

there's a few men at work but they might not go along with it. There's no one else suitable, it'll have to be Jack O'Brien.'

CHAPTER 23

Kate's in a frenzy. 'You want to ask Jack for what? The loan of his sperm? You mean you plan to return them afterwards, slightly used, one careful owner?'

'Well of course I can't return them, they'll be dead after they've fertilised my eggs – they can't survive for long outside the body,' explains Gloria.

Heavens above, she thinks, Kate's acting like a maniac – anyone would think she wanted to sleep with her ex-lover. Besides, Kate's already established that's a forgivable offence as far as Eimear's concerned.

'There'll be no physical contact,' explains Gloria.

Kate looks like someone who thought she bought a cinema ticket for a slusherama but finds herself sitting through a slasher flick.

'He'd only have to ejaculate into a glass container. I wouldn't even be in the same room with him,' continues Gloria helpfully.

'Right, and then you'd have his baby and there'd always be this bond with him. Look, you're talking about Eimear's husband, Gloria, you'd both be the child's parents. You haven't thought this through, it would never work. Eimear's bound to learn the truth sooner or later, she'll be in ribbons – it could destroy her.'

'She might never find out – she might not even mind if she does discover it years from now, when she's not so raw.

There's no point in speculating; sure, how do we know till we give it a lash?' Gloria suggests.

'You don't have to stick your hand in the fire to know it burns,' protests Kate. 'And believe me, I've singed my fingers in Jack O'Brien's grate, you really don't want to go down that road. The man's a romantic arsonist.'

She tugs at a delicate gold chain on her wrist with an indelicate amount of force.

'Glo, dote,' Kate's tone is kinder now, 'I know you desperately want a child and I hope it happens for you, I genuinely do, but you must forget this crazy idea. Go back to Mick, he's your husband, he's the man you should be having a baby with. Patch up your quarrel and use his sperm.'

Kate's taking sides. The wrong side, as far as Gloria's concerned. She's on the verge of tears as Kate continues.

'Mick didn't mean it, he has a temper on him like a fire-rocket and he's been under a lot of stress, he probably regretted the words as soon as they left his mouth.'

'But what if he does mean it?' Gloria barely holds her tears in check. 'What if I arrive at the hospital for my extraction and there's no sign of him? The eggs are almost ready – they have to come out now, they can't stay inside me indefinitely.'

'Gloria, Jack O'Brien is probably the last man living you should consider to father your child. You want a decent fellow like Mick, not a rampant womaniser.'

'But my baby wouldn't be like Jack, it would be like me,' wails Gloria.

'How do you know?' demands Kate.

'Because I'd raise it to be like me,' she sniffles.

'There's no accounting for genes.'

Gloria pretends to abandon the idea, Kate's opposition is wearing her out. And she has to concede that her friend is making sense – except sensible behaviour doesn't attract her right now.

'You win, this was a mad stratagem but you know how I'm fixed, it's the –'

'Hormones,' says Kate.

Gloria shrugs theatrically. 'I'll apologise to Mick, I'm not sure for what but I'll do it anyway.'

'Sensible child,' nods Kate – that well-known beacon of decorum, fumes Gloria.

'Off you go.' Kate looks encouraging. 'No dawdling, the quarrel is already a day old, you know you're not supposed to let the sun go down on a fight.'

Gloria levels the sort of glance at her your mother would call old-fashioned and Kate has the grace to blush. God in heaven, how she condescends to her.

Gloria delays going indoors when she finds herself back in Ranelagh: she collects a soft drink can from the pavement in front of the house and gathers some nasturtium seeds spilling on to the path. She has nowhere to put them so she makes a little pile by the step, meaning to collect them later, and then she can procrastinate no longer – she opens the door. The house is empty. No sign of Mick in the living room, no vestiges of him in the kitchen, she tries upstairs for some indication of his whereabouts.

There's a note on her pillow: 'Gloria, gone home for a few days, it's the only way I can stop you pressing ahead with this treatment. Mick.'

Not even 'Love, Mick' or 'Good luck, Mick.' She screws the note into a ball and bounces it off the wall. It flops on to the bed and she picks it up and flings it again. This time it's trapped in the radiator and she can no longer see it, treacherous piece of paper.

'He knows I'm having my eggs extracted in two days' time, how can he walk away from this?' Gloria yells at the pillow the note rested on.

The pillow doesn't look particularly sympathetic – then

again, it doesn't look unsympathetic either. Having it both ways, aren't you, you piece of feathery fluff.

'That's it then, he's lost his chance. I'm ringing Jack O'Brien and if he won't help me I'm approaching Paul at work and if he won't help me I'll fly Marlene's boyfriend home and if he won't help me I'll call on creepy Pearse and if he won't help me I'm starting at A in the telephone directory and I won't stop until I reach Z.'

Jack answers on the first ring.

'You're quick off the mark,' Gloria gasps, 'I haven't even rehearsed what I'm going to say yet.'

'Gloria?' He sounds amused.

'That's me. Hope I'm not disturbing you, Jack.'

'Not in the slightest. I'm starkers but if it doesn't bother you it doesn't bother me.'

She's flummoxed, he's never flirted so ostentatiously with her before, though she's seen him in action often enough.

'You mean you're naked?' she checks she hasn't misunderstood him.

'As the day I was born.'

'Are you just about to take a bath?' Gloria tries to ignore the nervous fluttering in her stomach.

'No, I like to wander around in the altogether, it helps the creative juices to flow.' His voice booms confidently down the phone line. 'It's a new technique I've discovered and I'm writing some really promising material this way. Abandoning clothes is a way of stripping yourself of artifice, checking out of the twenty-first century, clearing your mind of trivia so you can concentrate on essentials.'

'That's – er – great.'

The man is obviously deranged, she doesn't want his sperm after all.

'What can I do for you, baby girl?'

Drat, that voice gets to you, it's so seductive, it's like chocolate fudge cake with whipped cream on top. Gloria relents.

'Well . . .' Just because he's mad doesn't mean he'd have loopy children.

'Yes, Gloria?' he prompts.

'I have something to ask you, something a little bizarre, it's a favour really, but I can't mention it over the phone. Could we meet?'

'Come right over,' he invites.

'Now?'

'Seize the day, little Gloria, jump straight into your shiny yellow Corsa and come to Trinity. I'll be waiting in my lair, ready to pounce.' He laughs softly.

She's unsure if he's joking but doesn't stop to check. 'I'm on my way then, I'll be there in fifteen minutes.'

She's relieved, but disappointed too, when Jack answers the door in a black polo-neck and black jeans. Tight black jeans, the sort younger men tend to wear, but they work on Jack. He's barefoot and his naked brown feet lend him a predatory air. Maybe this isn't such a clever idea.

He kisses her cheek, just as he always does when they meet, but this time he cups her chin in a lingering gesture that reinforces her qualms.

'Sit down, Gloria,' he murmurs, 'you look ill at ease.'

It's early evening and still bright out but he's drawn the curtains and lit scented candles.

'They help me concentrate,' he explains. 'Electric light is so unconducive to poetry, I want to chase shadowy themes along the dimly lit corridors of my mind.'

Poetry books will be banned in her house if she has this baby, pledges Gloria, choosing a hardback chair as far from Jack as possible. He pulls up another alongside her, straddles it back-to-front and tips forward, regarding her minutely. She can feel her nose glow, it always turns scarlet when she's under pressure. If he doesn't stop looking at her like that her neck and ears will soon be mottled too.

'Jack, there's no other way to ask this than by coming straight out with it.'

She looks around to see what eejit said that. Dear God, it was her. He lays a finger against her lips.

'Where's your rush, Gloria?' he lulls her. 'I haven't seen you in such a long time, let's become reacquainted first. Has life been kind to you? Your sweet, small face looks troubled, a wan Ophelia approaching the riverbank. Will Hamlet spring forth from the reeds and effect a rescue?'

What gibberish he talks, she thinks later, but he manages to make it sound compelling at the time. He leans forward attentively and she longs to throw herself against his shoulder and pour out her woes. God this man is good, I mean bad, I mean good at being bad. But an image of Eimear floats into her mind and she hesitates. It's his fault for rambling on about Ophelia.

Get thee behind me, Satan, she cries (but not aloud, she's not that dense). Get thee behind me, Satan, I'm not interested in men, just babies.

'You said *carpe diem*, Jack, so we'll get cracking.' Gloria adopts a businesslike tone. 'Here's the situation: I need some sperm the day after tomorrow and I was wondering if you'd oblige.'

Jack looks dazed. 'Some . . . ?'

'Sperm,' she supplies the missing word helpfully. 'I'm up to my oxters in IVF treatment and Mick is sulking in Omagh. Talk about choosing his moment. Anyway, I'm in a bind because the eggs are nearly ready to pop and I have to find a donor. It's a nuisance because if I lived in England, I could just pay the hospital and they'd sort me out with something from a medical student but obviously Ireland won't be party to licentiousness like that so I have to find my own donor. Not to mention pulling a fast one on the hospital staff but it's worth a try.'

Gloria waits for Jack to speak but he looks stupefied.

'You don't have to do anything other than empty your sperm into a hospital container,' she explains. 'It shouldn't take more than a few minutes, I'll arrange for a taxi to take you to and from the Rotunda if you like. Then your sperm will be introduced to my eggs and with any luck a match will come of it. Maybe even a baby or two.'

Again she waits, still he looks baffled.

'Obviously I wouldn't regard you as the child's father, there'd be no liability, you'd simply be doing me a massive favour. So will you? Will you help me out here, Jack? I'm desperate.'

'I guess so,' speaks Jack slowly. 'The girl wants sperm and I've plenty of sperm, I can lend you a few million and not even miss them.'

'I really only need one but I'll take as many as you can spare. Oh, Jack, I'm so grateful, I can't begin to tell you how much this means to me. Thank you, from the bottom of my heart.'

Relief saturates Gloria and she reaches for him spontaneously – but his seductive mood seems to have evaporated and he hangs in her arms. Rather slackly, she notes.

'Well, I mustn't keep you back from your poetry any longer, you never know what shadowy ideas are flitting about in alleyways waiting for you to pounce on them. I'll ring tomorrow to finalise the arrangements. You won't' – doubt catches her by the throat momentarily – 'you won't change your mind, will you, Jack? Once you've had a chance to collect your thoughts? I know I should've offered you time to sleep on it but time is something I don't have.'

A ghost of a smile flits across Jack's still stunned face, 'You want my sperm. Not my body, not my brain – my sperm. There's a first time for everything, I hope this doesn't indicate I'm on a slippery slope. But it took courage to ask me, it'll take even more courage to face Eimear when she hears about it. She'll be incandescent.'

A speculative note enters his voice. 'Incandescent doesn't begin to describe how she'll react.' He beams. 'Gloria, my sperm are yours, do with them what you will.'

She glows back at him. 'I'm going to try and get pregnant with them, that's what I'm going to do with your sperm, Jack O'Brien.'

CHAPTER 24

'Who would you prefer to run away with, Antonio Banderas or Ronan Keating?'

Kate is playing one of her let's pretend games.

'I don't want to run away with anyone,' Eimear objects.

'I know but just say both asked you to decamp with them, which one would it be?'

She considers the options. 'Ronan makes sense because he lives in Dublin so you wouldn't have to run too far, but then again Antonio is very tempting – he has those flashing eyes and that accent.'

Both mime shuddering with desire.

Eimear carries on weighing up the pros and cons. 'Mind you, Antonio Should-Be-Banned-Eras might be a bit of a handful, all that Latin temperament to contend with, I'd say he'd be sulky if you didn't pander to him 100 per cent.'

'You'd have a problem pandering to Antonio Should-Be-Banned-Eras 100 per cent?' Kate's face radiates disbelief.

'Maybe not,' admits Eimear. 'But Ronan gives you the impression he'd be plenty of fun. The sort to spoil you to death too. There's a lot to be said for the boy next door, especially when he's drop-dead gorgeous, rich as Croesus and a famous pop star.'

'You're only choosing Ro-Ro from Boyzone because he's a local lad,' objects Kate.

'It's true that familiarity breeds content,' concedes Eimear.

'But I think he's more my type anyway – well-mannered on *The Late Late Show*, combs his hair, looks like he washes regularly.'

'Is that what you want in a man? Someone who showers daily and says please and thank you? Jaysus, Mulligan, you've lowered your sights.' She sounds incredulous.

'I just think El Banderas might be more trouble than he's worth.' Eimear is defensive. 'There'd be women crawling out of the woodwork offering themselves to him on a plate – even Madonna was at it – no matter how much he loves you, he's bound to be tempted. How could he help himself with all that Spanish blood pumping through his veins?'

'Stereotyping, Mulligan,' reprimands Kate. 'You see you have to pose the crucial question: would I like six days of paradise with one man or six years of earthly pleasures with another?'

'That's enough of your let's pretend games,' says Eimear. 'It's your turn to go to the coffee machine.'

They're sitting in the room they've christened Harry's waiting room, ready to collect Gloria after her egg replacement. It's actually the HARI unit waiting room, as in Human Assisted Reproduction Ireland. Mick is elsewhere – surprise, surprise, they should be grateful he turned up to ejaculate two days ago. Gloria told her he went straight off to Omagh afterwards, Eimear is appalled that he wouldn't stay and see it through with her.

If she were Glo she'd be calling Mick McDermott every name under the sun but his determined little wife doesn't even want to mention him – she says all her energies are concentrated on nurturing her embryos.

'They're mine, I've earned them,' she insists.

Gloria was upset that she only produced nine eggs this time, convinced her ovaries were starting to give up on her as well as her fallopian tubes, but Kate and Eimear reassured her she only needed three embryos.

Imagine having your husband's embryos whooshed up inside you and he's not even there to hold your hand, thinks Eimear. No wonder Gloria's on the edge. She and Kate are there to take Mick's place but can anyone really deputise for a husband?

'It's incredible that Mick isn't here,' Eimear complains as Kate returns with the coffees. 'I've a good mind to ring him up and let rip.'

'I wouldn't do that, Eimear, this is between Mick and Gloria, we can only be here for them.'

'I'm not here for Mick McDermott, I'm here for Glo and no one else,' fumes Eimear.

'There's just one problem about your choice of Ronan Keating.' Kate changes the subject with the finesse of a hatchetman. 'Are you not bothered that he might be too young for you?'

'Of course he's fa-ar too young for me. I was only going to run away with him in theory. In practice I'd have to organise someone to write him a sick-note for school.'

'You could be on to something all the same,' remarks Kate. 'It strikes me we're wasting our time on men our own age, we should be concentrating on fresh-faced, malleable ones, not cynical old scuts who've cantered around the block once too often.'

'Like us.'

'Like us,' she nods.

'Kate,' announces Eimear in her firmest voice. 'Stop wasting your energies thinking about men. Here comes Gloria.'

And they rush to her side.

They drive home in Eimear's pink Beetle, since three don't fit easily into Kate's Hurtle Turtle, and ease Gloria out with infinite tenderness.

'Stop treating me like a piece of Belleek china,' she snaps, irritated by their tender, loving care.

If this is motherhood, it obviously disagrees with her, thinks

Eimear. 'You were always criticising Mick's lack of attention,' she replies, stung.

Kate nudges her. 'Let's just get the soldier home from the wars. In we go, Glo, shall we piggyback you up the stairs or would you rather play leapfrog up them?'

Gloria elects to walk, holding on to the banister, her fingers disturbing a layer of dust. Surreptitiously Eimear checks the wooden trim on either side of the stairs where the carpet ends – dusty too. She doesn't understand why Gloria refuses to employ a cleaning lady if she can't be bothered polishing – she's always recommending her own Mrs Ahern.

'Shall I put the kettle on while you settle her into bed?' Eimear enquires of Kate.

'Ask her do I take sugar while you're at it,' snarls Gloria.

Eimear hesitates, Kate inclines her head towards the kitchen and she scurries off. Hormones are demons, no two ways about it.

In the kitchen waiting for the kettle to boil, Eimear's attention is drawn to the worktops. They look like they haven't had a decent scrub in weeks. She roots around in the cupboard under the sink for a cleaning agent, finds a nearly empty one and squirts and swabs thoroughly. Then she throws her dishcloth into the bin. Eimear inspects the inside of Gloria's teapot, it fails to pass muster so she dunks teabags in mugs, lips quivering with distaste, while she steeps the pot in the sink. She's not going home until it's sterilised, she promises herself, and sets off bathed in a virtuous glow carrying Gloria's poppy-patterned tray. Which could do with a wipe but she doesn't notice until she's halfway up the stairs.

Kate is expounding her theory on younger men to Gloria, who looks thoroughly disinterested.

'We don't need men, we need Beautiful Boys. We can boss them around and instruct them in the art of pleasuring us. They'll be grateful and devoted and they'll always remember us, like in the Bobby Goldsboro song where your one who's our age picks up with a wee lad of seventeen and takes his education in hand, so to speak.'

'I'd be embarrassed to admit I knew the words to a Bobby Goldsboro song,' says Eimear, setting the tray at the end of the bed.

Kate is unrepentant. 'Some lyrics sneak into your brain and won't be dislodged. Anyway that song has one of the best pay-off lines in history –' she warbles at the top of her lungs, hands on her heart – '"And I saw the sun rise as a man."'

'If you don't stop massacring Bobby Goldsboro songs I'll ring the guards, Kate McGlade. I'm sure there's a by-law against it,' objects Gloria.

'OK,' she agrees. 'But back to our Beautiful Boys. We don't want seventeen-year-olds like Bobby's fellow, that's vaguely pornographic. They have to be at least twenty and not living with their mammies. We want ready, willing Abels to run errands for us, like ordering rounds of drinks at the bar. We'll give them the money so they know who's boss, we don't want to be drunk in charge of minors, there's probably a by-law against that too. Mulligan has the right idea with her little Ronan.'

'He's not my little Ronan,' protests Eimear. 'He belongs to a model, as it happens.'

'It was your idea to run off with a young one,' Kate points out.

'It was nothing of the sort, you gave me a straight choice between Ronan Keating and Antonio Banderas and I said, if pushed, I'd take the Keating lad.'

'You turned down Should-Be-Banned-Eras for Ronan Keating?' Gloria looks animated for the first time since being collected from the Rotunda.

Eimear is apologetic. 'I just thought he'd be more reliable.'

Gloria falls back against her pillows. 'I need a drink,' she croaks.

'It'll have to be tea – think of your embryos,' says Kate, lifting the Elvis mug that flashes The King Lives around the rim when hot water is added to it.

Eimear decides it's time to move away from beautiful boys and on to bouncing babies.

'How are the babas, do you think they've made themselves at home? Do you feel pregnant yet?'

'I don't want to talk about them,' says Gloria, tugging moodily at the hairband she's taken to wearing in an effort to grow her fringe out.

'The golden rule is no teenagers: we have to remember we want to be seducers, not criminals,' Kate contributes.

Is she still harking on about toyboys, the woman's obsessing. Eimear shakes her head in despair. 'And where are we supposed to find them?' Her tone is sarcastic. 'You can't just wander into Dunnes Stores, eye up the lads stacking the shelves and say, "They'll do nicely, I'll take half a dozen assorted."'

Kate's eyes glaze over. 'When Cher spots a likely lad she commands, "Have him stripped, washed and taken to my tent."'

'Cher invents her own rules,' says Gloria. Wistfully, as it happens.

Kate obviously detects the same note and adopts a brisk tone. 'What we need is a Girls' Night Out to take our minds off our miseries. We need flings.'

Eimear nods meaningfully in Gloria's direction and Kate adds a caveat: 'Not Gloria, of course. You can just have a mental fling to show willing; you have to concentrate on reproduction not seduction. Mulligan and I will do the flinging for the three of us.'

Gloria is uncooperative. 'I have to spend the next week in bed – a Girls' Night Out is the West Cork, the South Pole, the ocean floor on my list of priorities. Couldn't you just write a letter to Santa for a Beautiful Boy?'

210

'Too long to wait, it's only August. Anyway we want to pick our own toys, not let some hairy fellow in a signature suit do it for us,' says Kate. 'Hey, we can make it a combined birthday celebration next month, that'll give you long enough to let the eggs take root, Glo, and it'll give me long enough to scout around and establish which nightclub Beautiful Boys go to . . . I'm a little out of touch.'

'I want mine to be called something cute with a "y" on the end like Nicky or Ricky,' says Gloria.

'You aren't having one,' Eimear points out. 'You're having a baby instead.'

'I want one who still remembers how to blush,' says Kate. 'And he'll be too young to have chest hair. What about you, Mulligan?'

Eimear would like one who's a student of her husband's so he knows how it feels to have your nose rubbed in it but she keeps this to herself. Instead she adopts a Sphinx-like demeanour and says, 'That's for me to know and you to guess.'

'She's being faithful to Ronan,' deduces Kate.

As Gloria and Kate start gossiping about the latest episode of *Coronation Street*, Eimear tunes out and considers the Beautiful Boys option. Maybe Kate's on to something, adoration from a younger man might be extremely gratifying. The only trouble is you have to go to ear-bleeding disco bars to meet them.

Something weird happens when you turn twenty-nine: you don't like loud music as much as you used to. You wake up one morning and realise conversations can be quite agreeable in pubs and so can occasional silences. But inflicting GBH on the eardrums might be worth it in the interest of meeting Beautiful Boys. She fantasises about lying on the patio with a magazine while one wanders around in jeans with his shirt off, weeding the flowerbeds.

The trouble with nightclubs is they all have bouncers (they call themselves door supervisors now) who seem to think it's clever to refuse people admittance for no proper reason.

'I've never seen you before, feck off.'

'You come here too often, feck off.'

'I don't fancy you, feck off.'

Imagine if they said: 'You're too old, feck off.' Eimear makes a mental note to fit in plenty of early nights before they hit the town.

'If we're going to pull we need to avoid the tarty look,' she tells Gloria and Kate. 'Beautiful Boys can get that from their own age group and we can't compete. So no Lycra and no cleavages. We're women, not chicks – the London derriere is restricted to two wiggles per minute, Kate. We want to look cultured, refined, cosmopolitan – not available.'

'But we are available,' Kate protests.

'Of course we are but we don't have to advertise it. We want to look unattainable so they can't believe their luck when we deign to notice them.'

'It's a ploy, it could work,' Kate ruminates.

Eimear sweeps on. 'We must remember that the chances of both of us scoring are low – don't look so hurt, Glo, the only result you want's from a pregnancy testi – so we have to forget about the usual rules where women are meant to be too loyal to dump their friends if one of them gets off with a man. This "all for one and one for all" notion can fall by the wayside when we're sharking. The chances of bumping into a brace of BBs on the same night are slight to zero.'

'BBs sounds like babies,' says Gloria mournfully.

'Maybe you shouldn't come with us,' Eimear tells her. 'You might be too maternal for this caper.'

'Please let me, I won't mention babies once in the night-club,' she promises.

'All right,' concedes Eimear. 'Now remember, it's down to business for the seducer who scores a bullseye and taxi time for the others – with the promise that every sordid detail will be recounted over a glass of vodka veritas at the earliest opportunity.'

Kate rumples her red hair exuberantly.

'My God, I've created a monster,' she exclaims. 'You've latched on to this big time, Mulligan. Let's go for it, girls.'

Eimear drops Kate off on the corner of St Stephen's Green. 'I must check my flat has all the vital components for Operation BBs,' winks Kate.

'Like a bottle of champagne?'

'He never replaced that,' she frowns. 'Tight git.' She pauses, then adds: 'Sorry Eimear, this must be painful for you.'

'Water under the bridge,' she assures Kate. 'Strictly speaking he's not tight, just distracted. His mind tends to be on higher things. Like fornication.'

Kate squirms beside Eimear in the car.

'Are you having trouble with the door? Let me open it for you.' Eimear leans across and fiddles with the catch, to put her out of her misery – and to put herself out of her own. No more thoughts of Jack.

I'm completely over him, Eimear thinks as she drives home past the National Concert Hall. Jack won't cross her mind once when she's frolicking with the young bucks of Dublin. She'll be too busy thinking how delectable it is to have a firm twenty-year-old body to grapple with instead of a nearly middle-aged one, even if it was in fine fettle. She may just happen to have a drink with one of these Beautiful Boys in Jack's local but it will only be a quick one, she doesn't need to parade the fact that she's an attractive woman in her prime whom many men find attractive. Even if he doesn't.

CHAPTER 25

Eimear lies in bed thinking about Kate. Her sleeping pattern's banjaxed since Jack left – actually it was constructive dismissal – and she's developed a succession of tactics that occasionally fool her body into thinking it's ready to go comatose. They include warm milk, hot-water bottles and a stack of sizzling page-turners but the heat treatment isn't working tonight. She resists switching the lamp on and curls around her pillow in darkness, contemplating Kate.

Although she's forgiven her, she didn't do it effortlessly – it was the toughest decision of her life. But no pain, no gain, isn't that what they say in keep-fit classes. Eimear's mind wanders restlessly. Forgiving means to be merciful; she remembers the first line of a speech she was forced to learn in third year from *The Merchant Of Venice*: 'The quality of mercy is not strained.' What did Portia the Prig know, the quality of mercy is extremely bloody strained. It's strained to screaming point. But what's she to do, lose her husband and a best friend in one fell swoop?

Eimear's being merciful to all three of them by forgiving Kate: to Kate, because she loves her, whether she deserves it or not; to Gloria because she was suffering, trying to accommodate both of them and in danger of pleasing neither; and to herself because she looks magnanimous and keeps a friend she doesn't want to forfeit, even if she failed her at the crunch.

She's known Kate more than quarter of a century, if she turns her back on her now she'll be nudging sixty by the time she builds up another friendship as long-lasting. Besides, she doesn't befriend people readily.

At first when Kate claimed Jack landed one on her, Eimear thought she was slandering him to winkle her way back into her good graces. No dice, sister, I don't buy it, she decided. Then Eimear realised she was starting to sound like something out of a gangster film. The stress was obviously getting to her – she'd wake up one of these days and discover she'd taken to wearing tight sweaters over push-up bras, like Lauren Bacall, and asking men if they knew how to whistle. Just put your lips together and blow. Still, a girl could have a worse role model.

Their slap without the tickle didn't ring true to Eimear. 'Jack's a lover, not a fighter,' she told Gloria. 'He couldn't even tell me face-to-face he was leaving me, he's no giant-killer.'

But Glo insisted he really had punched Kate and Eimear wasn't sorry, though she knew she should be. What pleased her most was that he'd cheated on Kate too, the castor oil remedy for both of them.

'So,' she told Gloria when she relayed the news, 'the great love affair is liquidated. Our very own answer to Dermot and Grainne, to Helelil and Hildebrand, to Rick and Ilse . . .'

'Who?'

'The lovers from *Casablanca*, Humphrey Bogart and Ingrid Bergman, you sap.'

'Right,' Gloria nodded.

'To Liz Taylor and Richard Burton,' Eimear continued, 'to Jane Eyre and Mr Rochester – oh, to hell with the analogies, so the lovers aren't very loving any more. Well, don't ask me to send a sympathy card.'

Eimear punches her pillow and rolls over on to her back. Her eyes stray to the clock. Nearly 2 a.m. and she has work tomorrow. What on earth was Kate thinking of, luring away

215

her husband – even if he is the most easily tempted man in the cosmos? If friendship is supposed to stand for anything, surely it's for incorruptibility in the face of husbands propositioning you.

But . . . oh boy, does Eimear have the whip hand now.

'You abandoned me,' she told Kate, who acquiesced in an extremely satisfying manner.

'You've turned the unthinkable into the unmentionable,' Eimear accused her.

Kate bowed her head humbly.

Sometimes there's a flash of what – mutiny?

'I've wronged you,' Kate struck a silent-movie era pose. 'Let me devote myself to soothing your sting.'

'Try first-degree burns,' Eimear retorted, and Kate was silenced.

Eimear pads out of bed and across the room to the bedroom curtains. The moon is a slice off being full, by tomorrow it'll be Dean Martin's big pizza pie. Everyone imagines she forgave Kate because she's magnanimous, thinks Eimear, as she wraps her arms around herself and hugs tight.

Wrong, she did it because she's a manipulative cow who knows she'll always have a hold over Kate. This will rear its head between them while they have breath in their bodies. Kate will be doing penance till the end of her days. She'll be doing penance into the afterlife, if there is one. She'll be doing penance if they're reincarnated. She may as well carry a bell and chant, 'Unclean, unclean.'

One of the ways Eimear punishes Kate is by forcing her to recount explicit details of their lovemaking. Of course she punishes herself too, in listening, but she's driven to it, she has a compulsion to hear of her husband's adultery and her friend's perfidy.

Did they remove all their clothes or only some? Did she always orgasm? Did he brush her hair afterwards? Did he call her baby girl?

Kate hates answering Eimear's questions but she's always able to make her, she can't refuse Eimear anything. 'Aren't I the happy camper,' says Eimear.

What she hates most is the thought of them kissing. Who invented kissing, anyway? It seems such a strange way of signalling sexual desire. It's caught on big time, that's for sure, although the Eskimos seem to manage very nicely thank you without it. She imagines the reception for the first person in a loincloth who latched on to a snog.

'Listen, lads, I've found this great way of passing the time. You fasten your face on to a woman's and then you suck till the saliva banks up or you run out of breath.'

Eimear giggles as she visualises the catcalls.

But then she sees Kate and Jack kissing in her mind's eye. The image incenses her; sleep is out of the question, she may as well go downstairs and brew up some camomile tea.

Time to put Kate's new-minted loyalty to the test.

'Read these poems,' Eimear orders, presenting her with a sheaf of her scribbles.

Kate scans the first couple, eyebrows disappearing into her hairline.

'Your own work?' she ventures.

'Every last verse,' Eimear smiles beatifically. 'Tell me truly what you think of them, you know how I value your opinion.'

Kate falters.

'I'm thinking of offering them for publication,' Eimear continues, with just a hint of wickedness. 'You could be my legal representative and help me haggle with the publishing houses for the best deal.'

Kate is horrified. 'I deal with conveyancing, I don't know that I'd be much good to you when it comes to bargaining with publishers, Eimear.'

'Nonsense,' she chuckles. 'You were superb in the souk

that time we went to Morocco – remember how you had the prayer-mat salesman on his knees to Allah while you bartered him down.'

'Holiday souvenirs,' she remonstrates, 'it's hardly in the same league as book deals. I know nothing of the publishing world, apart from the fact that poets don't tend to make a lot of money. Most of them have day jobs, which isn't a sign that the world is heaping them with earthly gain.'

'True, but my poetry is very marketable, wouldn't you say? Graphic imagery, topical material like child molestation, impotence, date rape. And then, I'd make excellent copy for the interviewers, we could talk about Jack's priapic tendencies, source of my inspiration, the reviewers will revere me.'

'Eimear, the poetry's abysmal,' Kate says with a hunted look on her face.

'So it is. But why should that be any barrier to success?'

Kate laughs. 'You never fail to amaze me, Mulligan. Maybe your verses will bring you fame and fortune, no one deserves it more. When were you thinking of sending them off?'

'I already have. To Bitchin' Babes Press, they've invited me in for a chat – I think they're interested.'

'That's a stroke of luck.' She's impressed.

'Good luck, bad luck, who knows?' jokes Eimear. 'I may end up a laughing stock, I may be sacked from my nice safe job at nice safe Rathmines Library for writing poetry with profanities in it.'

'Where were the profanities, I missed them.' Kate flicks through the pages. 'Hey, you've rhymed penis with genius here, the guys will love you for that.'

'Not if they read on. I also rhyme bum fluff with dandruff in "Teenagers Never Buy Shampoo But They Sometimes Borrow Yours".'

'You should pen an ode about sharking Beautiful Boys, it might give us some inspiration for our night on the town,' she suggests.

Eimear sucks in her cheeks. 'They make too much noise, those Beautiful Boys/But there are compensations for their loud exclamations/And I could sing hymns to their gilded limbs,' she recites.

'Mulligan, you invented that off the top of your head.' Kate is astonished. 'What will you call it?'

'Paean To Pain,' she pronounces.

'But it's pleasure, not pain,' complains Kate. 'Beautiful Boys are about playtime for grown-up girls.'

'Pleasure has a price above punts and pence,' Eimear tells her.

'That's not another poem, is it?' she asks suspiciously.

'No, just some of my homespun wisdom – or Gloria's, in fact.'

'You're suggesting we'll go off and fall in love with one of these cherubs and end up broken-hearted,' Kate protests. 'Of course that won't happen – we'll be flinging flungs with our eyes wide open, it'll be fun on the run and no expectations.'

'Have it your own way,' Eimear shrugs. 'Do you fancy coming to the publisher's with me? I'll ring Gloria and see if she wants to be part of the gang too. Bitchin' Babes Press will love me, going everywhere with my gal-pals.

'We'll have to work that into the biography for the back of the book. "Eimear O'Brien, who quit librarianship after she won the Nobel Prize for Literature and married the Hollywood star Aidan Quinn, is inseparable from her two dearest friends."'

'Gloria won't come, she's still hibernating,' Kate reminds her. 'The eggs haven't had their full week's bed rest yet. We should go to Ranelagh and check on her later.'

'True, you couldn't rely on Mick the Hick to look after her,' agrees Eimear.

'Mick's still at his mother's. And if he's a hick, so are we.'

'At his mother's!' Eimear is outraged. 'What in the name of God is he playing at?'

Kate shrugs. 'That's between the two of them.'

'Who's looking after her?' demands Eimear.

'I am, I stop by every night to cook her an evening meal – well, bring her a takeaway – and I leave sandwiches and a kettle by her bed to take her through the next day.'

'You'll be canonised next. Why didn't you tell me? I'd have helped out.' Eimear feels excluded.

'Gloria didn't want you to know.'

'What have I done to offend her?'

'Nothing.' Kate presses her eyelids, leaving a dark smear around each one. That's why she's looking so tired, thinks Eimear, Florence Nightingale probably had her mascara half-rubbed off too.

Kate continues: 'Glo's just behaving a little oddly at the moment. She probably thinks I've been so wicked I need to do penance, and what better way than tending a sickbed, while you deserve some peace and quiet.'

'It's ludicrous that they're trying to have a baby.' Eimear is nettled. 'Gloria's convinced a child will work miracles, make Mick her devoted slave. God love her wit – their troubles would be only beginning.'

Kate doesn't want to know.

'All we can do is leave them alone to sort out their own problems,' she replies. 'I think we should drop the subject.'

Eimear is too pumped up to abandon anything. 'Kate, I know you like Mick but he isn't treating Gloria well, even you have to admit that. His disappearing act when she's trying to have his baby is disgraceful. I wouldn't want to share a house, never mind a bed, with a man like that.'

'Your poetry's getting to you,' says Kate. 'You've painted them so black it has you thinking all men are beasts.'

'They are when it comes to money,' Eimear complains.

'Jack being miserly?'

'He wants us to sell the house so he can have his half of the lolly,' she elaborates.

'Selling up sounds fair enough, the property's in your joint names,' Kate suggests cautiously.

'But it's my home,' wails Eimear. 'I don't want some other couple moving into it, it belongs to me. I planted the lilies in the back.'

'Take them with you.'

'Lilies don't travel well,' she carps.

'This has nothing to do with lilies, Eimear. Now let's think it through: could you buy Jack out?'

'No. Maybe.'

'That's helpful,' she smiles. 'Is that a "No. Maybe" as in yes or a "No. Maybe" as in possibly?'

'I thought my poems might drum up some cash. And my hotshot lawyer is pressing for a share of Jack's royalties.'

'The sums won't add up, angel,' Kate explains gently. 'Jack may well owe you some royalties and you may indeed get your own poems published, but it's dicey to expect a golden egg, never mind the goose that laid it into the bargain.'

'I know, I know, but I want to keep the house, I'll never find anywhere I like so well.'

'Can you afford the mortgage on your salary?' Kate is brisk.

'No.'

'So how are you managing?'

'Jack is still paying half the mortgage.'

'Obviously he won't want to do that forever. Could you take in a tenant, use the rent to repay a bank loan and buy Jack out that way?'

'I'd still have to find all the mortgage on my own and I couldn't do that.' Eimear sighs.

'There's only one way forward then, Mulligan,' she chews a strand of red hair that just about stretches to her mouth. 'You know what it is you have to do.'

'Tell me anyway,' she suggests, hoping Kate's version will be more palatable than her own.

'Slap up a "For Sale" sign, walk away and start again. Your equity will buy a little cottage somewhere.'

'But not in Donnybrook, I love Donnybrook, I don't want to live anywhere else.'

'Not in Donnybrook,' Kate agrees, 'but this Dublin 4 address is a lot of nonsense anyway.'

'That's rich coming from someone who can see the trees on St Stephen's Green from her living-room window.' Eimear wanders the room moodily.

'True, but I don't have a semi-detached period house, I have a minute flat with a brown stain on my bathroom ceiling from my overhead neighbour's leaky shower and I have a bedroom a few feet away from the lift, so if anyone uses it at night I hear every creak.'

'You seem to like it there.' Eimear is surprised at her unalluring description.

'I do, but nothing's perfect – welcome to the real world, at the age of almost thirty-three. Being independent isn't all about no queue for the bathroom and having the freedom to wear a face mask in bed. There's a down side too.'

'Donnybrook suits me,' whines Eimear. 'I like the delicatessen on the main road and there's a handy flower shop near the house, the dry-cleaning staff know me by name and I've made friends with my neighbours.'

'Stop your carry-on, Eimear O'Brien, you've only lived in Donnybrook a couple of years, you were perfectly happy in Portobello before that and in Harold's Cross before that.'

Eimear reflects on her previous addresses: she's perfectly right, there was life before Donnybrook.

'You pays your money and you takes your choice,' continues Kate. 'Perhaps you could afford a small flat in Donnybrook if you're determined to stay. Or maybe you might cast your net further afield and try for a cottage in Milltown – you never know what's out there till you start looking. You could head for the hills, you could end up by the seaside, it'll be an adventure.'

An adventure. When she puts it like that . . .

'I haven't had an adventure in years,' remarks Eimear, buoyed up. 'I think I'm ready for one of those yokes.'

CHAPTER 26

Eimear's feeling fluttery. Jack's just phoned and she wasn't expecting to hear his voice on the line. She's over him, of course she is, but she prefers advance warning before speaking to him. So she can settle her emotions, steady her voice, measure her heart-beat. That unreliable organ is still pumping erratically ten minutes after the receiver's been replaced.

'Be still my beating heart,' she instructs it aloud, hoping the sheer nonsense of the admonition will give her a reality check. It doesn't. She eats a square of chocolate to calm herself, wishing she hadn't thrown away that last half-empty packet of cigarettes in a fit of self-improvement.

She was minding her own business, channel-hopping, when the call came.

Jack: 'This is Jack, Eimear.'

Eimear: 'I'd never have guessed.'

(That sounds caustic, why is she starting the conversation on such a negative note?)

Jack: 'We need to talk.'

Eimear: 'Of course.'

(Promising – does he want a reconciliation?)

Jack: 'About the house. We have to move this situation on, sell up and divvy up – I can't afford to keep you in luxury in Donnybrook while I huddle in a couple of minuscule rooms at the top of a building that should be demolished brick by brick.'

Eimear: 'You put it so poetically, my dear.'

(You put it so bluntly, you heap of dung.)

Jack: 'We have to accept the marriage has failed.'

Eimear: 'There's no question about that.'

(So the reconciliation's off.)

Jack: 'My poetry's suffering, I need to get my life in order.'

Eimear: 'I thought writers were supposed to crouch in garrets, summoning their muse by gaslight.'

(He miscalculated badly, he thought he'd have a nest at Kate's as well as a bolthole at Trinity. But she rescinded your parking permit, didn't she, my Jack-in-a-box.)

Jack: 'That's nonsense. I wrote some of my best poetry in Donnybrook.'

Eimear: 'Too bad you turned to your groin for inspiration, you lecherous layabout.'

(Ditto.)

Jack: 'Let's not dredge up old scores, Eimear. We were tearing each other apart, one of us had to be strong for both of us.'

Eimear: 'Big brave boy.'

(Little cowardly man.)

Jack: 'So are you going to be reasonable? About the house?'

Eimear: 'There's an estate agent coming by on Saturday.'

(I'm doing this for me, not you.)

Jack: 'Excellent. Well, I won't take up any more of your time.'

Eimear: 'Feel free, you've wasted five years of my time – what's another five minutes.'

(Shove off and never speak to me again.)

Jack: 'There's nothing much else I had to say. Except – how's Gloria, is she pregnant?'

Eimear: 'Possibly, she doesn't know yet.'

(What's your game?)

Jack: 'When will she know?'

Eimear: 'Later this week.'

(There's something going on here.)

Jack: 'Right, give her my best.'

Eimear: 'Do you have a best? I thought you only had a worst.'

(He's getting to me.)

Jack: 'I'll say goodbye now, Eimear. I'll be in touch again about the house.'

Eimear rustles the chocolate wrapper and speculates about Jack's uncharacteristic interest in Gloria's pregnancy. Is it a wind-up because he knows Eimear wanted their baby? And who told him Glo was having another IVF attempt anyway? Is he trying to imply that he's still in touch with Kate and that she's keeping him informed?

Her brain hurts. Jack O'Brien insinuates himself under her skin like no other man. Imagine having to force-feed herself chocolate just to recover from a telephone conversation with him. Eimear knows she has to take her mind off this, she needs to speak to someone. She lifts the phone again.

'Gloria, it's Eimear here. How's the hatching going? That's good news, fingers crossed – legs too. You sound tired, Glo, I hope you've not gone back to work too early. Any word of Mick? You're kidding, I wish I had a boss like his who'd let me swan off indefinitely. I've just had a phone-call from Jack, he's being his usual arrogant self, ordering me to sell the house so he can get on with being Ireland's Greatest Living Poet in comfort. Apparently he doesn't like his rooms at Trinity as much as he thought he would.

'Anyway I have every intention of selling the house – of course I have, Glo, I decided it ages ago, Kate and I talked about it and I decided to put it all behind me, start a new chapter. It'll be an adventure. Sorry? Well I did mean to talk to you about it but you've been busy with the embryos and I didn't want to distract you from that vital task. No, I'm not being flippant, honestly, Gloria, you're so touchy these days. Look, can we start again?

'The update on my life is that the marital home is now about to be advertised for auction, furniture included. I'm not being rash, I just want rid of it all now. Yes, I know l love my tables and sofas but they're only things and you end up being the one possessed by possessions. Feel free to ask for anything that tickles your fancy – you always liked that hall-stand, it's yours if you want it. Gloria, stop, it was meant as a friendly gesture, I don't know where you come by the notion you'd be a vulture. Offer me twenty pounds if it makes you any happier. Kate's welcome to anything that catches her eye too. Well, she's already had the most important asset of mine that appealed to her, why stop now?

'I know, sometimes resentment oozes out but mostly I can handle it. I have forgiven her, truly I have, it's just when I talk to Jack, pus starts seeping from barely sealed wounds. Anyway I'll be completely free of Jack once I've sold this millstone. I don't know where I'm going, that's the whole point of the adventure, it could be that I'll find a little artisan's cottage in Dundrum that needs renovating. Of course I can handle builders, you must think I've been wrapped in cotton wool all my life. Where did you get that idea from?

'Certainly I like Donnybrook but I'm not wedded to it – there's a divorce coming up, remember. Of course I'll find somewhere I like just as much as Donnybrook, I don't know why you keep banging on about it. New home, new life, new video shop.

'Jack the Rat was asking after you. Gloria? Are you still there, it sounded like you dropped the receiver. You have to go and lie down? A stitch in your side? Mind the embryos, don't lie on your front, take it very, very easy. I'll come straight around. Fair enough then but you rest yourself and I'll call by tomorrow.'

Poor Gloria, thinks Eimear, all alone with three embryos. 'Entombed in the Womb', that would make a good title for a poem – or maybe it's too bleak. How about 'Womb-Mates'?

Hey, she's really thinking like a poet, she's awash with ideas. That woman from Bitchin' Babes will discover she's signed the find of the century.

Euphoria is replaced by reality as she remembers she hasn't enough pieces for a collection, she has to drum up some more. Where's the paper, must get cracking while the tide's in.

The phone side-tracks her.

'What's cooking, Mulligan?' Kate's voice sparkles down the line.

'My brain cells, they're in overdrive. I'm in poetry writing mode. What can I do for you, oh fan of my art?'

'Got a brilliant wheeze,' Kate announces. 'We're all going to a fortune teller.'

'Zippidy-doo-dah.'

'You don't think it's a brilliant wheeze?'

'Oh, I do, from the fortune teller's point of view,' Eimear assures her. 'It's masterly – you troop three gullible women into your tent, invite them to cross your palms with silver, promise them the moon and then show them the door.'

'I don't think silver works any more,' says Kate. 'Fortune tellers have been converted by Ian Paisley, they insist on a silent collection.'

'Look, I tell you what I'm going to do, Kate, I'll hold a few notes against my lighter and promise myself there's an irresistible man waiting to enter my life, plus an inheritance on the sidelines. Then I'll set fire to it and I'll be saved the bother of schlepping off to darkest Ballybogeyman, or wherever your dodgy seer lives.'

'Oh, ye of little faith.' Kate sounds saddened. 'This woman is the Real McCoy. Isabel at work swears by her. She's been house-hunting for a year and had all but given up on finding something. She goes to the fortune-teller, who says she'll be living under her own roof within a few months and hey presto, the next week she hears about a house before it's officially on the market, makes an offer and it's accepted.'

'That's miraculous,' breathes Eimear. 'You don't think that after a year of trying, she was bound to come up with a place sooner or later?'

'But how did Mrs Gilmartin know she was looking for one?' asks Kate triumphantly.

'So that's her name, Mrs Gilmartin, not Gypsy Rose or Madame Olga. It sounds normal enough.'

'She is normal, she just happens to have an abnormal gift. She lives out in Ashbourne, she's a widow, she keeps hens in her backyard, she was babysitting her granddaughter the night Isabel went along. What do you say, Mulligan, will we round up Gloria and make an expedition of it?'

'It's a sinful waste of money but why not. At least you're not bringing us to one of those soothsayers off O'Connell Street that all the tourists visit.'

'Would I?' Kate injects an aggrieved tremor into her voice.

'Yes, you would. Remember the time you tried to force me to hunker down at the foot of the Molly Malone statue and have that dark-haired fellow who sits there with his Tarot cards sort out my future for me?'

'That was nothing to do with fortune telling, I just wanted a closer look at your man,' admits Kate. 'It's not often you get a lad telling fortunes, the girls have the job stitched up.'

'Is that because women are more intuitive?'

'Nah. They just have more time on their hands. So I can definitely count you in then, Mulligan?'

'I may as well, it might spur me on to another poem. "She held my loveline in her hands/And said the track was broken . . ."'

'No more doggerel please,' pleads Kate.

'I'm glad you're not the managing director of Bitchin' Babes Press,' complains Eimear. 'When are you planning this expedition – before or after we go sharking for Beautiful Boys?'

'After, definitely. We want Mrs Gilmartin to give us the

229

low-down on the highfliers we've lined up. I've worked out which nightclub we should hit, it's the Den of Iniquity, the name sounds promising.'

'An omen,' remarks Eimear. 'What about a meeting place, I suppose we have to go to one of those disco bars?'

'It doesn't much matter which one we pick so long as we steer clear of Temple Bar and the stag party herds over from England for the weekend – they'll all be too drunk to be much use to us.'

'Too old, as well.'

'Positively withered.'

'There isn't a rugby international on the same night as our shindig, Kate, is there?' Eimear's panicked. 'We don't want to be distracted by hordes of maudlin fans celebrating their sporting victory over our boyos.'

'Not as far as I know, but I'll double-check. Anyway why should you assume they'll be crowing it over our supporters?'

'Have a titter of wit, woman, when did the Irish team ever win a match, especially on home ground?'

'True.'

'Isn't the Den of Iniquity popular with Trinity students?' Eimear asks casually.

'As far as I know,' Kate responds, instantly cagey. There's a pause, then she continues: 'Is that a problem? I don't think it would be the lecturers' scene if that's what's worrying you.'

'The last thought on my mind,' she assures Kate. 'I have nothing against Trinity students, wasn't I one myself. It was an idle thought, no hidden agenda.'

'I've just remembered something else about Mrs Gilmartin,' says Kate. 'At the end of your visit she tells you to concentrate on whatever you want most in the world, hold the thought and then she lets you know if it will happen for you.'

'We might as well toddle back to the Killiney angel,' says Eimear. 'I'd rather wish on him than on Mrs Gilmartin with her hens in the back yard in Ashbourne.'

'He wasn't bad, our winged totem, he made my wish come true.'

'What was it?' Eimear is curious, it's not like Kate to be so forthcoming.

'The three of us friends again, no more cheating and evasion.' Her voice has an uncharacteristic catch. 'How about your wish?'

'I've forgotten what I asked for,' lies Eimear. 'I'm going to watch television now, there's a film on RTE I want to see.'

'Chick flick? I'll tune in myself if it is.'

'*Splendor in the Grass*.'

'Oh boy,' Kate exclaims, 'the chick flick par excellence, Warren Beatty and Natalie Wood, consumed with unconsummated lust at high school in Kansas. Which channel did you say it was on? Here come the titles, catch up with you later, Mulligan.'

Eimear switches on the television set but keeps the sound to mute. Warren is necking energetically with Natalie in an open-topped car, while a waterfall pounds in the background. Very subtle, Mr Director. Warren climbs on top of Natalie, she pushes him off, he thumps the door in frustration, she's apologetic.

Women are far too conciliatory, thinks Eimear, as she pulls the notepad towards her, not to write poetry but to compile a list.

She writes PRIORITIES IN MY NEW HOME, underlines it and starts with

Period Features

She crosses that out and replaces it with

With built-in shelves for all her awards, she giggles. And a side entrance for all her lovers. Why not aim high?

CHAPTER 27

It's Eighties Night in the Den of Iniquity (chance would be a fine thing) but the DJ has jumbled up his decades and is urging the punters to get dancing in the street. Kate, Eimear and Gloria are tempted to take him at his word and jiggle amid the traffic outside because the dance floor is jammed to capacity. A heaving mass of bodies are writhing – like one of those scary dark canvasses by artists in the pay of the Vatican showing the contortions of the damned. It's a vista that calls for alcohol. Fast. Kate hacks her way to the bar and orders a bottle of wine, just the house white but she's dazzled by the price.

'Unless it's the strobe lighting kicking in,' she tells Eimear.

All Kate and Eimear can say for the wine is that it's wet. Presumably it's alcoholic too because halfway down the second glass apiece they decide to Walk Like an Egyptian – there's a very insistent voice over the speakers recommending it. They toy with the idea of undulating with feet and hands at right angles around the table but discard it on the grounds they can shimmy at their own kitchen tables any day of the week. They're on a Girls' Night Out and they intend to have fun.

So off they bolt for the dance floor, desperate to do their Bangles impersonations before the song is over; naturally it ends just as they find a space to cavort seductively – and another space for their handbags but, hey, Gloria assures them, it's cool to bop around your Jane Shilton these days.

A slow set starts up so they file back towards the Argentinian vino.

'Isn't it amazing how even a few seconds of dancing leave you gasping for expensive cheap wine,' remarks Kate.

Eimear is tapped up, as they used to say at school discos – literally tapped on the shoulder by a lad of seventeen or so, who jerks his head towards the dance floor and reaches for her hand.

'Go for it, Mulligan,' Gloria and Kate yell encouragingly, as she suffers herself to be led, pantomiming extreme reluctance. This is too entertaining to miss, at the risk of looking like wallflowers they elbow a space at the side of the dance floor to watch. Eimear is back beside them halfway through the song, however, when they've only had a chance to run hands up and down their bodies suggestively a few times.

'Ah Lord, could you not have given the poor lad till the end of the dance at least,' protests Gloria. 'Such an innocent, and he wearing the shirt that his mother ironed for him only a few hours earlier.'

Eimear arches an eyebrow. 'I need a drink. That innocent has just told me he was voted best at head in his class and that only regular practice can keep him, um, ahead.'

They troop back to their table, sorrowing at the forward behaviour of the younger generation. Someone has emptied the bottle in their absence and stubbed a cigarette out in Gloria's glass of Ballygowan. She's had a positive pregnancy test so she's with the girls in spirit but sticking to water.

Gloria volunteers to trek barwards for another bottle – 'Is it Chateau Vinegar Hill I have to ask for?' – and Eimear and Kate contemplate the dribble in their glasses in her absence.

Kate leans across to gossip about Gloria's annunciation but it's impossible to make Eimear understand.

'What? You're what? You'll have to speak up, Kate, it's like living inside a tom-tom drum here. Without wanting

234

to sound like my mother, we're probably doing irreversible damage to our eardrums just sitting here.'

Kate gives up and sways along to the Floaters instead. 'Float, float on,' she mouths, the words gobbled by the sound system.

'I'm sure that was a hit in the seventies; this DJ doesn't know his stuff,' Kate complains, but Eimear doesn't see her lips move, she's watching the action on the dance floor.

'Cancerous, and my name is Barry,' Kate's singing, still with the Floaters, as Gloria returns from the bar with their nectar of the gods – they're easily pleased by this stage.

'The next time we want a bop, we should do it around the bottle as well as our handbags,' Kate shrills in a gap between songs. 'No point in being taken for saps twice.'

'Sound idea,' agrees Eimear.

Gloria cradles her bottle of Ballygowan possessively.

'We'll dress up in ra-ra skirts and frilly shirts and comb sugar through our hair to achieve the Steve Strange electrocution look if we come here again,' says Eimear.

'Quick, look,' says Gloria, 'there's a fellow out there who's the spit of Mr Collins, our first-year geography teacher.'

They peer through the weaving dancers, past a Boy George lookalike, and catch a glimpse of an Adam Ant pirate who does indeed bear a fleeting resemblance to the idolised Mr Collins. He only lasted one year at the convent but he metamorphosed during those three terms from someone in a collar and tie to a man who wore polo necks and let his hair grow and then, in the penultimate week, to a free spirit in denim flares with bumble bees and butterflies rioting up the sides. Kate smiles. How the nuns must have fretted when he pitched up for class looking like someone who stepped out of a commune, but he was working out his notice by then and they were powerless.

'He was a complete child of the sixties in his cheesecloth shirts and flares,' recalls Gloria wistfully.

'Except we were more than halfway through the seventies by then,' Eimear points out.

'True, but Omagh always was a decade behind,' interjects Kate.

They sigh in unison, thinking of their deprived youth in a backward country town. Kate was amazed, the last time she went home, how much it had come on. Or maybe she's getting old. 'Desist, you evil thoughts, I'm here to drink myself comatose and prowl for Beautiful Boys,' she rallies herself.

'Whatever happened to Mr Collins?' asks Eimear.

'He travelled around Europe for a year or two, then went back to teaching in the end. Married a teacher he trained with, who wore little round granny specs, and they're living in Dundalk now,' Kate tells her.

'I heard they called their first baby Free but it turned out to be Fee, short for Fiona,' adds Gloria.

They digest this depressing information, until Gloria snaps them from their reveries.

'I know they're a bit passé but how about we give a Seventies Nights a go, get into all that Bee Gees disco beat, it'd be a hoot.'

'We laughed at it first time round,' protests Kate. 'Can't we laugh at something different now?'

'We fancied John Travolta though,' admits Eimear.

'True but we were ashamed of it,' the others remind her.

They're distracted by a slender drunk wearing a pair of dungarees – 'Dexy's Midnight Runners fan or a farm boy too rushed to change?' speculates Kate – who walks a wavy line towards their table and enunciates slowly and distinctly, 'You ladies are each so gorgeous you take my breath away. Would one of you do me the honour of a dance?'

'Feck off,' says Kate.

'For God's sake, Kate, we came here to boogie,' hisses Gloria. 'I'll dance with you, sonny,' she adds, rising to her feet.

'I was really hoping for the good-looking one,' he complains as he lurches after her.

'He meant you,' Kate tells Eimear, who shrugs and takes a drink.

'Don't you know he did,' Kate insists.

Eimear scrutinises her coolly. 'My pretty face didn't keep my husband interested.'

Spandau Ballet are singing an interminable song about cutting a long story short, but failing to deliver on their promise. Kate doesn't know how to answer Eimear.

Finally she responds: 'Neither did my plain one.'

They look steadily at each other. 'Bastard,' they spit in unison, and then dissolve in giggles.

'I don't know what they've put in this wine but it works for me,' chokes Eimear.

'Alcohol,' Kate tells her. 'They've put alcohol in the wine, it's never known to fail.'

Gloria returns, minus her pixilated infant, and demands to know what the joke is.

'Is it your man? I know he was making a show of me on the dance floor but what could I do,' she complains.

'Regard it as your good deed for the day, he looked about the right age to be a boy scout,' says Kate, and seconds later they're gasping and waving their legs in the air.

'Come on, now, seriously, I thought we were on the pull,' says Eimear, after they've wiped away the tears, thumped Gloria on the back for her hiccups and had a calming drink of wine. 'We mustn't keep turning down fellows who ask us for a dance, we might regret it, there could be a shortage of them.'

'Who was it said, "How extravagant you are, throwing away men like that. Someday they may be scarce"?' asks Kate.

'It was the chief of police in *Casablanca*,' says Eimear. 'And he said women, not men.'

'Same idea,' she shrugs. 'Maybe we are being profligate. We don't seem to be meeting many Beautiful Boys.'

'That's because there aren't any here,' Kate points out. 'Obviously the Den of Iniquity isn't their happening habitat any more.'

'Never mind,' says Gloria, 'let's have another dance.'

Eimear and Kate ignore her as they mournfully survey the lack of talent.

'The options are limited,' admits Kate, after a profitless scan. 'There's maudlins and toddlers, the choice is yours, Mulligan.'

'You mean the lack of choice.'

'If you were so keen on being picked up, why didn't you skip off with the lad you danced with?'

'Do me a favour,' protests Eimear. 'He was both drunk and under-age – I have my standards, it's either or.'

'Fair enough,' Kate concedes. 'But why should we sit around waiting for one of them to approach us? We're modern, vibrant, unattached women (apart from Gloria, who doesn't count) in the prime of life, let's each select a man and put the moves on him ourselves.'

They stare at her, aghast.

'There's being independent and there's being independent. Surely you're not suggesting we ask fellows to dance,' exclaims Gloria.

'They'll think we're sluts,' Eimear backs her up.

'Times have changed and Irishmen with them,' Kate reassures them. 'It's cool to ask a man to dance, he won't think any the worse of the woman that does.'

They regard her doubtfully, then Eimear empties her glass and stands up purposefully.

'You're right, Kate. I'll show them mine if they'll show me theirs. Here goes.'

She walks across to a tall, dark-haired man leaning against the bar. How did they miss this one, he looks both soberish and thirtyish. The catch with no apparent catches (yet) bends his head to listen to Eimear and they speak for a moment. Then she turns and walks back to her seat.

'Did he say no – what happened?' They're agog.

Eimear serenely refills her wine glass, gulps from it and replies: 'I bottled it.'

'You mean you didn't ask him for a dance?'

'No, I asked him if he knew what time last orders were.'

They carry on drinking until the bottle is empty and Gloria suggests they may as well dance with each other since no one else seems inclined to manhandle them. She also insists on taking the empty bottle with her to boogie around, an astonishingly drunken suggestion from someone awash with water.

When they return to their table, the tall, dark-haired stranger is waiting with a bottle of wine – not the house gut-rot they've been knocking back – and four glasses.

'I hope you don't think I'm being too forward but I'm bored senseless over there on my own and wondered if you ladies would mind having a drink with me. I'll go quietly as soon as you tire of me. You've only to ask.' He flashes a smile at each of them in turn. A disarming smile.

His name is Christy Troy and they agree later that he looks a bit like Pierce Brosnan, only real. He's been on the fizzy water all night because he's chauffeuring his sister and a group of friends who're helping to celebrate her twenty-first birthday.

'I'll just have the one glass of wine, then it's back on the wagon for me – the guards will be out in force on a Saturday night,' he explains, as he offers up a toast.

He has pale grey eyes fringed by the blackest lashes, Kate notices; she's a pushover for long lashes. Someone told her once premature babies often have long lashes but she doesn't think there's anything premature about their new acquaintance – he's arrived at exactly the right time. Lucky for him he's not wearing a flying jacket or she'd ravish him here and now.

'To beginnings,' announces Christy, and they chorus 'beginnings', exchanging covert glances.

This man is too good to be true. An Irishman who doesn't drink and drive and who gives up a Saturday night to look after his little sister – it has to be a front. He must be a drug baron or a student priest or a nutter. Still, if he's a looper he's easy on the eye.

'Which is your sister?' asks Gloria.

He gestures towards a manic throng of girls in the centre of the dance floor.

'That young one over there with the suede pixie boots and the pedal pushers,' he points.

Kate peers but can't detect anyone with a family resemblance at this distance. Specs are needed but not just yet – she's the St Augustine of the optically challenged.

'Could they not take a taxi home?' she asks, more to encourage him to look at her than because she cares about the answer.

'Sure who's able to find a taxi on the streets of Dublin these days?' shrugs Christy. 'It's not every day your baby sister turns twenty-one, I can manage one night among the tots in the Den of Iniquity. I'm not sure how many more fizzy waters I can stomach though, they have my insides churning – do you know they cost the same as a beer, it's criminal.'

They chat for a while, roar actually, the DJ seems to be increasing the volume as the night wears on. It turns out Christy's a press photographer and renovating a Victorian railwayman's cottage a couple of miles from his parents' home – what a relief, thinks Kate, she thought they might have bagged one of those lads who stay at home till they're thirty-seven and then decide to get married because the Mammy's not able to wait on them hand and foot any more.

He has to be over thirty because he lets slip that he finds eighties nostalgia nights depressing – it seemed like only ten minutes ago he was driving around Dublin with his 'Who Shot JR?' bumper sticker listening to a tape by a hot new band called U2.

It's difficult to say which of the three Christy Troy is interested in. He takes them out one after another for a slow dance, starting with Gloria.

'But that could be because he's sitting next to her,' Kate and Eimear hearten each other while they're watching them shuffle.

He moves on to Kate, who has Christy in stitches when she tells him the proper manner of inviting a woman to dance in her part of the country is to ask, 'Would you face me?'

'They don't really say that in Tyrone, do they?' he demands.

'No,' she admits regretfully. 'Probably not. Except maybe in VERY remote areas.'

Christy finishes the set with Eimear, to Kate's disappointment. She was hoping to hang on to him for a couple of dances once they were out there on a dance floor bearing an increasing resemblance to Sodom and Gomorrah before the plug was pulled on the party. Kate looks at him smiling down into Eimear's face and sighs. He saved the best till last, like Angel Clare carrying Tess across a water-logged road in *Tess of the d'Urbervilles*.

Christy sticks to his word and returns to the Ballygowan after his single glass of wine.

'Did he do anything he shouldn't have when he was dancing with you?' Kate asks Eimear.

'Sadly no,' she responds.

'Me neither.'

Gloria looks horrified when the same question is put to her. 'I'm not on the market, Mick and I are simply taking a break from each other,' she says. Then she smirks. 'Mind you, a few more smoochy sessions with that fella and Mick could be consigned to history.'

Eimear grabs her by the arm. 'Are you saying he smooched you on the dance floor?' she demands.

'There, there, Eimear,' says Gloria. 'It was just an expression. He was the perfect gentleman. Dammit.'

'Maybe he doesn't fancy any of us, he's just putting in an evening the best way he can while he's building up bonus points for heaven via his sister,' Kate suggests, and all three look gloomy. The effects of the alcohol seem to be wearing off.

Christy has left them while this conversation is going on, claiming he needs to check on his sister; just as it occurs to his trio of admirers he's sloped off because he's bored to tears with elderly dollies when he could have his pick of nubile teenagers, he returns. As charming as ever, full of stories about the nightmare of doing up an old house and how his mother keeps dropping by with flasks of tea and banana sandwiches and then staying all day so he can't get any work done. They're so engrossed, collectively, they hardly realise the DJ is saying:

'Good night, drive carefully and God bless. You groovy animals.'

That's added after the God bless in case it sounds too square.

The lights come on when they're least prepared for them and they're pink-faced and blinking, with their lipstick sucked off from wine and giggling. Except for Eimear, who looks as dazzling as she did at 8.30 p.m. when they met up. Christy offers them a lift home but they say his sister is his priority and they're known for their uncanny ability to track down taxis in this cab-challenged city, so off he goes. But not before arranging to meet the trio in a couple of days' time at the film centre, where a Marx Brothers season is starting.

'It's a bit odd that, wanting to meet all three of us – he isn't into some group sex kick, is he?' Kate tests out her theory on the others.

'Only time will tell,' says Gloria, while Eimear smiles secretively.

'It's harder the older you get, this picking up fellows malarkey,' Kate muses as they queue for their coats.

'Was it ever easy?' asks Gloria.

'What are you smiling about, Mona Lisa?' Kate confronts Eimear. 'Do you have certain information you need to share with the group, about Christy-can-any-man-be-this-perfect-and-not-a-psychopath-Troy?'

'No,' she fiddles with her blonde bob, still smiling cryptically.

'No talking till we reach the taxi queue, it's lengthening by the micro-second,' Gloria interrupts, shepherding both towards the door.

Kate glances at Eimear.

'You're at it again with that smiling,' she says. 'It's down to Christy, isn't it?'

'Maybe,' she concedes.

'And?' Kate's inflexible. Jealous, too.

'I just have a feeling about him,' says Eimear.

'What sort of feeling?' asks Gloria, still chivvying them taxi-wards.

'A feeling that we'll all be seeing a lot more of Christy.'

'Is that so,' Kate responds, as the icy air roars around their ankles. 'So one of us has managed to pull. The million-dollar question is, which one?'

'I don't think even Christy knows that yet,' answers Eimear. 'The field is wide open and may the best man win.'

'I always wanted to be a best man but nobody ever asked me,' complains Gloria.

'Let's put this child to bed,' Kate tells Eimear, who nods in agreement.

'It's not the winning or losing that counts,' Kate adds, as

Gloria starts working out how many are ahead of them in the queue.

'It isn't?' Eimear sounds surprised.

'No, it's the shagging.'

CHAPTER 28

'That wasn't a very profitable tally on the Beautiful Boys hunt,' complains Kate, as they lounge in her flat dissecting their evening. Sunday papers are scattered around, coffee rings decorating their covers. She notices Eimear looking about and shuddering.

'The Mr Sheen is on the shelf above the washing machine,' Kate tells her, 'feel free to polish while we chat.'

She ignores her and picks up the *Sunday Independent*, which has a photograph of Grace Kelly on the front of its Living section. Eimear looks a lot like Grace Kelly, if you can imagine her without the hat and gloves, thinks Kate, looking over her shoulder.

'Maybe there aren't any Beautiful Boys in Dublin,' suggests Gloria. 'Perhaps you have to go to Sicily or Corfu to find them.'

Kate can see Eimear checking her mug for stains before she drinks out of it – she catches her eye and takes a guilty swig.

'We didn't do too badly in the end,' Eimear says, setting the mug down on Grace Kelly's pearl choker.

'You mean St Christopher?' enquires Kate, 'patron saint of little sisters and rescuer of bored damsels in nightclubs?'

'My head hurts,' says Eimear, 'I drank too much last night, I've filled my poor body with toxins. Of course I mean Christy, who else would I be talking about?'

'He could turn out to be a pig in a poke,' remarks Kate.

'We're not buying him, just going to the pictures with him. Now never mind about Christy Troy, what about the fellow in the leather jacket and designer stubble you danced with, the one who said at the end of the set, "Don't fall for me, babe, I'm trouble." Was he for real?'

'No, he lived in Cloud-Cuckoo-Land.' Kate sniggers as she remembers her self-styled heartbreaker. 'Oh, don't make me laugh, Eimear, it feels as though my head might fall off my neck and bounce on the floor when I do that.'

'If we'd any sense we'd have a hair of the dog, that'd cure us,' says Eimear.

'Could you face alcohol?' Kate is amazed.

'Absolutely not, but I'd kill for a cigarette,' she replies. 'I'm going to have to run out for a packet.'

'Will power, Mulligan,' she admonishes. 'Gloria, quick, think of something to distract Eimear.'

'There's a lot to be said for drinking water,' she responds.

'Don't be so sanctimonious,' Kate objects. 'If you weren't pregnant you'd be as hungover as the two of us.'

'No, for a hangover, I mean. Your body is dehydrated, it's crying out for oceans of water, not' – and she looks pointedly at Eimear – 'nicotine.'

'Gloria,' Eimear says, 'explain to me again how come you're finally pregnant but you and Mick aren't dancing on air. How come, in fact, that you seem to be going your separate ways, since he's applied for a job in Omagh and you say you have no intention of leaving Dublin.'

'Kate . . .' Gloria looks imploring.

Eimear purses her lips suspiciously. 'You two are in cahoots; what am I not being told?'

'It's up to Gloria to fill you in,' shrugs Kate.

'Gloria?' Eimear's eyes swivel back towards her.

Gloria turns scarlet, then white, then scarlet again. 'It's not Mick's baby,' she mumbles.

Eimear's astonishment is so pronounced it resembles caricature. She turns to Kate for confirmation, registers her nod and regards Gloria again.

'Whose is it, Glo? You haven't met anyone else, how could you just magic up a father for your baby?'

Gloria throws Kate a beseeching look.

'She doesn't know who the father is, she had donor sperm,' says Kate.

Eimear's eyes are like saucers – flying saucers – she couldn't radiate any more astonishment if a little green alien appeared and said, 'Take me to your leader.'

'I didn't know you could use donor sperm in Ireland, I thought that sort of freewheeling behaviour only went on in America or England,' Eimear finally manages to speak.

Gloria is still so resolutely silent, but looking completely dismayed, that Kate feels dishonour-bound to supply all the answers.

'No, we do it here too,' she lies glibly, 'but the hospital doesn't like to advertise it or the hell-and-damnation pickets would be out in force.'

'So Gloria doesn't have a notion who her baby's father is.' Eimear studies Gloria with the same detachment she'd examine a specimen in a glass case.

'Not a baldy,' Kate agrees cheerfully. 'It'll be quite exciting, won't it, Gloria, wondering what he'll look like and who he takes after if he turns out to have brown eyes.'

Gloria's green eyes flash daggers but she's mute.

'I can't get over it,' says Eimear. 'Our Glo carrying a mystery man's baby. How does it feel, dote?'

Gloria shifts in her seat. 'I'm not sure yet, it's taking some adjusting.'

'Of course it must be. Didn't Mick do the business then?'

'No, he refused to provide the necessary sperm so I was given a donation,' says Gloria. 'For which I'm extremely grateful, but I don't know anything about the father – nor do I want to. He's not the father at all as far as I'm concerned.'

'He's just a sperm bank in the sky,' suggests Kate.

Malevolent doesn't begin to describe the look Gloria flings in her direction.

'Mick must be raging,' remarks Eimear. 'He must feel cuckolded.'

'You've been reading Chaucer again, haven't you,' interrupts Kate. 'Men haven't been cuckolded since women gave up wearing wimples.'

'How is Mick taking it, anyway?' Eimear presses.

'He's moving 112 miles away from me, that must give you some indication of his feelings on the subject,' responds Gloria.

Unexpectedly, Eimear bursts out laughing. She's doubled over and choking with mirth, incapable of speech. When she finally wipes away the tears, she gasps, between chuckles: 'You dark horse, Gloria McDermott, you sly dog, you crafty puss . . .'

'That's enough animal imagery,' Gloria interrupts. 'I need afternoon naps these days since the morning sickness keeps me awake half the night. I think I'll head home, see you guys later in the week.'

'Aren't you coming to *Duck Soup* with Christy?'

'No, you and Kate go without me, I was only sharking with you two to show willing last night. I'm not all that gone on men at the moment.'

'Join the club,' says Eimear. 'We're only seeing Christy so we can punish him for the misdemeanours of his gender.'

'Speak for yourself, Mulligan, I want to shag him.'

'How will that punish him?' enquires Eimear.

'He'll be gutted when I stop.'

Kate and Eimear stand at the window and watch Gloria climb into her Corsa, parked on a double yellow line that matches it exactly, but minus a ticket since it's a Sunday.

They wave enthusiastically but she doesn't look up.

'How come you knew about this immaculate conception and I didn't?' demands Eimear.

Kate debates how much of the truth to tell her. 'Mick rang me,' she says, having stalled for time by drinking some cold coffee.

'Why?'

'He trusts me. I need more coffee and I'm out of beans, will we wander down to Bewley's?'

'Use instant. Why did he ring you?'

'My brain cells won't work without a double espresso. Are you coming or not?'

Eimear is stern. 'Kate McGlade, sit down on this footstool thing of yours immediately and tell me everything – repeat, everything – you know about Gloria's baby.'

Kate holds her hands up in surrender. 'OK, ma'am, I'll cough, only ple-ee-ee-ase let me inject some caffeine into my jaded veins first. We'll go to Bewley's, my treat, and I'll reveal all over a jam doughnut.'

'An iced one,' Eimear stipulates, lifting her denim jacket and flicking her blonde hair over the collar.

'I bet Grace Kelly never wore a denim jacket,' says Kate, pulling on an oversized black sweatshirt with Notre Dame emblazoned on the front. The university, not the church with gargoyles, she's always telling the people who pause to read her chest.

'Has Grace Kelly anything at all to do with Gloria's baby?' Eimear asks.

'Nothing,' admits Kate, glad she can answer at least one of her questions honestly. Though it's downhill from here on in, she expects.

As they cut through the Green to Grafton Street, each lost in their thoughts, Kate mulls over how much of the real story she can tell Eimear. This is Gloria's mess, she doesn't know why she's suddenly the contract cleaner. Then again,

Gloria did stand by her when she lost her head over Jack. But, complains the Greek chorus in her brain, Eimear's sure to find out eventually that you lied to her yet again. You're only just off the hook over Jack, it's a miracle she forgave you – cover up for Gloria and you're likely to be dangling again, without any prospect of a reprieve.

'We should've brought some bread for the ducks,' Eimear interrupts the wrestling match in Kate's conscience.

'The bread-bin's empty.'

'Is there never any food in your flat, Kate?'

She reflects. 'There's a tin of tuna in the press and a French stick in the freezer. I think I have a jar of olives somewhere too.'

'Enough to feed the five thousand,' Eimear congratulates her. 'And there was me thinking your cupboard was bare.'

'I live slap-bang in the centre of Dublin, if I want food it's just a few steps away at any time of the day or night.' Kate defensively rubs at a toothpaste smear on her sleeve.

'A fridge is just a few steps away too. It wouldn't hurt you to feed it with salads and fish or meat occasionally, the sad little box must think it's forgotten,' Eimear points out.

'Don't you worry about my fridge, it gets plenty of wine and beer to look after. I bought it a lemon the other day, it should count itself lucky. Imagine if it belonged to a horrible man who shoved it full of sausages and black pudding, or to a family who had it packed to the gunnels with microwave chips and chicken nuggets.'

By now they're at Bewley's and Eimear nabs a table while Kate queues.

'Deferment officially over,' pronounces Eimear, as Kate gulps the black coffee. 'Spit it out.'

Kate points to her doughnut quizzically but Eimear doesn't even pretend to find that amusing. So she takes a deep breath and starts talking.

'Mick rang me from Omagh the day of Gloria's egg extraction

and asked me to drive her home. He realised she'd have to get the eggs taken out but what he wasn't banking on was donor sperm,' she explains.

'What a creep, letting Gloria go through the treatment and then leaving her in the lurch at the pivotal stage.'

'It wasn't the kindest action but he obviously decided they weren't ready for parenthood. He argued it would be more irresponsible to charge on and have a baby in a creaky relationship.'

'I don't understand where it all went wrong for them,' Eimear laments. 'They were devoted to each other. Does nobody stay in love forever any more?'

'Our parents seem to be meandering along amicably enough.'

'That's because they make do. They've turned it into a virtue. They aren't necessarily happy, they've just stopped asking themselves if they are.'

'Maybe we pose the question too often.' Kate turns her doughnut around and around, trying to decide which side the jam is likeliest to squirt out from. 'Maybe the secret of happiness is to stop wondering if you are and just get on with being. If that makes sense.'

'It doesn't,' answers Eimear, picking icing off her bun.

'Look, Mulligan,' she tries again, 'Gloria and Mick have been together since she was sixteen. That's getting on for seventeen years now. You're not the same at thirty-three as you are at sixteen, it stands to reason. Do you honestly think Romeo would've felt the same way about Juliet ten years down the line? He'd have been declaiming soliloquies about her warts and bad breath.'

'Suppose so,' says Kate. 'But I still wish . . .'

'Save it for Mrs Gilmartin. In the meantime, Glo's having a baby on her own, and it's a conscious choice because she can't expect Mick to take on the child. So she's going to need our support.'

'So much for that high-minded "I want the family package and baby makes three" lecture she gave me.'

'She did want the family package but sometimes you can only play the cards you're dealt,' Kate reminds Eimear. 'Another doughnut, Mulligan? We'll have you eating like a real woman yet.'

'I'll get the doughnuts in,' she laughs. 'And I already eat like a real woman.'

'True, but only on alternate days.'

She watches Eimear glide through the crowds to the cake counter – heads turn as she passes but she doesn't notice. Eimear hasn't a notion that Jack is the father of Gloria's baby – sweet Jesus, let it stay that way.

CHAPTER 29

Christy leaps to his feet as they approach the corner table he's saved in the café area of the Irish Film Centre. 'Good Grief, a gentleman,' Kate whispers to Eimear. And one who's taller than her too, double brownie points all round.

'Only two of us, I'm afraid. You've been stood up by Gloria,' Kate tells him.

'I'm the luckiest man alive, meeting two glamorous women, it would be gluttony to expect three of you,' he assures them.

Irishmen, thinks Kate, honey just drips from their tongues.

'Nothing wrong with a bit of healthy greed.' She accepts the chair he holds for her.

Christy's effort to attract the bar-girl's attention is futile.

'I'm useless at impressing women,' he grins, and walks to the counter to place his order.

'Coffee?' Kate asks Eimear, surprised, when they're alone.

'Nobody's stopping you drinking wine, I just happen to like the coffee in here,' she shrugs. 'Anyway I've been bevying too much lately, it's playing havoc with my skin.'

'Your complexion, oh Helen of Troy, is as lovely as it was on the day Paris first sighted it,' Kate teases. 'As well you know.'

Eimear smiles back. 'Why do any of us need men when we've friends to keep our ego levels topped up?'

'It's a mystery, Mulligan,' agrees Kate. 'Let's walk away right now before Christy comes back with the drinks.'

'We will not.' Eimear's voice rises in alarm. 'I like Groucho Marx, I want to see the film.'

'Course you do, angel. That's why you're wearing the turquoise earrings that match your eyes – you always colour co-ordinate to go sit in a darkened cinema.'

Christy's return checks their sparring match.

'You've probably forgotten which is who,' says Eimear, accepting her coffee gracefully. 'This is Kate, Gloria's the one that got away and I'm Eimear.'

'I don't need reminding.'

There are faint freckles on Christy's nose and he's wearing a navy linen shirt with a button-down collar that turns his eyes from silver to dark grey.

Snap out of it, McGlade, Kate admonishes herself, it's Eimear he's connecting with. She should do the decent and slope off while neither of them are looking. But she sits on and sips her wine.

'You're the librarian,' he tells Eimear, 'and you're the solicitor,' his gaze turns to Kate. 'I have a good memory.'

'Did your sister enjoy her twenty-first?' Kate wonders.

'Every last alcoholic minute of it; it made me feel my age though.'

'Which is?' Kate asks.

'I'll be thirty-two next birthday,' he answers. 'That must sound ancient to the pair of you.'

'Antique,' Kate assures him. 'That's why we're only willing to go to the flicks with you, they turn the lights out. We're terrified of being spotted in public beside you, it would do our swinging image untold harm.'

'Ouch, you believe in telling it like it is, Kate. So what made you take pity on an old man like myself?'

'Charity work,' she explains. 'We belong to a voluntary organisation called the Compassionate Sisters – we're pledged to brighten the dull life of a thirty-something man on a weekly basis. We do it in pairs, to protect our virtue. You wouldn't believe the advances these geriatrics make on a novice do-gooder.' Kate looks downcast at the wickedness of the world.

'Is this true?' Christy appeals to Eimear.

'On my honour,' she replies gravely.

'Which is a pearl beyond price,' Kate tells Christy, who's staring from one to the other as though they're bats.

'It's not too late to escape, you can pretend you're stepping over to pick up a programme and then run like the wind,' Kate stage-whispers to him.

He regards her indulgently. I'm entertaining him, but it's still Eimear he fancies, she thinks.

'I'd say it's showtime,' he says. 'At least another kind of showtime – shall we buy our tickets for *Duck Soup*?'

He sits between the girls during the film, which prevents them from discussing him sotto voce at the boring bits. It shows he knows women – of course he has at least one sister.

Kate leans across to him. 'How many sisters do you have, Christy?'

'Four,' he replies. 'Three younger, one older.'

Rats, he'll be privy to inside information, she thinks. They're not going to run rings around this one.

'One's probably about your age,' adds Christy. 'How old did you say you were?'

'I didn't,' Kate explains. 'Classified information – I could tell you, but I'd have to kill you.'

'Sssh, the film's starting,' scolds Eimear.

In the bar afterwards, Eimear volunteers to fetch the drinks.

'That's some girl,' says Christy appreciatively.

Defeated, Kate decides to be magnanimous. 'She's a poet too, a woman of many talents is our Eimear.'

He gazes at her back with renewed interest, if that's possible. 'Would I have read any of her work?'

'Not yet, she has her first collection coming out in a few

months, but I'm sure if you speak nicely to her she'll show you something in advance.'

'I always speak nicely to lovely ladies, I make it a rule,' he responds.

Just as well it's Eimear he's enamoured of, much more of this syrup and her teeth would rot. Eimear returns, balancing three glasses – the coffee's fallen by the wayside, she's decided Christy's safely in her coils and her complexion's passed muster. As she hands Kate her wine, she notices something different about her left hand. She checks the other one to be certain – yup, her wedding band has finally been removed. Eimear's wearing a signet on her ring finger, as though too self-conscious to leave it bare.

'How do the two of you fancy a day by the seaside on Saturday?' asks Christy, waiting for his Guinness to settle.

'Afraid I have something arranged for this Saturday but you're free, aren't you, Eimear?' Kate kicks her under the table.

'Ouch!' she says.

'Is that a yes or a no?' Christy enquires.

She hesitates, glances at Kate and says, 'Can I let you know?'

'By all means,' he agrees. 'I'll give you my mobile number. I'm out and about a lot so it's a safer bet than the home or office lines.'

He produces a white card with Independent Newspapers printed on it and his name in smaller type at the bottom.

'So it's the *Irish Independent* you work for.' Eimear strokes the card's embossed surface. 'It must be a fascinating job.' She stares deep into his eyes and winds a skein of blonde hair around her finger.

Talk about feeling superfluous. Would they even notice if she stood up and left, wonders Kate.

'People always imagine that it's glamorous but it's just a job really, it has boring days and exciting days like any other,' says

Christy, angled so far forward towards her it's a wonder they don't abandon all pretence at decorum and leap on each other then and there. Body language, the ultimate giveaway.

'Although I did go up to Aras An Uachtarain yesterday to photograph the President,' he adds.

'I suppose that's the advantage men have over Beautiful Boys,' Kate comments to no one in particular.

Christy looks puzzled, Eimear furious.

'They have jobs they can crow to you about, Beautiful Boys don't,' she elaborates.

'I wasn't boasting – I mean, I hope I didn't come across as being flash,' stutters Christy. 'I've only just been taken on staff at the paper, I'm fairly junior in the department.'

'Don't worry, you weren't swaggering,' Kate tells him. 'Boasting would be if you started listing all the supermodels you'd photographed. You know, "I had that Claudia Schiffer in the back of my lens."'

Christy's face swings from relieved to baffled again. 'What was that about Beautiful Boys, Kate?'

Now it's Eimear's turn to kick her but Kate's wearing ankle boots, she's immune to prodding.

'You see, Christy, it's like this,' Kate says expansively, swilling wine around in her glass, 'the three of us – that's Eimear, the missing Gloria and myself – had a scheme to find ourselves some Beautiful Boys because we decided we're tired of men. We thought Beautiful Boys might tickle our fancy and tackle our fencing – or any other odd jobs that needed doing around the house.'

'I'm a very passable odd-job man myself,' remarks Christy.

'I've no doubt you are. But you still don't qualify as a Beautiful Boy – you have to shave every day, don't you?'

'Sometimes twice a day,' he admits, running his fingers along his jawline.

'That'll be the black hair,' Kate reminds him.

'And were you being thoroughly modern by deciding

to interview Beautiful Boys for your escort vacancy?' he enquires.

'Not at all,' Kate rebukes him, 'we're following in the footsteps of Queen Maeve.'

'The Cattle Raid of Cooley Queen Maeve, the one who lived thousands of years ago?' Christy's brow is furrowed. 'Is there any other?'

'There's Queen Maeve of Binchy, high priestess of the Hibernian page-turner,' suggests Eimear, who's finally decided to leave Kate's ankles alone.

'So there is,' agrees Kate. 'But there's no evidence that she pays the slightest bit of attention to Beautiful Boys. Whereas Queen Maeve of Connaught had a decided penchant for them. She called them her thigh-friends and bragged that she never had one but the shadow of his successor lay across him.'

'What did she do when she was bored with them?' asks Christy.

'Sent them off on cattle raids, of course. Everyone thinks the raids were to harry Ulster and purloin our magnificent bulls, but obviously the real reason was to rid herself of inconvenient lovers who'd passed their sell-by date.

'"Off you go to the wars now, Fiachra. Watch out for those nasty Ulstermen and their spears, especially that Cuchulainn character. Step forward, Conn, aren't you a fine figure of a lad. Shall I explain to you what being my thigh-friend involves?"'

'It's a descriptive phrase,' says Christy, 'I doubt if they needed much coaching.'

'So you see,' concludes Kate, 'we're simply following Queen Maeve's stirring example in our hunt for Beautiful Boys. A hunt, by the way, which you stymied, Christy Troy.'

'Sorry about that, girls,' he says. 'If I'd known I was hindering a historical appreciation society drumming up warriors for another Cattle Raid of Cooley I'd have left you in peace at the disco. You just seemed to look as out-of-place as I felt.'

'We were,' Eimear butts in. 'The Den of Iniquity was a cattle market, not a cattle raid. And we definitely won't be going back there again.'

'You were the one who suggested togging ourselves up in ra-ra skirts the next time we went,' Kate protests.

'Tell us about this cottage you're renovating, Christy,' invites Eimear, making more eye-contact than seems strictly necessary to Kate on the substitutes' bench. 'I'm looking for a place that needs fixing up myself.'

'Don't do it,' he groans. 'Take a spin out to the Bog of Allen, dig a hole, bury all your money in it and then drive away without a backward glance. You'll still be putting your cash to better use.'

'Expensive?'

'Crippling. And time-consuming too. I used to have a social life until I took on this albatross.'

'Still, it must be lovely to look at it as it progresses and think, "All my own work,"' Eimear radiates encouragement.

'Not quite all my own,' he admits. 'I can do the labouring jobs but I have to hire plumbers, plasterers and bricklayers for anything that requires skill rather than muscle. I did all the electrics myself, though – you must come out and see for yourself.'

'I'd love to,' she breathes.

Kate looks at her, waiting for it. Yes, sure enough, here it comes. Her head is thrown back, her arm sweeps up and her hair is scrunched into a hand-held bun, emphasising her cheekbones. Christy is lost in admiration.

'I should really bring you on my house-hunting expeditions,' adds Eimear. 'Kate's come out with me' – she acknowledges her presence briefly, thanks for that nano-second, Mulligan – 'but neither of us knows what to look out for. We can't check for damp or dry-rot, we're just looking at superficialities like fireplaces and coving and, fetching though they are, they're simply the icing on the cake. You need to be sure your ceilings are going to stay up before you start worrying about ceiling roses.'

Kate can't believe her ears, she's parroting word for word the exact lecture she harangued Eimear with after being dragged to Booterstown to look at a heap of stones labelled 'full of potential' by an optically challenged estate agent. Eimear cooed over a rambling rose framing the doorway, while Kate attempted to point out that half the roof was missing.

'It's so reassuring to hear you say that,' Christy tells Eimear. 'You've no idea how many people turn sentimental when you mention cottages with exposed beams, but they don't realise most of them need complete restructuring before they're habitable. People buy these rundown places and then fall apart at the seams when they realise how much work is involved. They'd be better off with a flat in town.'

'Like me,' interrupts Kate. 'I'm delighted with my tiny place at the top of the Green. It has no period features, unless you count a creaky lift, which I have to share with thirteen other flats, there isn't even a balcony so I have no herbs in pots, and if I have a leak I call the porter. In other words, I eat there sometimes, I sleep there most times, I hang my clothes there all the time and I never give the flat a second thought. Whereas everyone else of my acquaintance, and sadly I can't exclude present company, are turning into property bores. If you're not visiting salvage shops for extra-wide skirting board, you're congratulating each other on how much equity your house has accumulated in the past twenty minutes.'

'Kate has socialist tendencies,' explains Eimear. 'They're only leanings, she doesn't follow through on them, she is a solicitor after all, and she owns this flat she's busy castigating.'

'I suppose you're going to call me a champagne socialist because I keep bubbly in my fridge,' Kate complains.

'I thought you'd given up on that since Jack – I mean, since the last bottle was emptied in unfortunate circumstances,' says Eimear.

Good old Mulligan, she knows when to pull the leash. Kate purses her lips.

'Tomorrow's a work day.' Kate springs to her feet. 'No, don't stand up, Christy, I'm only a hop, skip and a jump away from home. See you again, you must have Eimear bring you to my decadent capitalist penthouse sometime.'

As she walks along Dame Street, not even noticing when she passes her office, Kate scolds herself. Why does she even bother trying to compete with Eimear? Kate launches into a mental lecture: she's had revenge enough on Eimear with Jack, be grateful she's been given a verbal warning and leave well enough alone. Besides, there's a time-bomb ticking away in this circle of friends and Kate doesn't want to be pricked into detonating it.

The time-bomb in Gloria's stomach.

CHAPTER 30

'You're in a right pickle and no mistake, aren't you, little Glo.' Kate looks at her kindly.

'Don't pretend you're reading that book because you haven't turned a page for fifteen minutes,' she adds.

Gloria is holding the *Complete Thomas Hardy* in her inert hands – now there's a man who didn't expect much from relationships. They're supposed to be keeping each other company in Ranelagh while Kate has an electrician install recessed lighting (she's had a rush of blood to the head and started home improvements). The plan was to loll about doing their usual Saturday chores but that doesn't suit Kate, to Gloria's intense irritation – Kate always has to be niggling.

'Mick rang me,' Kate volunteers. 'He was pumping me to find out whether you were on your hands and knees yet, ready for the inevitable crawl back to him. I was so dumbstruck I must have made him suspect there was something afoot. He started quizzing me; I took the Fifth Amendment but don't imagine it will stay a secret forever, you know what this town is like – never mind the valley of the squinting windows, this is the dark pool of wagging tongues. You ought to throw yourself on Eimear's mercy and confess all before Mick discovers it from someone else. Now that he's asking questions he's like a terrier. It's a matter of when, not if, he finds out.'

Gloria is aghast. 'Eimear couldn't cope with it, it would be too much on top of losing Jack and that desperate business with you. Besides, confessions have repercussions.'

'Eimear's as tough as old boots,' objects Kate. 'Anyway, she has a certain big brawny distraction.'

'I'd forgotten all about your date with the nightclub pickup – how did it go?'

'Gloria,' Kate reproves her. 'You're using Christy Troy as a way of distracting yourself from the subject of donor sperm belonging to donors who ought to know better than to go around donating them.'

Gloria tries to drum up a sense of indignation but it's an uphill struggle.

'You're a fine one to be lecturing me on morality,' she says weakly. 'At least I didn't go to bed with Jack O'Brien.'

'I'd think more of you if you had. Mine was honest-to-God passion of torrid proportions, what's your excuse for acting like someone with half a brain?'

'Tell me about Christy,' insists Gloria.

Kate shrugs. 'He and Eimear are seeing each other, he's obviously smitten, as most men are by her, and she's trailing him around derelict cottages the length and breadth of the county. Which is very convenient since her car has given up the ghost and you'd manage precious little house-hunting if you were relying on our bus service.'

Gloria pushes her hair away from her face – it seems too heavy now that she's pregnant, she'll have to overcome her baby-induced sloth and make an appointment for a haircut – and speculates: 'Are they doing it, do you think?'

'It?' she enquires mockingly.

'You know: *it*.'

'That would be a breach of confidence,' Kate responds.

'Kate!' squeals Gloria. 'You're holding back on me. Tell me everything you know at once or I'll, I'll' – she casts around for a suitable threat – 'I'll name the baby after you.'

Kate looks horrified, she's always detested her name.

'Eimear wants to jump into bed with him in theory, she's just not sure if she's able to go through with it in practice. Not even to practise,' she explains.

'Why not?' Gloria's puzzled. Also distracted by her stomach, which is making digestive noises. 'Steady, boy,' she whispers under her breath. She just knows this baby is a little Jack. No, not a little Jack, a little James, he'll be modelled on her father, not the man who fathered him.

Kate paces before the living-room window, trailing her hands along the radiator. She has nun's hands, as slender and translucent as Sally Bowles' in *Cabaret*.

'Eimear's lost her confidence,' she says finally. 'I'm afraid I took it from her with Jack. She was always so unruffled, so composed in her beauty, but now she questions it. She looks in mirrors – when did you last see Eimear glance in a mirror? She complains about her nose and frets over her hair and worries about the size of her thighs.'

'Just like a normal woman.'

'Just like a normal woman,' agrees Kate. 'But that was never Eimear.'

She resumes her pacing.

'What does that have to do with sex?' asks Gloria, mystified.

'Everything,' Kate throws over her shoulder, fingering the curtains.

Gloria waits. And waits.

'You've lost me there,' she says finally. 'It's so long since I've had sex I've forgotten what the rules are.'

Kate stares pointedly at her stomach. 'What's that, trapped air?'

'This has nothing to do with grinding loins, pregnancy doesn't come any more hands off,' shrugs Gloria.

Kate smiles as she fiddles with the curtain tiebacks.

'I'll get you your own set if you like,' offers Gloria.

Kate looks puzzled.

264

'Of tiebacks,' she explains. 'You can have fringed or un-fringed. Hours of entertainment guaranteed.'

Kate relinquishes them and joins her on the sofa.

'Eimear's worried that her boobs have started to droop,' she expands. 'She's embarrassed to take them to bed with Christy in case he's disgusted, so she prefers to have him think she's playing hard to get. She's also discovered a little dry patch of discoloured skin on her bottom which she can't get rid of, she's even been to the doctor's about it in case it's malignant but it's just unsightly, nothing more.'

'How unsightly?'

Kate sounds exasperated. 'I don't know, Glo, I haven't been studying her backside at close range, I only have Eimear's word for it.'

'I'm sure her boobs can't be that droopy,' Gloria frowns. 'Her chest isn't big enough, for starters. You have to be born with one of those obscene double D-cup chests to develop saggy breasts or they might go a bit pear-shaped if you were breastfeeding your fifth child or something. I bet she's imagining it.'

'My prognosis entirely, Doctor Feelgood. But the point is, there's no dissuading Eimear. She's convinced she's on the slippery slope and once Christy sees what a wreck she is he'll bolt.'

'So why doesn't she wait till the light's off before going about in the nip like the rest of us?'

'Gloria,' Kate reprimands. 'I don't think you're taking Eimear's problem seriously.'

'That's because it isn't a serious problem.'

'You're right,' she nods. 'Heave-ho with your best friend's husband, now that's a serious problem. Accepting donor sperm from your best friend's husband and keeping shtoom about it, now that's a serious problem. The remote possibility of saggy bits is not a serious problem. Except to Eimear, who occupies a parallel universe on such issues.'

'So has she explained this to Christy?' enquires Gloria. 'You never know, he might be the one man in a million with a fetish for droopy boobs.'

'Doubt it. She's told him she's not ready yet and he says he's prepared to wait until she is. Sure where's the mad rush, they've only been seeing each other a few weeks. And in the meantime, they continue her house-hunting.'

'Very convenient,' remarks Gloria. 'Trust Eimear to land on her feet. And stay off her back. Is she keen on this Christy fellow then?'

'Your guess is as good as mine, Glo. He's good for her ego and he's diverting her from the horrors of the division of spoils between herself and Jack. He may be a stopgap, he may be The One. Technically he's only supposed to be her Interim Other, before she meets the man she's really meant to be with. But sometimes people skip a stage.'

'Kate,' Gloria is severe. 'You've been reading magazines again.'

'It's true,' she admits. 'I keep meaning to get stuck into something mind-improving, like all the authors on this year's Booker Prize shortlist, but I can't help myself. I walk past Centra and I look through the window and there they are, stacked in neat little racks, calling to me, calling, all shiny and pristine and begging to be handled. I go in thinking, "I'll just flick through them," but before I know it I find myself at the till with two or three in my hand and then I scurry home and curl up in bed with them.'

'It has to stop,' warns Gloria.

Kate turns rebellious. 'What harm am I doing? I pull out the face-cream samples, I read the magazines and then I put them in a pile by the wardrobe. There's worse I could be doing in bed, I could smoke and flick ash on the pillows or I could paint my toenails and drip polish over the sheets.'

'You know it's not as simple as that, Kate. You're not just

reading lifestyles of the rich and famous, you're poring over silly articles about Significant Others and Dubious Others. And then when your Adjective Other doesn't act out the scenario the article predicts, you're dismayed in case you're doing something wrong.'

Kate caves in unexpectedly. 'I'll be straight down to Eason's tomorrow and buy something you'd approve of, Glo. I'll make you proud of me, really I will.'

'Sarcastic scut. Will we go for a walk?'

Kate is dubious. 'Are you on some health kick with this baby?'

'Only as far as Gammell's for brown bread,' Gloria reassures her. 'Of course we'll have to walk past Centra, so I'll be able to watch if you're really trying to cure this addiction of yours or simply fobbing me off . . .'

As they stroll along, it starts to drizzle.

'Ah, the gentle Irish autumn. Indistinguishable from the gentle Irish spring and summer. Don't look on this as rain, treat it as a bit of moist air,' remarks Kate. 'Do you know there's a desert in Chile where it hasn't rained for four hundred years.' She pulls up the hood of her bronze silk mac, bought in last year's sale at Powerscourt Design Centre on Eimear's instructions.

'I like those Chilean wines,' replies Gloria. 'Or at least I used to' – she turns pathetic – 'in the olden days when I was allowed to drink.'

'Poor Glo.' Kate wrinkles her freckled nose and slips an arm through her friend's. 'Put your hood up – we don't want you catching a chill. Are you missing the demon drink?'

'Not as much as I expected to. But I haven't had a food craving yet, maybe it's too soon. I'm quite excited to see what it'll be. Ice-cream with chilli sauce? Sausage and peach sandwiches? My mother had a craving for liquorice allsorts when she was carrying me. Daddy kept a packet permanently in his coat pocket to be on the safe side or she'd have had him out scouring the streets at midnight. You didn't get twenty-four-hour shops then.'

'And do liquorice allsorts appeal to you at all?' Kate smiles, as they pass the Indian restaurant and the off-licence.

'Not in the slightest,' Gloria admits. 'But at least I don't have an aversion to them, which is a marvel considering I was probably ingesting tonnes of the stuff inadvertently for nine months.'

'Have you told your mother yet?'

'No, I'm waiting till I reach the three-month stage,' Gloria admits, as they come to a halt by Gammell's. 'They said at the hospital your chances of miscarrying are higher during the first trimester so I'll leave it till I'm over that hurdle.'

'Hey, Glo, you have all the jargon. And have you thought about what will happen with Mick?'

Mick. Deep down Gloria knows she's disowned him unfairly. She could argue that she wasn't thinking clearly when she threw herself on Jack's mercy and passed him off as Mick at the Rotunda for impregnation purposes. Good job it wasn't one of the nurses who'd met Mick on duty that day. But Gloria did know what she was doing, she weighed the consequences and went ahead anyway. It was a husband or a baby and she chose the baby. Husbands aren't so hard to come by, babies are a sight more difficult.

'Gloria?' Kate's voice jolts her from her reverie.

'Let's take you inside for a cup of tea,' she says in her head prefect voice. 'There's a table by the door. Not the most private spot in the world but you have a bird's-eye view of the cakes.'

She ushers Gloria into Gammell's and keeps up a steady flow of chatter that requires no answer as they remove their coats and place their order.

'It's Mick, isn't it?' Kate looks steadily at Gloria, after a decent interval.

'It is,' she admits, stumbling over the sentences as though

268

English doesn't come naturally to her. 'I've acted' – she searches for the word – 'dishonourably by him. There'll be a price to pay somewhere down the line. But I'm willing to pay it. For the baby, you see.'

'You mean, Eimear, is she the price?'

'Maybe. Or it could be something else, something totally unexpected. You never know what the tallyman will demand.'

Even Gloria realises she's raving, while Kate's blue eyes have widened with worry.

'It's OK.' Gloria stretches across the table and touches her hand. 'I don't mean to spook you. I almost said I was having a qualm of conscience but it isn't even that, because I have no reservations. I'm just being superstitious.'

Kate smiles. 'So what's new? The day you stop being super-stitious is the day I join the Scientologists. That reminds me, I've booked our session with Mrs Gilmartin.'

'Give me a clue, Kate. Manicurist? Aromatherapist? Feng shui expert?'

'Fortune-teller, woman, you've a memory like a sieve. And no blaming it on your handy hormones, you've always been like that. The three of us are going to throw ourselves on the fortune-teller's mercy and hear what the fates have in store for us.'

'I'm not sure I want to go,' Gloria protests.

'You must, it's arranged,' Kate sounds aggrieved. 'Eimear was the backslider I expected to have trouble with, not you. You could probably pitch your tent and set up in opposition to Mrs Gilmartin anyway. "Gifted Gloria: she tells it like it is."'

She finds herself giggling and Kate joins in.

'Tell me, Gifted Gloria, what do you see for me?'

Gloria shakes the teapot. 'There's no leaves in here, it'll have to be a palm-reading.'

She pretends to study Kate's slim, freckled hand.

'I see a fair stranger,' she intones huskily. 'I see a seaside wedding. I see a beautiful bride.'

'That's enough about Pearse,' she objects. 'What about me?'

'Sure, your guess is as good as mine,' Gloria returns to her real voice.

'What are you going to do about Mick, Glo?'

That's Kate for you, lightning conversational changes are her speciality.

Gloria shrugs. 'Buy him out of the house, set a divorce in motion, invent a new life without him.'

'You and your baby,' notes Kate.

'Got it in one. I'll wish him well and that'll be that, he'll move to Omagh and I'll stay here – our paths are unlikely to cross again.'

'And he's happy for you to keep the house?'

Gloria considers. 'Happy doesn't come into it. He doesn't want it, he's been accepted as assistant manager at the bank in the street next to his mother's house so it's no use to him now. I think I can just about afford to give him half of the equity. I have some money Daddy left to me and I can top it up with a loan.'

'Maybe not from Mick's bank,' remarks Kate.

'Maybe not from Mick's bank,' concedes Gloria.

She carries on in a rush: 'We have a good deal on the mortgage already on account of Mick, which I suppose I'll inherit, and if I budget carefully I'll be grand. I'll give up buying clothes, sell the Corsa and I have a few pieces of jewellery I can probably flog off if I get really strapped. Money will be tight, especially when the baby comes along, but I think we should just about manage. It's lucky we didn't sell up and move to a larger house – we discussed it last year – then I really would have been in over my head.'

Gloria thinks of her little two-bedroom terrace with its patio garden and imagines it with a baby in residence. Sterilisers on the kitchen worktop, a cot by the bedside, perhaps a swing in the yard. One might just about fit if she shifts the flower pots, just a tot's swing.

They're halfway home when Kate mentions Eimear again. Gloria can't handle it now, she has to head her off. Inspiration strikes as she recollects her brown loaf still sitting on the café table.

'I'll run back to Gammell's for you,' offers Kate.

'I couldn't ask you to do that.'

'Certainly you could, we can't have you jiggling about in your condition. I'll catch you up,' she insists.

'This isn't a ploy to sneak into Centra and buy a few magazines?'

'My dastardly plan is foiled,' Kate twiddles an imaginary moustache. 'Walk slowly.'

As Gloria rounds the corner towards her street, she sees a tall, lean figure waiting on the doorstep. She hesitates, panic sets in, she turns away but he spies her and calls out. 'Gloria, I was just about to put a note through your door. I need to talk to you.'

It's Jack.

CHAPTER 31

'I can't talk to you here, Kate is right behind me.' Gloria glances over her shoulder.

Jack allows himself a supercilious smile. 'Kate hasn't transformed herself into your moral guardian, has she?'

She disregards the snipe. 'Jack, you have to leave, I'll ring you when it's safe for you to call by.'

'When, baby girl?'

He's still smiling, leaning casually against his scarlet BMW. It's exactly the colour of car you'd imagine him driving.

'Tonight or tomorrow, soon,' she gabbles, watching out for Kate.

'Tonight.' His white teeth shine against the tan of his face. 'Don't bother to ring, I'll call here at eight.'

'Make it nine, Jack, now please leave.'

He laughs, folding his arms, chin pointing skywards.

'What a hurry you're in. You must learn to take life easier, Gloria, especially now there's a baby to consider.'

She feels her cheeks flame as she stares at the ground. So that's what he wants to talk to her about, she suspected as much.

Suddenly Jack takes pity on her.

'See you at eight then, baby girl.'

'Nine.'

Her eyes challenge his.

'You're the boss.' And with a last mocking laugh, he climbs into his car and drives off.

Gloria props her shoulder against the garden wall, shaken. There'll be tears before bedtime – that's what her mother used to say when Marlene, Rudy and Gloria were playing too exuberantly. It's a mercy Kate didn't come upon them, she'd be convinced Gloria was knee-deep in something clandestine.

Kate materialises around the corner, swinging her bread in a plastic bag.

'Bumped into someone from work,' she calls. 'I didn't realise Isabel Eccles lives in Ranelagh now. She's just bought a house with her boyfriend, behind the picture framer's, I've promised to call round and inspect it before I go home. Do you fancy a snoop? It's legalised voyeurism, looking at other people's houses. Even better when they aren't at home, of course, but you can't have everything. Or so we're led to believe.'

'To tell you the truth, Kate, I'm feeling a bit tired. I could probably do with a nap. It must be the –'

'Hormones,' she finishes Gloria's sentence for her. 'That's fair enough, Glo, we'll get you inside and settled, then I'll be on my way. A chat with Isabel and it's back to vacuuming up after the electrician and playing with my new dimmer switches. What a full life I lead.'

To tell you the truth, Kate. Sentences that start with that are never about honesty, Gloria reflects. As true as I'm standing here, honest to goodness, no word of a lie . . . all fabrications. Oh God oh God oh God. What does Jack O'Brien want with her?

He rings the doorbell at ten minutes to nine. She's in the hall, studying her reflection in the mosaic-tiled mirror hanging there to hide a mistake in the wallpaper pattern. Too much lipstick. Dark shadows under the eyes, confirmation she's having trouble sleeping. Jack's bulk is visible through the stained glass, he shifts impatiently on the step and rings again. Hold your horses, man.

'Gloria, you look delightful.' He proffers a bunch of pink roses.

They're her least favourite colour of roses in all the world. Jack's eyes scan Gloria, size her up. She knew she shouldn't have changed into a dress, she plucks nervously at its cotton denim folds; he'll imagine she did it deliberately for him. Which she did – not to impress him, but to bolster her confidence against him.

He radiates self-assurance, big bold Jack. It's the brown eyes, they snap at you. He doesn't wait to be invited into the sitting room, he breezes in ahead of Gloria and she finds him sprawled on the sofa.

'I'll just put these in water,' she stammers.

'Any chance of a drink while you're out there?'

'I haven't any wine or beer. I'm not drinking at the moment because of . . . I'm just not drinking.'

'Anything will do,' he shrugs. 'Rustle me up a gin and tonic or a drop of Mick's whiskey or a cooking sherry if all else fails.'

'I'll see what I can find. I can't promise anything, mind.'

When she returns with a few inches of whiskey in a glass, she's slightly scandalised to see he's kicked his shoes off.

His eyes follow hers to his bare toes.

'You don't mind if I make myself comfortable, Gloria, these deck shoes are pinching,' he smiles and pats the sofa beside him. But she moves to the fireplace and props herself against it, she feels safer standing – more in control.

'So, how are you feeling, baby girl?' He swigs half his whiskey and sets it down with a thump that startles her. He notices and a dimple twitches in his narrow face.

'Grand, thanks, and yourself?' she responds automatically.

'I'm fine too, but then I'm not pregnant.' His smile never wavers.

'And what makes you think I am?' she tries to stall him.

'I rang up the hospital claiming to be Mick McDermott and they told me.'

This man is turning into the Cheshire cat, he's going to vanish inside a gigantic smile, thinks Gloria, looking down on him from her not so advantageous vantage point.

'And have you come to congratulate me?' she manages, after a spiky pause.

'Of course, roses for the rose in bloom,' he gestures expansively towards his bouquet.

There's another pause during which they gauge each other.

'It's not your baby, Jack.' She takes the initiative.

He raises a bantering eyebrow. The man's enjoying this, he's a slug, thinks Gloria.

Eimear's well rid of him, Kate too.

'I mean, technically it is but you're not really the father. It has no father, there's only me.'

She wishes forlornly that she could control her skin, fiery patches are flaring on her neck.

'Only you,' he repeats, although it doesn't sound like he's agreeing with her.

He gulps the remainder of his drink.

'Any chance of a refill?'

'I'm afraid that's the last of the bottle,' she fibs. Then she seizes her courage. 'Anyway, aren't you driving?'

'Such a sensible creature,' he remarks, running a finger along the lunar contours of the glass. It's Tyrone crystal, a wedding present. 'I'll have a coffee then, since you're so touchingly worried about the guards catching me.'

She longs to order him to leave but instead finds herself in the kitchen digging out some beans from the bottom of the fridge – Jack O'Brien doesn't look like an instant coffee sort of man.

Gloria looks up and he's standing in the open doorway, watching her; she's caught off-guard and drops the coffee, she didn't hear him pad along the passage in his bare feet.

'You never struck me as the nervous type.' He watches her retrieve the packet.

She occupies herself with the grinder, uncomfortably aware that he's studying her every move.

Jack sprawls at the kitchen table, feet resting on the supports of a chair. Still grinning – doesn't his jaw ache with all that smirking? He's removed his jacket and she's aware of the curly dark chest hair at the base of his throat. It's spilling out above the open buttons on his shirt and she smells a lemon scent; not aftershave, not deodorant. It must be Jack.

'Well, Jack, what can I do for you?' Her nonchalance is assumed.

'Nothing,' he replies, just as airily. 'I just wanted to check up on you. Is it true you and Mick are splitting up?'

'Your spies have been busy. Yes, we are.'

'And does he know who the baby's father is?'

'No, and I'd like to keep it that way.'

'What about Eimear?'

'Ditto.'

'You don't look pregnant, baby girl.' His eyes glint as they roam over her.

There's invitation in them and a gleam of something else, another emotion she can't quite pinpoint.

Unexpectedly he stands up. 'I won't detain you, I just wanted to let you know I'm here for you if there's anything you need.'

She makes an effort and composes her face into an agreeable expression.

'There's nothing I need, thanks all the same. I'm grateful you helped me out when I was at my wits' end and, though I don't mean to sound ungracious, I think we should leave it at that. All there is between us is that we have Eimear in common – and we won't even have that much if she gets wind of what we've been at.'

'Partners in crime,' he remarks.

Gloria cements her lips together.

He regards her thoughtfully. 'She forgave Kate.'

'So she did, but somehow I don't think she could forgive me. It's one thing to have it off with your husband but another matter altogether to have a baby by him.'

'You have a point.'

The hall-light is shining directly on his thick dark hair now, highlighting russet strands, as he pulls on his footwear. Gloria realises she's unconsciously admiring it and turns away.

Jack looms directly over Gloria. His eyes return to her stomach and she feels it somersault. The baby's not supposed to move yet, it's too soon. He leans towards her cheek to kiss it, she looks down quickly and he skims the top of her head. As he straightens, a hand reaches out and strokes her stomach.

'Stop that!' she shrieks.

Jack steps back, dazed. It's the first time she's seen him wrong-footed.

'It's my baby, mine, not yours,' Gloria howls, pushing him towards the door.

God in heaven, what came over her, she pants as soon as she's alone. Talk about overreacting.

'Get a grip, Gloria,' she instructs herself, sitting on the bottom stair. The adrenaline has ebbed and she feels too weak to walk into the living room. She hears the phone ring but can't summon the energy to answer it. It rings off and immediately starts shrilling again. Its noise is an imperative: she totters in and lifts the receiver.

'Gloria? Thank heavens you answered. I was worried about you. Kate told me you were stopping in tonight and I couldn't understand why there was no reply.'

It's Eimear.

'I must have dozed off,' Gloria mumbles.

'Listen, I've great news – Christy took me to see the perfect cottage in Dundrum, I'm putting in an offer on it on Monday. It's an executor's sale, it's only just gone on the market and it's simply gorgeous.'

'Great,' says Gloria; Eimear's so caught up in her dream home she doesn't notice the dearth of enthusiasm.

'It has three bedrooms – well, two and a cupboard – and an enormous kitchen with an inglenook fireplace, flagged floor and exposed beams. The bathroom's on the poky side but I might be able to knock it through to the landing to add more space.'

She rambles on about her view of the mountains; Gloria only half-listens until she's pulled up short.

'And the baby could have the cupboard-sized room and . . .'

'What baby, Eimear?'

'Yours, silly, how many babies do we have?'

She's won her full attention now. 'Eimear, why would my baby want your spare bedroom? You're surely not planning sleepovers already, I'm only a few months gone.'

'Gloria, have you been listening to a word I've said? The cottage is perfect for the three of us, you, me and the bump. You're being incredibly brave having the baba on your own and I can't find a word low enough to describe Mick for leaving you in the lurch. But you don't have to go through it on your own, Glo, I want you to come and live with me and I'll lend a hand any way I can with the baby.'

If she only knew, laughs Gloria. It sounds suspiciously like one of those hollow laughs you read about but never actually hear.

'What's so funny? Don't you like my brilliant idea, Glo?' Eimear's voice is hurt.

'Not much,' she admits. 'We tried living together before, it was a lethal combination.'

'It would be different with a baby.' Her tone is eager. 'You don't know what you're letting yourself in for as a single parent – all those dawn feeds and grungy bottles to clean, and the teething and the nappies and there's the loneliness too. Single parents never meet anybody, it's a two-dimensional life.'

'You make it sound so desirable,' Gloria jokes.

'Well of course it's not all bad, there are compensations, but it would be easier with both of us – we'd be company for each other and there'd be more money to go around and . . .' She hesitates, her voice lowers: 'I'd like to share your baby, Glo, truly I would.'

'What about Christy? He's not going to like his seduction scenes interrupted by squawks from the baby monitor.'

'Never mind Christy, I can handle him.'

'But he won't be able to handle you, not with a baby in the way,' Gloria points out.

'Just because you've had a few dates and done a bit of house-hunting with a fellow doesn't mean you have to plan your entire life around him. I like him, he's been extremely helpful, but I'm not intending to grow old with him.'

'He must be expecting some kind of reward for all this house-hunting, Eimear. The man would need to be a martyr just to do it from the goodness of his heart.'

'He can expect all he likes.'

Eimear turns huffy and rings off, having extracted a promise from Gloria to inspect her cottage.

Gloria needs a treat: she clatters upstairs to the bedroom, roots around in her underwear drawer and extracts a tissue-wrapped oblong. It's a christening robe; she had her wedding dress cut into one the year she started trying for a baby. She took to keeping the robe at the bottom of her underwear drawer for ease of access and because she knew it was the one place Mick would never stumble across it. You don't ransack the frillies of a woman you have zero interest in bedding. She doesn't have to hide the christening robe any more now that Mick's gone but habits die hard. He went ballistic when he saw her with it once, he called it tempting providence.

279

Comfort seeps into her from the ivory silk cloth she holds against her face. Its tiny perfection gladdens her like an embrace: lace collar, lace cuffs, adorable skullcap. She imagines her son wearing it, like one of those ancient-eyed infants that peek from gloomy oil paintings. She brings it to her nose and inhales its soothing fragrance. Not a baby scent yet but soon.

CHAPTER 32

'You first,' Kate jostles Eimear.

'No, you,' she elbows her back.

'Gloria then,' Kate suggests.

Eimear is indignant. 'Kate McGlade, it was your idea to traipse out to Ashbourne to see this Mrs Gilmartin. We're here now so get out of the car and ring her doorbell, isn't the woman expecting us.'

Reluctantly Kate steps out, muttering, 'I vas only following orders,' and approaches the door of a fifties semi with a cherry tree in the front garden. Before she touches the bell, the door is opened by a benevolent-faced woman in her sixties.

'Come in, my dears, I've been watching you sitting out there in the car for the past ten minutes. Don't worry, most people are nervous the first time.'

She ushers the trio into the sitting room, where a blonde girl of five is watching Disney's *The Little Mermaid* on video.

'That's Ariel,' the child indicates the heroine. 'Her hair is the same colour as yours.' She looks at Kate.

'Mine's shorter,' replies Kate, touching her newly shorn crop of red hair diffidently.

The little blonde one examines her. 'It might grow,' she says.

'Are you all right, Michelle?' asks Mrs Gilmartin. 'You don't mind these ladies watching your video with you until I take them into the kitchen for Granny's special business?'

Michelle shakes her head and returns her attention to the television set, already bored by the intruders.

'Now, who'd like to start?' Mrs Gilmartin waits while they shuffle their feet. She homes in on Kate. 'How about you, dear, will you follow me down to the kitchen?'

Eimear and Gloria sit on a crimson velour sofa as Ariel sells her voice to the sea-witch in return for a pair of legs.

'I'm going to Copenhagen to see the Little Mermaid statue one day,' says Eimear.

'Everyone needs an ambition,' replies Gloria.

'Where's Coping-that-word?' pipes up Michelle, who's wearing orange fleecy pyjamas with bunny rabbits cavorting on them.

'It's in Denmark, that's a country a long way from here,' says Eimear. 'It's about the same size as Ireland, except they're clean and don't throw chip wrappers on the street.'

'Do they have real mermaids there?' Michelle's interest is sparked.

'Yes.'

'And princes?'

'I'm not sure.' Eimear turns to Gloria for clarification. 'Does Denmark have a royal family?'

'I think so, isn't it that country where the royals cycle around and behave like ordinary people?'

'No, that's Holland. Of course it might be Denmark too. Yes they have princes,' she tells Michelle.

'Then I'm going there to marry one when I grow up,' announces the child, and returns to her video.

'Are you nervous, Glo?'

'As a kitten. Do you think she'll realise I'm pregnant? I don't show.'

'If she doesn't she's in the wrong game,' says Eimear.

'Kate seems to be taking her time.'

'Did you tell Christy where you were coming?'

'Catch a grip, I don't want him thinking I'm any more

mental than he has me already pegged for – as it is he says I'm not A1 mental health.'

'What are you?'

'A-flawed. Apparently that's quite sound for a woman – Christy has this theory that none of us are A1.'

'And of course men are,' Gloria snaps. 'He sounds a right one, your lover boy.'

'He's not my lover boy, he's a friend.'

'Aha, so you still haven't done the dirty deed. He's patient, I'll grant him that. You see, men have some advantages over Beautiful Boys – you'd never get a BB to hang around for a few months while you dither over whether or not to admit him to the delights of your body.'

Eimear half-smiles as she confesses: 'Actually, I have decided. Well, not exactly to sleep with him, to be guided by whatever Mrs Gilmartin says. If she's in favour of my tall dark stranger, then it's portals of bliss time. And if she says I have a malignant dark presence in my life, it's *adios amigo*.'

'What's a dirty deed?' pipes up Michelle.

Eimear looks startled. 'It's something nasty, you don't want to hear about it.'

'I do,' protests Michelle.

'No you don't. So you live with your granny, do you?'

'Mammy's gone away so I sleep in Granny's bed now.'

'What about your daddy?' Gloria enquires gently.

'I haven't got a daddy.'

She thinks of her own baby. 'Would you like one?'

Michelle considers. 'Maybe. Granny says the two of us rub along together very well as we are but Daddies buy nice presents, Louise at school told me. She's my friend, I have two friends, Louise and Justin.'

'Which do you like best?' asks Eimear.

'I like them both the same. Louise can make a loud noise with her knuckles and Justin can ride his bike the fastest, he wants to be a pizza delivery man when he grows up.'

'You're next, Mulligan.'

Kate flops down on the sofa on the space vacated by Eimear and rolls her eyes at Gloria when she mouths, 'Any good?'

'Magic,' she whispers. 'I'll tell you all about it later.' She transfers her attention to Michelle. 'Have you any other videos?'

The two of them chat about *The Lion King* – Kate's comfortable with kids, she has a niece and a nephew, unlike the others – and Gloria thinks about what revelations Mrs Gilmartin might have in store. She's carrying a notebook in her bag so she can write down everything, otherwise she'll never remember the half of it. Eimear is back quicker than Kate and Gloria is on her feet and out the door before she's even taken her seat on the crimson velour.

Mrs Gilmartin is smoking at her kitchen table. 'I'll be with you in a moment, dear, as soon as I finish this. It helps me switch off between readings,' she smiles.

'Take your time.' Gloria's eyes travel around the neat little kitchen. There are a few pots of herbs on the windowsill. Gloria recognises parsley and rosemary, mint too. There's a splashy red and blue painting of a house attached to the fridge by a magnet, obviously Michelle's handiwork.

Mrs Gilmartin stubs out her cigarette, carries the ashtray over to the sink and returns to her place opposite Gloria. 'First I'll read the cards and then I'll look at your palm.' She handles an ordinary deck, not the Tarot cards Gloria is expecting.

'Do you mind if I take notes?' Gloria produces her pad.

'Work away, whatever suits you suits me.' Mrs Gilmartin reaches her the cards. 'Now I want you to give these a good shuffle, choose half a dozen cards and place them face-down on the table in the order you pick them.'

She follows instructions, shuffling clumsily – it's years since she had a pack of cards in her hands, it reminds her of playing pontoon for buttons with Marlene and Rudy. Mammy confiscated the deck when Rudy had them substituting pennies for buttons.

When the six cards are isolated from the deck, Mrs Gilmartin asks her to hand the top one to her.

'Your life is going through a huge change, almost an upheaval,' she says. 'Have you recently moved house or switched jobs? No? Well, if it hasn't started, the change is just about to begin. Everything you've known for the past decade or more is about to be turned on its head.

'Don't be nervous, people need change, it keeps us on our toes. Take it easy though, be kind to yourself, don't get frustrated if it isn't all plain sailing and don't try to do too much at once.'

Gloria reaches over the second card.

'Your health hasn't been great for a while, dear; have you had an operation recently?'

'I had an ectopic pregnancy nearly a year ago.'

'Yes, I see a sadness in your life. I see lots of hospital visits in the past, sorrow attached to them, and more hospital visits in the future. There is trouble ahead but don't lose heart, everything will work out for the best.'

Gloria is anxious. 'Is there unhappiness attached to the future hospital visits?'

'I can't see, dear, but I do see you going through the doors of a hospital. You're walking beside a dark-haired man, you're not on a stretcher, which is a positive sign.'

Mrs Gilmartin peers over the top of her glasses, shrewd eyes taking in the wan face opposite.

'You mustn't neglect your health, dear, you owe it to your body to take care of it. It's a machine that needs maintenance. I start every day with a solid cooked breakfast. There's no use making do with a cup of tea and half a slice of toast.'

Gloria hands her the third card.

'This is the money card,' she explains. 'You've recently come into an inheritance but it's already earmarked for a purpose, you won't be using it for a holiday or new furniture. I don't see a lot of money surrounding you but you'll never be destitute. You'll have to work hard for your funds, dear, like all of us. Beware of bad financial advice.'

Gloria scribbles furiously as she handles the fourth card.

'I see a baby here, dear. A little boy. He's playing in your back garden, he has dark hair like you. He'll bring you much joy, you'll have waited a long time for him, but he's worth the wait.'

Her pen stops in its headlong flight across the page.

'He'll be with me soon, won't he?'

'Not for some time,' frowns Mrs Gilmartin. 'He wants to be born to you but it isn't the right moment. Be patient, he will come.'

Gloria's confidence in her abilities is diminishing as she picks up the fifth card.

'You're gifted in your friends, appreciate them. I see you surrounded by people who love you, they form a circle around you. But you must be careful not to break the circle. There is pressure on it from outside, you must withstand that pressure and nurture your friends. You're the sort of person for whom friendships are lifelong, you have an ability to love and be loved and to smooth away obstacles. Are you Gemini? No? Libra? I thought so, you like peace and order, you want life to be beautiful. There is ugliness ahead but friendship will help you through it.'

The sixth card is retrieved. Mrs Gilmartin runs her hand across her forehead wearily.

'Are you all right?' asks Gloria. 'Can I fetch you a glass of water?'

'I'm fine, my dear, just a weak spell, it's passed now. I need to concentrate so intensely during a reading that sometimes my energy levels drop.'

'I thought for a minute you'd seen something appalling in my card,' she half-jokes.

The older woman regards her seriously.

'My dear, it's not my place to predict tragedies, if I did see any I wouldn't say so, and besides, what the cards show me is what may come to pass, not what will inevitably happen. You have free will, you can choose one path above another and alter your own destiny. I can warn you of certain pitfalls, I can't predict you'll fall under a bus. But I can say, "Be careful in traffic, you have a tendency to daydream." You need to do something about the iron in your blood, I sense a deficiency there.'

Buy vitamin pills, writes Gloria, nodding obediently. It's not so different to being in a doctor's surgery, apart from the toaster in the corner of her field of vision.

'This is the romance card,' says Mrs Gilmartin. She sighs as she studies it. 'You had a great love affair, it ran its course for many years, but now you have doubts about it.'

'It's over,' agrees Gloria.

'This great love affair is over and you feel empty, cast adrift, unsure of yourself. You've been part of a couple so long you've · forgotten what it's like to be an individual. Regard this as an opportunity, explore yourself, learn to be on your own for a change, start to enjoy your own company. The solitary life doesn't suit you but go with it for now, it will bring rewards.'

She really doesn't have a clue about the baby, Gloria smirks, as she writes.

'I see a man in the distance, a man who has tender thoughts for you. But there's a barrier, maybe you feel it's too soon, maybe you feel he's not right for you. Trust your instincts. This man has recently given you a gift. Enjoy it, but remember, all gifts must be returned one day.'

Gloria's puzzled. 'I don't understand.'

'There is a man who wishes you well and a man who wishes you ill. You're connected to both of them.'

'How will I know which is which?'

'You'll know,' says Mrs Gilmartin. 'Now show me your left hand, dear.'

She runs her fingers lightly along it.

'This is the lifeline, you'll have a long life with no serious illnesses. This is your loveline. You aren't interested in hordes of men, you prefer loyalty and continuity. What's the expression they use now, serial . . . ?'

'Monogamy,' Gloria tells her. 'It's true, I'm the original practitioner of serial monogamy. Much good it does me.'

'It's your nature, dear,' says Mrs Gilmartin. 'You can't buck your nature. Or if you do there's a tangle to unknot. I see one great love affair which has ended and another one waiting to begin.'

'When?'

'Not for some time. A nature like yours can't cast off one lover and take on another, you need time to adjust. Let yourself take that time, don't be in a hurry, it's out there waiting for you. Now make a wish, dear. Concentrate on it, fill your mind with it.'

Gloria thinks of her baby, eyes tightly closed. 'Grow healthy and strong,' she urges him. When she opens them, Mrs Gilmartin is watching with an unfathomable expression.

'Shall we go through to the front room and find your friends? It's long past my granddaughter's bedtime.'

'What about my wish? Will it come true?' asks Gloria.

She puts a finger to her lips and Gloria notices for the first time she's wearing frosted pink lipstick that's bleeding slightly where it's been applied shakily. 'Everything comes in its own time, dear.'

The three friends pile into a pub called The Hunter's Moon on the main road back to Dublin.

'That woman is beyond brilliant,' proclaims Kate. 'What she told me about my life is uncanny. She knew about Pearse, about the job, the flat, everything.'

'What did she say about the future, Kate? You're not paying her to tell you things you already know.' Eimear is less than enthusiastic about their Ashbourne psychic.

'She had plenty to say about the future,' insists Kate. 'I'm going to travel with my job and I won't settle down for years and years. When I do she sees me in a happy home surrounded by sunshine and laughter. And I've been wasting my time with the wrong sort of men, I'm to be choosier and have confidence in myself.'

'All very general,' sneers Eimear, splashing the tonic into her vodka. 'You could point to every woman in this pub and tell her she's been wasting her time with the wrong sort of men and she'd say you were a genius.'

'How did it go for you, Eimear?' asks Gloria. 'Is Christy the one for you or are you wasting your time with wrong uns too?'

Eimear taps the table. 'That woman was useless. I'm supposed to stop worrying about material things. "Possessions will only end up possessing you," she told me. I'm to chill out and let the dust mount up and take time to get to know myself.'

'I have to get to know myself too,' exclaims Gloria. 'It must be her party piece. What about you, Kate, are you supposed to take this voyage around yourself too?'

'No, she didn't mention that, I'll be travelling in hot countries and I'm to go easy on the drink, apparently there's a danger I might get too fond of it. Whose round is it?'

Eimear is still playing with her vodka, too annoyed to drink it.

'Any word of men, Eimear?' enquires Gloria. 'I've two of them after me, apparently, though I haven't spotted even one yet.'

'There's the usual tall dark stranger hanging around but

he isn't Mister Right,' she snorts. 'He isn't even Mister Keep-Me-Going-Till-Mister-Right-Arrives, I'm to stop using him and learn to make my own way. That woman claims I've never been without a man since I was fifteen and I'm far too dependent on them for my own good.'

'She wasn't far off the mark there, Mulligan,' interjects Kate, sucking her lemon slice in the absence of further alcohol.

'It's the implications of the remark I object to, as though I'm using men as props – as chauffeurs, as decorators, as financial advisors, as bed-warmers.'

Kate winks at Gloria and she winks back. This Mrs Gilmartin doesn't just foretell the future she dispenses sound advice too.

'Put it this way,' Gloria addresses Eimear. 'Would you be bothered with Christy if you weren't house-hunting and didn't find it useful to have him ferry you around?'

She's indignant. 'Just because the Beetle's conked out and I can't afford to have it repaired doesn't mean I'm stranded. Can't I get a lift off either one of you if I need it.'

'True, but we weren't able to tap pipes and peer under floorboards to tell you if the house with clematis framing the door you were so keen on was a dream purchase or a nightmare waiting to engulf your bank account.'

Eimear tosses her head. 'She didn't mention my collection of poetry, she didn't mention my separation, she didn't mention my job.'

'But she did say there was a creative force within you that needed expression,' Kate reminds her.

'That could mean anything.'

'So what happened to *"Adios amigo,"* if Christy didn't get the Mrs Gilmartin imprimatur?' asks Gloria.

'The Troy Boy, in lieu of anything younger,' remarks Kate.

Eimear raises her drink defiantly. 'I'll show that old biddy who's using who,' she vows. 'I'm going to make this work with Christy Troy, I'll ring him as soon as I get home and invite him over for a meal on Friday night. Candles, Puccini, the works.'

'Does that mean passionfruit ice-cream for dessert?' enquires Gloria.

'It means I'll be having my roots seen to before Friday,' promises Eimear. 'The man doesn't know it yet but he's in for the time of his life.'

'Fighting talk, Mulligan,' applauds Kate. 'I'll lend you my fornicating tape to help create the ambience.'

'You're not still using that to pull men,' says Gloria.

'Certainly I am. Wall-to-wall Lionel Ritchie and the Righteous Brothers, it's never been known to fail. There's just one condition, Mulligan.'

'Name it.'

'You have to memorise the Christy conquest and titillate us with it. And I mean every detail, from which item of clothing he removes when, to the words he whispers in your ear at the crucial juncture.'

'You drive a hard bargain, Kate McGlade,' says Eimear. 'But for the ultimate fornicating tape – it's a deal.'

CHAPTER 33

Talk about an anti-climax, chafes Eimear. Christy couldn't see her last night, he was working. So the fornicating tape is sitting in its plastic container, still waiting to be unleashed on him. So much for her fooling herself he's putty in her hands.

'Come to dinner,' she purred, in her Sharon Stone starter kit voice.

'Love to but I'm on the rota,' he said.

He must have detected a drop in temperature because he suggested she accompany him on this afternoon's job – she's waiting to be collected now.

'I can't go to work with you,' Eimear protested. 'I'll look like a groupie.' But she agreed anyway.

She's watching from the window for his car when the phone rings.

'Are you sure all over? Is your body a throbbing mass of sated lust? Is he still captive in your boudoir?' It's Kate, avid for some tantalising titbits.

'Go take a cold shower, Kate; it didn't happen.'

'He passed up dinner for two *chez toi*? The man's unnatural. That's bad news.'

It's too good an opportunity to pass up. 'Good news, bad news, who knows?' Eimear shrugs. 'Maybe I was panicked into inviting him.'

'Stop right there, Mulligan, that sounds suspiciously like backsliding. Why did he turn you down?'

292

'He had to work. He offered to call by afterwards for a drink but he said it would be midnight and it didn't seem worth it. I want to tease him lingeringly over the course of an evening, not reach him a can and jump him while he's pulling the tab.'

'So it's game on,' whoops Kate. 'This is only a postponement, not a cancellation. Give him the works tonight, a few bars of "You've Lost that Loving Feeling" and he'll be a pool of water at your ankles.'

'Kate, I have decided to have sex with Christy. I have promised to share the gory details with you. Now shag off and leave the when and where up to my discretion.'

'Touchy.'

'It's just struck me,' says Eimear, 'that it's not beyond the realms of possibility I'm planning to seduce a man with the same tape you used on my husband.'

The connection crackles with electricity between them.

'Am I right?'

'Would I display such a taste deficit?' Kate responds.

'Yes.'

She can hear Kate breathing. 'Let me read your stars, Eimear,' she suggests finally. 'See if tonight's a propitious time for you to put the moves on Christy.'

'You make me sound like a predatory female. As it happens, he's more than keen to oblige.'

Kate reads: '"A pairing of Mercury and Mars heightens the pleasure of sharing, especially for September Librans, for whom this planetary duo may materialise in the guise of a virile male presence." Hey, that's it, the chequered flag. The planets are telling you to go for it.'

The doorbell rings.

'That'll be Christy,' says Eimear.

'He must've read your stars too and decided to strike while the girlfriend is hot.'

'Kate, contain yourself, he's working.'

'Asked you along to hold his spare roll of film, has he?'

'Just to keep him company. And I have to confess I'm curious to see him in action.'

'You shouldn't have to step outside the door to see that if you play your cards right.'

'Kate,' Eimear remonstrates with her, 'any more quadruple entendres and I'm withholding all further information from you. Gloria too, in case she leaks it to you.'

'Eek, you wouldn't be so cruel. Well run along and let the lad in. At least he doesn't sound the horn at you, my mother always warned me about men who beep.'

'See you.'

'See you, Mulligan – and remember you've been promised a virile male presence. It could be just what the doctor ordered.'

Eimear is giggling as she answers the door, Kate really is irrepressible.

'Hiya, Little Miss Happy.' Christy kisses her lightly, his breath tasting of Polo mints.

'I could go in and come out again as Little Miss Misery Boots,' she volunteers.

'Whoa, Neddy, we have to hit the road,' he smiles. 'I'll take you as you are. And I've no complaints, I may add.'

Eimear feels a twinge when she looks at the SOLD sign by the garden gate – she's living on borrowed time in the house now. Christy's Astra is a tip on wheels, crammed with chocolate bar wrappers, out-of-date newspapers, notebooks, biros, anoraks and boots. She snoops in the back and distinguishes a frying pan.

'Is this in case you find yourself stuck in traffic on the N11 and fancy a few rashers?' She holds it up for inspection.

'So that's where it went to, I was looking for it the other night.'

'What on earth are you doing with a frying pan in the back of your car or is that a stupid question?'

'For the Pancake Tuesday shot – s'obvious, innit.'

'Right,' Eimear agrees. 'I won't root around any further in case I unearth a turkey.'

'Why would I have a turkey in the car?'

'For the Christmas shot. S'obvious, innit.'

Christy hums as he drives, elbow leaning on the open window.

'Where are we headed?'

'Skerries. Only a wedding but it's an editor's must. The bride is a niece of the chief executive's.'

A warning bell sounds in the back of her brain. 'What's the name of the bridegroom?'

Christy shrugs. 'I forget his name. It's written on this piece of paper here.'

He digs about in one of the multiple pockets that criss-cross his beige photographer's waistcoat and produces a scribbled scrap. Eimear reads aloud with a sinking heart:

'Wedding of Pearse Coleman and Gertrude English, 3 p.m. Church of the Redeemer, Skerries.'

'I'm not able to go,' she tells him. 'You'll have to take me home.'

'I can't do that, I'll miss the bride's arrival.' He's scandalised.

'I'll have to stay in the car then, I can't be seen.'

Christy runs a red light before replying. 'What's the problem?'

'I know the man.'

'An old flame?'

Eimear shudders. 'One of Kate's; he's still sore at her so I don't think it would be in the best taste to have me popping up with a box of confetti.'

Christy drums on the steering wheel.

'You've suggested the solution yourself. Stay in the car, I have to hang around for an hour to catch the couple emerging from the chapel and then I'll spin by the office to drop off the negs. After that, I'm all yours. We could take another look at your cottage, if you like.'

Pearse is wringing his hands by a tombstone as they arrive, looking more than passable in his Windsor grey, although he's had a savage haircut. Someone should have reminded him to go to the barber a fortnight ago, thinks Eimear. There's a red rosebud in his buttonhole which he plucks between bouts of hand-squeezing.

'Is that him, Kate's ex?' Christy opens the boot to extract a tangle of cameras and flashes.

'Ssh, he'll hear you,' she hisses, sinking into the seat.

'Not unless he's bugged the church wall,' observes Christy, parked insouciantly on a double yellow line. 'I'll leave the keys in the ignition in case a traffic warden shows up.'

'Why don't you just pay for parking like everyone else?'

'Nah, too tame. I like to walk on the wild side, me.' And he blows a kiss and heads Pearse-wards.

Women with floppy hats teeter up the path to the church, hands clamped to the crown of their heads to foil the sea breeze. They mill around Pearse, kissing and cooing, and at ten minutes before the off he disappears into the church. Just in the nick of time, because a black limousine rounds the corner, slows by the entrance and then drives off again.

'She's keen,' mutters Eimear. 'She might have the decency to be a few minutes late.'

The limousine returns, an elderly man in morning suit steps out and holds his hand out to the bride.

'Over here, love,' invites Christy, who's elbowed the official photographer out of the way.

Why is he calling a woman he's never seen before 'love', Eimear wonders. Photographers seem to transmogrify into chirpy Cockneys once they start clicking, even if they've never been anywhere near the sound of Bow bells.

The bride, half in and half out of the car, spilling scrawnily from a white confection designed for a younger woman, smiles hesitantly up at him; she has a gentle hazel-eyed face, no beauty, but she looks like someone with a loving disposition.

'Well done, Pearse,' Eimear addresses him mentally. 'This one will last the distance, she's a much better choice for you than that skit of a Kate.'

Eimear watches her gather her mass of petticoats as she billows towards the porch. Brides are supposed to be good luck – or does she have to see a chimney sweep as well for the magic to work? And do chimney sweeps still exist or did Dick Van Dyke's version hound them out of the profession? She's pondering this as Christy flings his camera carelessly into the front seat – obviously it belongs to the newspaper.

'There's a café down the hill, I'll grab us a couple of take-away coffees while we wait for the closing titles.'

At least he doesn't call her love.

Contemplating Pearse with his bride Gertrude clinging to his arm, shyly accepting the congratulations of their guests, Eimear turns maudlin – weddings have this effect on her. It's all that faith and hope, she doesn't think charity comes into it because the women are eyeing each other's ensembles critically.

'Back to Middle Abbey Street, then the world's your lobster,' grins Christy, slamming the car door.

Time to shake off her wedding miseries, resolves Eimear – the thought of all those best frocks and best intentions are unsettling her. 'I know what I'd like to do,' she tells him.

Grey eyes turn enquiringly towards her.

'I'd like to cook that meal for you we had to adjourn last night. Drop me at Dunnes at the top of Grafton Street and make yourself scarce for a couple of hours, I'll expect you at eight.'

*   *   *

There's a lasagne cooking in the oven, a salad in the fridge, home-made (but not by Eimear) onion bread waiting to be sliced and red wine uncorked. The fornicating tape is playing, to ease her into the mood, as she polishes crystal glasses ready to reflect dozens of tiny candle flames.

She did think about rustling up something more adventurous but decided she didn't want to be in the kitchen until two minutes to eight, slicing and peeling and puce in the face. Meal under control, Eimear changes the sheets, tidies the bedroom, pours a small glass of wine and runs a bath. She nips back to the bedroom to squirt some perfume on the pillows before immersing herself in scented suds. Her knees peeping pinkly from the froth catch her attention: they must be the least alluring part of the body after elbows.

'You're a desirable woman in the prime of her life, about to take a relationship on to the next stage from choice,' she rallies herself.

Opening the wardrobe door, Eimear dithers over vampish or romantic. Her high-necked black jersey dress, which undulates over every curve and peters to a halt an indecent distance above the knee, or her floaty gold shift which swirls after her when she walks and makes her feel like a Merchant Ivory leading lady? Faint heart ne'er won fair lad; she wriggles into the black number – besides, she can wear a padded bra with the dress that fools you into thinking she has a bosom. She pins her hair to the back of her head to show off her diamante drop earrings, an anniversary present from Jack. She hesitates at the reflection in her full-length mirror. Perhaps she ought to abandon the earrings, too many memories. No, Christy's going to exorcise Jack, the earrings are staying.

The doorbell rings as Eimear is placing salmon, wheaten bread and lemon slices on the table, after turning the fornicating tape to smoocherama part II.

'You look sensational, Eimear,' breathes Christy, no slouch himself in a midnight blue shirt and stone-coloured trousers.

Mental note to self, she thinks: don't splash red wine on his legs.

As well as a tissue-wrapped bottle, he's carrying lilies.

'Some people are superstitious about having them in the house, they think they're funeral flowers,' he extends them awkwardly. 'But my mother loves them and I thought you might too. You look like a lily yourself.'

He's self-conscious, as though he's been practising that speech in the car. Nice one, Eimear thinks, he mentions his mother and works in a compliment to her at the same time. This lad's been around the block.

'Lilies are my favourite flowers,' she reassures him, inhaling their heady fragrance.

He troops after her into the kitchen while she hunts for her tall white china vase.

'It's on the top shelf, I can't reach it.' Eimear points to her dresser. 'Would you mind?'

As he hands it down, he leans across and kisses her fleetingly on the mouth.

'Hello, you,' he whispers.

'Hello back.' Her heartbeat pounds in her eardrums.

'I love your hair up,' he touches her chignon.

(Steady, lad, it's not that safely pinned.)

'Keeps my hair out of the way while I'm cooking,' she replies. 'Can't have you fishing blonde hairs out of the food.'

(Why did she say that? It's spoiled the mood.)

'I wouldn't mind,' says Christy. 'So long as they're yours and not cat hairs.'

(He has it bad; she hugs herself, this is going to be a cakewalk.)

'Let me pour you a drink,' Eimear offers. 'I'm on the red wine, do you fancy that?'

'Inspirational, where's yours?'

299

'By the side of the bath, I'll find another glass.'

'Drinking in the bath? You decadent woman, I can't wait to find out what other louche habits you have.'

Eimear's flummoxed. A photographer who says 'louche'? Wait, he said 'loose' habits. Concentrate – he's flirting, she must return the ball.

'You'd be surprised,' is the best she can drum up. 'Come through to the sitting room,' she adds, tap-tapping ahead of him in her spindly femme fatale heels. They say men love a woman in high heels because she looks like she's on the brink of toppling over – a sort of knee-jerk caveman reaction to having her at your mercy. Of course women know this and wear them because they realise it's a sure-fire way of having *him* at your mercy.

Eimear sits on a sofa and waits to see if he chooses a sofa to himself or shares hers. He eases himself into a corner of the one she's perched on, near enough to be flattering, not so close as to crowd her. Ten out of ten so far, Christy, now comes the litmus test.

'Did you find a parking space near the house? The street can get very crowded with cars at the weekend,' she asks.

'I called a cab. I want to enjoy a few drinks without having to look over my shoulder for the guards on my way home. The taxi driver gave me his number and promised to pick me up again, he's on duty till 6 a.m.'

Bingo! He's available to stay the night but he isn't expecting it, this man deserves a refill.

'Let me freshen your drink,' smiles Eimear.

(Why did she come out with such an inane remark? It must be the excitement. Real people never offer to freshen drinks, it's only something they do in Pinewood films. It sounds like you're offering to squirt deodorant into the glass.)

'Love the music,' says Christy later, as she clears away the dinner plates. 'I take it you don't have a vast collection of tapes?'

'Choose something different while I bring through the dessert,' she suggests. She probably doesn't need the fornicating tape any more anyway.

In the kitchen Eimear digs out her make-up purse, secreted in the saucepan cupboard, and checks on her appearance. Red wine goes straight to her nose. A dab of powder, another slick of lipstick, and she's carrying a crème caramel into the dining room. Sensuous and tactile. Like she plans to be.

'You're spoiling me,' he smiles, as Micky Dolenz warbles about thinking love was only true in fairytales.

He's found her old Monkees record, he must've really been poking around in the press.

She looks seductively at Christy as she spoons out the crème caramel. That's a mistake, a gloop of toffee-coloured gunge slips from the spoon and plops on the table. Tactfully he ignores it.

'How did the Skerries photos turn out?' she asks.

'Just another wedding, we'll run a pic in Monday's paper. Can't imagine the groom as Kate's type.'

His eyes stray to her wedding picture on the mantelpiece. Hell, she meant to take it down. It's in a square silver frame: Eimear's looking straight into the camera thinking, 'I wonder if the train on my dress is straight,' and Jack is gazing worshipfully at her.

'You look younger there.' Christy nods at the photo. He realises this isn't the most flattering remark in the world and adds hastily: 'I don't mean you look old now, just different. More mature.'

'Marriage ages you.' Eimear's teeth are gritted. 'Did you never fancy taking the plunge yourself?'

'I did but she wouldn't have me, she said we were too young. She's married to a dentist in Clontarf now.'

'And were you too young?'

He spreads his hands. 'I was willing to risk it if she would. We were both twenty-six, not young and not old.'

Never trust a man without baggage, that's what Eimear read in one of Kate's magazines. Baggage can be inconvenient but it also shows you're dealing with a man who isn't afraid of loving and being loved – even if it means hurting and being hurt. She's no use for one of those lads who make an art form out of being a thing of beauty and a boy forever, she wants a man with a few emotional scars.

She feels a rush of attraction for Christy as he sits there opposite her, hair as black as Jack's but offset by silver eyes instead of brown. She toys with the idea of inviting him to adjourn to the sofa there and then, but reluctantly decides she needs time for her food to digest. Her stomach is still protruding, even though she only picked at the meal.

'Are you excited about the cottage?' he asks.

Her offer has been officially accepted.

'Euphoric. I can't wait to ship out of this place. Too many memories.'

Christy regards her for a long moment across the dining table, eyes glittering in a way that makes her shiver with anticipation. 'Your husband needs his head examined. If you belonged to me I'd never let you out of my sight.'

Heady stuff, her heart starts thumping. Of course he could be a manic obsessive and mean it literally . . .

'Shall we move into the other room?' She sways her hips deliberately as she steps through the partition into the sitting room, perches on a sofa and waits for him to join her. He's sitting so close she feels his breath on her face. Christy has an expression of intense concentration as he removes her glass, setting it carefully on the coffee table. He takes her face between his hands, the tips of his fingers tangling in her hair.

That was the best part, it always is, she thinks in the aftermath. Damp sheet, damp body, dry mouth. A street light filters through the unclosed curtains, bouncing off the laddered stockings on the floor – he removed them a little too enthusiastically.

'I'm roasted, I need a glass of water.' She attempts to disentangle herself from Christy's embrace.

'Stay where you are, gorgeous, I'll go down to the kitchen for you.' He bounces from the bed.

At least he doesn't prance around in the nude like Jack, he pauses to pull his trousers on.

'I brought the rest of the wine up as well,' he waves the remains of their second bottle.

I hope you don't imagine you're here for the night, pal.

'Mind reader,' she smiles. 'Shall we draw the curtains to keep the neighbour's jealousy at bay?'

When the wine is finished, Eimear offers to phone for a taxi for him. His face falls.

'I hoped we might spend the night together. I could bring you breakfast in bed or we could go out to a café for a fry-up.'

She's horrified but pastes on another smile. 'I can't let you near me first thing in the morning, I look such a mess, I wouldn't see your heels for dust.'

'I seriously doubt that.'

He drops a kiss on her shoulder.

'I'm sure you look just as amazing as you do now.'

He drops a kiss on her neck.

'I am completely, totally, utterly smitten by you, Eimear.'

He drops a kiss on the ticklish patch of skin behind her ear.

He tugs at the sheet, clamped firmly across her chest by her arms; there's a momentary tussle before she concedes. She'll look ridiculous if she refuses to uncover her breasts to the man she's just made love with. He starts nuzzling a nipple, she risks a downward glance to check how floppy her boobs are. Not too bad, of course the nipples are erect which helps, but they'll pass muster.

As his hand trails downwards across her stomach, she realises he's game for another session. She'll have to put a stop to this. She captures his hand on the pretext of kissing it, lacing her fingers through fingers.

'This is so difficult to do but I'm going to have to throw you out now.' Eimear watches from under her eyelashes. 'You've worn me out, I'm desperate for some sleep and that's going to be impossible with you in my bed – there's no way I'll keep my hands off you.'

(Has she over-egged the pudding? No, Christy has a sweet tooth.)

'I surrender,' he laughs. 'I'll ring that taxi number now. On one condition – you come over to my place tomorrow and stay the night.'

'No problem,' Eimear smiles into his eyes. She can always back out of it by phone.

By the front door, he loiters to kiss her, tongue massaging tongue.

'See you tomorrow, gorgeous.' He cups her face. 'You're the best thing that's ever happened to me.'

'See you tomorrow, Christy,' she agrees, returning his kisses.

No chance.

CHAPTER 34

Gloria and Kate are mystified.

'It just wasn't right,' Eimear explains lamely.

'Did he rush through it and forget about what you'd like?' asks Kate.

'No, he was very considerate.'

'Was he wearing boxers with cartoon characters on them?' presses Gloria.

'No, a respectable pair of white Calvins.'

'Was there too much tongue?' says Kate.

'No.'

'Spittle?'

'No.'

'Did his teeth clash against yours when you snogged?'

'No, he kissed me very sweetly,' she protests. 'He even remembered to turn his head to one side and didn't stick his nose in my eye.'

'Did he fall asleep straight afterwards?' asks Gloria.

'No, he pulled me close and stroked my hair.'

'Did he make strange noises when he was coming?' Kate wonders.

'Not particularly, a bit of heavy breathing but nothing out of the ordinary.'

'Did he leave his socks on?' from Gloria.

'No, he stripped to the skin.'

'Did he have a peculiar willy?' asks Kate.

'Peculiar?'

'Covered in moles or bent at an awkward angle,' she expands.

'Not that I noticed but I didn't take a torch to it.'

Kate and Gloria regard one another.

'Mulligan,' concludes Kate, 'you're mental.'

'I know,' she agrees miserably. 'I've met the perfect man and he does nothing for me. He kisses me – zilch. He caresses me – zilch. He jiggles up and down on top of me – zilch. I must be frigid.'

'You just don't fancy the man, it's not a crime,' says Gloria. 'Chemistry's a funny business.'

'I fancy him in theory. He's lovely to look at, exactly my type. But all I could think about as he lay on top of me was: "This is a mistake and I can't wait for it to be over." He thinks we're meeting tonight for a repeat performance.'

'You'd better cancel,' advises Kate. 'No point in doubling your torment.'

'Unless you want to offer it up for the suffering souls in Purgatory,' interjects Gloria helpfully.

'I don't think the suffering souls in Purgatory would thank her for it,' says Kate. 'It's not exactly the sort of sacrifice they benefit from.'

Kate studies Eimear. 'Have you ever felt this way before?'

'Which way?'

'Indifferent while another human being is straddling you, thinking he's carrying you along on a wave of passion,' Kate expands.

'Frequently.' Eimear hangs her head in shame. 'But,' she lifts her head again, 'last night I decided I don't have to do it any more. If the sex isn't right with someone, I'm not going along with it. In the past I've been too embarrassed to call a halt.'

'Well said, Eimear,' agrees Gloria. 'I can't pretend there was much surfing in the sea of love these past few years with Mick but I just went with the flow – mainly because I was so surprised when he climbed on top of me it seemed ungracious to expect excitement too.'

'You girls have been selling yourselves short,' sighs Kate. 'I can see I'll have to do something about this – open a geisha school.'

'Geishas are trained to please men,' objects Eimear. 'We need training on pleasing ourselves.'

'You've made a grand start,' says Kate. 'Now pick up the phone and tell Christy you don't want to see him any more.'

She does as she's ordered, except she only finds herself cancelling tonight's date – she can't bring herself to end the romance over the phone. He deserves a face-to-face explanation.

'Coward,' says Kate.

'I'd prefer to do it in person, it's more humane. After all, we've had sex, it puts everything on a different footing.'

'Eimear's right,' Gloria backs her up. 'Since when did we start treating decent men indecently.'

'So does this mean we're back to sharking for Beautiful Boys?' Kate has a hopeful gleam in her blue eyes.

'You can count me out, Kate,' says Gloria. 'I'm nearly three months pregnant, the only Beautiful Boy I'm interested in is the one I'm carrying around with me twenty-four hours a day.'

'Have you been told it's a boy?' asks Eimear.

'No, I just have a feeling about it,' explains Gloria. 'I'll be glad when I'm past the three months mark, I'll start to relax, tell work and my mother and people.'

'You still haven't told your mother?' Eimear is incredulous. 'But Mick knows – what if he blurts it out to her? They only live a few streets apart after all.'

She's ashen. 'God oh God oh God, Eimear, I hadn't thought of that. I'll ring her immediately.'

While Gloria's in the hall, Eimear tackles Kate.

'You hear from Mick from time to time, why is he set so implacably against this baby? He should have softened by now.'

A shrug.

'Is there something you're not telling me, Kate?'

Eimear detects a faint blush spreading across her face. 'Kate, you're holding out on me, give.'

'I'm not, Mulligan,' she protests. 'Cross my heart and hope to diet. Mick just doesn't fancy fatherhood.'

'He ought to have thought of that before they started fertility treatment.'

'Maybe he didn't expect it to work. So will we chase a few Beautiful Boys next weekend?'

'I'm not ready for another relationship, besides I still haven't blown Christy away.'

'Piece of cake.' Kate flaps her hand dismissively. 'Anyway Beautiful Boys aren't about relationships, they're about instant gratification – the only kind worth having.'

'Give me a break,' complains Eimear. 'I'd rather concentrate on moving house. I've mountains of organising to do, I need to find a plasterer and a plumber.'

'Shame on you, Mulligan. Imagine preferring the Golden Pages to a gilded youth. Well, I'm planning to grow old disgracefully even if you're sinking into its hoary arms without a murmur.'

'You can shark on your own, can't you?'

'Ah, you see, that's where you're wrong,' explains Kate. 'I've been pondering this and it's my conclusion that successful sharking is always carried out in pairs. A woman on her own looks desperate, three women together look self-contained – a pair of women look available but not too predatory. It's the optimum combination.'

They're laughing as Gloria returns from the phone.

'How'd the Mammy take it, Glo?' asks Eimear.

'The good news is, she's started knitting.'

'And the bad news?'

'She's going around to Mick's to sort him out.'

'Oops,' says Kate. 'That could be tricky.'

'You're being too pessimistic, what can he say other than that he's not ready to be a daddy and you went ahead without him.' Eimear shrugs.

Gloria and Kate look ill at ease.

'Did she suggest you called the baby after your father?' asks Kate.

'Naturally. But to wind her up I said I was thinking of Fergus. She protested that everyone would call him Fergie. So then I said maybe I'd carry on the family tradition and plump for a film star's name – either Cary or Spencer.' Gloria chuckles. 'I was paying her back for the baby story. She launched into it yet again – you know the one she told everyone at my first holy communion AND my confirmation AND my graduation AND my wedding, and just about every occasion where she can inflict maximum embarrassment before the widest audience.'

'That's the one about you being jealous of your new brother,' Eimear says, more from manners than interest – she's right, Mrs Mallon does repeat it ad nauseam. And Gloria may well have inherited the trait.

Gloria beams. 'I watched Daddy in front of the fire fussing over a strange baby and I suggested we pitch him in on top of the coals to see if that wouldn't heat him up.'

'You divil,' laughs Kate, who's heard the story as often as Eimear.

'I was only three,' Gloria defends herself. 'It's the oddest thing, I was in the house when both Rudy and Marlene were born and I don't remember so much as a whimper from my mother's room. When you see women having babies on television they're bellowing fit to wake the dead and shouting, "You bastard!" at their husbands.'

'She was protecting you, wasn't she,' Eimear points out. 'She knew you were downstairs, she didn't want to terrify you so she obviously bit on a pillow. Now when are you coming with me to see the cottage?'

'Soon,' Gloria hedges.

'Looking at it won't commit you to anything. It's not as though the house will stretch out grisly tentacles and hook you in against your will.'

They banter for a while, then Kate drops Eimear home. She's contemplating that rejection routine call to Christy when the phone rings. It's Mick McDermott, of all people.

'I've just had a visit from Mrs Mallon,' he begins.

Eimear attempts to judge if he's been drinking from his pronunciation – he seems sober.

'That was sociable of her.'

'It wasn't a social call – far from it. She wanted to remind me of my responsibilities. Except, as I had to point out to her, they aren't my responsibilities.'

'Mick, why are you telling me this?'

'Because it concerns you.'

Eimear is baffled.

'Obviously,' he continues, 'since I didn't impregnate the bitch, somebody did. So I made a few calls to Dublin. Kate knew all about it but she wasn't talking. You women are all the same, thick as thieves. But I worked my way along to Jack and he had some very interesting information to shed on this novel situation.'

'My Jack?'

'Loyal of you to call him that under the circumstances. Or downright stupid. He knew all about the pregnancy, in fact he's the man behind it.'

'I'm not following you.' His voice booms inside Eimear's head, ricocheting around it.

'Your Jack, as you like to call him, is the father of Gloria's child. And Kate knows all about it.'

310

'You're lying,' she says, and presses the button that breaks the connection.

But Eimear knows he isn't lying, she knows it as surely as she realises there's no going back now, she's alone in the world. No Gloria, no Kate, no friends. No Jack, no Christy, no lovers. Only herself alone. On automatic pilot, she rings Gloria.

'Is it Jack's baby?' Eimear asks.

There's a painful intake of breath.

'Is it?' she repeats. Her voice sounds odd to her.

'Yes.'

Eimear hangs up.

A few minutes later, the phone rings again. It's Kate. 'I'm coming around to see you.'

'I won't open the door.'

'I have to talk to you, Gloria's distraught.'

'Kate, I'll only say this once. Between the two of you, you've blighted my life. Stay away from me.'

'Mulligan, listen, I know you're hurting. We can sort this out, give me a chance to –'

Eimear lays the handset on the table and walks out of the room, Kate's voice splintering fainter and fainter behind her.

PART THREE

CHAPTER 35

'I'm so proud of you.' Christy hugs Eimear.

They're at her book launch, surrounded by people she's never met before and will probably never encounter again. They don't pay much attention to Eimear, they seem preoccupied by the free drink and miniature spring rolls.

Bitchin' Babes doesn't have a huge promotions budget, its marketing director Josie explains to her. She's been eating cheese and onion Taytos, Eimear flinches from her breath. So the venue isn't a hotel, it's in their managing director's office, which could do with a lick of paint. The furniture's been moved out to her secretary's cubby hole but even so, it's anything but roomy. Not that they need a lot of space, there's sixteen people here including Christy, Eimear and the Bitchin' Babes team.

What HAS this mythical publicity budget been spent on, she wonders. Certainly not the wine, they obviously give this gut-rot away free. Maybe they overspent on blowing up posters from the publicity shots of her, although Christy didn't charge for taking the photograph. Enlarged and unfamiliar versions of her face, airbrushed to look misty, adorn the walls: they've turned me into a Sacred Heart picture, she realises with a jolt – her eyes follow you around the room.

Eimear O'Brien the Poet is windswept, which is natural enough when you're standing on a beach, and encased in an

315

Aran sweater – a garment she usually leaves to the tourists. But the publishers insisted: they wanted to push the Celtic goddess line, although she seriously doubts if a Celtic goddess would be caught dead in a knitted jersey.

The book is called *Mna*, which makes it sound like a public convenience, but Josie talked her into it. 'They won't know it's a jacks in Sydney,' she explained. She could schmooze for Ireland, flattering her into thinking Aussies will be queuing up to buy her collection.

'Imagine,' Christy's arm steals around her waist, 'all these people are here because of you.'

She regards them, knocking back glasses of wine and spilling spring-roll filling down their fronts. Isn't she the lucky one.

'They're just professional liggers,' Eimear complains. 'I don't know a soul apart from you and Josie.'

'Sorry you didn't change your mind about inviting Gloria and Kate?'

She treats him to her most disdainful glare and his arm drops from her waist.

She never did give Christy his marching orders; she may be simple but she's not completely dense. No point in ordering a general evacuation of everyone in her life. Besides, the adoration is reassuring, it makes Eimear feel less . . . abandoned. She's been keeping busy since it happened. Moving house, putting the finishing touches to *Mna*, pleading with builders to finish her bathroom. You have to hop over a hole in the floor where floorboards used to be and negotiate some exposed pipes just to use the loo – it's like an obstacle course. Her bladder is learning admirable self-control. Still, she's settling into her cottage much quicker than she expected – she can have as many swagged curtains as she likes, without anyone complaining.

Eimear frowns, remembering the letter she had from Gloria, a self-serving epistle purporting to justify her behaviour – and which reassured her, as though she gave a fiddler's, that out of loyalty she never actually went to bed with Jack. She's just having his baby. So that's all right then. She ignored it, and the second letter that followed it. Gloria has a funny definition of loyalty. Eimear grinds her teeth, wondering which dictionary she's using.

'How's it going, Christy?'

A familiar-looking man in his late thirties, in an expensive linen suit that manages to look cheap on him, sidles up. He's wearing grey suede shoes. Eimear's mother calls all suede footwear brothel creepers, implying the men who wear them are fiends in human form. In this man's case, she's inclined to agree – he'd surely sizzle under a splash of holy water.

'Eimear, this is Manus. Eimear O'Brien, Manus Comiskey. Manus is our arts correspondent,' Christy does the honours.

'So you're the poetess.' Manus has one of those Dublin 4 accents that sound English to everyone but the English.

'Poet,' she corrects him.

'Right. I haven't read the book but I hear you come across like a man-hating harpy in it.'

'That's because I am a man-hating harpy,' she smiles blindingly.

'Splendid, I'll set up an interview so,' Manus grins. It's an unfortunate one which sucks in the lips above the teeth and exposes the gums. 'I need to circulate here, there's a few people I must have a word with, but I'll be back. No slipping away while my back's turned, now, Eimear the man-hating poetess.'

He half-turns, pauses, and says to Christy: 'You wouldn't take a snap of your woman Landers over there with the youngster beside her, would you? I suspect he's her latest squeeze, it should make for some idle speculation in the gossip column.'

'No, I wouldn't, I'm off-duty,' snorts Christy, 'Steve's supposed to be covering this.'

'No sign of him.' Manus scans the room.

'Not my problem,' shrugs Christy, and pointedly drapes an arm around Eimear.

Manus makes a beeline for the drinks table and stays resolutely within inches of it, so much for the need to circulate.

'He gets my goat,' Christy says. 'He thinks he's such a lady-killer, he has the confidence of a king.'

'Prince Charles never struck me as very confident,' she responds. 'Of course he isn't a king yet.'

As Christy broods about Manus Comiskey, she fits the face to the picture byline she remembers seeing on Thursdays in the *Irish Independent* – the photo is at least ten years out of date, which is why it's taken her a while to recognise him. He should be had up for misrepresentation.

'Working press, be charming to them,' hisses Josie in her ear.

Eimear's startled – some saliva has bounced off her lobe. 'Where?'

Josie indicates three bored-looking individuals propped against the table doubling as a bar. Along with Manus there's a balding swinger with shoulder-length sandy hair wearing a biker's jacket with the collar turned up and a girl with too much black eyeliner who doesn't look old enough to be allowed out on her own.

'Go over and beguile them, it's worth a few inches,' she adds, still in an undertone.

'Especially the girl, she's the *Sunday Business Post*'s latest find.'

'The twelve-year-old?' exclaims Eimear. 'I thought she was here with her mammy.'

'The benefits of keeping a portrait in the attic,' sighs Josie.

'Anyway I've already met the Comiskey fellow, he wants to fix up an interview later.'

Josie appraises her. 'You're a fast worker, I'll grant you that. There's a lot to be said for a head of blonde hair.'

'Will I take you home now, Eimear?' suggests Christy.

'I don't think I can leave just yet, it's supposed to be my bash.'

'All the best people snub their own parties. Let's slip away and split a bottle of wine somewhere quiet, this stuff's vile, I can feel my gastric juices complaining already.'

'It's not so bad,' she tells him. 'You get used to it.'

Obviously all those years on the Blue Nun before she knew any better have built up a tolerance.

Manus Comiskey shuffles up, two glasses in his hand. Eimear imagines he's about to offer her one, but he explains that the barman has intimated he's about to shut up shop, so the second glass constitutes emergency rations.

'Of course,' he looks lopsidedly at her, 'if I take you on somewhere for a bite of supper, and do the interview over that, I'm automatically on expenses.'

'She has other plans,' says Christy.

'She'd love to,' says Josie.

'Sorry, I can only invite Eimear,' says Manus. 'The eckies don't run to more than a table for two.'

Eimear vacillates. On the one hand he's obviously an obnoxious little toad, on the other hand she needs the publicity.

'You're not to go,' whispers Christy.

It's a red rag to a bull.

'Ready when you are,' she smiles straight into the pink-rimmed eyes of Manus Comiskey. He blinks, downs one of his drinks, hesitates over the second, sets it on a nearby table and sweeps an arm gallantly to indicate Eimear should precede him. Then he has second thoughts about the untasted wine and retrieves it for a final gulp.

'I'll call you tomorrow, Christy,' she promises with a quick kiss.

She knows she's misbehaving, but she also knows he'll let her away with it.

'Business before pleasure,' she murmurs quietly, as Manus's Adam's apple negotiates the wine.

Christy's eyes blur with hurt.

Now that she's alone with Manus Comiskey, Eimear feels much less confident. She doesn't like the way he accidentally-on-purpose bumps his knee against her under the table. She's not keen on being squirrelled away in the darkest corner of Bucci's restaurant. And she's not sure she wants to press ahead with her plan to dish the dirt on Jack. Revenge may be a dish best eaten cold, but there's such a thing as indigestion. It's retaliation enough proving to him he's not the only Famous Seamus in the family. Her collection of poetry must be sending him into a lather.

Manus seems unable to settle until he has a bottle of wine on the table in front of them. He can't concentrate enough to listen to the answers to questions he poses half-heartedly – if this is his interviewing technique, it stinks. But there's a transformation as soon as he holds something liquid in his hand: he focuses, he looks closely at Eimear and murmurs: 'I don't know how such a beautiful woman was able to put up with Jack O'Brien for as long as you did. You must be extremely patient. And forgiving.'

She considers: now's her chance to play the injured party to the hilt.

'I've heard,' Manus leans forward conspiratorially, 'he had a weakness for the under-graduates.'

Eimear widens her eyes. 'You mean . . . ?'

Manus nods sadly.

'I'm astonished.'

'You didn't know?' He raises an eyebrow.

'I know he's an extremely conscientious lecturer who devotes himself to his students.'

Both eyebrows shoot up this time.

'And it never occurred to you his interest might be more than professional?'

'I really can't imagine what you're suggesting, Mr Comiskey.'

'But you are separated, you have sold the family home.'

'That's true,' she nods.

'And that would be because . . . ?'

Now it's Eimear's turn to lean forward in collusion. 'I haven't known you very long but I feel I can trust you.' He nods avidly. 'This is strictly confidential. The reason Jack and I separated was because he refused to engage in marital relations with me. The women are a cover – off the record, he prefers men.'

He pushes the glass to one side, eyes bulging. Her instinct was right – he is a toad; if a fly drifted past she'd swear his tongue would flick out.

'There's never been a whisper of this before,' he gasps. 'Jack O'Brien trades on his reputation as a literary Casanova.'

'It's all a sham. Of course I'm relying on you to keep this strictly entre nous. I'm only telling you because you seem so genuine, so committed to the arts, so interested in my book. I want you to understand where my poetry springs from, the salient influences.'

'Oh yes, your book, Men Are something,' he says.

'Mna,' Eimear corrects him. 'Do you think you'll be able to mention it somewhere in your wonderfully authoritative and entertaining column?'

(Is she going over the top here? No, he seems to inhabit an irony-free zone.)

'I hate to ask but I know Jack is using all his literary contacts to block publicity about my little collection. He's probably approached you already but I've always heard how incorruptible you are.'

(Now she has overstepped the mark, there's a quizzical expression on his face.)

But he's still thinking about Jack's predilections.

'Naturally I'll give you a mention, a photogenic lady like yourself could write a laundry list and still get her face in the paper. You are sure, aren't you, about your husband's sexual preferences?'

Eimear is too preoccupied with fuming to answer.

Belatedly, he realises he might have offended her and adds: 'Not that your wonderful book is a laundry list, far from it, it's a page-turner, I have a copy by my bed.'

'You told me you hadn't read it yet.'

'I meant read as in savoured and appreciated; naturally I've dipped into it and I must say it's spellbinding.'

'Which is your favourite poem?'

That's flummoxed him: the unsavoury grin reappears, gums shining wetly, and he fumbles for an answer. She watches him squirm for a while before putting him out of his misery.

'People generally like the one about cystitis, where I compare the sting of urine to elastic bands being snapped against the girl's genitalia,' she explains.

'Such a graphic analogy,' he ad-libs, wincing only slightly 'When did you first realise your husband might have these leanings?'

The waiter arrives with his chicken and her fish.

Manus waits while he fusses around, offering black pepper from a grinder the size of the Leaning Tower of Pisa – but without the incline – and attempting to refill their glasses.

'I can manage that, thank you.' Manus brushes him away.

I'm sure you can, thinks Eimear. Keeping a glass brimming is a labour of love for you.

'But there's adultery and adultery,' he insists, when the coast is clear.

'There is and there isn't,' she prevaricates.

She can see he's itching to scribble on his napkin but is afraid she'll stop talking. She also notices he's stopped drinking.

'Manus,' Eimear brings her face so close to his that the

features swim, 'you do realise I'm telling you this as a friend, not as a journalist. I know we've only just met but there's something solid and reliable about you, you have the power to make a woman feel, well, safe. I sense an innate chivalry in you.'

Then with one hand she gathers her hair into a loose bun, exposing her neck and shoulders, concentrating on looking vulnerable, and leans her chin on the other hand.

He kidnaps the hand she's resting on, presses his lips to it, then turns it over and tickles the palm. Yuk! Eimear heaves her stomach back into position and focuses on maintaining her defenceless aura. (What colour is a defenceless aura, she wonders idly. Probably something pastel, maybe lavender. But back to business.)

'If Jack knew I'd been talking about him in such an intimate way I don't know what he'd do to me – he's capable of anything,' she shudders. 'But it's such a relief to confide in someone as understanding, as supportive, as intuitive as yourself.'

He strokes the hand he's held pinioned since the kiss. Not noticing that his sleeve is dipped in the tomato sauce coating his chicken.

'Your wife is such a fortunate woman,' Eimear murmurs. 'I believe Christy bumps into her from time to time.'

It's a shot in the dark because he isn't wearing a ring but it has the desired effect. He drops her hand with unseemly haste, grabs his glass and swallows deeply.

· The meal passes with Manus trying to elicit specific details about Jack which she's unable to furnish because she doesn't have any. He thrusts, Eimear parries, and before long she's on her way home with nothing more unpleasant than a clumsily groped bottom as she jumps into a taxi.

Next morning she rushes to buy the *Independent* on her way into work. She flicks through it quickly but can see no mention of Jack. She tries it again more thoroughly during coffee-break, but still nothing to be quarried. Strange, she'd have bet her shirt on Manus being a man for whom the word 'confidence' was always shortened to con. Then she remembers – it was nearly midnight before she headed for the hills, probably too late for him to start spinning his tale.

She checks again the following day and there's the story, on page five, along with Eimear's woolly goddess publicity shot and a photo of Jack in full flow at a poetry reading. She speed reads the text: her book is mentioned, except there's a misprint and it's billed as *Nna* (now there's an endorsement); Eimear is described as 'the radiant, estranged wife of prize-winning poet Jack O'Brien' and later 'the blonde poetess'. God almighty, how many times does she have to tell that man she's a poet?

She returns to the start and reads through properly. The piece is honeycombed with suggestive language. The gist of it is that Manus claims a source (that's Eimear!) close to the poet (not Eimear!) reveals the couple's marriage has irretrievably broken down because his wife feels she can no longer turn a blind eye to his outside interests. For Jack O'Brien, it divulges, who toured American campuses two years ago with an acclaimed series of lectures on Oscar Wilde, has taken to emulating the master in more ways than one. His broken-hearted wife, meanwhile, is consoling herself with her own collection of literature, *Nna*, which unsurprisingly displays a certain animosity towards the male sex. It's all a bit nudge-nudge, wink-wink, but there's enough for any self-respecting mathematician to put two and two together and reach seven.

Her answerphone is bristling with messages when she arrives home from the library.

First Jack: 'Have you been speaking to the press? I'll wring your fecking neck if you have and you can kiss goodbye to a share of my pension.'

Then Manus (how did he get her number?): 'Your husband's solicitors have been on to us, they're threatening to sue for libel. The editor's breathing down my neck, can you call?'

Another message from Jack: 'And *Mna*'s a pile of shite, by the way.'

Manus again: 'The editor's turning nasty, my job's on the line, I really need you to ring me back. O'Brien is definitely suing.'

Next Christy: 'I told you Manus Comiskey wasn't to be trusted, you'll find you've bitten off more than you can chew. I can't make Friday night, I'm working.'

And finally Kate: 'Way to go, Mulligan. I know you hate me, and I don't blame you, but I have to say "bullseye". I thought you'd hit him where it hurts when you hammered Black Jack for cash, but this latest scam is sheer bloody genius. You've turned bad news into good news, you devious cow, you're a star.'

Eimear rewinds the tape so she can listen to Kate's voice again. She's not softening, but maybe Kate didn't know about Jack and Gloria. She misses her. Then she thinks of Gloria having Jack's baby, the one she wanted, and the shutters fall. Eimear erases the message.

CHAPTER 36

Kate is reading aloud to Gloria, who's swollen up like a bal-
loon since she hit the six months mark. She's like a bowl of
Angel Delight, thinks Kate: blubbery-shuddery cheeks, bottom (she'll need her London derriere man's number after the
birth) and belly.

Gloria isn't impressed by what Kate's reading from the
newspaper advertisement: 'What every woman's hips, thighs
and buttocks have been waiting for.'

'Is this to do with liposuction?' asks Gloria, serially chewing
winegums.

'Save me a yellow one.'

'You don't need winegums, Kate, you can drink your own,'
she complains, extracting a couple of sweets and aiming
them at her.

'No, it doesn't mention liposuction, it's a little battery-operated
gizmo called Cellesse that wages war on your cellulite.'

'Cellulite is the least of my worries.' Gloria's mouth is
crammed full of jelly and E numbers. 'What do you do with
the gizmo?' Gloria turns the bag upside down to flush out
the last sweet clinging stickily inside.

'You massage yourself. There's a picture of a woman's lower
regions, with a strategic towel, and they've stamped "Cellesse
here" all over the danger zone.'

Gloria studies the advertisement. 'She wouldn't recognise
cellulite if it knocked on her door and introduced itself as her

long-lost cousin. And the day's a long way off before that one has to massage herself, men are probably whimpering to do it for her.'

She hauls herself to her feet with difficulty and peers into Kate's fridge.

'Still empty,' she sighs. 'Have you nothing to eat? I'm permanently hungry these days.'

'It's not empty,' protests Kate, 'there's a bottle of vodka and a carton of cranberry juice in there. Possibly even some cheese.'

'The cheese crawled .out when I opened the door,' says Gloria. 'And the vodka and juice may be convenient for your cranberry coolers, you crypto-hipster, but they're not much good to me.'

'Have a cream cracker,' offers Kate, having ransacked the press but failed to turn up anything more substantial.

Gloria bites in, complains it's soft and chomps on. Crumbs spill down the front of her sweatshirt with 'Let me out!' emblazoned across the front.

'Been back to the IVF clinic?'

'Nope, finished with all that. Once you're pregnant it's a case of here's your hat and where's your hurry. They shunt you sideways into the hospital's pre-natal unit.'

'Do you feel strange going to appointments on your own?'

'It's no big deal, there's loads of single mothers there, even a lesbian couple who syringed the conception with the help of a contribution from an accommodating neighbour, so they told me – when Ireland embraced the permissive society there were no half-measures.'

Gloria pauses, looking thoughtful, fingering the tartan bow in her ponytail. 'Sometimes I think it might be nice to have Mick there. At my last appointment I watched a man and woman do a crossword puzzle together while they waited for the doctor and it seemed so . . . companionable.

'But mainly Mick never crosses my mind. I've bought him

out, he's emptied the house of his belongings – some of mine too while he was at it – and apart from the odd letter that needs readdressing, I don't think about him. He claimed he'd get a flat in Omagh but so far there's no shifting him from the Mammy's, sure why would he want to move out when he's living off the fat of the land. She even butters his toast in the morning.'

'So you don't miss him?' asks Kate. 'There isn't a gaping Mick-sized hole in your life?'

'Only a yawning Mick-sized dip in my mattress – I'll have to buy another. Amazing how we turn into our parents – my father always maintained there was no substitute for a sound night's sleep. You don't miss Pearse, why would I be lonesome for Mick?'

'Pearse and I were only together for four years, it's hardly in the same league as you pair of teenage turtle doves.'

'Look at how well we're managing without Eimear,' Gloria points out. 'If we can get by without her we can handle anything.'

Gloria has convinced herself that Eimear can be erased from their lives as easily as you'd press a delete button on a computer. Kate is amazed at how conveniently she's blocked out the fact she used Eimear's husband to father her child, it's as though she simply went to a sperm bank and selected sample number 271. Her baby has taken Eimear's place in the troika – they're still a trio as far as she's concerned.

Of course Gloria's cocooned herself in fantasy bubble-wrap but it's not up to Kate to burst it. Gloria will have enough reality poking through when the infant arrives. For starters, the child's father is not going to be so easy to shake off as she imagines.

'Jack still pestering you?' The enquiry is posed casually.

Gloria regards her friend suspiciously. 'Why, what have you heard?'

'Nothing. Really and truly, oh little red dragon.'

'He still leaves the odd plaintive message on my answer-phone, asking after the bump, but I ignore them. Granted, I'd have no bump if it weren't for his donation but he was never interested in me. It was an act of random generosity. Once I turned into a carrier for offspring sharing his incomparable gene pool, however, I became instantly beguiling to him.'

'It would be worse if he didn't give a fiddler's,' Kate suggests, wondering why she's bothering to defend Jack. 'It shows the man has a spark of humanity.'

'So let him take himself off to the foreign missions if he wants to turn do-gooder, there's no scope for him here in Ranelagh.'

'It's obviously his midlife crisis,' explains Kate. '*Image* magazine says men often turn broody in their late thirties, it's fear of forty syndrome.'

'You and your syndromes. What can I eat now?'

'I can't keep up with you, Glo, are you sure it isn't a tape worm instead of a baby you have in there?'

'I'd be skinnier if it was a tape worm.' She looks complacently at her stomach.

'We can't have you dying of malnourishment, I'll dial a takeaway,' Kate offers.

'No, run me home, I can rummage for something there – pregnancy is making me incredibly territorial. I hate to be too long away from the nest.'

'Shall I come in with you?' Kate helps untangle Gloria from the seatbelt.

'You might as well if you've nothing planned – no hot dates then?'

'Not even a lukewarm one – whatever I had, I've lost it.'

'Nonsense,' laughs Gloria, her stomach shaking alarmingly. 'You just haven't decided if you want a Beautiful Boy or a wrinkly old man.'

'Is there no halfway house?'

'You mean like a wrinkly boy or a beautiful old man?'

'Not quite,' giggles Kate, as they stroll up the path.

Gloria half-stoops to pull at some weeds edging out her marigolds as she passes them but thinks better of it. Bending is something she's had to abandon. A familiar figure emerges from a car parked at the top of the street.

'Hello, Gloria, Kate,' he says.

'Hello, woman-beater,' Kate responds.

He looks pained; meanwhile Gloria fumbles for her keys and turns the lock.

'Inside, quick,' she hisses, pushing Kate ahead of her.

'Gloria,' says Jack pleasantly, 'either you invite me in or I conduct our business via a megaphone from the pavement. It's entirely up to you.'

She turns helplessly to Kate.

'You have to live here,' Kate reminds her. 'I'll leave you to it.'

'No, don't,' Gloria clutches her arm. 'I'll let him in on condition you stay.'

'What are you afraid of?' Jack seems mystified. 'I don't bite – I may have the odd nibble but I promise you no one's ever complained.'

Kate's lips curl as she looks at him, lolling there with his foot on the step and his brown eyes mocking them. In her mind's eye she sees him watching her, just as confidently, the day she found him in her bed with one of his students.

'I'm not afraid of anything but I don't see why Kate should be forced out just because you want to come in.' Gloria faces him defiantly.

'What is this strange obsession you have with Omagh girls?' Kate says conversationally, as he follows them indoors.

His eyes ignite but he doesn't respond. Instead he concentrates his attention on Gloria, charm oozing from every pore. 'Continuing to blossom, I see.' He smiles devastatingly.

Despite everything, Kate's heartbeat speeds up, but Gloria appears unaffected. 'State your business,' she snaps.

'It's not so much business as pleasure.' He tries another disarming smile but this, too, falls on stony ground. 'I thought you might be finding it difficult to manage on your own by this stage and I wanted to offer you the services of a cleaning lady. Just to help out with the heavy work until the baby comes. She works in the college, I can recommend her unreservedly, and it would be my pleasure to pay her wages. Say twice a week for a couple of hours, would that be acceptable?'

His grin sets new standards in smugness. Still, Kate has to concede it's a generous offer – Gloria does need help. She can offer moral support till the cows come home but Kate's not so handy with a vacuum cleaner. Gloria's anger is palpable.

'You can shove your cleaning lady, you can shove your self-satisfied face, and most of all you can shove your money. I never want to see you again, Jack O'Brien, in fact never's too soon.'

Jack's expression registers his astonishment at her venom.

'I think you'd better leave now,' suggests Kate, leading the way. He follows docilely but hesitates by the front door.

'She could be seeing me every day of her life in the baby's face,' he says, before walking out.

Gloria is shaking when she returns, not from anger but from fear. The adrenaline is dwindling and her face is pinched, green eyes borderline tearful.

'You need a brandy, pet,' Kate tells her.

'I can't, the baby wouldn't approve,' Gloria protests, quivering.

'Tea then,' and Kate guides her into the kitchen where she plugs in the kettle and fishes around for mugs.

Tea, the great panacea, the camomile lotion that soothes all stings. Any crisis can be dealt with by a cup of tea – death, unemployment, separation. It gives people something to do in the wake of bad news, this ritual that occupies the hands and disengages the brain.

Gloria watches her dunk teabags in mugs.

'Eimear would complain to the high heavens if she saw you doing that,' she says.

'What she doesn't know can't hurt her,' winks Kate, slinging the used teabags in the sink.

They sip in silence but behind the peaceful exterior Kate is railing inwardly: she's ageing before her time, life is all tea-drinking and no champagne-swilling. And she hasn't had sex for months, she'll have forgotten how to go about it if this lasts much longer – she needs a refresher course. Soon. Seeing Jack has rekindled some sensations – Kate always prided herself on being the sort of woman who, asked what sort of sex she liked, answered 'frequent.' She doesn't want Jack back, but she's reminded how physical their relationship was. She's jolted from her flesh-toned reverie by Gloria.

'He's after my baby, Kate.'

'A share in it, maybe.'

'Has he any rights?'

'I don't know, Glo, it's not my area of expertise. I can look into it for you if you like.'

'He's my baby, I don't want to share him,' Gloria says fiercely. 'Especially not with Jack O'Brien. I don't want a man like him anywhere near my child.'

Kate strokes her dark hair. 'He's not all bad, Glo,' she tells her, again wondering why she's championing him. 'He did supply the sperm when you were desperate – without Jack there wouldn't be a baby.'

'I know,' she howls, tears spilling out at last. 'Oh, Kate, I'm so frightened he'll take my baby away from me.'

Kate calms Gloria down, piles her off to bed for an early night and slips out quietly. She's looking forward to a long drink in a tall glass, with ice-cubes clinking around the bottom and a slice of lemon if her fruit bowl can run to it. A hand covers Kate's as she unlocks the car door, simultaneously another hand muffles her incipient shriek.

'Don't panic, Kate, it's me, Jack,' he whispers, mouth close against her ear.

Fury lends her strength and she breaks free, whirling around to challenge him.

'What on earth are you playing at?'

'Ssh,' he flaps a placatory hand. 'I need to talk to you – can I sit in your car for a minute?'

'On your granny.'

She jumps quickly into the Spitfire.

His hand snakes in after her and grips the door frame – if she slams it, she'll crush his fingers. He's so close she can smell his fresh sweat and she's lost, she can't do it.

'Get in,' Kate murmurs, head slumped against the steering wheel.

'This is about Gloria,' he begins, his body angled towards hers in the narrow confines of her mucky green car. She never seems to find the time to wash it.

Kate looks ahead, she can't risk turning towards him.

'Gloria needs me.' He regards her at close range. 'She doesn't realise what she's letting herself in for as a single parent, nor what she's depriving her baby of.'

'She has her friends and family.'

'The Mallons are all in Omagh or London – there's only you here in Dublin. You're surely not counting on Eimear to melt when she hears there's a bouncing baby to dandle.'

'So what are you offering, to marry Gloria and play Mammies and Daddies?'

Now Kate does turn to look at Jack.

His face creases. She notices he has a suntan, he must have been abroad because there's been no sun in Dublin.

'Even if I wanted to, I'm not in a position to marry anyone, Eimear and I have to be separated for four years first. Besides which, I don't love her.'

'Naturally not.' Her tone is caustic. 'Your notion of love is very self-contained – it's Jack O'Brien first and last.'

'Maybe,' he shrugs, unleashing his little-boy-lost look on her, the one that always had her reaching to comfort him.

Kate quashes the rising tide of emotion and returns her gaze sternly to the streetlight a few doors up from Gloria's house.

'Kate, please intercede with Gloria for me, she listens to you.'

'Why should I?'

'For Gloria's sake and for the baby's.'

'No mention of the benefits to you, Jack.'

'I know you have no reason to do me any favours, I don't have a right to ask on my own behalf.'

'And what is it exactly that you want from Gloria?'

She's still looking resolutely ahead, memorising every line of that streetlight.

'Just to share her baby, to be there for both of them. Not to play Daddy, as you put it, but to have a part in his life.' His tone alters, become guttural with emotion. 'You see, Kate, I know what it's like to grow up without a father. I know the emptiness and the neediness, I've lived with the conviction I'm the reason why my mother and father aren't together, that I'm somehow unlovable.'

She steals a glance at his face and is moved, in spite of herself, by its bleakness. Jack's voice cracks as a story emerges that she doesn't think even Eimear knows.

'My father left home when I was five. "I'll write to you, son," he promised, "and I'll be back before the summer's out." Every day I scanned the road, watching for him. I bolted my breakfast and climbed the tree at the bottom of the garden for a better view of the way he would come, I hardly wanted to go in for my dinner. But the leaves fell off the tree and still no sign of him. Christmas came and went without a card. Finally my mother said he'd moved to Australia to start a new life and it was better that way. She said I should forget him.' His voice trails off and he gazes sightlessly ahead, then he takes up the story again. 'He used to keep a bar of chocolate for me in the breast pocket of his jacket. I'd run to him when I saw him coming from work and he'd swing me up into his arms and I'd push my hand into the pocket to find it. It had a purple wrapper. I can remember the chocolate bar vividly but I can't see his face.'

A splattering of rain raps the windscreen, Kate contemplates turning the key in the ignition to activate the wipers but decides she prefers looking at the world through a haze.

'Did you never try to contact him when you were older?'

Jack knuckles his eyes. 'When I was twenty or so I started making enquiries through the Australian embassy. It wasn't easy, all we knew was that he'd arrived in Sydney fifteen years earlier but it's a vast country and there was no way of knowing where he'd ended up.

'Finally I located him in Broom, in Queensland. But I was a few months too late – he'd died of cancer. I visited his grave on a lecture tour of Australia in 1992. His tombstone said: "Jack O'Brien, born Tipperary, Ireland 1929, died Broom 1981. Sadly missed by his wife Jennifer and sons Ned and Joe."'

'So you have brothers,' Kate exclaims. 'Did you go looking for them? You always wished you weren't an only child.'

He brings his fingers to his forehead and rams them hard along his eyebrows. 'My parents never divorced. He must have married that woman bigamously. How could I approach her and her children with news like that? There were fresh flowers on the grave, they obviously cherished his memory. I had no right to defile it.'

She reaches out and holds his hand. He grips Kate's, crushing the bones. She glances towards Gloria's house and is relieved to see it's still in darkness.

'Shall I drop you back to Trinity, Jack?' asks Kate after the longest time.

He starts, as from a trance. 'No, my car is at the top of the street, I'll drive myself.'

He touches her chin, stroking the dimple, and opens the car door. Before he steps out Kate speaks, stumbling in her rush: 'I'll speak to Gloria for you.'

'Thank you.' The ghost of his old smile flits across his countenance. 'You always were a pushover for a sob story.' And he's consumed by the night.

CHAPTER 37

'He's a poet, he has something called an imagination to play with. It's obvious he's lying.'

Gloria's voice curls derisively.

'You didn't hear him, Glo, he was breaking his heart hauling all that buried grief to the surface. You wouldn't invent a story like that.'

Her mouth is twisted out of shape. 'Hearts don't break. Arms, now they break, legs break, so do necks. But hearts? I don't think so.'

'Gloria, I have no reason to think well of Jack O'Brien, I have no reason to plead his case with you. This is the man who clocked me one, this is the man who used my flat for a tryst, who wooed his pop-tart with my champagne.'

'Which he never replaced,' Gloria intones, before Kate has a chance to lodge her usual complaint.

'Right,' Kate agrees. 'There are some betrayals a woman can never forgive, he crossed my Rubicon with that one. However I still say – don't write him off. I learned something about him last night and it's not important any more whether we approve of him or forgive him. He's a product of circumstances, like all of us, of choices – his own and other people's. He's not admirable or evil but a mixture of both. I think he needs this baby as much as you do. Give him a chance.'

'If I give him an inch he'll take a mile,' Gloria protests. 'Jack

O'Brien is sugar-coated arsenic. Look at what happened when he meshed with you, it nearly drove Eimear to breaking point. And see the result of my encounter with him – he couldn't keep his gob shut and now we've both lost Eimear and there's no way she'll come around a second time. There are no bridges to build there, the ground has turned to quicksand. And if all that isn't enough, the man has me tormented, he's forever pestering me, he's even swayed you to his camp – the one person who should know better. He has to learn that he can't have everything he wants for the asking.'

'You're terrified of him, aren't you, Glo? What is it that petrifies you – are you wary of his charm, frightened of falling in love with him? Are you attracted to him, is that the problem?'

Kate is chancing her arm but the barb hits home. Gloria looks startled, then guilty, then mulish. 'I'm not going to dignify that ridiculous allegation with an answer.'

But Kate knows and Gloria knows she knows.

'So,' muses Kate, 'Eimear has his name, I had his body and you'll have his baby. The wife, the mistress, the mother. Jack's shared himself out equally among the three of us, like a sheikh servicing his harem. Except we haven't been glad to take turns with him, have we, we've scrapped over him and become enemies because of him.'

Gloria shrugs. 'We're better off without him, the man's a jinx. Let him in the door and who knows what might happen, you and I could be at each other's throats. I say he's history – ancient history, like Nero. Jack O'Brien doesn't exist.'

Gloria has developed a taste for intransigence during this pregnancy. Kate deems it best not to thwart her and retires, defeated – for now.

'Have it your own way, Glo. He's bad, badder, baddest. He's irredeemably wicked and we're both plaster saints. Still, I won't push you any more; I promised I'd put in a good word, I didn't offer to brainwash you. Now, Isabel Eccles says there's a new and very Beautiful Boy working at the Put A Cork In It, an American backpacker on a year out from college – will you come out with me till we give him the once over?'

Gloria smiles, relieved the unpleasantness is at an end. 'When did you have in mind, oh seducer of fresh-faced buckos?'

'Would-be seducer. Why not tonight? Fun and games have fallen by the wayside around here, time to put that to rights.'

Gloria looks doubtful. 'I fancied a bath and an early night to be honest, Kate. I'm finding it heavy weather standing about on my feet in the classroom, my back aches by going home time – still, only another month or so to go.'

'And you will have an early night, my sweet,' promises Kate. 'I just want a gander at our All-American boy, I don't plan to pinion him on the counter and deflower him then and there.'

Gloria dithers. 'Do they serve food in the evenings?'

'Food?' Kate spoofs. 'Isabel says it isn't food, it's manna and yes, they serve until 9 p.m. Put your shoes back on and I'll treat you to a banquet of gastronomic superlatives.'

'I probably won't be able to get into them.' Gloria huffs and puffs as she struggles to ease on her flat-heeled courts. Her ankles are swollen and she's already wearing a size up.

'Never mind shoes, slip on some sandals,' Kate is business-like; she's spotted a pair under the coffee table.

'It's hardly the weather for open toes,' Gloria objects, push-ing her feet into the navy sandals. 'This had better be door-to-door service, I'm not sashaying through the streets of Dublin in these.'

'Your chariot awaits you, ma'am.' Kate executes a sweeping bow and ushers Gloria into the Hurtle Turtle. But Spitfires weren't designed for pregnant women and it is with con-siderable difficulty that she finally folds her friend in.

Isabel is right: the new waiter is a gift from the gods. Six feet four inches tall, eyes the colour of antique pine, curly blond hair and a chest like a teddy bear's. He's exactly Kate's type – unfortunately every woman in the Put A Cork In It feels the same way. There's so much oestrogen floating around the man's in danger of being either smothered or mothered to death, she thinks, fluffing out her red hair. Just in case he notices her.

'Now, ma'am, what's your pleasure?' The American reaches their table, order pad in hand, and lowers himself into a chair with easy familiarity. His voice is southern states, one of the Carolinas maybe, and his grin is as wide as Georgia. This IS a suitable object of lust, Kate hugs herself, as she asks for some Ballygowan and a glass of house white.

'I can recommend the Dublin Bay oysters,' he beams, producing menus from the pocket of his dark green bar apron. 'I had some for lunch. One of the perks of the job is I get to eat as much as I like. That's why I do restaurant work, I'm always hungry.'

And with another flash of the killer grin, he heads for the bar.

'He can whistle Dixie to me any day of the week,' Kate whispers.

'If I didn't look like a beached whale I'd be dangling bait at him myself,' agrees Gloria.

'Wonder if there are any more like him at home. Glo, I'm entering that lottery for American work visas if he's a representative sample.'

'As soon as I can drink, I'm going to ask him for a mint julep – just to make him feel at home,' says Gloria.

'Do you know what's in a mint julep? What if you don't like it?'

'Of course I do, there's mint and um, alcohol. And liking it is irrelevant.'

His return interrupts their drooling session. 'You fine ladies decided what you'll have?'

They haven't even opened the menus.

'You couldn't give us a minute,' suggests Kate, capsizing into his golden eyes.

'You can have as long as you need, ma'am.'

He prepares to move on to the next table but she detains him.

'You're American, aren't you? What's your name?'

'Brad, ma'am, Bradley P. Kelly.'

'Kelly, so you're Irish?'

'Yes, ma'am. I have Irish, Polish and Lithuanian blood. Also some Cherokee on my mother's side.'

'That's quite a combination,' notes Gloria. 'What are you doing in Dublin, Brad, researching your roots?'

'Yes, ma'am, but there doesn't seem to be any of our branch of the Kellys in Dublin. My great-great grandfather came from County Galway so I'm going to call on the Kellys there.'

'All of them?' Gloria is taken aback. 'You'll have your work cut out.'

'Are there a lot of Kellys in County Galway, ma'am?'

'There are hordes of them in every county in Ireland, Brad. But good luck to you, I dare say you'll rustle up a handful willing to claim kinship with you.'

'And what do you work at back home in America, Brad?' enquires Kate.

'I'm still a student, ma'am, I'm on a year off from college. I've taken my degree and I hope to go back to do a master's in international law. My father's an attorney, he's real keen for me to follow in his footsteps.'

'Fascinating,' she breathes, 'as a matter of fact I'm a lawyer myself. Maybe I could get you into our office as a runner for a couple of weeks, give you a chance to see how we do business here.'

'Ma'am, I sure would appreciate that.'

'What other plans have you for your year off?' smiles Kate, sending so much 'I'm yours for the asking' radar towards him it's a wonder jet planes aren't diverted off-course from Dublin Airport.

'Well,' he leans his elbows on the table and she notices tiny hairs glint on his bare arms. 'I thought I'd travel around, see a bit of the old country. I've only been here four weeks and most of that time has been spent finding somewhere to live and this job.

'I was in London for a month before that but I wasn't so keen on it, people seemed in too much of a hurry and the air was so thick you could take a knife and fork to it. I may go on to Poland in a couple of months or I may hang out in Ireland for the rest of the year, I haven't decided. Galway isn't far from Dublin, right?'

'Couple of hours,' says Gloria. 'You don't want to go haring off to Poland, Brad, you've only just arrived here. Tell us what you think of the place.'

'The people sure are friendly and the air seems clean but it's colder than I expected. Is it always this wet?'

'Always,' Kate confirms. 'We're a south European people trapped in a north European climate, it's a national tragedy. We're awarded five days of sunshine a year, seven if the hole in the ozone layer rips again, and winter lasts from October to May. It's not Ireland at all but Direland you've come to.'

Brad laughs. 'Bord Failte must be paying you guys to drum up business, right?'

'Well done,' she smiles back. 'You're picking up the language already. Another couple of weeks and you'll be giving the specials of the day *as Gaelige*.'

'Ass what?' Brad looks faintly scandalised.

'In Irish,' Kate translates. 'But you're making such a good fist of the English with all those elongated Southern Comfort vowel sounds, perhaps we oughtn't to lure you away from it.'

'Brad,' shouts a harassed barman, 'any chance of a hand over here this side of Christmas?'

He smiles apologetically and strides off, every female eye in the room boring into his back.

'That,' sighs Kate, 'is most definitely a Beautiful Boy.'

'I'm hungry,' complains Gloria, 'he forgot to take our order.'

Kate brightens. 'Excellent, that'll give us another chance to monopolise him. I'll offer to take him on a sightseeing trip on the pretext I want to talk about his work experience with us. If he's circumnavigated the city already I'll lure him up to the Hill of Tara, tell him it was the traditional seat of the Kellys.'

'You could explain young contenders for the chieftainship used to challenge each other to single combat on top of the mount, get his blood all fired up,' suggests Gloria.

'Or I could tell him there's a prophecy that Ireland will never be united until the day a Kelly from a far off land comes home to Erin and wins the love of a native-born maiden from the Clan McGlade,' Kate elaborates.

'Maiden,' ponders Gloria. 'They say Americans can be gullible but I don't think they're as soft as all that.'

'Behave yourself, or I'll tell Brad you're always this huge,' threatens Kate, and they subside, giggling.

The door opens and Eimear walks in with Christy. She's en route to a party, in a crimson Chinese dress which accentuates every curve, hair piled high and secured with oriental pins. She doesn't see the others until they're squeezed on to seats at the corner of the bar; when she does catch sight of them she stiffens and seems inclined to bolt.

Gloria, too, is tense: after an initial sibilant 'look' she fiddles with her knife and fork, clattering them against the empty plate. Kate is expectant – should she go over to Eimear? Her heart pounds as she wonders what to do for the best. Christy seems to be the only one unaffected. He bends his head towards Eimear and then approaches their table.

'Hiya, Kate, Gloria, how's it going?'

'Grand, Christy, and yourself?' replies Kate.

'Never better,' he smiles awkwardly. 'Can I buy either of you a drink?'

'We're all right at the moment but maybe you'd like to join us?' invites Kate.

He looks over his shoulder but Eimear has her back unyieldingly presented towards all of them and is lighting a cigarette.

'Why not, for a minute,' he says. 'I shouldn't leave Eimear too long though, she tends to feel ignored. You know?'

'Tell me about it,' mutters Gloria.

'Can't you persuade her to talk to us, Christy?' asks Kate.

He shrugs helplessly. 'Eimear's Eimear, she's not easily persuaded to do anything she objects to.'

Kate takes pity on him sitting opposite, grey eyes bewildered by this strife among women. 'Go back to her, give her our love. Tell her we're here for her when she wants us. And, Christy, be kind to her.'

He smiles at her. 'She's easy to be kind to, she's so beautiful.'

'She is.' Kate smiles back.

'You need to be kind to yourself too,' interjects Gloria. 'Eimear will take all your solicitude and hunger for more, you'll never satisfy that one.'

He looks uneasy as he returns to her. Eimear stands up immediately and walks to the door, leaving her drink untouched on the counter. He follows, catching up with her on the pavement. From Eimear's expression, Gloria and Kate know there's trouble in store.

'How do you think Eimear's looking?' asks Kate.

'Ravishing, naturally.'

'But a little strained, perhaps. I thought I saw loneliness in her eyes for a moment before the shutters slammed down.' Kate watches Gloria, hoping for signs of a thaw, but her face remains resolutely blank. 'Poor Christy,' continues Kate, 'she won't make him happy. And he certainly can't make her happy.'

'He's a big boy,' shrugs Gloria.

'Speaking of big boys . . .' Her eyes stray towards Bradley P. Kelly. 'What do you think the P stands for, Glo?'

'Patrick, of course.'

'Let's ask him,' suggests Kate. 'I'll have a coffee and you try a pud.'

When he returns with Gloria's Mississippi Mud Pie (especially chosen to please Brad), she poses the pertinent question.

'Gloria here thinks your P is for Patrick but I think you look like a Peter myself. Which of us is right?'

'Neither, I'm afraid, ma'am,' he beams. 'It's Ptak.'

'What sort of name is that?' enquires Gloria.

'It's Polish, ma'am, my grandfather was called Lech Ptak. You don't pronounce the P.' His grin illuminates the room.

After he's gone, Kate tells Gloria in a mock-portentous voice, 'He will be mine, oh yes, he will be mine.'

Gloria chokes on her spoon. 'I can see you've got the bit between your teeth, McGlade, there's no hope for the poor lad – he's irretrievably lost.'

'Besides which,' Kate continues in her normal voice, 'there's something I desperately need to find out about him.'

'Which is?'

'Will he still call me ma'am in bed?'

CHAPTER 38

'It's built in such a way that at the summer and winter solstice, the light illuminates the central burial chamber. The Egyptians weren't the only ones with a knowledge of mathematics and astronomy and all that malarkey,' explains Kate.

They're standing at Newgrange in the Boyne Valley: Neolithic treasure, feather in Ireland's tourism cap, impressive beyond words and a source of limited interest to the ravishing young Kelly blade.

'That Slane Castle place where they hold rock concerts is near here, right?' he asks. 'I hear the Verve played a cool gig there the other summer.'

'They did,' confirms Kate. 'It clashed with the Bee Gees so I didn't go.'

'You went to the Bee Gees instead of the Verve?' His look is as sceptical as his tone.

'No,' she admits. 'I didn't go to either. But I have to follow your countryman's dubious advice and confess I cannot tell a lie. Given a straight choice, I'd have preferred to see the Bee Gees. You see, one of the joys of turning thirty, Brad, is that you no longer have to pretend to be trendy. You can hold your head up and admit you have Bermuda shorts in your wardrobe and country and western music in your CD rack.'

This torrid affair with a Beautiful Boy is proving harder work than Kate bargained for. Gratifying though it is to find herself in bed with a young man who demonstrates his ardour as often and as satisfyingly as though he'd swallowed an entire bottle of Viagra, there is a down side. A down slide, in fact.

Everything's fine and dandy when they're in bed, but with the best will in the world they can't spend all day every day under the duvet. For starters she has to go to work; good God, Kate yelps, horror-struck, she actually enjoys work.

'Gee Katie,' he rests an arm on her shoulders and she near-buckles under the weight.

'Kate.' She removes the offending limb.

'Sure thing. You know it's been three weeks already.'

As long as that? she wonders.

'Is that all?' she asks. 'It seems like only yesterday that I coiled my lasso at you like a rootin' tootin' cowgal.'

'I've told my mother about you,' he confides.

Kate stiffens. 'Brad, how old is your mother?'

'Forty-three, Katie. Why do you ask?'

Relief courses through her – ten years older, that's a decent gap. 'No reason – what did you tell her?'

'Just that I'd met a wunnerful Irish lady who's really kind to me.'

'You could be describing your landlady,' objects Kate.

'You are a sort of landlady, I spend so much time at your apartment,' he squeezes her waist. 'Except I don't pay any rent – I remunerate you in a different way.'

He picks Kate up and whirls her around – he's so physical, like a playful grizzly bear.

'Down boy,' she gasps, when she regains her feet. 'Let's get you over to Slane if you'd prefer to see it – you can drive, use up some of that excess energy of yours.'

Be careful what you wish for, it might come true. Another of Gloria's old crone sayings. Here she is with a Beautiful Boy and she's as glum as they come. He's so ardent, he's so enthusiastic, he's so energetic, he's so wearing. He's so young.

'Brad,' she says later to her Virginian (she was a state out) back in St Stephen's Green, 'I think I'll head over to Gloria's tonight, see how she's managing.'

'Cool, I'll come too.'

'No, it'll be too boring for you. It'll be all girl talk, you wouldn't like it.'

'I would,' he radiates confidence. 'I love girl talk, my sisters say I'm better at it than them.'

'This is different,' explains Kate. 'Gloria's heavily pregnant, she'll need some tender loving care.'

'I can do that. I give great back rubs. I'll have her spine singing in no time.'

'Brad!' Kate's tone is sharper than she intends it to be. 'Don't they need you at the wine bar tonight?'

He looks shifty. 'I've been meaning to talk to you about that, Katie, I quit my job.'

'Why?'

'Because –' he bounds across the room and lands on top of her with the finesse of a puppy – 'I want to spend more time with you.'

'Oh, Brad, this simply won't do,' she sighs, and allows herself to be swept off to bed.

Gloria's face is puffier than ever, she's resting her ankles on a footstool.

'So let me get this straight,' she says. 'He's sensational in bed, you can't walk down the street with him but you're the envy of every woman, he absolutely adores you and he's even told his mother about you. Maybe I'm being dense here but IS there a problem? You're worse than Eimear was after jiggery pokery with Christy.'

'He's suffocating me,' moans Kate.

'Doesn't take his weight on his elbows?' she enquires mischievously.

Kate lobs a cushion at her.

'He wants to go everywhere with me, he meets me after work, he tries to take me to lunch, he runs baths for me, he carries my shopping, I can't even go to the hairdressers without him peeking in at me through the plate-glass window.'

'And the real problem is?' Gloria pushes her dark hair away from her hot face as Kate writhes.

'I feel like his mother!'

'So dump him.'

'I'm willing to dump him, I'm wanting to dump him, I'm waiting to dump him,' moans Kate.

'Just do it.'

'I will.'

'When?'

'Soon.'

'Tonight.'

'Maybe.'

'Yes.'

'All right.'

'How are you anyway?' Kate tears her attention away from her over-active love life and contemplates the bump. 'You sure you're not ready to pop, Glo? You look more than nearly eight months to me.'

'I do, don't I, but the doctor says another five weeks to go. Shame he won't be a Libran, like us; he'll be Gemini, but that's nearly as good.'

'He could have a split personality – Gemini isn't the twins for nothing. But, speaking of stars' – Kate hunts around in her bag – 'you should hear our prognosis for the week ahead: "Prepare yourself for great news. This is the best of times. Mars gives you the drive and flair to develop your creative brilliance. The focus is on interesting experiences."'

'Spectacular,' Gloria nods. 'Mind you, I don't feel particularly creative right now, I feel lethargic to the point of sloth. That's one of the seven deadly sins, isn't it? I haven't the energy to commit any of the others. Well, maybe gluttony, but that's definitely it.'

'But you are being creative, angel,' Kate tells her. 'You're creating in the best way known to woman, you're producing another human being.'

'Yuk,' she squirms. 'You've been reading those wimmin's books.'

'How much longer do you have left at school?' asks Kate before Gloria starts ranting about her books – it's true, she does have a pile of them by the bed but they're mainly there instead of a bedside locker, she rests her clock on them.

'I finish next Friday, it can't come a day too soon,' she yawns and stretches. 'I wanted to stay on as long as possible to give me extra time after the baby comes but I can't last any more than eight months – it takes all my energy just to totter out of bed in the morning and come downstairs. I break out in a sweat if I walk any further than the bottom of the street – it's lashing off me now and I'm not even standing.'

'I'll fix you a nice cold drink,' Kate tells her. 'A gin and tonic without the gin.'

'Better still, send Brad over, he can show us how to make the ultimate mint juleps,' Gloria chuckles. 'I looked them up in my cookery book with a cocktails section. You need a bottle of wine, lemonade, soda water, some Pernod, a dollop of crème de menthe and cucumber to garnish. Serve chilled on a warm day.'

'The best we can manage is warm on a chilly day. Sounds like a lot more julep than mint in that recipe, you're not fantasising about being able to drink again, perchance, Glo?'

'I am,' she confesses. 'I've been stockpiling bottles of wine for the great day. As daydreams go, they're even more satisfying than my Tom Cruise one. Which hasn't recurred, before you ask.'

'Probably just as well,' Kate tells her. 'Nicole Kidman's not an easy woman to follow. You know it might be all in the mind, this fancying a drink. A magnum of champagne might not be your priority when labour's over. It could be like a Lough Derg pilgrimage – you fast until midnight on the last day, pound home and line up all the goodies you're raring to eat, then find your eyes are too big for your stomach.'

'Spoilsport, would you let me alone with my fantasies,' exclaims Gloria. 'If the thought of diving headfirst into a crate of Chardonnay keeps me going until next month, where's the harm?'

'Just so you're warned. Did you see that article about Eimear in the Sunday paper?'

'No, what did it say?'

'It was an "at home with . . .". Her cottage looks idyllic. She was photographed arranged wantonly over various items of furniture – the bed, the sofa, the kitchen table. Obviously she was doing it to plug her book but writers must feel like prostitutes.'

'I think you're being a little hard on writers,' says Gloria. 'Besides, they're not all doing it to make pots of money, some might enjoy seeing their photographs in the paper.'

'More fool them. I like to be able to shut the front door on the world, not invite it into my downstairs lavatory. Not that I have one.'

'Any mention of that business with Jack and his homosexual leanings in the article?'

'Alleged homosexual leanings,' Kate specifies. 'Retracted allegations of homosexual leanings. I hear the paper crawled on its hands and knees over barbed wire and paid him a juicy out-of-court settlement. Apparently a journalist lost his job over the story, too.'

'So Eimear did Jack a favour,' says Gloria. 'That must be niggling her no end.'

'As you reap, so shall you sow.' Kate shrugs. 'You know what we're doing here, don't you?'

'Gossiping, of course,' says Gloria, rustling the inevitable

351

packet of winegums. 'They say your hair falls out after you have a baby but I think my teeth are going to be the first to parachute out.'

'No, we're engaged in one of the fifteen great longings of Homo sapiens.'

'Thought there was just one and that was sex,' munches Gloria.

'Only according to Freud. There's a group of American psychologists who claim they've outlined the fifteen fundamental desires that underpin all human activity and one of these is the urge to communicate.'

'Doesn't that mean intense discussions about the meaning of life and whether God's a man, woman or hermaphrodite?'

'No. Apparently we're the most communicative species on earth and most of our talk is trivial. But that's all right because it's forging relationships. Other animals bond by grooming each other, we do it by gossiping. And where we win hands down over the other species is because our bonding technique is more effective: you can only groom one at a time but you can gossip with a roomful of people. Brilliant, isn't it. No wonder we're the dominant species.'

'We're not,' objects Gloria. 'Don't they say when the bomb drops there'll be nothing left on the planet but cockroaches?'

'True, but in the meantime they're not building Taj Mahals and sending rockets to the moon.'

'What are the other major human desires?' she asks, mouth stuffed with sweets.

'Eating winegums, that counts as the food imperative, family groups, sex of course, social order, power – nothing as important as gossip. I read it in the same newspaper that had Eimear's "at home with". You look tired, Glo, aren't you sleeping?'

'I can't get comfortable. The bump's a brute, he starts kicking as soon as I settle down at night. I try dozens of alternatives but none of them satisfy him so I end up having to prop myself against the headboard with pillows, but then I develop a crick in my neck. They didn't mention any of this at the IVF clinic.'

'Would it have made any difference?'

Gloria reflects: 'Not a bit of it.'

'Well then, just mark the days off your calendar. Won't your mother be down soon?'

'Not until a fortnight before my due date, there's no point in having her hanging around indefinitely. And they say first-timers often go well over on their dates. Cruel, isn't it?'

'Monstrous, Glo.'

Kate's decided it's as well to agree with Gloria these days, she's apt to burst into tears if you say anything controversial – 'I see the slugs have been at your peonies' or 'They've postponed *Fair City*, there's a football match on.' Cue waterworks.

'He's kicking again now, would you like to feel?' Gloria invites Kate.

'No,' she shudders, 'that's too much like nature in the raw. Why's he kicking, anyhow?'

'To remind us he's here. As though there's any danger of me forgetting. Are you still game to be present at the birth?'

'Absolutely,' Kate promises her.

After all, she thinks, she's going to end up as this child's godmother – Gloria has to ask her, who else is there?

'Provided,' adds Kate, 'there's no screeching, no blood, and you can guarantee the doctor delivering you will look like George Clooney out of *ER*.'

'No problem, it'll be a dawdle. You can chat up my medic while I quietly give birth in a corner of the room, doing my best not to interrupt the pair of you.'

'As long as that's settled. Jack been prowling around lately?'

'No sign of him, Kate,' admits Gloria. 'Perhaps he's finally got the message.'

'Nah. He's busy doing a crash course in gynaecology so he can deliver the baby for you. He probably thinks you won't recognise him behind his surgical mask.'

'Not funny.' She looks at Kate reprovingly.

'Sorry,' she apologises, in case Gloria's hormones decide to take an interest in their conversation. 'Thought about the christening yet?'

'I've been giving it a great deal of thought,' she admits. 'They don't actually expect me to do any work at school these days, it's enough that I turn up, so I've been making lists.'

'Is that so? Obviously a woman who means business.'

'I'm going to spend my few remaining paltry punts and throw a party – let's face it, this is probably the only baby I'll have so I may as well mark his arrival in style. I'm going to round up all the distant cousins, book caterers, have a chocolate cake in the shape of a crib and buy myself a new frock. James Spencer Mallon is going to have a christening day to remember, even if he won't. Remember it, I mean.'

'Spencer? So you weren't kidding your mother?'

'I was at the time but the name grew on me. My father was a big fan of Spencer Tracy's. He liked Henry Fonda too but I can't bring myself to call the blob Henry, not even for a second name. What if he grew up to have six wives?'

'At least he won't be allowed to decapitate them these days,' Kate comforts Gloria. 'So we're to prepare ourselves for the mother of all parties, sounds good to me.'

Gloria regards her defiantly. 'And I'm inviting Eimear.'

Kate is taken aback. 'Are you sure about that? I mean, I think it's a splendid idea but what if she wrecks the occasion, what if she's determined to cause a scene in front of your family and friends? It could be awkward.'

'Eimear's not a scene-causer. A scene-stealer, yes, but she'd never throw a wobbler in front of witnesses,' says Gloria. 'It's up to her if she accepts the invitation, I can only extend the olive branch.'

Kate examines her scheme for flaws. 'You've nothing to lose and a friend to gain, it's worth a try. Just so long as you don't rub salt in her wounds by inviting Jack too.'

'I'd sooner ask Mick,' she shudders. 'Now he IS someone who'd probably turn up specifically to cause maximum embarrassment.'

'Poor Mick,' murmurs Kate.

'I know,' Gloria's regretful. 'Where did it all go wrong.'

'Now, now.' Kate's determined to avoid the threatened mood swing. 'Back to the party. You can't have it too soon, you must lose some of the flab first.'

'This isn't fat, it's all baby,' she insists.

'Of course it is, and I'm Sinead O'Connor.'

'Well, give us a song then, how about "I Wish I Were A Maid Again"?'

'Too late for that,' Kate tells her. 'You'll have to go on a diet after the boy wonder arrives – there's a price to pay for all those winegums.'

'I'd better enjoy them while I can then.' Gloria opens a new bag. 'Anyway I've come up with a way of making sure Eimear comes to the christening.'

'What's that?' Kate asks, liberating a yellow winegum.

'I'm going to ask her to be godmother.'

CHAPTER 39

A woman who wishes to conceive should walk naked in her vegetable patch on Midsummer Eve.

That's one way to do it, Gloria supposes. She wishes she'd known this years ago, a fortune could have been saved at the fertility clinic. She's propped up in bed reading the invaluable advice from *Paganism: A Beginner's Guide*, bought in a discount shop.

Pagan christenings are all the go, she's seen photographs of them: fellows who kit themselves out as druids and conduct open-air ceremonies, where the infant is held aloft and blessings invited from the four elements.

'What do you think?' Gloria addresses her bulge. 'Will it be a windswept hilltop or the Church of the Holy Name? I think so too, indoor services are infinitely more civilised.'

No more work, she stretches languorously. Just her and James, no noisy pupils, no homework to mark, no queuing for lunchtime sandwiches. No one to talk to though, she decides to give Kate a call.

'Ms McGlade is in a meeting right now, can I take a message?'

It's Bridie, her relentlessly efficient secretary. Is Kate really in a meeting or is Bridie shielding her from time-wasters? Gloria can't leave the message she wants to, that she's baking a ginger cake in the afternoon and she'll save her a slice. It sounds far too trivial.

'Just tell her Gloria called, nothing urgent, I wanted to ask her to drop by later if she's free.'

The day stretches endlessly. Gloria wanders into the kitchen and peers into the cupboard, half-hoping she's out of flour. No such luck. Nine months is a gargantuan gestation period, you should be allowed time off for good behaviour. Mind you, she wouldn't be entitled to any remission – she blotted her copybook on the day of conception.

James Spencer Mallon's conception. Gloria is reminded of Jack, part of him was there at the conception, after all. Against her will, Kate's story about a five-year-old boy dangling from a tree, aching for his father, resurfaces. Such a pathetic scene, the expectant child on sentry duty day after day. It doesn't excuse him for the way he is but it certainly goes a long way towards explaining it. She sets flour, treacle and ginger on the worktop and extracts margarine from the fridge.

'This is useless, you have to be in the mood to bake cakes and I only fancy eating them,' she says.

Gloria wanders out to the garden, deadheading a few late tulips. 'Trollops from Amsterdam,' she sings to entertain herself, but it doesn't work. She could bring a deckchair out and sit in the sun, except the rays aren't warm enough for basking – you have to keep walking to drain any benefit from them.

'I'm lonely,' she complains to some dying daffodil stalks.

She'll be obliged to ask her mother to stay, she's desperate for company. Her mother's probably lonely herself and missing Daddy. A pang of guilt pierces Gloria: she hasn't been particularly attentive since her father died, she assumed Rudy and his wife would take care of her since they live so close.

'I've been preoccupied with my own life,' she scolds herself.

Plus – and maybe she's being hyper-sensitive here – she can't help feeling that her mother watches Gloria with puzzled eyes, wondering how her life has taken such an unexpected hairpin bend. They've had long phone conversations, Gloria's been up for a couple of weekends, but she hasn't had her mother to Dublin to stay with her and that's selfish. She'd have loved a wander along Grafton Street and a cup of coffee in the Shelbourne. She's hardly a demanding house-guest.

'I'll make it up to her,' Gloria promises the daffodil stalks, before retreating into the house. 'Suppose I may as well get dressed.' She's still wearing her bathrobe and it's nearly lunchtime. 'Can't let my standards slip.'

Two o'clock and still nothing to do. She's washed, dressed, lunched, and only an hour and a bit has been used up. She tries reading her Thomas Hardy but it's so depressing, you need to be feeling positively ebullient before tackling *Jude the Obscure*. She replaces the marker in the book just one page further along and wills the phone into life.

'Ring,' she orders, with her most determined thought waves. It stays remorselessly silent.

Wouldn't you think that Kate might have phoned her back. She checks the connection in case it's off the hook, it isn't.

'I bet Bridie didn't give her the message in case it diverted her from work. That's the trouble with Kate when she's between men, she hurls herself into the job. If Bridie had her way she'd never look sideways at a fellow again.' She decides to give Jude another chance to be less obscure.

Gloria wonders if Jack is better than no father at all. She knows he has a track record that stinks when it comes to women but that doesn't mean he's hopeless with babies.

Uh-oh, she thinks, I know where this train of thought is leading.

She takes a deep breath. 'Get thee behind me, Satan!'

He did give her the sperm to make this baby, though, she couldn't have managed it without him. And what if he's right, what if she does see his face every day reflected in her son's? And what if the baby grows up resenting his lack of a father or imagining he's unlovable, the way Jack did?

358

Gloria lifts the Golden Pages down from the shelf, looks up the number for Trinity College and dials.

'Professor O'Brien is giving a lecture, would you care to leave a message?'

Would she? Gloria is dubious. In fact, she's unsure why she's calling his office.

'Caller – would you care to leave a message?'

'It's Gloria Mallon, he has my number.'

She rings off, feeling like she's run a marathon. She hopes she doesn't regret this.

Gloria switches on the television set as the opening titles of *Pillow Talk* flash up. Her spirits lift – Rock Hudson and Doris Day, just what she needs. It's extremely suggestive, in an innocent sort of way. Rock's a womaniser and Doris is disgusted by his philandering.

'If there's one thing worse than a woman living alone, it's a woman who says she likes living alone,' says Doris Day's daily help.

Gloria stores that gem away to contemplate later. In the meantime she's fascinated by Rock's bachelor pad; if that apartment was a dog it would have to be spayed.

The phone shrills, just as Rock and Doris are in a nightclub and he's rescuing her from the clutches of a drunken admirer.

'Gloria? It's Jack, I've just been handed your message.'

Why did she leave her name, it was boredom – she'll fob him off.

'It was nothing important,' she begins but he interrupts, concern pitching his voice higher than usual.

'Is everything all right with the baby?'

The baby, that's all he cares about. She could be on a life-support machine but as long as the baby was growing safely inside her it wouldn't take a fidget out of him.

'MY baby is perfectly well, thank you.'

'I'm glad to hear it. How are you managing on your own –

do you feel like company? I'm finished for the afternoon, why don't I stop by and see you? Just for a few minutes. I could bring you some groceries if there's anything you need.'

'Well . . .'

She's tempted. She's out of winegums, milk and fresh fruit. Gloria's been delaying an expedition to the shop, she can't muster the energy even to go the length of Centra on the Ranelagh Road. He detects her hesitation and pounces.

'I'm on my way, tell me what you need.'

Gloria watches Rock escort Doris home (he takes her key to open the door for her – now why don't men do that for us any more) and considers pulling a comb through her hair. But she feels too lethargic; besides, he's coming to inspect the bump, she could be a shop mannequin for all he cares. The doorbell rings; the man must have broken land speed records getting here. She struggles from the sofa with the grace of a walrus and in comes Jack, arms full of shopping.

'I thought I'd cook you a meal if you'll let me,' he smiles in a way she'd have called bashful if she didn't know him better. 'I'm renowned for my peppered steak.'

'I can't manage spicy food, the baby objects,' Gloria says with ill grace.

'Then you'll be even more enamoured of my steak in mushroom sauce.' He hands her the Colossus of Rhodes masquerading as a bag of winegums and makes for the kitchen. 'Go back to the television and put your feet up, I'll bring you through a cup of tea.'

'Thanks for permission to do what I want in my own home,' she mutters.

Tea with fresh scones and raspberry jam are on a tray on her lap minutes later. They watch the film in companionable silence.

'I had such a crush on her when I was a kid,' remarks Jack. 'Me too.'

Part of her is thinking, 'This is beyond weird, Mallon,' and part of her is thinking, 'It's lovely to have a man about the house.' Don't think, just watch the box.

Long before Doris and Rock – what a name, he'd never get away with it today; just imagine, Rock Stallone or Rock Willis – long before Doris and Rock have melted into the inevitable clinch, Jack lifts the tray and heads purposefully for the cooker. Chopping noises and sizzling smells drift up the corridor and the radio plays softly in the background. She closes her eyes and drifts away.

'I thought we'd eat in the kitchen.'

She opens her eyes, startled. God oh God oh God, she must've looked like a trout with her mouth open, snoring away.

'Fine by me.' Gloria attempts to rise and fails miserably because her left leg thinks the rest of her body is still asleep.

Jack bends to lift her but thinks better of it. She chuckles, although the joke's on her.

'I wouldn't try any gallant gestures unless you want to rupture something, just lend me an arm to lean on.'

He guides her towards the kitchen, illuminated by a pair of candles flickering on the table and the light above the cooker – it's still daylight but she recalls Jack's penchant for candlelight from her visit to his Trinity rooms.

Gloria raises an eyebrow. 'Surely you're not setting the scene for a seduction?' she asks, rather bravely considering. But an eight-month bump lends courage.

'Old habits die hard,' he shrugs. 'I thought it looked more inviting this way.'

'So it does,' she agrees, although by far the best sight is the plate heaped with steak, mushrooms, mashed potatoes and broccoli. There's an uncorked bottle of red wine on the table and two glasses.

His eyes follow hers to the wine.

'I didn't know if you'd be able for half a glass, maybe diluted with water?'

361

'Heavens above, I'm pregnant.' Contrition sets in when she sees his wounded expression. 'Doctors say there's nothing wrong with the odd glass of wine but I don't care to take any chances, I want to give this baby the best start I can. I'm probably being over-protective but it just seems the right course of action.'

'Of course it is.' He guides her to the seat furthest away from the oven, one padded with cushions from the living room. The man's a saint. A reformed sinner anyway.

They chat over dinner – not about pregnancy, or Eimear, or Kate, but about current affairs (she has so much time on her hands she reads the newspaper from cover to cover instead of just turning to the television guide). He clears the dishes and produces a trifle.

'Did you rustle this up too while I was sleeping?' Gloria pushes straggling hairs behind her ears.

'Shop bought,' he confesses. 'But I whipped the cream myself.'

'That counts as home made.' She accepts a huge helping. 'Eimear never told me what a dab hand in the kitchen you are.'

'That's because I wasn't around her, to my shame,' he refills his wineglass.

The wine is black-red, Gloria watches a drop splash on the pine table and spread out in a spiky pattern.

'She's so capable in the kitchen, as she is in all areas of her life, that I simply didn't bother. When I tried to cook a meal it wasn't a treat for her, she worried about whether I was burning the saucepan or making too much sauce.'

'You poor dear, how you've suffered. No wonder you were driven to affairs,' Gloria snarls.

He's taken aback. 'You certainly have mood swings. But you're right, I can't use her as an excuse for my behaviour.'

He lifts his glass nervously and half-empties it. Can this be the same man who had her on tenterhooks at his flat, feeling like a lamb who's trotted off for a quick gambol in the meadow, taken a wrong turn and ended up in the slaughter-house?

'And what excuse do you use for hitting women?' She's relentless.

The glass is lifted, drained and refilled before he answers. 'No excuse at all. I've never done it before, I'll never do it again. I'm bitterly ashamed, I don't know how to make it up to Kate so I haven't even tried – which is cowardly of me but there you have it. I waste my time impressing nineteen-year-old girls and embarrassing nineteen-year-old boys so the girls will be even more dazzled by me. I'm verging on forty, living in rooms at the university and spending my evenings showing off at poetry readings in return for some fawning admiration and a couple of free drinks.'

He gulps and continues: 'The joke of it is, I haven't written a line in six months – for all I know there may be no poetry left inside me. I may be just another of those poets with a promising career that fizzles out. Not even a war to enlist in, so I can die a hero's death and have people say of me, "What early talent he showed . . ." '

'Very convenient,' observes Gloria, although she's impressed by the self-loathing that's palpable in him. 'Kate takes a clout on the ear and you say, "My oh my, I don't know what came over me, it'll never happen again." '

He shrugs. 'Pitiable, isn't it? I almost expected her to call the guards, I wouldn't have defended myself if she did. I deserve to be punished, it was brutish and primitive of me. All I can say about the incident, and I've replayed it and agonised over it a thousand times, is that I snapped. I saw yet another person leaving me, walking out of my life, and I couldn't handle it. You see it's fine for me to turn my back on other people but they're not allowed to do it to me.'

The bottle is drained now, he takes his glass to the tap and fills it with water, emptying it in one gasp. 'And there was something else about Kate,' he picks up his thread again, standing at the taps. 'About the relationship between her and me – it was extremely . . . physical. Perhaps that's how I allowed myself to overstep the mark. It's an explanation of sorts.'

Jack turns a tortured face towards her and Gloria feels the baby kick. She's suffused with an urge to soothe the suffering on such handsome features.

'Quick,' she calls him urgently, 'put your hand on my stomach.'

He approaches her bulge with some trepidation and lays a hand gently on her tent-like checked shirt, fluttering with the force of Junior's blows. His eyes are incredulous.

'So what happens now?' asks Gloria, as he clears the dishes and prepares to wash up.

Jack shrugs. 'Your guess is as good as mine. We threw away the rulebook when we started this baby, I think we'll have to make it up as we go along.'

She attempts to stand so she can dry the dishes.

'Sit where you are, Glory,' he orders. 'Drip-drying's more hygienic.'

She cradles her chin in her hands and watches him immerse plates in suds. Glory, she likes that. Much better than baby girl.

'Make it up as we go along,' she muses. 'What would you like to see happening?'

He faces her. 'I'd like to see us become friends so we can both be there for our baby.'

'It's not our baby.'

'But it could be. I want to be here for it.'

She considers the prospect. 'You mean like a friendly uncle, or a godfather?'

'That would be grand, Glory.'

'It might be hard on Kate, she has to take precedence over you, I depend on her.'

'I'll make my peace with her,' he vows. 'Don't ask me how but I'll do it.'

'And then there's Eimear, I'm planning to ask her to be godmother.'

'Making my peace there might be more difficult,' he admits. 'But I'll give it a lash.'

'This is *Twilight Zone* time,' she murmurs.

'So's turning up on my doorstep and asking me for a few million sperm,' he points out.

'True. It's so weird, we might just pull it off.'

CHAPTER 40

Gloria's mother's been on the phone to her, she's pitifully upset because Mick's going around the town making unpleasant remarks about her daughter. Gloria asked for specific details and when her mother told her she had to admit they were true. In theory. It's just the spin he's putting on them.

Granted, Eimear's estranged husband is the father of her baby, and yes, he's also the man who had an affair with Kate which shattered his marriage. But Mick's making it sound as though the three of them are hens in a barnyard and Jack's their rooster – and it's not like that. The trouble is, he's not hurting her by dredging this up in every pub in Omagh but it's distressing for Gloria's family.

She despises him for dragging her family into their dispute but she also realises he must be hurting like fury to react in this way. She supposes he must be counting her dates, it has to rankle that she's close to – what's the word her mother uses? – confinement. Perhaps that's why the vitriol is spilling over. They had so many happy years together, herself and Mick, if only they could wave a magic wand and eradicate the bitter ones.

But there are no spangly sticks with stardust leaking from them and her attempts at apology or explanation were dismissed by him as self-justifying. She noticed a little pool of phlegm at the corner of his mouth as he spat the words out.

'He hates me, he genuinely hates me,' she realised.

Gloria sighs. It's a miserable feeling, knowing there's some-one out there in the world who harbours an enormous grudge against you. Who isn't willing to let bygones be bygones. She realises everybody can't like her but it's particularly indigest-ible to recognise that a man who once loved her now detests her like no other. Loving and loathing, two sides of the one coin, isn't that what they say? The omniscient 'they'.

Kate rings, foreshortening her wallow.

'You'll never guess what Mick is saying about us, Kate – he's claiming we belong to a kinky sect which advocates sharing one man among all the women.'

'Wistful thinking, he's hoping to be invited to join the cult,' she hoots.

'You're not taking this seriously,' Gloria complains. 'My mother and brother and an assortment of aunts and uncles have to live in that town.'

'Ten-minute wonder, they'll have found someone else to talk about by tomorrow. But Mick McDermott should know better than to drag me into this, I'll have a few words for him when I see him. Bridie's just told me you rang yesterday, I was out all afternoon and I'm only catching up on phone messages now. Everything all right?'

'Fine, couldn't be better, apart from feeling like an elephant and having a drunk with a flick-knife tongue for an ex-husband.'

'Poor little Glo. No point in reminding you, I suppose, that you longed for a belly the way some of us crave rocket rides to the moon.'

'No point at all. Besides, I don't think it was a gut the size of Rockall I was particularly yearning for, a baby by special express delivery would have suited me just as well.'

'Sure the worst is over. The stork is poised at the starting gate, even as we speak, tiny bundle of joy in its beak. You know, like in *Dumbo*. Now, are you eating properly, shall I drop over with some Chinese food later? You have to keep

367

your strength up for labour, I've been checking *EveryWoman* in preparation for this Awfully Big Adventure. Apparently I'm to smuggle Mars Bars into the delivery suite to keep you going and a bottle of vodka for myself. Doesn't leave a smell, the nurses will never suspect.'

'I'm sure you didn't read that in *EveryWoman*,' says Gloria.

'Honest to God. It's a page-turner, it makes labour sound so captivating you want to rush out and get yourself impregnated, just to try it out.'

'You could be in luck there, Kate. Apparently all you have to do is wait until Midsummer's Eve and find a vegetable patch.'

'Potatoes or carrots?'

'I don't think it matters.'

'You're cracking up, Glo,' she says kindly. 'You're obviously hallucinating for lack of food. Man cannot live by winegums alone.'

'Actually,' Gloria begins, and trails off. 'Actually,' she tries again, 'Jack O'Brien called by yesterday and cooked a meal.' The words tumble out.

Gloria waits – but Kate's waiting too.

'You were right about him, Kate, he may not be as black as he's painted.'

'Well,' Kate says. 'You certainly know how to spring a surprise.'

'It was yourself told me to give him a second chance.'

'I did, Glo, but you were set so adamantly against him that I never thought you would. Your chances of patching anything up with Eimear after this are about as likely as breathing life into the Dead Sea Scrolls.'

'I'm just willing to be friends with him, I'm doing it for the baby's sake,' protests Gloria.

'Tell it to the marines. And you do know he hits women, don't you? Of course you do, you saw my face when I had a rainbow painted across it.'

'Kate, I don't understand,' wails Gloria. 'You told me to give him the benefit of the doubt, now you're reacting as though I'm inviting a sabre-toothed tiger into my cat basket.'

'You're right,' she sighs. 'Obviously some unresolved issues between Jack and me are muddying the water here. Of course you and Jack should try for an amicable footing, it's the sensible course of action. And I don't think it was justifiable but I don't harbour any ill-will over the punch – it's not ideal but there are more painful ways to end a relationship. So good luck to you both. But don't count on Eimear taking you up on your offer to be godmother; you may have to make do with me.'

'Kate, you're so understanding. When did you get to be so mature?'

'Crept up on me, I guess. Hey, Jack and Mick must be the two men in your life Mrs Gilmartin mentioned, one who bears you malice and one who wants to do good turns.'

'Could be,' Gloria agrees. 'Does that mean you're about to jet off to the Tropics in fulfilment of her predictions for you?'

'No such luck. Unless there's an equatorial climate in Waterford, I have to go down there on business tonight.'

'Thought you were bringing over emergency supplies of monosodium glutamate?'

'Can do, before I set off.'

'No, I'll find something in the freezer,' Gloria tells her. 'You may as well hit the road straight after work instead of detouring here. Besides, I have the second half of *Pillow Talk* on video to watch again.'

'You taped it?'

'Certainly, I want to watch the scene again where Rock Hudson implies he might be gay so Doris Day is obliged to abandon her Ice Queen pose and initiate lovemaking.'

'Kind of ironic, under the circumstances,' Kate comments. 'Don't record over that video, Glo. Better head off now, the calls are banking up. The Seventh Cavalry will be with you tomorrow, hold out as best you can until then.'

'You're bringing reinforcements?'

'Only me, my sweet, but I can pretend to blow a bugle if it makes you feel any better.'

CHAPTER 41

The letter arrives as Eimear juggles drinking orange juice with overloading her eyelashes with mascara on a Monday morning. It's on crested notepaper and comes from her old Latin teacher, Miss McGinn.

It reads: 'Dear Eimear, the teaching staff at Loreto Convent are delighted by your literary success and are following your career with great interest. We always knew you'd make your mark on life. The head nun, Sister Xavier, has asked me to invite you to speak to our sixth-formers who could learn a great deal from you. Perhaps you'd contact me if you can fit us in on your next visit to Omagh. Wishing you all the best, Yours sincerely, Maura McGinn.'

Bingo! At last she'll see inside the staff-room, none of the pupils were ever allowed past the door. What they could detect of it looked intriguing: armchairs, wreaths of smoke and locked cupboards stacked six-deep in bottles of the hard stuff, or so Kate claimed.

'I wonder if Amo-Amas-Amat McGinn is still doing a line with that ancient accountant Ronan Donnelly, or did he abandon her on the grounds that he came, he saw but he couldn't conquer,' Eimear conjectures.

This is her chance to find out – her marketing guru Josie says she's to accept all invitations, no matter how minor, because they lead to book sales.

Her imagination revs into overdrive – if she plays her cards right, maybe *Mna* will end up on the school syllabus. But a hint of reality creeps in and Eimear realises it would have to be a doctored version – some of the poems are too, er, adult for textbook consumption.

Naturally Christy will want to come with her, he can't bear to let her out of his sight. Eimear is finding his worship suffocating. He's hounding her to allow him to move in with her, he's always leaving clothes and CDs and other possessions at the cottage as though it gives him squatter's rights. One of these days she'll pile them all into a cardboard box for him to take away – but not just yet, it might be construed as provocative.

Eimear lifts the photograph of her that Christy took only last week on the Ha'penny Bridge, its curving metal roof framing her like an upturned heart. She likes Christy and it's flattering that he permanently wants to take pictures of her but she wishes he'd give her a moment's warning to straighten her hair instead of shoving the camera into her face and snapping. He carries a photograph of her around in his wallet – Jack didn't do that. And Christy never notices other women when he's with her, unlike some people.

But he seems suspiciously keen on commitment – a handful of nights of passion and he wants them to set up home together. She's at a loss to know why women are meant to feel complimented when men suggest they move in with each other.

Something bizarre has happened since she was single first time around, men have become model citizens, desperate for responsibility. Lads used to hyperventilate at the thought of being tied down, now they suffer more severe panic attacks at the idea they're not tagged and accounted for.

'Whatever happened to "I like you and you like me, let's hang out, go drinking and shag"?' Eimear asks the photograph.

Christy's even planning an expedition to Ikea in London,

she marvels. Not a trip to London to go to Harvey Nicks or take in a few shows, oh no. They're supposed to go across on the ferry, dump the car somewhere north of Wembley, spend hours in a warehouse full of Scandinavian plastic objets d'art and then crouch doubled up on the homeward trip to make room for blinds which don't fit Irish windows and toasters too small for Irish bread.

Eimear likes her home as much as the next woman, she has a new one to decorate after all, but she draws the line at organising holidays around a trip to Ikea. All Jack expected blinds to do was pull down to shade his hangover; Christy requires his to make a statement.

'What kind of statement, Christy?' she asked him.

'A statement of who I am,' he replied.

'Who's that then?' she asked him.

'Why are you being difficult?' he replied.

Maybe she is a difficult woman, but so what. She'd rather be awkward than amenable – she'll never be anybody's trophy girlfriend again. She used to be teased about being fussy, Kate and Gloria always said she was too preoccupied with having a perfect home, but Christy is borderline obsessive. It's enough to put anyone off housework; Eimear looks at the smears on her television screen and decides they're staying.

He scolded her for the way she washed the dishes the other night – she didn't rinse the suds off before placing the plates on the rack.

'There's such a thing as gravity,' Eimear explained. 'The suds will slide down all on their own and then they'll fall off.'

Christy becomes anxious when she's snotty and backs down instantly but it's increasingly intolerable all the same. Imagine noticing in the first place. She wouldn't mind but they were her own plates in her own drying-up rack in her own kitchen in her own house. The litany of Christy's shortcomings reminds her of Kate, with her complaint about

Jack drinking HER champagne in HER bedroom in HER flat. Eimear smiles, then realises to her surprise that she's just thought about Kate without an accompanying smarting sensation.

There's something else about Christy that's bothering her: she's noticed he has a hygiene fixation about everything to do with the house – not the car, it's a wasteland. But he won't touch the TV remote control without wiping it with a tissue first and she actually caught him squirting disinfectant down her loo once. And he bought her one of those anti-bacterial sprays the other day. Eimear plots revenge: she's going to spit in his coffee one of these days when he isn't looking, that'll give him something to chew on in the germs department.

Christy has his uses, though, she'll grant him that. He sorted out the ancient electricals in the cottage and he was able to recommend a builder who's converted her bathroom just the way she wants it. He charged her a grand more than she expected and didn't return for two weeks to make good but it's done now and money well spent. Even if the rest of the house is a no-go zone she can retreat to the bathroom and sink into luxury.

Eimear's noticed Christy prefers it when she's helpless and he can take charge. Sometimes she's willing to go along with it and sometimes she's not. He was furious when she used her own plumber instead of the one he suggested and once when she turned around in the cinema and asked the man behind to stop kicking her seat, Christy said she should have told him and he'd have sorted it out. As if she didn't have a tongue in her head. Eimear didn't let him sleep over that night.

But she has to go out with somebody. Of course she does, she can't sit at home on her own. And Christy is very keen on her, which is reassuring. He keeps telling her she's gorgeous; Eimear needs that, her confidence took a hammering with Jack. If it weren't for Christy she'd have to resort to evenings out with Nuala Ryan from the library, who buys all her clothes in House of Style in Thurles. Eimear keeps volunteering to go shopping with her and organise a makeover but Nuala reacts as though she's on a mission to corrupt her.

'Nuala Ryan takes a close interest in corruption,' remarks Eimear to the empty room. She's always seeing evil around her – she's convinced the Italian and Spanish language students about town are setting a bad example, with their exposed tummy buttons (some pierced).

'You see what I'm reduced to for a friend,' complains Eimear. 'Christy's foibles pale by comparison.'

She wonders what she should wear to this question-and-answer stint with the sixth-formers. A sharp suit to indicate she's a career woman who means business, a trendy number so she doesn't come across as antiquated or something hand-painted and poetic?

She may need to go shopping. Jack used to say Eimear's policy was 'I spend, therefore I am' – that was back in the days when he paid half the credit-card bill. She doesn't do too much shopping at the moment – she has assorted builders to keep in luxury. Still, there's nothing to beat the narcotic high of a new purchase, especially if you retain the receipt and return it the next day. The adrenaline hit without the credit-card strike.

Shopping takes her mind off men. The only fellows you see in shops work there. Even Christy, who shadows her, quakes at the idea of an afternoon in Grafton Street. Eimear remembers how she and Gloria had some satisfying shopping sessions, but Kate only shopped when she wanted something specifically – never on the off-chance. Eimear smiles and then stiffens; she doesn't need them, they were false friends.

'Why couldn't they have gone somewhere you'll find men by the yard if they were looking for action, why did they have to target mine?' she grumbles. 'They could have tried the pub or the snooker hall or the betting shop.'

Maybe not the betting shop, she can't see either of them

saying: 'I'll just nip into Odds On and lay a couple of trebles, you never know what talent might be losing their shirts on the same race.' And snooker halls are probably too dimly lit to have a proper look at the fellows cueing up. Eimear supposes pubs aren't all that promising either ... there's always a million to one chance some hunk will approach and ask if he can buy you a drink but the reality is being pestered by drunks wanting change for the cigarette machine.

Nuala Ryan is looking for a man: she told Eimear supermarkets in England have singles only nights and it's high time her Spar in Harold's Cross introduced the same idea.

'But, Nuala,' said Eimear, 'you don't need to pitch up between 8 p.m. and 9 p.m. on Unattached Wednesdays to spot the singles – five bottles of wine and one small pizza in a basket is as obvious as a kiss-me-quick hat.'

The more she talks to Nuala, the more Eimear realises she ought to hold on to Christy. According to Nuala, it's difficult enough to meet someone when you're in your twenties but terminal weariness has set in by the time you hit thirty.

Nuala has taken to scrutinising those initial-ridden ads in the personal columns of newspapers and regaling Eimear with details of the TDH males with GSOH applying to meet 'earthy' or 'fun-loving' or 'tactile' females – all euphemisms for nymphomaniacs, so far as Eimear can judge. Not that any of those adjectives apply to Nuala Ryan – she wears Aran cardigans. Baggy ones. Are there enough sex addicts out there to meet the demand from the male population? There's Kate and Gloria for starters, although Gloria's currently out of commission in the advanced stages of pregnancy. She must be due soon, Eimear realises with a pang.

Eimear has been studying the personals with Nuala – the library is awash with newspapers and every one is cluttered with column after column of men advertising themselves. They've been trying to estimate how many are truly single.

376

The ads are all ageist, with fellows of forty-five saying they want women aged between eighteen and thirty-five.

'Is it a crime to date women their own age?' asked Nuala indignantly during their lunch-break.

'Apparently,' shrugged Eimear. 'It leads to loss of face, loss of sex drive and loss of ego.'

There's something else they've noticed about the personals. When men advertise their wares they choose the oddest attributes for their come-and-get-me-girls pitch: they say they're 'solvent' or 'non-smoking' (another excuse for initials, NS) or even 'spiritual' – this from a man who wants to meet an 'Asian babe'. All the men are handsome, genuine, affectionate and cultured. Who's admitting to alcoholism or a violent temper or parsimony?

Some try to be provocative to stand out from the herd – they'll ask for women with PhDs only . . . but she still has to look like a Baywatch lifeguard. Then there are men who imagine a string of puns will provoke response. Eimear memorised one classic example: 'Stake Me Out. Transylvanian male, 40s, seeks attractive acolyte 20–35, to open the lid on his social life.'

She felt like writing to him to say, 'Stay in your box, perv.'

But then the ads from women aren't much better:

'One Jaguar, one Mercedes, sought by two beautiful women, 24, to be driven wild in the city.'

When she reads the personals, Christy doesn't seem so bad – at least he's normal. And when Eimear compares him with Jack, he's a saint. One with some oddities, admittedly, but then you don't have to be a saint to become a saint. Look at Saint Kevin, who sat up a tree and threw missiles at women because he thought they were the source of iniquity.

'Who am I trying to kid? Christy's a pain,' sighs Eimear. 'Perhaps I'd be better off with one of Kate's Beautiful Boys. He might not know his way around an electrical circuit but at least he wouldn't supervise my washing-up operations. Or be trying to drag me off to Ikea.'

Your gut reaction is all you have to go on in relationships. Right from the start she sensed that Jack was a Don Juan but she disregarded it, convinced she'd be woman enough for him. Which she was, for all of ten minutes. Then there's Christy. Her instinct tells her he isn't the love of her life but she's too cowardly to risk being alone.

'I knew he wasn't right for me as soon as we had carnival knowledge of each other and it turned out to be no funfair,' she tells Nuala after work, when they try out the Happy Hour drinks in the new pub on the corner. Nuala sticks to Coke, while Eimear swallows Moscow Mules in rapid succession, which is why she's talking about her sex life to an avid (but disapproving) Nuala Ryan.

'But here I am still seeing him,' Eimear continues 'allowing him to describe me as his girlfriend, failing to object when he leaves a change of clothes at the cottage. At least with Jack it was love. "I wasn't in full command of my senses, your honour."'

She even tells Nuala about Gloria's pregnancy and the identity of the father.

'That's what hurts most.' Her voice is dismal, the Moscow Mule lashes out inside her 'I wanted a baby so badly and I couldn't manage it. My useless body that Christy desires and Jack before him and God knows how many others before them.'

Sandy-haired Nuala pulls her paisley-patterned skirt primly down over her calves, at once envious and censorious of the effect this glamorous new friend has on men.

'In another week or so Gloria will be cuddling the baby I should have had,' says Eimear. 'I don't understand why Jack went through with it, unless he wanted to punish me. It's not as if he has the least interest in children – he's an only child, self-centred. He flipped when he realised I was trying to get pregnant and that's the real reason the marriage ended.

'He stormed out of the house and moved into rooms at the college, it was nothing to do with me finding out about him and Kate. He accused me of cheating on him by trying to have a baby without his prior consent – he saw a child as a rival and couldn't bear the idea of sharing his woman with a child. I think it's because he never had to share his mother with anyone, not even a father. He died when Jack was five.'

'I have to catch the 7.23 p.m. bus, Eimear.' Nuala attempts to climb decorously from the bar stool and fails miserably. Eimear ignores her.

'Christy's everything that Jack's not and it's driving me crazy,' she wails. 'You'd think I'd cherish a man who idolises me as ostentatiously as Christy, who lavishes me with compliments and is forever telling me he loves me. I have to break free of him, Nuala; the irony is, I could have done it with Kate and Gloria's support. I think about them all the time. I speculate on whether Kate found herself a Beautiful Boy. I wonder if Gloria's having a boy or a girl.'

As Nuala slides out, staggering only slightly under the onslaught of her colleague's drink-fuelled despondency, Eimear wonders if she'll ever find friends to replace Kate and Gloria. Nuala Ryan's a poor substitute, with her long face and longer skirts. But there's no point in having friends she can't trust.

CHAPTER 42

Eimear is physically restraining herself from ringing Kate. The local free-sheet is lying on the mat alongside her letters and, between bites of toast, she finds an article she knows would have Kate rolling about the floor. She cuts it out for her automatically, it's exactly the sort of nonsense Kate would frame and hang in her loo.

It's from Albert Einstein to his wife on their tenth wedding anniversary – a list of requirements. He tells her she has to ensure his clothes and linen are kept in order, that he's served three regular meals a day and that his bedroom and study are tidied but no one touches his desk. Eimear doesn't know whether to laugh or cry as she reads on:

'You will renounce all personal relations with me except when these are required to keep up social appearances. In particular you will not request:
  That I sit with you at home
  That I go out with you or travel with you
You will promise especially that:
  You will expect no affection from me and you will not reproach me for this
  You must answer me at once when I speak to you
  You must leave my bedroom or study at once without protesting when I ask you to go

You will promise not to denigrate me in front of the children either by word or deed.'

Talk about a control freak; and this is the man whose face appears on T-shirts. Christy doesn't seem so bad with his washing-up fetish and his habit of prowling the house with a bottle of bleach in his hand.

She realised something shocking recently, something even Moscow Mules wouldn't help her confess to Nuala Ryan because she's so ashamed: she'd like Jack dead. She doesn't want to kill him but she prefers not to think of him breathing and laughing and loving either. Eimear was hunting on the shelves for a copy of *Pride and Prejudice* for a fourteen-year-old with an essay to write when she drifted off, fantasising about identifying Jack's body after a road accident. He hadn't a mark on him and death was instantaneous so it's not as though she imagined him suffering the torment of the damned, but there he was all the same, still as the grave. It was a particularly satisfying daydream.

Naturally she was mortified when she resurfaced and realised she had an impatient teenager and a nasty flaw in her personality to contend with. Eimear knows it's nothing to be proud of, picturing someone lifeless just because he doesn't love her any more. She supposes it means she's not over him, perhaps she'll never be over him.

The newspaper story didn't work out quite as she'd planned – Jack ended up making money from it and she was pestered by the journalist who lost his job. He seemed to think she could go to his editor and straighten it out.

'Fat chance,' snorted Eimear. 'Maybe next time he'll think twice before sabotaging someone's name on the strength of another's say-so. It's power with responsibility, my friend, not power with an expense account.'

Anyway she heard he landed on his feet with another job on one of the English tabloids trying to make inroads into the Irish market. So she has nothing to berate herself about.

'Eimear Mulligan, I'd recognise you anywhere.'

Miss McGinn takes Eimear's hand in both hers and gazes fondly at her; Eimear finds it most disconcerting. She hasn't changed either, she's still encased in a fusty suit. It's not the same one she wore when she was teaching them but an identical twin.

'I suppose we should be calling you Eimear O'Brien but old habits die hard,' adds Miss McGinn.

Eimear nods with as much grace as she can muster. She never felt like a Mulligan.

'Now the girls are all waiting for you, they're dizzy with excitement at having a published poet come to speak to them,' says Miss McGinn. 'But first I must bring you to the staff-room. You'll see a few familiar faces there.'

'I'm looking forward to meeting my old teachers, Miss McGinn,' Eimear tells her.

She throws up her hands in horror. 'Call me Maura,' she insists. 'Miss McGinn sounds far too elderly.'

The sense of smell is a fast-track to the past – one whiff of the school's characteristic odour of floor polish and gym shoes and Eimear's a first former again, wearing a blazer one size too large and puzzling over how to find the science lab. She'd never have managed without Kate, her older sisters coached her in the layout. It's all exactly as Eimear remembers, except scaled down to half-size.

The staff-room is smaller than she expects too, acrid with the scent of cigarette smoke – and she's a smoker – and littered with coffee cups. Sister Xavier is waiting with a reception committee but she's the only one Eimear recognises. In fact she hardly recognises the nun at all because she's not wearing her black robes; she's traded them in for a navy suit with a silk blouse underneath and her hair is visible because she's discarded her veil. Stylishly cut hair, Eimear notices with some surprise.

She stutters over Sister Xavier's name, to her evident delight. She touches her salt-and-pepper bouffant self-consciously as she extends a hand to Eimear and explains that she's reverted to her own Christian name, Sister Anne.

'You're welcome back to the school, Eimear. Well well, it's always a pleasure to receive our old girls. Whatever happened to those two friends of yours, Gloria and ah, Kate? Are they still in Dublin with you? My goodness the three of you were inseparable, we used to call you the triplets.'

'Yes, they're in Dublin but I don't see so much of them these days,' Eimear replies. 'You know how it is, you grow apart. Gloria has a little job in a school and Kate helps out in a solicitor's office.'

'Does she indeed? I thought she'd trained for the law but maybe the course was too long. Well well, she had a fine brain. And what about yourself, a poet now. Are you working on anything at the moment?'

'Inspiration is creeping up on me every day,' Eimear assures her. 'Snatches of conversation overheard in bus stop queues, odd lines from a pop song, you never know where ideas will strike.'

'Is that so – maybe we'll end up inspiring you here,' smiles Sister Anne. 'Well well, mustn't keep the sixth-formers waiting – Miss McGinn will bring you back for some refreshments before you leave.'

Eimear grinds her teeth as she follows 'Maura' along the corridor. Inspiration is not hitting her every day, nor even every week. In fact she's writing drivel since she finished her debut collection. Obviously she's a one-hit wonder, won't Jack be thrilled.

The girls look older than seventeen or eighteen, despite their brown and yellow uniforms. They exude sophistication and – Eimear realises with a sinking heart that she could be in for a bumpy ride – boredom. So much for thinking this will sell books and winkle her on to the school curriculum. Old Amo-Amas-Amat radiates encouragement from the back of the room, along with another teacher Eimear doesn't know, their English teacher.

'I want to keep this informal so I'm going to read a few poems aloud to you and then perhaps we could discuss them, you may have some questions,' she begins.

Perhaps the hand-painted cream silk dress and scarf were a dodgy idea – she should have opted for the businesslike image after all.

The girls listen politely but the silence is complete when she invites questions. Humiliatingly blank looks are directed at her. Fortunately their teacher, a curvy strawberry blonde wearing what Eimear evaluates and dismisses as a cheap summer dress, poses one.

'Where does your inspiration come from?'

This is easy, she can slip into her bus stops and pop songs spiel. But she can't spin the answer out forever and again the stillness is mental torture. 'Maura' steps in.

'Did you always want to be a poet and when did you realise you could write poetry – was it one particular event which galvanised you?'

The answer to that's an extremely interesting one, thinks Eimear grimly, but she's not going down that particular cul-de-sac to entertain a crowd of tedious sixth-formers who probably won't even buy her book anyway. Ex-husbands, affairs with best friends, therapeutic ranting about perfidy and serpent's teeth on a blank page . . . nope, let them keep those bored expressions.

'I always used to scribble odd lines – I kept a notebook and fired down ideas as they occurred to me,' she chatters. 'And then one day I knew it was time to turn all those jottings into a collection of poetry.'

A sea of indifferent faces loom up at her. She's impressing

nobody – what is it with teenagers nowadays. There's nothing for it but to head off for a coffee with Sister-Xavier-reincarnated-as-Anne. Or would she rate a thimbleful of sherry? She could use something alcofrolic.

Wait, a genuine question, be still her beating heart.

'I notice a blanket resentment of men in your work, why do you portray them all as fiends and ravishers – don't you think you're generalising and being somewhat unfair?'

Watery eyes blink innocently up at Eimear from behind gold-rimmed glasses. Little cow.

'I think you're misconstruing my intention. It's not to present men in a negative light but to show women in a positive one. For the purposes of this work I'm not sufficiently interested in men to vilify them, what I'm attempting to do is to demonstrate how women are powerful enough to overcome mistreatment, how they refuse to allow themselves to become victims even if circumstances – or indeed their men – attempt to channel them into such a role.'

'But there isn't a single redeemable man in your entire collection. I've worked my way through it and found a child molester, two pimps, a bigamist, a Peeping Tom, a phone pest and several sadists. That's not representative of society.'

Who let this girl in? And who gave her a copy of *Mna* to read – Eimear wants it confiscated immediately.

'What's your name? Karen? Karen, I'm flattered you've taken the trouble to study my poetry so conscientiously, you must bring me up your copy after we're finished here and I'll sign it for you.

'Let me explain something about art to you. It's not a writer's function to hold up a mirror to society to reflect exactly what goes on – in some instances it's more productive to exaggerate the flaws you perceive, the better to draw attention to them. Now patently there are decent men in the community and there are deviants and equally patently the perverts are far outnumbered. However there's such a thing as poetic licence and I make it my responsibility to focus on those warped few in order to fire a warning shot – to eliminate complacency. Does that make sense, Karen?'

She smiles ingratiatingly at a scrap of a girl with glasses and a scowl.

'So you're being economical with the truth for dramatic impact?'

Her spectacles had acquired a threatening glint.

'Perhaps my vision of society is slightly different to yours, Karen. Outlooks tend to change with age. And experience. Any more questions?'

Later in the staff-room, Sister Anne raises a similar point – Eimear is starting to think it's a conspiracy.

'You've encountered some extremely dubious men in your time, Eimear,' she remarks, clattering her cup into her saucer. (Eimear didn't merit the sherry, she noticed.)

'You've been playing with your crystal ball, sister,' she replies.

'Well well, there's no need for mystic mumbo-jumbo. There isn't even any need to read more than a few pages of your book, I can see you've been exposed to a nasty lot.'

'I've had my share of feckless fellows.' Eimear studies the peacock pattern on the Royal Tara china and feels a stirring of self-pity.

'It seems such a waste, an attractive girl like you.'

Eimear's self-pity is threatening to engulf her, she has to take a gulp of coffee.

Meanwhile Sister Anne (she'll always be Sister Xavier to Eimear) cocks her head.

'And did you never think of giving them up?'

'Men?' Eimear is astonished.

'Yes, did you never think of the celibate life? It has its compensations – it offers serenity and space and time for contemplation.'

'I never felt I had a vocation, sister.'

'Some people are born with vocations and others develop theirs. I think perhaps you may fall into the latter category, it could be that your pretty face has been a distraction from your true calling. I'm not suggesting that a woman should join a religious order from cynicism about the opposite sex, that would be a negative reason for making a choice intended as an affirmation. But my intuition is generally sound, Eimear, and it's telling me that God may have singled you out to dedicate your life to him. Well well, think about it, at least, pray for guidance and I'll remember you in my prayers.'

Eimear doesn't even go to Mass on Sundays any more; she's appalled at the turn their conversation has taken. The comfort that church attendance offered during Jack's affair with Kate didn't last the distance when it came to Gloria. Besides, she's in a relationship with someone. She can just see herself landing back to Dublin in the car Christy lent her and saying, 'Great trip north, I've decided to join a convent.' He wouldn't be reaching her the keys to his Astra again in a hurry at that rate.

'So much for me being feted as the conquering hero returning to her alma mater.' Eimear purses her lips, as she walks back to her mother's house.

She's been branded a man-hater by a skit of a schoolgirl who probably doesn't know any men let alone have an aversion to them and Sister Xavier/Anne has a hunch she's nursing a vocation.

'I'm surprised she didn't suggest I ring up Gloria and Kate and organise a mass entry to the order, three for the price of one,' thinks Eimear.

However laughter froths up inside her as she stalks through the convent grounds, past the grotto where they used to sing 'May is the Month of Mary' and crown the statue of the Virgin with flowers. Sister Anne doesn't realise she's separated – she's inviting a married woman to take the veil. So much for her legendary intuition, perhaps she should invest in a crystal ball after all.

The sheer nonsense of their conversation puts Eimear in such high good humour that she peels off towards the town for some window shopping instead of heading straight home to her mother's Spanish Inquisition. She can stop off at the bookshop in the main street and check they have *Mna* positioned somewhere appropriate. At the front of the shelf.

It's an unfortunate decision. For rounding the corner, she comes face-to-face with Mick McDermott. He looks about as thrilled to see her as she is to encounter him.

'Eimear,' he nods.

'Mick.'

She attempts to keep walking but he blocks her path.

'Thought you'd be in hospital doing some hand-holding around now.'

'Gloria has Kate to play patty-cake with, she doesn't need me as well.'

'Whatever happened to that all-for-one solidarity, don't tell me you've finally decided share and share alike isn't the best policy when it comes to men.'

'Mick, you're being offensive. I'd like to get past please.'

'Offensive? Is that what you call offensive? I have a different interpretation. I call lending out your husband as a stud offensive – standing in front of someone on the pavement doesn't come close. But you always had different standards to the rest of us.'

'Mick, I can see you're angry and you've every reason to be, but you've no right to take it out on me. You're not the only one with a collapsed marriage around here, mine's in flitters too, when all I did was love my husband and try to be the best wife I could.'

'I do believe I hear violins,' he sneers. 'Unless it's the sweet sound of self-righteousness blowing in the wind. No, it's just hot air. Your marriage didn't fail because of Jack or Kate or even because of Gloria, trollop that she is. It fell apart because of you.'

Eimear doesn't know where it springs from, but she's infuriated by Mick calling Gloria a trollop.

'Mick, you are a pathetic excuse for a man and I'm not going to waste my time bandying words with you in public. Whatever Gloria did or didn't do, she made the best decision of her life the day she kicked you out. And I'm sure she thanks God you haven't fathered her baby because what woman in her right mind would want to carry a child with your DNA.

'Now step out of my way before I start yelling.'

His lip curls. 'Shout away.'

A rush of adrenaline floods Eimear. She opens her mouth and feels a scream ripping against the walls of her throat. It soars up and is released, flapping into the air. She sees Mick's aggrieved face and the astonished glances of passers-by.

'Stop it, what will people think,' he pleads.

Eimear continues to scream but now she points a finger up the street. He scurries off and, vastly satisfied with herself, she danders into the bookshop and rearranges the display to give *Mna* its due prominence.

CHAPTER 43

Has to be the nesting instinct, rationalises Gloria, knee-deep in cake recipes. Her urge to bake, slice, freeze, share or if all else fails eat a ginger cake can only be explained by some primeval impulse. The only drawback is that the spirit is willing but the flesh is fat. She's already puffed out just waddling about the kitchen gathering together ingredients.

However, she needs to distract herself from the countdown to motherhood so she presses ahead and is up to her elbows in flour when the doorbell rings. It's Jack, who announces he's taken a half-day from college with the insouciance of someone assured of a welcome. He's brought more roses, she'll have to explain how she feels about roses: over-blown, over-romanticised, over-valued. Especially red ones. Of course these are pink, she reminds herself. The colour you'd bring your mother or a sick friend in hospital, not flowers for a lover.

He settles himself at the kitchen table, sniffing his own roses appreciatively in their square glass vase, and watches her send flour clouds billowing into the atmosphere.

'I've stumbled upon a scene of domesticity, I didn't know you modern women still baked cakes. How's my pal and her passenger?'

'Grand,' she responds, rubbing margarine into crumbs with her fingertips.

(Why do people react as though you're demonstrating how to split the atom when you bake a cake?)

'Tickety boo.'

(Tickety boo! He'll be asking for ginger pop next.)

She slides a glance at him from under her fringe. Confidence like that has to be assumed, or learned as a defence mechanism – it can't be innate.

'Here for anything in particular, Jack?'

'Bonding process, Glory. We're building bridges, laying foundations, cementing the friendship.'

'Sounds like back-breaking work. I take it you supply hard hats on these sessions.'

He laughs. 'Give us a break, Glory. I was humble Jack O'Brien yesterday, I can't keep that going two days in succession. I'm my usual insufferably charming, or charmingly insufferable, Jack O'Brien today.'

'And a fine fist you make of it. I'll put the kettle on as soon as I shoot this cake into the oven.'

'Did I ever tell you my confirmation name?' he asks; he has a way of looking at her, from under his heavy black brows, that makes her feel self-conscious. Even with the insulation of being almost nine months pregnant.

Gloria shakes her head and stirs treacle through the mixture.

'Jude. As in St Jude, patron saint of hopeless cases.'

'Are you calling me a hopeless case?'

'No, myself.'

She's giggling as she bends to the oven but, straightening up, a drumbeat of pain throbs in the pit of her stomach. Her expression alerts Jack; he's on his feet in an instant and leading her to a seat.

'Is it the baby?'

'Too soon,' she shakes her head. 'Probably just a false alarm. Could I have a glass of water, please?'

She drinks slowly, monitoring her breathing. All those screaming sessions with Mick are paying off, they taught her more about diaphragm control than her pre-natal classes.

'Panic stations can stand down now.' She manages a shaky smile. 'It was just James Spencer Mallon showing me who's big white chief.'

'If you're sure,' he steps back dubiously. 'You still look pale – I'll make you some tea.'

'That would be heavenly,' she says gratefully. 'There should be some Mikados in the biscuit tin.'

'I can do better than that, I stopped off at Gammell's for a rhubarb tart. We need to keep your strength up.'

Gloria is unaccountably touched – rhubarb tart was her father's favourite.

'You're fattening me up,' she protests half-heartedly. 'I'm already beef to the heels like Mullingar heifer.'

'You look divine,' he assures her, and goes straight to the press where the tea caddy lives. He must have a photographic memory.

Gloria lifts her bloated ankles and balances them on another chair, as he carries the tea-pot to the table. He's even produced some pastry forks she didn't know she possessed.

She attempts to massage the swelling but her stomach mound blocks her.

He takes an ankle in his hand and rubs it rhythmically.

'Maud with her exquisite face/And wild voice pealing up the sunny sky/And feet like sunny gems on an English green . . .' he quotes.

'Is that one of yours?'

'Lord Tennyson. He had it bad for the rose-lipped Maud. I don't admire much of his poetry but that girl certainly had something going for her.'

Gloria is firing up like a match as he massages the second ankle, she bends her head so the hair obscures her face. 'You have a perfect voice for reciting,' she whispers, 'perhaps you'd let me hear some of your own work.'

'Afraid I can't do that, Glory.'

She's surprised – and slightly bruised – by such a direct

refusal; couldn't he have fobbed her off?

He looks her in the eye, still holding an ankle. 'Reciting poetry to women is part of my technique. It doesn't even have to be my own verses, a few cantos of *The Rape of the Lock* usually does the trick. And that's exactly what it is, a trick. I derive a perverted pleasure from seducing women with poetry by a man called Pope.' A smile chases across his face. 'But I don't want to play those games with you, Glory. Friends, remember?'

She nods, at once offended that he isn't attracted to her and flattered by his honesty.

'Rhubarb tart time.' Jack brandishes a knife. 'Did I hear you correctly when you referred to the sprog as James Spencer Mallon?'

'You did,' she confirms. 'James for my father and Spencer for Spencer Tracy.'

'You're a fan of his?'

'My father was. It's a family tradition, we're all called for film stars.'

'I think James Depp Mallon has a ring to it, myself.'

'Stop your nonsense,' she splutters. 'And cut me a bigger slice of tart.'

As she holds out her plate the pain hits a second time, sharper than the first. An involuntary groan escapes; Gloria feels beads of sweat spring up on her forehead and she doubles over, arms wrapped around her stomach. Jack is by her side in a flash, her head is pressed to his shoulder.

'Glory, listen to me, I'm calling an ambulance, I'll be straight back.'

'Don't leave me,' she sobs, rasping her face against the tweed of his jacket.

'We have to get you to a hospital, the baby may be on its way.'

Another stab of pain rips through her stomach, she bites her lip but can't forestall the moan.

'I'm driving you there myself, we won't wait for an ambulance. Can you put your arms around my neck? Good girl. I'm going to carry you outside, don't protest, if I put my back out you can console yourself that you're wreaking revenge on behalf of the female sex. The legendary lover with a slip disc. Ready? Let's go. You're being very brave, Glory.'

'Wait,' she commands. 'My house keys.'

She points to her handbag, he somehow manages to lift it while still holding her and carries it in his teeth to the car.

'If your students could see you now,' she grins weakly, as sweat trickles between her breasts. 'The debonair Professor O'Brien with a ton of lard in his arms and a handbag dangling from his mouth.'

'If you make me laugh I'll drop you,' he warns, resting her against the bonnet of the car while he unlocks it.

'Jack, stop!' she shrieks as he pulls away. He slams on the brakes and looks at her, aghast. 'My cake, it's still in the oven.'

'Feck your cake,' he spits out, sliding into first gear.

'Feck yourself.' She holds her stomach protectively. 'I'm not leaving the place to burn down while I'm in hospital giving birth to my baby, we need a house to come home to. And . . .' she breaks off while another thrust sweeps through her body, jack-knifing it, 'I may need a slice of ginger cake if it's a long labour. Hospital cake is like sawdust.'

Jack jumps lights and weaves between lanes like a maniac; nobody pays him the least bit of attention, it's normal Dublin driving. The pain is intense now, Gloria can't concentrate on anything but the way her insides feel like they're being filleted by a giant carving knife. She's being ritually disembowelled.

'Talk to me, Jack, distract me,' she begs.

'About the weather? About work? Summer's almost here but it's cool still, cast ne'er a clout till May is out. Hang on in there, Glory, you're beautiful, we're nearly at the Rotunda.'

'We're not, we're only at Dawson Street. Recite some verses to me, give me some of *The Rape of the Lock.*'

Jack gulps. '"This nymph, to the destruction of mankind/Nourished two locks, which graceful hung behind/In equal curls, and well conspired to deck/With shining ringlets the smooth iv'ry neck."'

He pauses to cut up a bus, which flashes disgruntled lights, and continues: '"There lived a sage in days of yore/And he a handsome pigtail wore/But worried much and pondered more/Because it hung behind him."'

'That doesn't sound like the same poem at all,' she objects, between groans.

'Sorry, Glory, I can't concentrate, just let me overtake this car. Why don't I have a mobile phone, then I could ring the hospital to let them know we're coming. For God's sake why is there so much traffic on the road, does nobody walk any more?'

She can scent his fear and it aggravates her own.

He's still talking as they swing into Dame Street but she only hears odd words now from across a vast distance. She's neither conscious nor unconscious, but swimming somewhere between the two states. Her head rolls around on her neck and feels insecurely attached – one more jolt and it might plop off. That would give Jack a fright.

'Brave . . . there . . . lights . . . park,' he says.

Gloria doesn't remember any more.

Something's not right. She concentrates. Something's missing, she can't work out what. She tries to open her eyes but they're glued down. Gloria struggles with her lids, there's a burning sensation at the back of her eyeballs. One eye pops open, leaving a gritty residue in the corner, then the other copies it.

At first she can't distinguish anything, she's groping in the midst of a fog. Gradually it dissipates and she sees a pale green ceiling. Not a soothing green, it's a bone-chilling colour. She doesn't recognise this ceiling. A white paper lampshade covers the bulb. That proves it, she can't be at home, she doesn't have any paper lampshades. She tries to move her head to the side to look for clues but the adhesive they squirted on her eyelids has been applied to the back of her neck. She's rigid. Instead she swivels her eyes and sees a drip and tubes. Someone's arm is attached to them.

A wave of misery slops over Gloria, leaving her trembling with grief and something else, a nameless fear. She's suffused with dread but can't work out what it is that terrifies her. There's something dark and suffocating just over the horizon of her memory. She doesn't want to think about it, it's waiting to swarm down and smother her.

The door opens and a nurse appears.

'Imelda?' a voice croaks. It's her own voice.

'No, I'm Frances,' she smiles. 'Let me prop you up.'

She leans across, fabric conditioner wafting from her uniform, and adjusts the headboard. Now Gloria can distinguish apple green walls and a window. Branches belonging to a tree she can't see wave jauntily at her from the right hand corner of the window.

'Imelda,' she gasps. 'What happened?'

'I'm not Imelda, I'm Frances,' she corrects her gently. 'You nearly died, Gloria, your husband sat up all night with you, you've a sound man there. He's just gone to the canteen for some breakfast, he shouldn't be long.'

Someone must have sent for Mick at the bank, his office isn't far from the Rotunda. Poor Mick, he'll be so worried. There's something about Mick that bothers her; she frowns, thinking what it might be, but her brain aches. She squeezes at her memory, trying to pop out the missing constituent like an orange pip, but all she's left with is a pounding headache. She looks towards the tree, its leaves whisper softly in the wind. The sibilant sounds are moving closer. It isn't the tree, it's people murmuring outside her room.

The door opens again and Jack and Kate walk in. She's puzzled to see them together, then her memory returns. Jack and Kate love one another, they want to be together forever. Kate told her so, in this hospital bed. Was it this bed? She doesn't remember the room being green, Gloria thought it was orange. Perhaps they moved her to a new room.

Kate goes to sit on the end of the bed, thinks better of it and pulls a chair close to her. Jack walks to the window and looks out.

'Eimear won't like this.' Gloria's voice squawks like a rook's.

Kate simply takes her hand and strokes it.

'You can't let her find you two together, she might get suspicious,' says Gloria.

She's exhausted by the effort of constructing a sentence and turns her face to the pillow. It feels damp, there are tears rolling down her face – she's not even aware she's crying.

'She doesn't know,' says Kate.

She soon will, thinks Gloria. But Kate isn't talking to her, she's addressing Jack.

'She doesn't know,' repeats Kate.

A man's hand rests on her head. 'Glory,' he says. Why is he calling her Glory?

The disturbing mass hovering on the horizon edges nearer, it sneaks into her consciousness. Kate and Jack have left the door ajar. Down the hall, she hears a new-born baby cry. The name flashes into her mind. James Spencer Mallon.

'My baby! What are they doing to my baby, why is my son crying?' screams Gloria.

She claws at the drip, in a headlong rush to drag herself from the bed. Arms restrain her and she flails, screeching. Primeval wails. Jack calls and a nurse comes running, there's a needle and she sinks into oblivion.

*   *   *

Gloria opens her eyes and there's the mint ceiling again. This time it's only Kate sitting by her bed reading a magazine: Gloria watches her for a few moments before she realises she's awake.

'Gloria.' She sets the magazine down.

'Tell me what happened to my baby.' Gloria turns insistent eyes towards Kate. Desolate eyes.

'He's dead.'

She registers the information. 'He's dead.' She turns the sentence around and examines it. No pain, no surprise. Nothing.

'I'm so sorry, Gloria, your baby's dead. I wish there was a better way to tell you, I wish I knew how to prepare you.'

'I want to see him.'

'Do you think you should? He's . . .' she hesitates.

'I want to see him.' Gloria's speaking decisively, there's no shrieking this time. No more needles.

They carry her son in, wrapped in a lemon blanket. He has black hair, like Jack. Or Mick. His eyes are closed. She wonders what colour they are. She'd like to open the lids but she can't, that would be defiling him – they were never opened. Gloria hopes they're green, like her own. His face is waxy, blue-white, its features perfect miniatures, feathery black eyebrows. He's twenty-one days early. She touches his skin, it's cold. She pulls the blanket away and her gaze is drawn to his neck, encircled by an ugly scarlet band, a fiery necklace that scalds his white skin.

Gloria turns outraged eyes to Kate, who looks helplessly at the nurse. Gloria wraps her baby carefully in the blanket and brings him under the covers to warm him. Kate and the nurse are staring but she ignores them.

After a while, the nurse says, 'Shall I take him for you now, Gloria?'

'Where are you bringing him?' Gloria doesn't look up. Her eyes are on her baby's face.

'To another room,' says Frances.

'Can't he stay here with me? He's no trouble, I like having him by me.' Gloria can sense her hesitation but still she doesn't look up.

'Five more minutes,' says the nurse.

Gloria nods. 'You two wait outside,' she orders them.

Again there's indecision.

'Five minutes,' she tells them firmly. 'James and I want to be alone together.'

When the nurse returns for her baby, she hands him over without an argument. She's memorised his face now.

'How did it happen?'

Kate takes her hand. 'He was strangled by the umbilical cord as you gave birth. It was a tragic accident, no one could have foreseen it. The cord wrapped itself around his neck, the doctors did all they could to save him.'

Her voice carries on, waves crashing against jagged rocks. Gloria doesn't bother listening, she feels empty. She moves her left hand, the one without a drip attached, to touch her stomach – perhaps it's all been a mistake and James is still safely inside her. Her hand jerks from her front as from an electric shock, it's agonising to touch.

Gloria looks at the tree again, the corner of it that she can see. Little boys like to climb trees, little boys like James. God oh God oh God.

'I've sent for your mother,' Kate's voice breaks through her mental barrier. 'She's due to arrive this evening. Rudolph's driving her down.'

'How did I reach the hospital?'

'Jack drove you in. Apparently you went into premature labour and he bundled you into the car and flew like a bat out of hell with his foot through the accelerator. He's been desperately worried about you.'

She nods indifferently.

'Your mother and Rudolph want to bring you home to

Omagh to recuperate as soon as you're well enough to travel,' Kate goes on. 'But if you'd prefer to stay in Dublin, I'll take some time off work and move in with you.'

Gloria remains mute.

'The doctor will come by this evening and explain exactly what happened,' says Kate. 'That's if you want to know the details – if it isn't too soon.'

She trails to a halt and fidgets with the bedspread. Gloria closes her eyes and feigns sleep. Kate waits a moment and then tiptoes from the room.

Gloria's not surprised she lost her baby, he never belonged to her. She didn't come by him fair and square, she swindled him out of fate. She's an impostor. There are only so many babies to go around and she didn't wait her turn, she ran off with someone else's. She wasn't meant to become pregnant by that IVF session; it wouldn't have happened if she'd used Mick's sperm instead of Jack's.

'I pulled a fast one,' thinks Gloria, 'but I didn't get away with it.'

Mrs Gilmartin said she saw a dark-haired boy playing in her garden but not yet. It's too soon, she told Gloria, he's not ready yet.

Fertility treatment. Futility treatment. Gloria sighs. People go to the futility clinic and they hand over their money and expect miracles.

'We have faith in our doctors and scientists the way our ancestors relied on their shamen, their witchdoctors, their druids, their priests. But doctors can't work miracles, any more than priests. They can only help nature along. Nudge her, kick-start her, supply a missing component. Sometimes it works, sometimes it doesn't,' Gloria recites her hopeless credo.

'What do you mean there's only a one in four chance, doctor? This is the twenty-first century. We can clone animals, we can probably clone people only no one's prepared to admit it yet. So why can't I have a baby?'

Gloria screws her eyes shut but still her brain torments her. The world is full of women having babies, there are teenagers with defiant bellies congregating around the doors of this very hospital, puffing nicotine into their lungs as hard as they can. Drinking cans of lager, maybe doped to the eyeballs. But they're pregnant, they'll have healthy babies they may not even want. Oh, sure, they'll love them once they're born, they'll do their best by them, but they couldn't love their babies more than she loves hers. It's not fair.

This is natural selection and, guess what, she's been deselected. Her face contorts with despair.

'Dear Ms Mallon, we are sorry to inform you that you are not eligible for motherhood. Please reapply in your next life.'

Fuck that.

Her mind is playing tricks on her, looping back to her ectopic pregnancy. She remembers the elderly nun who visited with the holy picture of Virgin and Child: 'Pray for us sinners.' Prayers won't help Gloria's baby.

'I'm a sinner, I deserve to be punished, but what did he do wrong?' she beseeches, although she's unsure who she's importuning.

'Come to think of it, what did I do that was so terribly wrong? I want my Madonna and Child moment too.'

Mother most pure, mother most chaste, mother inviolate, mother undefiled.

The words of the Rosary return to Gloria, her parents said it every night of their marriage. Perhaps her mother says it still, on her own. Gloria's not pure, or chaste, or inviolate. The medics have defiled her with their syringes and probes, their promises that were as empty as her arms, their caveats that didn't prepare her for failure.

Virgin most prudent, virgin most venerable, virgin most renowned.

She's not a virgin, never mind a 'virgins of virgins', but the

Catholic Church doesn't worry about tautology. Do you have to be a virgin to get pregnant?

Spiritual vessel, vessel of honour, vessel of singular devotion.

All these vessels, containers, receptacles – this Virgin Mary they're told to use as a role model isn't a woman at all, she's a giant womb.

'Listen, God, if you're out there, if you exist, I'm willing to be a womb too. It's what you created me for, isn't it? But you won't let me, you changed your mind, you gave me a womb and then blocked up the entrance. That's some joke, isn't it. And the joke's on me.'

Gloria tries to cover her face with her hands but the right arm is still immobilised by the drip. She's too tired to rant, it's over now. She tried to buck the system and she failed. No guts, no glory. Jack calls her Glory. Eventually maybe the best she'll feel is . . . resignation. For now she's too weary for any sensation.

'Visitors to see you, Gloria,' says Frances.

She's wearing trousers, nurses have been allowed to wear trousers since the last time Gloria was in hospital. You see how life moves on, whether you care or not.

It's her mother and Rudy. Her mother bursts into tears as soon as she sees her shrunken daughter. Dispassionately Gloria watches her face explode into blotches. She has an old lady's perm; when did her mother become an old lady? Gloria watches her and wonders who she's weeping for: Gloria, herself, her baby?

So many tears shed in a lifetime. People cry because they cut their finger or because someone makes a cruel remark. And then they lose someone they love and all anyone can do is cry again, there is no other mechanism to express sorrow. But tears run out, sooner or later, their tracks dry and start to itch, gulping sobs quieten, shoulders stop heaving.

Gloria and her family talk, but not about the reason for their visit.

'Was there much traffic on the road?' 'Did you stop for a break?' 'Did you find your way through the city easily?'

Questions requiring answers that pass the time.

'How's Noreen?' Gloria asks.

Rudy shifts in his seat. She's not supposed to enquire about his wife, who's pregnant too. Only four months but she still has her baby safely inside her. Her womb is like the Virgin's, fulfilling its purpose, Noreen's pregnant and she's empty.

'How's Noreen?' she repeats.

'Grand – we thought it best for her to stay at home,' Rudy answers.

'Naturally,' she agrees. 'She has the baby to consider.'

Rudy's jumpiness increases.

'Why don't you go outside for a smoke,' Gloria suggests. 'If you light up in here they'll have to evacuate the building, there'll be so many alarms flashing. There should be a pay-phone out there somewhere, you can call Noreen and tell her you arrived safely. You don't want her worrying more than she has to. Under the circumstances.'

'Come home with us,' says her mother, as soon as they're alone.

'I don't think they'll be letting me out just yet. And I suppose there has to be a funeral, I can't miss that.'

'You don't have to arrange the poor mite's funeral, surely Rudy or Kate can sort that out for you.'

'I want to do it, Mammy, I want to see my son laid to rest. He didn't live in the world but he lived inside me, for nearly nine months.'

'Where will you . . . ?'

'I haven't thought.' Lines criss-cross her forehead. 'I suppose they must have a plot here in the hospital, or there's a holy angels' plot in Glasnevin Cemetery for dead babies, maybe he should go there.'

'Gloria, tell me if I'm interfering, but there's always the family grave.'

'In Omagh? But I don't belong there any more, my life is in Dublin.'

'If only your father were alive,' she sighs. 'He might know what to say to help you through this, his religion was a great consolation to him.'

Daddy.

Of course, Daddy.

'I'll bury my baby with his grandfather, they'll open the grave for him, won't they? There's room, isn't there?'

Her mother smiles and tentatively touches her hair. 'That's exactly what you should do, love.'

And consolation, of sorts, embraces her. Gloria falls asleep.

CHAPTER 44

'Ring the psychic hotline for a sincere and personal reading,' invites the chocolate voice on the radio. 'Calls charged at £1.50 a minute.'

Eimear is tempted, she has to admit she's tempted. She doesn't have anyone to talk problems over with now that she's had to amputate Kate and Gloria. Nuala Ryan has the life experience of a goldfish, she just opens her mouth and closes it if Eimear says anything she can't cope with – it's a wonder how she got through college. Or maybe not; she lived at home and caught the bus in to Dublin from Laragh every day, then it was back to the mountains for her.

Eimear can't even turn to her mother because she's still disgusted with her for splitting from Jack. Eimear sniffs: she belongs to the suffer-in-silence school of wives. Her notion of coping with a Clintonesque husband is to roll her eyes heavenwards and intone: 'All for thee, oh Sacred Heart of Jesus, all for thee.'

That psychics ad seems to be on the radio every twenty minutes, there's no escaping it. Eimear knows she's scraping the barrel but she has to call.

'Hello, caller, you're through to the psychic hotline, my name is Liz. Have you anything in particular you want the cards to help you with?'

'I have doubts about a relationship.' Eimear is grateful for the anonymity of the telephone line. She's as incognito as if she stepped into the confessional.

'I take it you mean a romantic relationship. Concentrate on it while I shuffle the cards.'

She fills her mind with Christy and his insistence that they either move in together or call it a day. Eimear hates ultimatums but he's inflexible.

Liz's voice is calm and unhurried. She sounds about forty-five: Eimear imagines an apple-cheeked woman – a farmer's wife who bakes soda farls on her kitchen table and drives her strapping sons to GAA matches.

'What on earth am I doing?' Eimear scolds herself. Until recently the nearest she came to a fortune teller was the booth in Bundoran on holidays, when you slid in a penny and out dropped a card. 'A chance meeting will bring you luck.' Now Kate's had her out in Ashbourne hearing lectures about using and abusing men from somebody's granny and if that isn't bad enough, here she is paying premium rates to listen to cards being shuffled.

'Are you a farmer's wife?' Eimear asks.

Liz's laughter peals down the line. 'I'm not married. The last time I set foot on a farm was on a school trip to County Kilkenny. I trod in something nasty and stank the bus all the way home.'

That decides Eimear. She isn't going through with this. 'Liz, I'm late for an appointment, I'll have to hang up.' And she breaks her cardinal house rule by slamming down the receiver.

Eimear sinks on to the sofa, heart pounding like someone who's just had a narrow escape. It's not the cream sofa she used to have in Donnybrook, part of a pair, Jack took custody of them. It's a battered old one she bought at an auction but it doesn't look too bad with a paisley throw. At least she kept the painting: she looks at her seascape above the fireplace. It never fails to soothe her – it could be anywhere and nowhere in this country, with its harbour at one end of a horseshoe shaped strand. In the distance there's a purple mountain; sea, sand and mountains, an unmistakably Irish landscape.

Eimear's glance strays around her living room – she expected to be more impatient about renovating the cottage but now that she's in situ, she's lost interest in sanding and polishing and checking wallpaper samples against swatches of curtain material. Perhaps the home beautiful fixation belonged to her Donnybrook life, perhaps she's in her home mediocre phase. She still loves all the interesting trinkets she's collected over the years but she doesn't feel so bothered about creating the perfect backdrop for them.

Eimear is relieved she resisted the temptation to rely on a telephone psychic for the answer to the mysteries of life, the universe and number 42 but there's still the problem of who to talk to.

Perhaps she could write to one of those problem pages. She lifts a pen from the china pot by the telephone and starts scribbling on a notepad. But she can't decide which agony aunt to unburden herself to. She seems to remember there's a newspaper where they only print one problem but you get three different experts responding to it, that might be the one to opt for.

'Time for tea,' she rouses herself. 'I'll think about this later, too much introspection is bad for the health.'

As she passes the phone she realises it's off the hook and replaces the handset. It rings as she's plugging in the kettle; it's Christy and he sounds aggrieved.

'Whoever you've been talking to it must have been an interesting conversation, I've been trying to get through to you for ages.'

Eimear smothers a laugh – she can hardly admit she was pouring her money into a psychic hotline in the hopes of a message from the cosmos about their relationship.

'I was just having a chat with a friend,' she says.

'Which friend?'

What is this, the third degree? Christy's possessiveness is becoming monotonous.

'Nuala Ryan – you don't know her, she works with me at the library,' she lies, annoyed with herself for pandering to him. She should just tell him it's none of his business – she pays her own phone bill.

'Was there something you wanted, Christy?'

'A fine welcome that is. As a matter of fact there is something. I'll call over later to talk about it, it's an answer to the question I asked you.'

'I don't have an answer, Christy,' she objects. 'You'll be the first to know when I do. You promised you'd leave me in peace to think it over.'

'You've had four days, that's long enough. It's not rocket science, you're turning it into a huge issue, a simple yes or no is all you have to come up with.'

'There's nothing simple about yes and no in this context. The words mean the end of a relationship or the beginning of a new type of relationship. You're bullying me for a quicker response than I feel ready to make.'

'I'm only trying to find out where I stand. I have strong feelings for you which don't seem to be reciprocated and I need to know if there's any chance they will be in the future.'

'Harassing me to move in with you isn't the best way to go about it, Christy. I'm only just settled here in the cottage, you're asking me to uproot myself all over again and move to another part of the city to share your home.'

'Not necessarily. I'm willing to move in with you if that's what you want or I'm equally happy for us both to rent out our houses and to find a new place together, in fact that might be the best solution. But I'm leaving it up to you – all I want is a guarantee that you believe we have a future together.'

'There are no guarantees,' she snaps. 'This is life, not an electrical appliances repair shop. Even if you marry someone there's no assurances that you'll be together for life. Hope, yes; good intentions, yes; a certificate from an underwriter, no.'

'Eimear, I'm not going to continue this conversation on the phone. I finish work in twenty minutes, I'll be straight over.'

'But it's after 11 p.m., I have work tomorrow.'

'I'll be with you by midnight.' He hangs up.

Eimear doesn't want to jettison Christy – he's kind to her, he brings her potted plants and makes her feel confident about herself.

'You can buy your own foliage,' she tells herself. 'You can work on your own self-assurance – there are classes you can attend, books you can buy.'

She remembers the boiling kettle and heads for the kitchen. Reaching into the fridge for milk, she sees a half-empty bottle of white wine and decides she needs a glass of it more than a cup of tea.

'You're not half-empty, you're half-full,' she observes to the bottle, as she pours.

She recently made a resolution to be more optimistic about life and this is an ideal opportunity to put it into action. The bottle is rapidly quarter-full, although the wine hadn't been resealed properly and is starting to turn sour. Eimear drinks it anyway – 'it's alcoholic, isn't it,' she tells the kettle.

She carries the bottle and glass through to the living room and riffles her CD rack for music. She discovers a Wet Wet Wet single Kate bought her to commemorate a particularly damp holiday and sings along. She's waiting for the part they used to love, ever since Kate heard one of her nephews get the words wrong.

'It's written on the window,' Eimear shrieks, 'it's everywhere I go.'

But it's not the same on her own. The doorbell peals

da-da-da-dum and she makes her millionth mental note to change it. The previous owner had a misplaced sense of drama.

Naturally it's her own dear Christy on the step, who else; she giggles as she sees through the glass that he has his camera over his neck, he obviously doesn't trust the neighbours not to break into his car. The idea of him coming a-calling with the tools of his trade dangling from his neck strikes her as so ludicrous the chuckle turns into a belly laugh. The wine is making her giddy, that's what she gets for skipping dinner.

'Christopher Troy,' exclaims Eimear. 'My very own Troy Boy, as Kate describes you. Step in. Won't you step inside my parlour said the spider to the fly, it's quite the nicest parlour that you did ever spy.'

'That has a familiar ring to it,' he smiles. 'If you try and pass it off as yours you'll be had up for plagiarism.'

'Drat. Another poem bites the dust. Come into my lair anyway.'

'You're in better form than you were on the phone. Anything left in the bottle for me?' He drops a kiss on top of her head as he squeezes past.

'I wouldn't recommend it, it'll leave a sour taste in your mouth. I forgot to use my gadget for sucking out the air when I put the cap on.'

'Never mind, I'll have a coffee instead.'

He walks into the kitchen and turns the kettle on.

Eimear returns to the sitting room and pours the last of the wine into her glass. It's definitely empty now, no amount of optimism can change that. The wine rack's empty too, she's been buying as she consumes instead of lining up bottles to take the bare look off the rack. It's called real life – not having the spare cash to buy wine for decorative purposes.

'Eimear,' says Christy, as he carries his mug into the room and collapses on the sofa beside her. She notices he's hunted about in the cupboard and discovered a chocolate bar too.

It's a tiny bit irksome the way he feels comfortable enough to help himself but she decides the emotion is ungracious and suffocates it.

'Yes, Christy.' She empties her glass and prepares to face the music.

'I heard something on my way out of the office you might like to know. It's about Gloria and her baby. Shall I tell you?'

Feck, feck, feck. He's going to tell her she's had Jack's child.

'No, don't.'

He runs a hand across his jawline, five o'clock shadow bristling.

'I really think you ought to hear – it's bad news. I'm sure you'd want to know.'

'Good news, bad news, who knows,' Eimear mutters automatically, as her heartbeat slows to a snail's pace. Gloria's dead, she thinks. Her heartbeat hovers, waiting for a reason to start pumping again.

He ignores the interruption.

'Her baby was stillborn – a problem with the umbilical cord, it's being buried in Omagh tomorrow.'

Her heart begins to operate again but this time it's sounding too quickly, it's careering all over her chest.

'Of course you won't want to go to the funeral,' he adds. 'But I thought you might like me to organise some flowers from you.'

'Yes,' Eimear agrees dully. 'I'll have to send a wreath. Is the baby really dead – there's no chance it could be a mistake?'

'No mistake,' he bites into the chocolate. 'No mistake and no baby. I expect you're relieved.'

CHAPTER 45

Kate realises their voices are rising as the discussion becomes heated – Gloria will hear them and she wants to avoid upsetting her.

'Wait here,' she tells him. 'You can't walk in unannounced, I need to prepare her.'

'I'll stay in the corridor,' he says.

'You won't,' she contradicts him. 'You'll go to the café and wait there, I'll come and find you if – repeat, if – she's willing.'

He shuffles off begrudgingly and Kate taps on Gloria's door. She's sitting with her back to it, staring out of the window. Kate can't see what there is to gaze at, apart from a nondescript tree. Her dressing gown is open and she ties the belt for her.

'Don't want you catching cold, Glo.'

'No chance of that in a hospital, it's like the Sahara Desert in here.'

'There's someone who'd like to see you.'

'That's nice,' Gloria mutters listlessly.

'It's someone I'm afraid might upset you.'

'I'm beyond that,' she shrugs. 'Besides, the doctor says I'm better now, I'm allowed to go home tomorrow.' Her eyes roam the hospital room. 'Back to Ranelagh and work and the real world. Normal service resumed.'

'You needn't go back to work for a while – I thought we'd take a holiday.'

'A paperbacks and palm trees holiday like the three of us used to go on?' Misery clouds her eyes to olive green.

'If that's what you want.'

'We could toast ourselves on the beach, drink ourselves into a stupor and go sharking for your Beautiful Boys.' Gloria's tone is conversational. 'Moroccan ones maybe.'

'Maybe,' Kate says guardedly, unsure where this conversation is headed, for there's a barbed edge to Gloria's voice.

'You'd love that, wouldn't you, Kate, you've never grown up. You still want to behave the way we did at twenty, you even fancy the same boys we did at twenty. Life is all about flirting and pulling and then dumping fellows when you're tired of them.'

A pink spot flares on each cheek as Gloria looks scornfully at her friend. 'Even Jack O'Brien is further along the evolutionary scale than you. He was prepared to acknowledge paternity of my baby, despite being more interested in his gas bill than in me. Shame on you, Kate, you're nothing but a lad.'

Kate strides from the room and leans against the corridor wall, brain whirring. The attack is so vehement she's reeling under it. She can't defend herself, how can you shine the quid pro quo home truths' beam back on someone who's been through what Gloria has? She's lashing out blindly. But just because Kate doesn't want marriage and babies doesn't make her deviant. She's different to Gloria, that's all.

Kate takes a deep breath and tells herself: 'She must be hurting like sin to turn on me so unexpectedly.' Then she opens the door and walks back in.

Gloria is still staring out of the window, her robe yawning open again. She turns her eyes to Kate and mute agony gapes from their depths. Kate puts her arms around her shoulders and rests her cheek on top of the dark head.

'Would you like me to wash your hair?' she suggests later.

Gloria nods.

'I always feel better when my hair is washed,' chatters Kate, leading her to the basin. 'There's nothing like lank hair for making you feel low. Where's your sponge bag – no shampoo. Rats, foiled in my efforts to test-drive a career change. Wait, the hospital shop is sure to sell some, I'll run down. Good job we didn't wet your hair before we checked, otherwise you'd be sitting here like a mermaid in all your dripping glory.'

Kate lifts her purse and sprints off. Alongside the shampoos are some scented soaps – she chooses a bar marked Roses of Tralee, Gloria must be weary of the squeaky clean smell from hospital issue – and gallops back with her purchases. Kate doesn't want her sinking into depression again while she's gone.

Mick's in the room when she returns.

'I told you to wait in the café,' she snaps.

'I did wait,' he complains. 'You took your time about collecting me so I decided to behave like a big boy and make my own way here. I'm not a parcel that needs delivering.'

She turns to Gloria. 'Is he bothering you?'

'No,' she whispers.

'Shall I ask him to leave?'

Her 'no' is barely audible.

'Right then,' says Mick triumphantly, 'if you'll excuse us, I have some matters to discuss with my wife.'

'Ex-wife,' Kate corrects him. 'You were married in the North, you don't have to wait years for a divorce.'

'Wife,' he repeats. 'The decree nisi hasn't come through yet, never mind the decree absolute. Close the door on your way out.'

Kate bends over Gloria. 'Do you want me to leave, angel?'

Her hand snakes out with unexpected speed and grips Kate's wrist. 'Stay,' she croaks.

'Gloria,' pleads Mick, 'I have personal business that I want to talk to you about. I've taken a day off work to come and see you, I drove all the way down from Omagh this morning. It really would be better to do this in private.'

She shakes her head.

He frowns and paces the floor, hands thrust into his pockets. He's wearing one of his pin-striped bank suits, as though at a business meeting. His hair is greyer than Kate remembers it; maybe life with the Mammy isn't as blissful as he anticipated.

'Have it your own way,' sighs Mick. 'Kate, would you at least go over there and sit on the bed so Gloria and I can make some semblance at discussing this one on one, without you stuck in the middle.'

Mick removes his jacket, plucks at his tie and pulls another chair next to Gloria. He brings his face parallel with hers and there's genuine affection in his expression.

'Glo, there's no denying episodes we're both ashamed of but we go back a long way and I've been married to you for too long to give you up without a fight. I want us to get back together again, leave the past in the past and concentrate on the present. Let's put the house on the market and find a new home together in Omagh – that's where we were happiest, when we first met, were married and planned our life together.'

Her hands are clasped as in prayer. He covers both with his fists and continues:

'No more fertility treatment, we'll raise a child the best way we can if one is sent to us, and if not we'll accept it. We'll each have the other, where's the point in railing against fate.'

Mick pauses, waiting for her to speak, and when she doesn't he lifts her chin. She makes contact with his eyes briefly before lowering her lids.

'Let's start again, Gloria. You and I will rub along together again well enough when all this madness is behind us, we managed well enough in the past.'

He's sweating by the end of his speech, dark pools spreading from below his armpits and staining the pink of his shirt.

Gloria disengages her hands from his. She pulls herself to her feet with difficulty, holding on to the chair for support.

'Goodbye, Mick, drive carefully.'

His mouth droops.

'You're turning me down?' he gasps.

'I am,' she admits, almost cheerfully.

'You'll regret it.'

'Every day of my life,' she assures him.

'You don't deserve a second chance.'

'You're too good for me, Mick.'

'I won't be back.'

'I suspected as much.'

'I was only being charitable and look where it gets me.'

'Sure you're wasted on me,' she agrees, with increasing high humour.

'You're mentally defective, that's your problem.' He's on his feet now and tugging on his jacket. 'My mother says all you Mallons have a want, it's in the blood.' He searches his vocabulary, face empurpled, and plucks 'deranged trollop' from its contents as he reaches the door.

'You always were a sweet talker, Michael,' she smiles, presenting her back to him.

Gloria slumps into the chair and directs a triumphant look at Kate. 'What about that shampoo you promised me?'

'I thought he'd have you in tears, I was poised to run out for the hospital security staff,' says Kate. 'Weren't you tempted to go along with him?'

'He's a Mammy's boy, Kate, he wanted someone else to fetch and carry for him. Did you hear the word "love" mentioned anywhere in that winsome invitation to pack up and move to Omagh with him? Me neither. I've wasted enough years of my life with that man, I'm going to grow old and crabby on my own.'

'Not on your own,' Kate protests, 'we can grow wrinkly and crotchety together. We'll buy a house with brocade wallpaper and a grandfather clock, fill it with cats, and we'll have eccentric habits and tea parties.'

'Sounds idyllic.'

'And we'll employ a young lad from the neighbourhood to come and cut the grass and tend to our flowerbeds and do our odd jobs.'

'Hold it right there, McGlade,' Gloria checks her. 'This house will be a Beautiful Boy no-go zone. Men are verboten, got it?'

'Have it your own way. But the garden will go to rack and ruin.'

'Girls are just as capable of pushing a lawnmower and changing light bulbs,' Gloria points out. 'We can take on an odd-job woman.'

Kate starts giggling and after a moment's hesitation, Gloria joins in.

'Why are we laughing?' she asks, when they finally draw breath.

'We're arguing over who'll cut our grass when we're too decrepit to do it ourselves,' Kate explains. 'We're both thirty-three.'

'What did I ever see in him?' she wonders, when Kate is combing out her newly washed hair.

'He knew the names of everyone in Roxy Music,' Kate reminds her.

'There must have been more to it than that.'

Kate reflects. 'He could snog for five minutes without coming up for air.'

'I told you that?'

'Guilty as charged.'

'We didn't believe in keeping secrets in those days, did we?'

It's a casual remark but one that silences both. Kate is

reminded of her affair with Jack; it's a safe guess Gloria is thinking about Jack too.

'Honesty wouldn't have improved the situation any, would it?' asks Gloria.

'Impossible to say.' Kate stops combing her hair and her hands fall to her sides.

Gloria shrugs. 'You couldn't have gone up to Eimear and said, "I fancy your husband, I'm going to have a fling with him," any more than I could have said, "I'm borrowing a few million sperm off Jack so I can have a baby – all right by you?" We had to be secretive, we were protecting Eimear.'

'Protecting ourselves,' Kate contradicts her. 'If we were concerned about Eimear, I'd have found someone else to have food-free lunches with and you'd have approached another man for a sperm bank deposit.'

Gloria's eyes mist over. 'My baby didn't live for even a second,' she whimpers. 'I never looked into his eyes and he never looked into mine. Imagine if he knew what sort of a world he was being born into and deliberately wound the umbilical cord around his neck – what if he chose not to be born?'

Kate is aghast, Gloria's plummeting into misery again.

'Snap out of it, Glo,' she orders her. 'That's superstition run amok. Babies don't make choices, that's a luxury saved for adults. You were incredibly unlucky, what happened to your baby is tragic and you'll never forget him, I'm sure you wouldn't want to. This will change you, but you'll still be yourself at heart. Just braver and sadder for a while but you'll come through this. You've taken a massive knock but you will recover, I promise you that. Life goes on, isn't that what people say when they dig into their store of trite expressions to cover all emergencies. It does though, whether your heart is singing or breaking. And take it from me, one day you'll dance again – you were laughing with me only a few minutes ago.'

'Don't remind me,' Gloria moans. 'How could I enjoy having you wash my hair and plan my future as an eccentric old biddy when my son is lying cold and alone in some Godforsaken part of this hospital.'

'You're a survivor. You turned Mick down and chose freedom and Dublin and –'

'Friendship,' Gloria finishes the sentence for Kate. And manages a wobbly smile.

'Dublin's not such a bad place to end up,' Kate tells her. 'Samuel Johnson said it was much worse than London but not as bad as Iceland. And that was in the eighteenth century, it's improved hugely since then, we have cappuccinos now.'

The smile looks less tremulous.

'You'd be dead by now if this was the eighteenth century, Glo,' she reminds her.

'From childbirth?'

'Old age.'

'With friends like you, who needs enemies,' she shakes her head.

'Just running through some reasons to be cheerful. Thirty-three doesn't count as ancient any more, there's life in us yet.'

'Speak for yourself,' Gloria sniffs. 'I'm ready for hibernation. And I'm finished with men – I've been in hospital twice in my life and both times it was because of an encounter with some fellow. If I steer clear of them there's a fair chance I can avoid hospital beds too.'

'There are advantages to a man-free life,' agrees Kate. 'You can abandon contraceptives.'

'True, they were a palaver.'

'Not as much of a palaver as in the olden days.'

'We're not back again in the eighteenth century, are we, Kate? I know you're trying to distract me from my woes but you can have too much of a good thing.'

'No, this isn't the eighteenth century, keep going backwards. Think 2000 BC, think scouring the banks of the Nile for crocodile dung to blend with honey for a spermicide. Egyptian women used to keep some handy in the boudoir.'

'You're making this up, Kate. This is a twisted ploy to take my mind off my problems, the "there's always someone worse off than yourself" approach.'

'It's the God's honest truth, Glo, I read it in a magazine. The dung's acidity altered the pH level in the vagina, killing sperm.'

'What use was the honey?'

'Some kind of obstacle course for the tougher sperm to negotiate.'

Gloria's face is wrinkled in disgust but at least she's not looking depressed. 'Is there a point to this, Kate, or are you simply entertaining me in your inimitable fashion?'

'There is a point,' she confirms. 'It's that condoms or pills aren't so bad.'

'I thought you said the beauty of not bothering about men any more is that you can give contraceptives a miss.'

'Now, Glo,' says Kate, 'it may take six months, it may take six years, but you will meet a man you fancy again and you may even decide to go to bed with him. In the meantime, there's something called life to get on with. And while it might seem like a heap of crocodile dung now, sooner or later you'll find some honey mixed in along the way.'

'Jesus, Mary and Joseph, you're labouring this,' Gloria mutters.

'Give us a smile or I'll tell you what Chinese women swallowed as a contraceptive.'

She grins. And adds: 'Tell me anyway, there's nothing on television.'

CHAPTER 46

It's a glorious day – a day for sundresses and sundowners. A day for the beach or the back garden. Instead Kate pulls a black jacket over her black T-shirt and wraparound skirt and walks through the heat haze to Gloria's house. She's sitting on the back step, watching a magpie.

'One for sorrow,' says Gloria.

'That's not a magpie, it's a black and white pigeon.' Kate joins her on the step.

Gloria's wearing a dress as green as her eyes, with a full skirt and scooped neck. She looks as fresh as a daisy in it.

'Aren't you changing?' Kate asks.

Gloria lifts a corner of the cotton frock and winds it around her finger; the material creases immediately in the heat.

'When I was a little girl,' she begins, 'I remember my mother wearing dresses like this. I don't see her in mini-dresses or slacks and cropped tops, she's fixed forever in my mind in knee-length gowns with splashy rose prints and nipped in waists. That's what mothers wear. I'm dressing like a Mammy today, for James.'

'Good idea, Glo.' Kate squeezes her hand. 'What time is the car coming?'

'Soon,' she says vaguely. 'Do you remember when it was just the three of us, Kate, before boyfriends and biological clocks elbowed their way into our triumvirate?'

'Like it was yesterday.'

'They were good times. We made wonderful wise men. I carried the myrrh, you had the frankincense and Eimear nabbed the gold. She was so exotic, in her turban and crown, with boot polish on her face and hands. She smeared it all over her mother's quilted dressing gown but Eimear didn't care, she knew her mother wouldn't scold her.'

'That's because she never chastised her, perhaps the odd slap on the backs of the legs wouldn't have done Eimear any harm,' says Kate.

'Kate, I'm surprised at you.'

'Of course I didn't mean it, Glo. The thought of Eimear makes me say stupid things.'

'I miss her. We destroyed her, between the two of us.'

Kate rolls her eyes. 'Gloria, trust me, you're overreacting on this one. Eimear's life is far from ruined: she has a new home, a new man and a promising new career as a crypto-feminist poet. Although her credentials for the sisterhood mightn't pass inspection.'

'I tripped on the belt of my robe climbing the steps to the stage and nearly dropped my box with the myrrh in it,' says Gloria dreamily. 'Eimear caught me by the elbow and winked at me.'

'Six-year-olds don't wink.'

'Eimear did. And she insisted we weren't wise men from the East, we were three kings from the Orient.'

'That sounds like her all right.'

'She'd have made a brilliant godmother,' continues Gloria.

Kate holds her tongue and glances up the garden to the rose bushes they used to asset strip to make rose water perfume, before Mrs Mallon caught them and put a stop to it.

Gloria is speaking again. 'Do you mind when we vowed eternal friendship – one night in summer camp, when we slept in tents and kept crawling out of our sleeping bags to look at the stars? You showed me the Plough. And do you remember how you'd been reading Enid Blyton books, about midnight feasts of plum cake and secret societies that caught smugglers red-handed, and you wanted us to make a fellowship pact and sign it in blood?'

The summer camp on the shores of Lough Erne crowds Kate's mind. The other two were terrified of every mooing cow and twittering bird – they wouldn't let her nick their fingers for blood so she had to use red ink, not nearly as dramatic as she'd imagined. They concocted a thrilling declaration between the three of them. Something to do with pledging eternal friendship through dungeon, fire and sword – they copied the line from a hymn sung at Assembly.

'We were about eleven, weren't we?'

'Ten,' corrects Gloria.

'Whatever happened to that piece of paper?'

'You drew skulls and crossbones on it and decided to bury it. Then you changed your mind in case somebody dug it up and the spell would be broken so you burned it in the camp fire on the last night.'

'So I did.'

They sit in silence, Kate recalls how difficult she found it to draw skulls without a picture to copy them from – they looked more like balloons and crossbones.

'Gloria, it's time to leave for the church.' Mrs Mallon appears at the back door.

Gloria flinches but makes no effort to move. Her mother looks helplessly at Kate, who takes her friend's face in her hands and whispers: 'Gloria, we have to do this now.'

Gloria nods slowly and stands.

It isn't a full-scale funeral Mass, just a simple service. Kate listens as Father O'Kane attempts to explain the inexplicable. Even he realises it's a lost cause. Kate scans Gloria's face but she seems to have drifted into a trance. Gloria looks – unusual – in her summer dress, surrounded by people in black. She's flanked by her mother and sister, while Rudolph and his wife Noreen are beside Marlene. Thank God Noreen doesn't look pregnant yet. Kate's in the pew behind.

Jack wanted to come to the funeral but she persuaded him to stay away. Warned him off, really. She painted an implausible scenario in which Mick arrived and squared up to him – under the fascinated gaze of assorted mourners. It was unlikely in the extreme but Jack seemed swayed by it. Kate still doesn't know if it was right to deter him; she simply wanted to minimise flashpoints.

Poor Jack, she sighs, he's grief-stricken too, they mustn't forget that.

She plans to tell Gloria, when she thinks she's able to hear it, about how distraught he is. About how he wanted to see their baby's body laid to rest. About how he longed to offer her what comfort he could.

'If it's consolation you have in mind for Gloria, stay in Dublin – you could create tension at the graveside,' she told Jack.

As the priest talks, Kate reflects on what Gloria said to her – that she's a lad, an emotional retard, so frightened of failure she pulls the plug on relationships as soon as they hit the bend for home. But Pearse and herself lasted more than four years – that has to be worth something. Anyway he's better off without her; she saw his wedding photograph in the paper and his wife looked gentle. He needs someone to make sure he's wearing a scarf on frosty mornings and to give him hot milk with whiskey in it when he has a cold threatening, Kate was too much like hard work for him with her gadding about.

Perhaps she is a commitment phobic, she starts feeling hemmed in when men make plans around her. Not going-to-a-party-on-Saturday-night plans, she's not that much of a sap, but the sort where they expect to spend Christmas Day with her. At least she knows her nature, she's not trying to fit her square peg into a round hole.

Kate is still trying to justify herself to the critical stranger inside her head at the graveside. The sun shines unrelentingly, Gloria looks cool in her summer dress compared to the others in their heavy garb. It's only the immediate family now – and Kate.

The coffin is lowered in on top of her father's and Gloria is watching dry-eyed, though Mrs Mallon, Marlene and Noreen are weeping openly. Even Rudolph is blinking and rubbing his eyes. Kate moves towards Gloria and puts her arm around her shoulders. As she does, she touches another arm being stretched around her friend's back. Kate looks over the top of Gloria's bowed head and meets Eimear's eyes.

'I only heard last night,' she says quietly. 'I had to come by bus, Christy couldn't lend me his car.'

Gloria raises her face to Eimear's. 'I knew you'd be here.'

The three friends stand, entwined.

Then Eimear reaches into her bag and produces three small boxes.

'For the grave,' she explains. 'A mirror for Gloria, frankincense for Kate and gold for me.'

She crouches down and drops her box on top of the coffin.

Eimear has an unnatural streak, thinks Kate, as she peers inside her box and sees a phial of massage oil marked 'frankincense'. But Gloria has a half-smile on her face as she copies Eimear so Kate replaces the lid and throws it gently on to the tiny coffin. It's spooky but if Gloria's willing to go along with it . . .

'What did you use for gold?' Kate asks Eimear.

'My wedding ring.'

They leave the cemetery, arm in arm.

'Mulholland's?' asks Eimear and Gloria nods.

As they approach the pub, however, she halts in her tracks.

'It's too bright a day to sit outdoors, let's walk by the river.'

They find a bench near the Camowen and sit down. It's a river as crooked as its name.

Its burbling sounds are soothing; there's a silver flash and a splash downstream, two boys with fishing rods approaching them break into a trot.

'For a while I wanted to die,' says Gloria. 'Just to lie in that hospital bed and not have the trouble of breathing. My thinking was scrambled. Or maybe it was my hormones.' A grim smile flits across her face. 'But I decided life might be worth living when Mick came to see me and suggested there was a spark left in our marriage.'

'Mick offered to take you back?' Eimear is incredulous.

'It's quite a story, I'll fill you in on it later,' Kate mutters.

'Yes, I think he felt I might be cleaned up and made worthy of him again, once I wasn't inconveniently carrying another man's child. So he came along and rearranged my life for me, outlining his master plan to start afresh in Omagh. As he spoke I felt something – it must have been rage – whatever it was it glowed like an ember inside me and I was consumed by a rush of this emotion and I ordered him out. When he was gone I knew that life could be worth living again, and if I could feel fury maybe some day I'd feel other emotions too. Healthier ones.'

'I know all about rage,' says Eimear.

Kate shifts uncomfortably in her seat but Gloria seems unconcerned.

'You've every right to,' she agrees. 'Is there something you want to say to me?'

Eimear looks from Gloria to Kate and back again. 'Now's not the time.'

They sit on, faces upturned to the sun. It's not exactly a companionable silence, but Kate is surprised by the lack of tension. Considering. She's just about to suggest they put in an appearance at the lunch laid on by Mrs Mallon when Gloria shivers, folds her arms across her body and says: 'I have to go home now.'

'We'll come back to your mother's with you,' Eimear volunteers.

'No, I mean home to Dublin. I have to see Jack.'

A wounded expression settles inexorably on Eimear's face. She pushes past Kate and Gloria and climbs the steps to the street.

CHAPTER 47

'Gloria!' Kate protests, kid gloves abandoned. 'What did you come out with that for? Haven't we damaged Eimear enough between the pair of us.'

Gloria regards her blankly.

'Don't move, I'll be back in a minute.' Kate rushes after Eimear, catching up with her by the traffic lights.

'She's half-demented with grief, she doesn't know what she's saying,' explains Kate, touching her elbow.

Eimear swings towards her, eyes navy with emotion. Two new vertical indentations are visible between her eyebrows.

'I'd want to be a block of wood not to mind,' she fulminates. 'I'm sick to death of turning the other cheek where you two are concerned, it just encourages you to take advantage of me all over again. I came here today because I loved Gloria, because I wanted to show friendship means something to me, but she's flung it back in my face All she cares about is Jack, a man who's the centre of his own universe.'

Eimear's face twists. 'I didn't notice him here today, Kate, offering a shoulder to cry on. Jack's only available for fun, when the going gets tough he wimps out. Christy said something to me once and it's time I put it into operation. When you're in a hole, stop digging. I'm throwing my shovel out of the pit and I'm climbing after it.'

She's shaking as she steps into the traffic without checking the road.

'Eimear wait!' Kate drags her back on to the pavement, as an Audi speeds past, horn blaring.

'You have it all wrong,' she absorbs Eimear's quivering body against her own. 'We know we're a pathetic excuse for friends but we love you, truly we do.'

Eimear tenses, straining away from Kate, then all of a sudden she uncoils and rests her forehead against the side of Kate's head.

'If only I could believe that. But every time I let my guard down something happens. How could Gloria say she's going back to Dublin to see Jack? It's beyond endurance.'

'I know, angel, I know,' Kate soothes. 'But Gloria's not thinking straight. She's not involved with Jack, she doesn't even like him, but the fact is he's the father of that scrap she buried an hour ago and I imagine she feels some connection with him. He's the only link she has with her child. We don't know what's going on in her mind, Eimear, but she's bound to be in torment. The trouble is that sorrow can leave you blinkered, she probably hasn't even considered your own link with Jack – he'd have no status to her other than as her baby's father. Can you understand any of that?'

Eimear nods reluctantly, her breathing less ragged.

They'd better move on, thinks Kate, cars are slowing down and people are craning their heads to study them.

'Eimear, Gloria's still by the river. I have to go back for her, she shouldn't be left to her own devices. Will you come with me?'

'No.' She shakes her head vigorously, blond tendrils escaping from the knot on top of her head.

'Will you wait here for me then?'

'I don't want to see Gloria.'

Kate is perplexed. She can't leave Eimear and she can't leave Gloria.

'Eimear, you'll have to do the big thing here. I'm going down to collect Gloria and then the two of us are escorting her home to her mother's, where hopefully someone will talk sense into her. You needn't speak to her, you needn't even look at her, but we're not turning our backs on her now.'

Eimear regards her feet; her black patent shoes have a rim of earth from the graveyard.

'Fine,' she mumbles.

By the river, there's no sign of Gloria. Kate looks left and right along the Camowen but the only movement is a hundred yards away where one of the fishermen reaches for bait.

Kate half-expects Eimear to have bolted too but she's standing where she left her by the traffic lights.

'She's gone ahead of us to Mallons, we'll catch up with her there.'

Mrs Mallon answers the door in a black skirt and blouse, a look just as dark on her face.

'I have a houseful of visitors and no Gloria,' she announces, as though it's their fault.

'Where is she?' Kate asks.

'She came flying into the house, completely ignored her Auntie Kathleen, grabbed her bags and dropped them in the car. Then she charged off towards the Dublin Road like a woman possessed, not a word of goodbye.'

'She's not herself, Mrs Mallon,' Kate apologises.

Eimear turns to Kate. 'What now?'

'We go back to Dublin and pick up the pieces – I'll give you a lift.'

They stop in Ardee for a coffee and sandwich. Kate studies Eimear as she picks at the tuna filling listlessly. She's changed in the past six months, she seems older – not in a negative sense, but there's more life experience there. As well as the indentations on her forehead there are two thin lines curving alongside each corner of her mouth. They're not unattractive, Kate decides, they lend her face character. She also has a restrained quality, an air of watchfulness, and

Kate realises with a pang that she and Gloria are responsible for that.

Eimear's still a head-turner, even in the black trouser suit which is too severe for her – Eimear was designed for pastels. A waiter rushes forward with a lighter when she pushes aside her barely tasted sandwich and produces cigarettes. Whatever resentment she once harboured towards Eimear is long gone, her fling with Jack must have lanced that boil.

Stirring her coffee restlessly, Kate realises she and Gloria always under-estimated Eimear. She wouldn't still be on speaking terms with a friend who stole her husband or used him to father a child. Obviously Eimear's need for them is greater than her resentment.

'You put me to shame, Eimear,' Kate tells her.

She inhales, eyes narrowed against the smoke, and looks at Kate enquiringly.

'With your ability to forgive,' she expands.

Eimear sighs. 'You have to let go so you can get on with life – my hostility was hurting me more than either of you. In truth it was never hatred, just injured feelings. I'd never do anything to jeopardise our friendship, it's been my lodestone all these years. Then when it was snatched away I felt destabilised: no Jack, no friends, no home – it's been dismal.

'But I've been considering what's happened between the three of us, I've been thinking about little else for the past few months. And what I've concluded is that friendship isn't something that simply evolves naturally, there's times you have to work at it and maybe this is one of those times. Sometimes, too, one of the friends has to give more than the others but it's swings and roundabouts, life has a way of balancing out. Perhaps you've supported me more than I've realised all these years. Or maybe I'm due a bout of temporary insanity and I'll need you two to stand by me in the future. Who knows?'

431

She stubs out her cigarette and inspects the dregs in her coffee mug. Kate is silent, reluctant to break the flow. Impatiently Eimear pulls a few pins from her bun and the white-blonde hair spills down her neck.

'I'm not trying to come across like Mother Theresa of Calcutta, Kate, there've been times I've raged and damned you both and I still can't believe you could be so stupid. It's been tempting to turn my back on the two of you and pretend you don't exist and I've tried that option, you've no idea how I've tried. But I've invested too many years in this friendship to jettison it and when I heard about Gloria's baby, all I could think of was her sorrow and how she'd need both of us by her side to help her through.

'It was a shock when she said she wanted Jack too, I didn't think I could handle that, I'm still not certain I can. But it's not because I still love him, it's more a case of thinking, "Good God above, am I never to be free of that man?"'

Eimear is plaiting the hair now, winding one pale skein around the other.

'I wanted his baby too, Kate, that's why it hurt so much when I heard about Gloria's pregnancy. I thought if I were the mother of his child it would copperfasten his love for me, give me an edge over all the other women he has an eye for.

'In a strange way, Kate, I didn't mind too much about his affair with you because it was just sex and I thought that Jack and I had transcended that – more fool me. I objected to his cheating with a friend because that was the real betrayal for me, not his adultery. I suppose I've always known one woman would never be enough for him. But after I calmed down, I knew you were probably suffering too and in a nasty little part of me, I realised I'd be able to count on your friendship for life because you'd always feel guilty over Jack.'

Eimear pushes her sandwich plate away, food spilling from its edges. 'But then Gloria turned out to be pregnant by my husband and it was a disloyalty too far – I felt abandoned and I panicked and shoved you both out of my life. The idea of her having his baby when I couldn't . . . it was misery.'

She grinds to a halt, staring sombrely ahead.

'Eimear,' Kate touches her arm, 'you do realise it wasn't a love affair, he simply supplied her with some sperm.'

'So she told me.'

'Gloria was frantic when Jack wanted an involvement in her life, when he seemed inclined to claim a share in the baby. And now there's no baby, there's no longer a reason for them to have any contact with one another.'

'So why did she hare off to Dublin to see him?'

It's a question Kate can't answer – she pays the bill and bundles Eimear into the car.

As they hit Dublin and drive down O'Connell Street, she's unsure where to head – to Jack's rooms in Trinity, to Gloria's house in Ranelagh, or should she deliver Eimear home to Dundrum? Eimear's been through an emotionally draining day, she spoke in monosyllables for the remainder of the journey. Kate realises she doesn't even know where her cottage is.

'I'll drop you home if you point me in the general direction,' Kate suggests, as they curl past Trinity College.

Eimear glances in through the entrance archway and shivers.

'Someone stepped on my grave. No, let's go to Ranelagh, it's my guess that's where Gloria is now.'

'Are you sure you're up to it?'

'What's the worst that can happen – I find her in a clinch with Jack? I've imagined that so often the reality can't harm me.'

Gloria's car is parked outside the house – and so is Jack's. Kate swivels towards Eimear again. 'They're both inside – is this wise?'

She hesitates, tugging at her earlobe. Then she reaches a decision.

'Since when were any of the three of us ever wise?' Eimear shrugs. 'I must face him sooner or later and I have to find out where I stand with Gloria, it may as well be now.'

She clutches Kate's elbow for support. 'I need to find out whether it's just the two of us now or whether we can ever be a threesome again.'

Kate unhooks her seatbelt and strains towards Eimear, as close as lovers in the Triumph Spitfire. 'Mulligan, whatever happens I'm your friend. I know I let you down once but I'll never do it again.'

Eimear eyes Kate as anxiously as a lost child.

'Promise?'

'Cross my heart and hope to die.'

Eimear's face breaks into a smile. 'Let's get this over with.'

'We're not afraid of Jack O'Brien,' says Kate, on the garden path.

'No, but we're afraid of what he means to Gloria.'

There are raised voices inside and Kate has to jam her finger on the doorbell before it's answered. If Eimear's nerves are in tatters, Gloria's must be twice as ragged, she thinks.

'Kate,' Gloria materialises in the hall and grabs her, 'come in. I've been kicking myself I didn't wait for you.'

She doesn't seem to notice Eimear, who drifts in after them. Kate cranes her head over a shoulder, checking she's coping, and Eimear nods almost imperceptibly

'So, the coven's assembled,' remarks Jack as they congregate in the living room. 'Time for some double, double, toil and trouble.'

Kate's taken aback: what's happened to the caring, shaken Jack she saw in the hospital – the cynical, drawling model seems to have taken his place.

'I've just been explaining to Jack that he's to stay out of my life forever.' Gloria's voice is defensively loud. 'That he was my friend's husband and he hadn't the sense to hang on to the best thing that happened to him. That he's brought

434

nothing but discord between the three of us and I accept a full share of blame for my part in it. That I made a mistake trying to have a baby with him because it was never meant to be. That I feel nothing but pity for him but it doesn't extend to wanting any further contact with him. That he's to go away and attempt to learn something from this miserable episode, as I'm trying to do.'

Jack sweeps the three with a disdainful glance.

'Omagh girls, you're more trouble than you're worth. You're all a bit long in the tooth anyway. Don't bother to show me out, I know the way.'

'On the contrary,' says Eimear, 'it's a pleasure to show you the door.'

And she slams it in his face.

'We shouldn't demonise him,' says Gloria when they're alone. 'We both buried a child today.'

'And he played the hero convincingly when he rushed you to hospital,' admits Kate.

'Plus there's the small matter of a sperm bank withdrawal,' Eimear points out. With only the suspicion of an edge.

The other two decide against answering the unanswerable. Kate races in: 'He can't help it, he's only a man. There's no getting away from that chromosome deficiency.'

There's a tense moment as the three women look at each other, unsure what to do next.

'I'm gasping for a drink,' says Gloria. 'I've a bottle of champagne put by for the christening' – her face turns to stone momentarily but she musters courage and continues – 'it's not chilled but at least it's fizzy. Fancy some?'

They nod.

'What shall we drink to?' asks Kate.

'To the three wise men,' suggests Eimear.

'As opposed to the three prudent virgins.' Gloria pulls a face.

They clink flutes tentatively – each of them knows the

friendship can never be exactly as it was before but perhaps the troika might survive intact after all.

'So how's your love life?' Kate asks Eimear after they've emptied the bottle and debated tossing a coin for a takeaway – head's an Indian, harp's a pizza.

'Is Christy still bowing at the foot of your pedestal?'

Eimear's chin sinks on to her hand. 'He's convinced we were lovers in a previous life. He photographed a woman who claims she's the reincarnation of Sarah Curran, Robert Emmet's fiancée, and he's hooked on the subject. Christy's got it into his head he was a soldier in Wolfe Tone's army of Frenchmen and we met after I hid him in the shed behind my father's tavern when they were defeated and the victorious mob went on the rampage.'

'So you were a buxom serving wench ladling out the ale and cavorting in the hayloft,' says Gloria.

'That's right.' Eimear extends her chest in a vain attempt to look buxom.

'That little fantasy says more about Christy than he might like to admit,' Kate smiles. 'How long has he had this fixation on barmaids?'

'Since the seventeenth century, obviously,' giggles Eimear.

Kate wrinkles her nose. 'I want to be reincarnated as one of those Japanese bulls that make the most expensive steaks in the world – you know, the ones they massage in gin to keep their flesh tender.'

'You could have trained that malleable young Brad boy of yours to perform that task,' says Gloria.

Eimear looks interested, Kate winces.

'It was a relief when he went south. Literally. I gave him his fare to Cork to investigate the Munster branch of the family.'

'I'm ratted,' complains Gloria. 'I haven't had a drink in so long, two glasses has left me legless.'

'You always were a cheap date,' Kate tells her. 'So, Mulligan, is this Christy fellow the love of your life?'

'Do me a favour,' she shakes the Veuve Cliquot bottle in the hope of rustling up some dregs. 'He was a bit of fun to start with but now he's a commitment bore and threatening to bin me if I don't agree to move in with him. So it looks like I'm flying solo again.'

'That's bad news,' says Gloria.

'Good news, bad news, who knows,' responds Eimear, falling backwards on the sofa. 'I never could take a man seriously who asked if it was all right to kiss me.'

'He did that?' Kate is wide-eyed.

'To begin with anyway. I suppose he thought he was treating a wounded damsel in distress with consideration.'

'Whereas really you wanted someone to sweep you off your feet and be masterful,' Kate muses.

'Pathetic, isn't it.' She's suddenly sober.

'But sure isn't it what we all want,' suggests Gloria.

'No,' Kate contradicts her. 'It's only what we think we want. When you encounter the reality, in the shape of a Jack O'Brien, say, it's not so alluring any more. Not after the initial euphoria.'

'Where does that leave us then, on the shelf at thirty-three, unloved and unlovable?' Gloria sounds glum, the alcohol's wearing off her too. 'Prawns caught and discarded in the fishing net of life?'

'It leaves us choosier,' Kate tells them. 'It leaves us unwilling to accept second-best just so we can have the comfort of coupledom. Maybe we'll be in pairs again one day, maybe we won't. But at least we'll always be a trio. Three wise men who grew up – and wised up.'

The other two look solemnly at her and Eimear opens her mouth to speak. 'Would you ever feck off down to the off-licence, Kate.'

'And while you're at it,' says Gloria, 'bring back some winegums.'

Lightning Source UK Ltd.
Milton Keynes UK
21 September 2010

160131UK00001B/18/P